FUTURE

Born in Manchester in 1917, Anthony Burgess was educated at the Xaverian College in that city and at Manchester University, from which he held a doctorate. He
served in the army from 1940 to 1956, and as a colonial
education officer in Malaya and Borneo from 1945 to
1960, in which year, his brief but irreversible unemploy-
ability having been decreed by a medical death sentence,
he decided to live by writing – and his output comprises
over fifty books. He was a Visiting Fellow of Princeton
University and a Distinguished Professor of City College, New York. He was created a Commandeur des
Arts et des Lettres by the French President and a
Commandeur de Merite Cultural by Prince Rainier of
Monaco. Anthony Burgess died in November 1993.

BY ANTHONY BURGESS

Fiction

The Long Day Wanes: Time For
  A Tiger
The Enemy In The Blanket
Beds In The East
The Right To An Answer
The Doctor Is Sick
The Worm And The Ring
Devil Of A State
One Hand Clapping
A Clockwork Orange
The Wanting Seed
Honey For The Bears
Inside Mr Enderby
The Eve Of Saint Venus
The Vision Of Battlements
Tremor Of Intent
Enderby Outside
MF
Napoleon Symphony
The Clockwork Testament; Or
  Enderby's End
Beard's Roman Women
Abba Abba
Man Of Nazareth
1985
Earthly Powers
The End Of The World News
Enderby's Dark Lady
The Kingdom Of The Wicked
The Pianoplayers
Any Old Iron
The Devil's Mode (Short Stories)
Mozart And The Wolf Gang
A Dead Man In Deptford

Autobiography

Little Wilson And Big God
You've Had Your Time

For Children

A Long Trip To Teatime
The Land Where The Icecream
  Grows

Theatre

Oberon Old And New
Blooms Of Dublin

Verse

Moses

Non-fiction

English Literature: A Survey For
  Students
They Wrote English (In Italy Only)
Here Comes Everybody: An
Introduction To James Joyce For
  The Ordinary Reader
The Novel Now: A Student's Guide
  To Contemporary Fiction
Urgent Copy: Literary Studies
  Shakespeare
Joysprick: An Introduction To The
  Language Of James Joyce
New York
Hemingway And His World
On Going To Bed
This Man And Music
Homage To Quert Yuiop
A Mouthful Of Air

Translation

The New Aristocrats
The Olive Trees Of Justice
The Man Who Robbed Poor Boxes
Cyrano de Bergerac
Oedipus The King

Editor

A Shorter Finnigans Wake

Anthony Burgess

FUTURE IMPERFECT

THE WANTING SEED
1985

V

VINTAGE

Published by Vintage 1994

2 4 6 8 10 9 7 5 3 1

Introduction
Copyright © Anthony Burgess 1993, c/o Artellus Ltd.

The Wanting Seed
First published in Great Britain by
William Heinemann Ltd, 1962
Copyright © Anthony Burgess 1962
Foreword © Anthony Burgess 1983

1985
First published in Great Britain by Hutchinson, 1978
Copyright © Anthony Burgess 1978

The author is grateful to Mrs Sonia Brownwell
Orwell, Secker & Warburg Ltd, and Harcourt Brace
Jovanovich, Inc., for permission to use
lines from 1984 by George Orwell

Vintage
Random House, 20 Vauxhall Bridge Road, London SW1V 2SA

Random House Australia (Pty) Limited
20 Alfred Street, Milsons Point, Sydney
New South Wales 2061, Australia

Random House New Zealand Limited
18 Poland Road, Glenfield,
Auckland 10, New Zealand

Random House South Africa (Pty) Limited
PO Box 337, Bergvlei, South Africa

Random House UK Limited Reg. No. 954009

A CIP catalogue record for this book
is available from the British Library

ISBN 0 09 922501 8

Printed and bound in Great Britain by
The Guernsey Press Co., Ltd., Guernsey, Channel Islands

1985 AND *THE WANTING SEED* – AN INTRODUCTION

1985 was written rather too close to the year it purports to deal with, demonstrating the impossibility of ever getting a prophecy right. But the novella with that title is merely a tail-piece to what the American publisher Little Brown requested. 1984 was a few years off, and it was thought that a reconsideration of Orwell's novel *Nineteen Eighty-Four* was needed. The term "Orwellian" was being very loosely used – to describe Dallas airport, for instance. It was being used where "Huxleyan", referring to *Brave New World*, would have been more appropriate. The essence of Orwell's prophecy could be summed up as the results of, through an impossible revolution, the imposition of Oxford idealism on the Western world, so that reality exists only inside the skull. Did Orwell, writing in 1948, really believe that such a metaphysical change could take place within thirty-six years? Certainly not, but he wanted a real date, not an impossible one like Huxley's A.F. 632, and 1984 seemed, at the time of writing the book, distant enough. The 1960s must have seemed similarly remote to Nevil Shute, who, in *On the Beach*, showed the end of the world coming through a kind of nuclear poison. Seeing the film of the book, we shudder rather than laugh when, to solemn music, we see 1961 on the calendar. But my own *1985*, which was written before the Thatcher revolution, must raise very sardonic guffaws when the nightmare is compared with the reality.

What the novella presents is a Britain totally in the control of the Trades Union Congress and therefore renamed Tucland. In the late 1970s the situation did not seem all that unthinkable, though its realisation in the terms I presented it was clearly impossible. For the principle of holistic syndicalism was too intellectual a concept (compare it with Orwell's Ingsoc), and the prospect of a new British constitution in which union leaders replaced members of parliament was hardly a tenable one. Paul Johnson, reviewing the book, thought that it contained the rhetoric of a possible tyranny and might profitably be filmed or televised. And then Margaret Thatcher came along and struck out at the unreasonable power of the unions. It is possible that the situation of syndicalist stupidity in the face of new technology will recur, but my nightmare is unlikely to be realised. Dystopias or cacotopias are only a kind of poetic warning to hang on to what freedom one has. Even the most bizarre of prophetic fiction has its use.

The other novel, *The Wanting Seed*, was published in 1962, the year when I published also *A Clockwork Orange*, and so it may be taken as my prophetic year. *A Clockwork Orange* I envisaged as depicting a situation that very nearly existed in the 1960s but might reach fulfilment, and consequent state retaliation, in the 1970s: I mean the cult of juvenile violence for its own sake. It is very much with us in the 1990s, but, though the book is still on sale, the brilliant film that Stanley Kubrick made of it has been, in Britain at least, banned by the producer-director himself. *The Wanting Seed* has not been filmed, though various cinematic proposals have been made. It has been filched from. Harry Harrison wrote a novel called *No Room! No Room!*, which dealt with the same theme as *The Wanting Seed* – a world population increase and a diminishing food supply – and this was filmed as *Soylent Green*. Harrison came to my apartment in New York to inform me that – there being no copyright on ideas – my cannibalistic solution to universal starvation had been adopted as an ending for the film. Did I have any objection? He consumed a whole bottle of my whisky while I told him I did not.

No date is fixed for *The Wanting Seed* – whose title, by the way, comes from an old folksong which cannot make up its mind whether seed is wanting or wanton. The future it presents is implausible, especially in the curious synthetic England in which its events take place. I had just come back from the Far East and, returning by way of India, had been appalled by the population explosions of Calcutta and Bombay. One did not dare give a rupee to a starving child: he would immediately have been torn to pieces. I thought of Thomas Malthus and his prophecy that, unless various natural checks operated, the growth of population would always be in excess of available nutriment. Could this really apply in the West, with its brilliant agronomic techniques and its use of contraceptive devices condemned by the Rev. Thomas Malthus? I let fancy have its way and produced an

England bursting with people and yet suffering a constant decrease in even synthetic foods, such as NUTS or nutritional units.

War has been unknown for some centuries, so one of Malthus's natural checks on population increase no longer exists. The world is divided into three major language groups – ENSPUN, RUSPUN AND CHINSPUN (English Speaking Union, Russian –, Chinese –) which are too much concerned with the problem of balancing population and nutriment to have aggressive ambitions. In CHINSPUN and RUSPUN pretty draconian measures are taken with those who, disobeying the law, have more than one child per family. In ENSPUN it is more a matter of playing the game and encouraging good citizens to become homosexual (IT'S SAPIENS TO BE HOMO) or even to castrate themselves: the highest posts in government seem to go to the Castros, as they are called. I have a pair of joint heroes, Tristram and Derek Foxe, twins, who respectively support the regime and rebel against it. Derek is a high official in the Ministry of Infertility, a post sustained because of his hypocrisy: he pretends to be homosexual but is in fact an ebullient member of the opposed camp: he is carrying on an affair with his brother's wife, Beatrice-Joanna. Derek teaches history in a boys' school. He knows that the process of historical change is cyclical, that tyranny alternates with liberalism, with a period of chaos known as an interphase coming between the dictatorial and the democratic.

The action of the novel takes place during an interphase. Near-starvation is making the country panic. A new police force is formed – the Poppol or Population Police – and rationing is at its tightest. The people revolt. The Catholic religion, long banned as irrational and also fertility-troped, returns to justify what is known as eucharistic ingestion: if God can be eaten, so can man. The chaos is countered by an improvised army, and wars, known as extermination sessions, return to the earth. These have one function only – that of providing cadavers for the food-processors. The sufficiency of canned meat in the world brings calm and increase. 'Everyone has a right to be born, but nobody has a right to live' sums up the new philosophy of life. The Ministry of Infertility loses its negative prefix.

The possibility that cannibalism, or anthropophagy,

could save a starving world was not acceptable in 1962. The notion was that human flesh was, at worst, poisonous, at best innutritious. With the Andes disaster, in which the survivors of an air crash survived further by eating the softer portions of their less lucky fellow-travellers, the edibility we share with most of the animal kingdom was made manifest. The survivors were healthy enough though terribly constipated. *The Wanting Seed* may be prophetic in a way too remote to be tested. But primarily it is offered as an entertainment.

Anthony Burgess 1993

A FOREWORD

This novel appeared in the autumn of 1962, with *A Clockwork Orange*, my other piece of futfic or future-fiction, pairing it in the spring of that year. *A Clockwork Orange* was squeezed out of my appalled observation of youthful behaviour in an England which had become new and strange to me. In 1954 I had left a Britain suffering from shortages to live a hardworked but moderately well-rewarded life in the Federation of Malaya. Returning to Britain for good, at least that was the intention, in 1959, I felt very much a stranger in a land that now seemed affluent, telly-haunted, and burgeoning with a cult of youth. If the violence of the young, coupled with a reaffirmation of the necessity of evil in a world still animated by the right of moral choice, was the theme of *A Clockwork Orange*, its matching novel was concerned with a phenomenon I had been well aware of while living in the East — the population explosion and the shrinking of the world's food supply. *The Wanting Seed* tries to show what England might be like if it suffered from the pullulation of India. The response to the prospect of overcrowding and starvation might well be a culture which favoured sterility by promoting homosexuality and rewarding self-castration. But, my instinct argued, nature might respond to human sterility with sterile patterns of its own, and the solution to the population problem could be more ruthless and more logical.

If the theological motto of *A Clockwork Orange* is 'We

I

must be free to make moral choices,' that of *The Wanting Seed* is 'Everyone has a right to be born.' Both assertions are traditionally Christian or, to be more specific, Catholic. The pattern of history presented in the book is based on a conflict between two modes of Christian belief – the Augustinian and the Pelagian. St Augustine taught that man was born in original sin, the British monk Pelagius denied the doctrine. Pessimism about man confronts a shining optimism. In terms of politics, conservatism faces liberalism or its later expression socialism. The history of a society is cyclical, as my hero Tristram Foxe teaches his overcrowded classes in a school of the future. Pessimistic convervatism, expecting the worst from man does not always get the worst and hence is modified in the direction of optimistic socialism. But this latter creed, expecting the best from man, is usually disappointed, and disappointment is expressed in a greater governmental rigour, ending with downright tyranny (many tyrannical régimes have called themselves socialist). But tyranny ends in revolution and a restoration of the Augustinian philosophy: Gusphase, Pelphase, Interphase, a perpetual waltz, as Tristram Foxe puts it, the circle turning for ever.

The book opens at the beginning of an Interphase, with the British government taking draconian steps – with such devices as the Population Police or Poppol – to control births and ration food. But the people revolt and solve the great problem through cannibalism, which they justify through a return to sacramental Christianity: indeed, they call anthropophagy 'eucharistic ingestion.' When order is restored with the return of a conservative system, the cannibalistic innovation is rationalised into organised warfare – men versus women, and the cadavers processed into canned protein in the supermarkets. But, as Tristram Foxe divines, this cannot last for ever. Liberalism will su[pervene], human life will be considered sacred, and the Pelphase will start all over again.

The book was, twenty years ago, regarded as a light, if dark, comedy, and nobody would take seriously that cannibalism might be the solution to the world's crowding and hunger. I was told that all human flesh was toxic. Then came the Andes disaster and the survival of the fittest through the eating of their fellows. The survivors proved, on examination, to be well nourished but terribly constipated. I think it possible that one day we will find cans of meat in our markets called Mench or Munch, human flesh seasoned with sodium nitrite, and that the corollary of the slogan 'Everyone has a right to be born' will be 'No one has a right to live.' This latter seems to me to be true, since, once born, we cannot quantify the life in store for us (some people die at eighteen, others at eighty and no one can scream about injustice), and men and women fighting in a just war (a war to maintain the food supply is undoubtedly just) have no cause to resent being killed in it: after all, their right to be born has been fulfilled. Abortion and birth control are both terrible sins; shooting a factitious enemy to fill the supermarket shelves is, conceivably, a venial one.

The book proclaims, in various of its lesser details, that it was written more than twenty years ago. Decimal coinage had not yet come in, and I believed that it never would. It pleased me to have coins like tosheroons and septs and even tanners. You may, if you wish, regard a tanner as today's pound grossly inflated, and the quid as the official name for forty of these. Some of the African states I mention have changed their names, but there is no reason why they should not, in the distant future, change them back again. Anyway, this is not so much the future as a hypothetical projection, into an impossible time, of certain historical processes which I consider all too possible. The world of *A Clockwork Orange* was meant to be a real future (1972 or thereabouts), and it has already become the past. I cannot foresee the highly schematic world of *The Wanting Seed* as ever coming to birth, but I think some aspects of it — the glorification of the homosexual, for instance — are already with us. The title, as I indicate in a prefatory note to the novel, comes from an old English folksong. This confuses *wanting* and *wanton*. The ambiguity is appropriate to my book.

Monaco   **A.B**
May 1982

THE WANTING SEED

TO THE UNSLEEPING GILLONS

One

THIS was the day before the night when the knives of official disappointment struck.

Beatrice-Joanna Foxe snuffled a bereaved mother's grief as the little corpse, in its yellow plastic casket, was handed over to the two men from the Ministry of Agriculture (Phosphorus Reclamation Department). They were cheerful creatures, coal-faced and with shining dentures, and one of them sang a song which had recently become popular. Much burbled on the television by epicene willowy youths, it sounded incongruous coming from this virile West Indian deep bass throat. Macabre, too.

> 'My adorable Fred:
>   He's so, so sweet,
> From the crown of his head
>   To the soles of his feet.
>   He's my meat.'

The name of the tiny cadaver had been not Fred but Roger. Beatrice-Joanna sobbed, but the man went on singing, having no feeling of his business, custom having made it in him a property of easiness.

'There we are, then,' said Dr Acheson heartily, a fat gelding of an Anglo-Saxon. 'Another dollop of phos-

3

phorus pentoxide for dear old Mother Earth. Rather less than half a kilo, I'd say. Still, every little helps.' The singer had now become a whistler. Whistling, he nodded, handing over a receipt. 'And if you'll just step into my office, Mrs Foxe,' smiled Dr Acheson, 'I'll give you your copy of the death certificate. Take it to the Ministry of Infertility, and they'll pay you your condolence. In cash.'

'All I want,' she sniffed, 'is my son back again.'

'You'll get over that,' said Dr Acheson cheerfully. 'Everyone does.' He watched benevolently the two black men carry the casket down the corridor towards the lift. Twenty-one storeys below, their van waited. 'And think,' he added. 'Think of this in national terms, in global terms. One mouth less to feed. One more half-kilo of phosphorus pentoxide to nourish the earth. In a sense, you know, Mrs Foxe, you'll be getting your son back again.' He led the way into his tiny office. 'Ah, Miss Herschhorn,' he said to his secretary, 'the death certificate, please.' Miss Herschhorn, a Teutonico-Chinese, rapidly quacked the details into her audiograph; a printed card slid out of a slot; Dr Acheson stamped his signature – flowing, womanly. 'There you are, Mrs Foxe,' he said. 'And do try to see all this rationally.'

'What I do see,' she said with asperity, 'is that you could have saved him if you'd wanted to. But you didn't think it was worth while. One more mouth to feed, more useful to the State as phosphorus. Oh, you're all so heartless.' She cried again. Miss Herschhorn, a plain thin girl with dog's eyes and very lank straight black hair, made a *moue* at Dr Acheson. They were, apparently, used to this sort of thing.

'He was in a very bad way,' said Dr Acheson gently.

4

'We did our best, Dognose we did. But that sort of meningeal infection just gallops, you know, just gallops. Besides,' he said reproachfully, 'you didn't bring him to us early enough.'

'I know, I know. I blame myself.' Her tiny nosewipe was soaked. 'But I think he could have been saved. And my husband thinks the same. But you just don't seem to care about human life any more. Any of you. Oh, my poor boy.'

'We do care about human life,' said Dr Acheson, stern. 'We care about stability. We care about not letting the earth get overrun. We care about everybody getting enough to eat. I think,' he said, more kindly, 'you ought to go straight home and rest. Show that certificate to the Dispensary on the way out and ask them to give you a couple of pacifiers. There, there.' He patted her on the shoulder. 'You must try to be sensible. Try to be modern. An intelligent woman like you. Leave motherhood to the lower orders, as nature intended. Now, of course,' he smiled, 'according to the rules, that's what you're supposed to do. You've had your recommended ration. No more motherhood for you. Try to stop feeling like a mother.' He patted her again and then turned a pat into a slap of finality, saying, 'Now, if you'll forgive me –'

'Never,' said Beatrice-Joanna. 'I'll never forgive you, any of you.'

'Good afternoon, Mrs Foxe.' Miss Herschhorn had switched on a tiny speech-machine; this was reciting – in the manic tone of a synthetic voice – Dr Acheson's afternoon appointments. Dr Acheson's fat rump was turned rudely to Beatrice-Joanna. It was all over: her

5

son on his way to be resolved into phosphorus pentoxide, she just a damned snivelling nuisance. She held her head up and marched into the corridor, marched towards the lift. She was a handsome woman of twenty-nine, handsome in the old way, a way no longer approved in a woman of her class. The straight graceless waistless black dress could not disguise the moving opulence of her haunches, nor could the splendid curve of her bosom be altogether flattened by its constraining bodice. Her cider-coloured hair was worn, according to the fashion, straight and fringed; her face was dusted with plain white powder; she wore no perfume, perfume being for men only – still, and despite the natural pallor of her grief, she seemed to glow and flame with health and, what was to be disapproved strongly, the threat of fecundity. There was something atavistic in Beatrice-Joanna: she instinctively shuddered now at the sight of two white-coated women radiographers who, leaving their department at the other end of the corridor, sauntered towards the lift, smiling fondly at each other, gazing into each other's eyes, fingers intertwined. That sort of thing was now encouraged – anything to divert sex from its natural end – and all over the country blared posters put out by the Ministry of Infertility, showing, in ironical nursery colours, an embracing pair of one sex or the other with the legend *It's Sapiens to be Homo*. The Homosex Institute even ran night-classes.

Beatrice-Joanna looked with distaste, entering the lift, on the embracing giggling pair. The two women, both Caucasian types, were classically complementary – fluffy kitten answered stocky bullfrog. Beatrice-Joanna nearly retched, her back to the kissing. At the fifteenth floor the lift picked up a foppish steatopygous young man, stylish in well-cut jacket without lapels, tight calf-length trousers, flowery round-necked shirt. He turned sharp eyes of distaste on the two lovers, moving his shoulders pettishly, pouting with equal disgust at the full womanly presence of Beatrice-Joanna. He began, with swift expert strokes, to make up his face, simpering, as his lips kissed the lipstick, at his reflection in the lift-mirror. The lovers giggled at him, or at Beatrice-Joanna. 'What a world,' she thought, as they dropped. But, she reconsidered, glancing covertly but more keenly at him, perhaps this was a clever façade. Perhaps he, like her brother-in-law Derek, her lover Derek, was perpetually acting a public part, owing his position, his chance of promotion, to the gross lie. But, she couldn't help thinking yet again, having thought this often, there must be something fundamentally unsound about a man who could even act like that. She herself, she was sure, could never pretend, never go through the soggy motions of inverted love, even if her life depended on it. The world was mad; where would it all end? As the lift reached ground-level she tucked her handbag under her arm, held her head high again and prepared to plunge bravely into the mad world outside. For some reason the lift-doors refused to open ('Really,' tutted the big-bottomed exquisite, shaking them) and, in that instant of automatic fear of being trapped, her sick imagination converted the lift-cabin into a yellow casket full of potential phosphorus pentoxide. 'Oh,' she sobbed quietly, 'poor little boy.'

'Really.' The young dandy, bright with cyclamen lipstick, twittered at her tears. The lift-doors unjammed and opened. A poster on the vestibule wall showed a pair of male friends embracing. *Love your Fellow-Men,* ran the legend. The female friends giggled at Beatrice-Joanna. 'To hell with you,' she said, wiping her eyes, 'to hell with the lot of you. You're unclean, that's what you are, unclean.' The young man swayed, tut-tutted, undulated off. The bullfrog lesbian held protective arms round her friend, hostile eyes on Beatrice-Joanna. 'I'll give her unclean,' she said hoarsely. 'I'll rub her face in the dirt, that's what I'll do.' 'Oh, Freda,' adored the other, 'you're so brave.'

Two

WHILE Beatrice-Joanna was going down, her husband Tristram Foxe was ascending. He was humming up to the thirty-second floor of the South London (Channel) Unitary School (Boys) Division Four. A sixty-strong Fifth Form (Stream 10) awaited him. He was to give a lesson in Modern History. On the rear wall of the lift, half-hidden by the bulk of Jordan, an art-master, was a map of Great Britain, a new one, a new school issue. Interesting. Greater London, bounded by sea to south and east, had eaten further into Northern Province and Western Province: the new northern limit was a line running from Lowestoft to Birmingham; to the west the boundary dropped from Birmingham to Bournemouth. Intending migrants from the Provinces to Greater London had, it was said, no need to move; they merely

8

had to wait. The Provinces themselves still showed their ancient county divisions, but, owing to diaspora, immigration and miscegenation, the old national designations of 'Wales' and 'Scotland' no longer had any precise significance.

Beck, who taught mathematics to the junior forms, was saying to Jordan, 'They ought to wipe out one or the other. Compromise, that's always been our trouble, the liberal vice of compromise. Seven septs to a guinea, ten tanners to a crown, eight tosheroons to a quid. The poor young devils don't know where they are. We can't bear to throw anything away, that's our big national sin –' Tristram got off, leaving old bald Beck to continue his invective. He marched to the Fifth Form classroom, entered, blinked at his boys. May light shone from the seaward window on their blank faces, on the blank walls. He started his lesson.

'– The gradual subsumption of the two main opposing political ideologies under essentially theologico-mythical concepts.' Tristram was not a good teacher. He went too fast for his pupils, used words they found hard to spell, tended to mumble. Obediently the class tried to take down his words in their notebooks. 'Pelagianism,' he said, 'was once known as a heresy. It was even called the British Heresy. Can anybody tell me Pelagius's other name?'

'Morgan,' said a boy called Morgan, a spotty boy.

'Correct. Both names mean "man of the sea".' The boy behind Morgan whistled a kind of hornpipe through his teeth, digging Morgan in the back. 'Stop that,' said Morgan.

'Yes,' continued Tristram. 'Pelagius was of the race

that at one time inhabited Western Province. He was what, in the old religious days, used to be called a monk. A monk.' Tristram rose vigorously from his desk and yellowed this word, as if he were fearful that his pupils would not be able to spell it, on the blueboard. Then he sat down again. 'He denied the doctrine of Original Sin and said that man was capable of working out his own salvation.' The boys looked very blank. 'Never mind about that for the moment,' said Tristram kindly. 'What you have to remember is that all this suggests human perfectibility. Pelagianism was thus seen to be at the heart of liberalism and its derived doctrines, especially Socialism and Communism. Am I going too fast?'

'Yes, sir.' Barks and squeals from sixty breaking voices.

'Right.' Tristram had a mild face, blank as the boys', and his eyes gleamed feverishly from behind their contact-lenses. His hair had a negroid kink; his cuticles half-hid blue half-moons. He was thirty-five and had been a schoolmaster for nearly fourteen years. He earned just over two hundred guineas a month but was hoping, since Newick's death, to be promoted to the headship of the Social Studies Department. That would mean a substantial increase in salary, which would mean a bigger flat, a better start in the world for young Roger. Roger, he then remembered, was dead. 'Right,' he repeated, like a sergeant-instructor of the days before Perpetual Peace had set in. 'Augustine, on the other hand, had insisted on man's inherent sinfulness and the need for his redemption through divine grace. This was seen to be at the bottom of Conservatism and other *laissez-faire* and non-progressive political beliefs.' He beamed at his class. 'The opposed thesis, you see,' he said, encouragingly. 'The whole thing is quite simple, really.'

'I don't get it, sir,' boomed a big bold boy named Abney-Hastings.

'Well, you see,' said Tristram amiably, 'the old Conservatives expected no good out of man. Man was regarded as naturally acquisitive, wanting more and more possessions for himself, an unco-operative and selfish creature, not much concerned about the progress of the community. Sin is really only another word for selfishness, gentlemen. Remember that.' He leaned forward, his hands joined, sliding his forearms into the yellow chalk-powder that covered the desk like windblown sand. 'What would you do with a selfish person?' he asked. 'Tell me that.'

'Knock him about a bit,' said a very fair boy called Ibrahim ibn Abdullah.

'No.' Tristram shook his head. 'No Augustinian would do that sort of thing. If you expect the worst from a person, you can't ever be disappointed. Only the disappointed resort to violence. The pessimist, which is another way of saying the Augustinian, takes a sort of gloomy pleasure in observing the depths to which human behaviour can sink. The more sin he sees, the more his belief in Original Sin is confirmed. Everyone likes to have his deepest convictions confirmed: that is one of the most abiding of human satisfactions.' Tristram suddenly seemed to grow bored with this trite exposition. He surveyed his sixty, row by row, as if seeking the diversion of bad behaviour; but all sat still and attentive, good as gold, as if bent on confirming the Pelagian thesis. The microradio on Tristram's wrist buzzed thrice. He lifted it to his ear. A gnat-song like the voice of conscience said, *'Please see the Principal at the end of the present period'* – a tiny plopping of plosives. Good. This would be it, then, this would be it. Soon he would be standing in poor dead Newick's place, the salary perhaps back-dated. He now literally stood, his hands clutching in advocate-style his jacket where, in the days of lapels, the lapels would have been. He resumed with renewed vigour.

'Nowadays,' he said, 'we have no political parties. The old dichotomy, we recognize, subsists in ourselves and requires no naïve projection into sects or factions. We are both God and the Devil, though not at the same time. Only Mr Livedog can be that, and Mr Livedog, of course, is a mere fictional symbol.' All the boys smiled. They all loved *The Adventures of Mr Livedog* in the *Cosmicomic*. Mr Livedog was a big funny fubsy demiurge who, *sufflaminandus* like Shakespeare, spawned unwanted life all over the earth. Overpopulation was his doing. In none of his adventures, however, did he ever win: Mr Homo, his human boss, always brought him to heel. 'The theology subsisting in our opposed doctrines of Pelagianism and Augustinianism has no longer any validity. We use these mythical symbols, because they are peculiarly suited to our age, an age relying more and more on the perceptual, the pictorial, the pictographic. Pettman!' Tristram shouted, with sudden joy. 'You're eating something. Eating in class. That won't do, will it?'

'I'm not, sir,' said Pettman, 'please, sir.' He was a boy of purplish Dravidian colouring with strong Red Indian features. 'It's this tooth, sir. I have to keep sucking it, sir, to stop it aching, sir.'

'A boy of your age should not have teeth,' said Tristram. 'Teeth are atavistic.' He paused. He had said that often to Beatrice-Joanna, who had a particularly fine natural set, top and bottom. In the early days of their marriage she had taken pleasure in biting his ear-lobes. 'Do stop that, darling. Ow, dear, that hurts.' And then little Roger. Poor little Roger. He sighed, then pushed on with his lesson.

Three

BEATRICE-JOANNA decided that, despite her tangle of nerves and the hammering at her occiput, she didn't want a pacifier from the Dispensary. She didn't want anything further from the State Health Service, thank you very much. She filled her lungs with air as if about to dive, then thrust her way into the jam of people packing the vast hospital vestibule. With its mixture of pigments, cephalic indices, noses and lips, it looked like some monstrous international airport lounge. She pushed to the steps and stood there awhile, drinking the clean street air. The age of private transport was all but over; only official vans, limousines and microbuses crawled the street crammed with pedestrians. She gazed up. Buildings of uncountable storeys lunged at the May sky, duck-egg blue with a nacreous film. Pied and peeled. Blue-beating and hoary-glow height. The procession of seasons was one abiding fact, an eternal recurrence, the circle. But in this modern world the circle had become an emblem of the static, the limited globe, the prison. Up there, at least twenty storeys high, on the façade of the Demographic Institute, stood a bas-relief circle with a straight line tangential to it. It symbolized the wished-for conquest of the population problem: that tangent, instead of stretching from everlasting to everlasting, equalled in length the circumference of the circle. Stasis. A balance of global population and global food supply. Her brain approved, but her body, the body of a bereaved mother, shouted no, no. It all meant a denial of so many things; life, in the name of reason, was being blasphemed against. The breath of the sea struck her left cheek.

She walked due south down the great London street, the nobility of its sheer giddy loftiness of masonry and metal redeeming the vulgarity of the signs and slogans. *Glowgold Sunsyrup. National Stereotelly. Syntheglot.* She was pushing against the crowds, crowds all moving northward. There were, she observed, more uniforms than usual: policemen and policewomen in grey – awkward, many of them, as if they were new recruits. She walked on. At the end of the street, like a vision of sanity, glinted the sea. This was Brighton, London's administrative centre, if a coastline could be called a centre. Beatrice-Joanna strode as briskly as the tide of the north-moving crowd would let her towards the cool green water. Its vista, taken from this narrow giddy ravine, always promised normality, a width of freedom, but the actual arrival at the sea's edge always brought disappointment. Every hundred yards or so stood a stout

sea-pier loaded with office-blocks or hives of flats, pushing out towards France. Still, the clean salt breath was
there, and greedily she drank it in. She held an intuitive
conviction that, if there were a God, He inhabited the
sea. The sea spelled life, whispered or shouted fertility;
that voice could never be completely stilled. If only, she
felt crazily, poor Roger's body could have been thrown
into those tigrine waters, swept out to be gnawed by
fish, rather than changed coldly to chemicals and
silently fed to the earth. She had a mad intuitive notion
that the earth was dying, that the sea would soon be
the final repository of life. 'Vast sea gifted with delirium,
panther skin and mantle pierced with thousands and
thousands of idols of the sun –' She had read that somewhere, a translation from one of the auxiliary languages
of Europe. The sea drunk with its own blue flesh, a
hydra, biting its tail. 'Sea,' she said quietly, for this
promenade was as crowded as the street she had just
left, 'sea, help us. We're sick, O sea. Restore us to health,
restore us to life.'

'I beg your pardon?' It was an oldish man, Anglo-
Saxon, upright, ruddy, mottled, grey-moustached; in a
military age he would have been taken at once for a
retired soldier. 'Did you address – ?'

'Sorry.' Blushing beneath her bone-white powder,
Beatrice-Joanna walked rapidly away, turning instinctively towards the east. Her eyes were drawn upwards to
the tremendous bronze statue that stood defiant, a mile
in the air, at the summit of Government Building, the
figure of a bearded man, classically robed, glaring at
the sun. At night he was floodlit. A cynosure to ships,
man of the sea, Pelagius. But Beatrice-Joanna could

remember a time when he had been Augustine. And, so it was said, he had been at other times the King, the Prime Minister, a popular bearded guitarist, Eliot (a long-dead singer of infertility), the Minister of Pisciculture, captain of the Hertfordshire Men's Sacred Game eleven, and – most often and satisfactorily – the great unknown, the magical Anonymous.

Next to Government Building, fronting the fecund sea without shame, stood the squatter, humbler building of twenty-five storeys only which housed the Ministry of Infertility. Above its portico was the inevitable circle with its chastely kissing tangent, also a large bas-relief of a naked sexless figure breaking eggs. Beatrice-Joanna thought she might as well draw her (so cynically named) condolence. It would give her a reason for entering the building, an excuse for hanging about in the vestibule. It was quite possible that she might see *him*, leaving work. He was, she knew, this week on the A Shift. Before crossing the promenade she looked on the busy crowds with almost new eyes, perhaps the sea's eyes. This was the British people; rather, to be more accurate, this was the people that inhabited the British Islands – Eurasian, Euro-African, Euro-Polynesian predominated, the frank light shining on damson, gold, even puce; her own English peach, masked with white flour, was growing rarer. Ethnic divisions were no longer important; the world was split into language-groups. Was it, she thought in an instant almost of prophetic power, to be left to her and the few indisputable Anglo-Saxons like her to restore sanity and dignity to the mongrel world? Her race, she seemed to remember, had done it before.

Four

'ONE achievement of the Anglo-Saxon race,' said Tristram, 'was parliamentary government, which eventually meant government by party. Later, when it was found that the work of government could be carried on more expeditiously without debate and without the opposition that party government entailed, the nature of the *cycle* began to be recognized.' He went to the blueboard and yellow-chalked a large clumsy ring. 'Now,' he said, swivelling his head to look at his pupils, 'here is how the cycle works.' He marked off three arcs. 'We have a Pelagian phase. Then we have an intermediate phase.' His chalk thickened one arc, then another. 'This leads into an Augustinian phase.' More thickening, and the chalk was back where it had started. 'Pelphase, Interphase, Gusphase, Pelphase, Interphase, Gusphase, and so on, for ever and ever. A sort of perpetual waltz. We must now consider what motive power makes the wheel turn.' He faced his class seriously, beating one palm against the other to clean the chalk off. 'In the first place, let us remind ourselves what Pelagianism stands for. A government functioning in its Pelagian phase commits itself to the belief that man is perfectible, that perfection can be achieved by his own efforts, and that the journey towards perfection is along a straight road. Man wants to be perfect. He wants to be good. The citizens of a community want to co-operate with their rulers, and so there is no real need to have devices of coercion, sanctions, which will force them to co-operate.

Laws are necessary, of course, for no single individual, however good and co-operative, can have precise knowledge of the total needs of the community. Laws point the way to an emergent pattern of social perfection – they are guides. But, because of the fundamental thesis that the citizen's desire is to behave like a good social animal, not like a selfish beast of the waste wood, it is assumed that the laws will be obeyed. Thus, the Pelagian state does not think it necessary to erect an elaborate punitive apparatus. Disobey the law and you will be told not to do it again or fined a couple of crowns. Your failure to obey does not spring from Original Sin, it's not an essential part of the human fabric. It's a mere flaw, something that will be shed somewhere along the road to final human perfection. Is that clear?' Many of the pupils nodded; they were past caring whether they understood or not. 'Well, then, in the Pelagian phase or Pelphase, the great liberal dream seems capable of fulfilment. The sinful acquisitive urge is lacking, brute desires are kept under rational control. The private capitalist, for instance, a figure of top-hatted greed, has no place in a Pelagian society. Hence the State controls the means of production, the State is the only boss. But the will of the State is the will of the citizen, hence the citizen is working for himself. No happier form of existence can be envisaged. Remember, however,' said Tristram, in a thrilling near-whisper, 'remember that the aspiration is always some way ahead of the reality. What destroys the dream? What destroys it, eh?' He suddenly big-drummed the desk, shouting in crescendo, 'Disappointment. *Disappointment.* DISAPPOINTMENT.' He beamed. 'The governors,' he said, in a reasonable tone, 'become disappointed when they find that men are not as good as they thought they were. Lapped in their dream of perfection, they are horrified when the seal is broken and they see people as they really are. It becomes necessary to try and force the citizens into goodness. The laws are reasserted, a system of enforcement of those laws is crudely and hastily knocked together. Disappointment opens up a vista of chaos. There is irrationality, there is panic. When the reason goes, the brute steps in. Brutality!' cried Tristram. The class was at last interested. 'Beatings-up. Secret police. Torture in brightly lighted cellars. Condemnation without trial. Finger-nails pulled out with pincers. The rack. The cold-water treatment. The gouging-out of eyes. The firing-squad in the cold dawn. And all this because of disappointment. The Interphase.' He smiled very kindly at his class. His class was agog for more mention of brutality. Their eyes glinted, they goggled with open mouths.

'What, sir,' asked Bellingham, 'is the cold-water treatment?'

Five

BEATRICE-JOANNA, the waste of life-giving cold water behind her, entered the open mouth of the Ministry, a mouth that smelled as though it had been thoroughly rinsed with disinfectant. She jostled her way to an office flaunting the word CONDOLENCES A great number of bereaved mothers were waiting at the counter, some – those who spoke with the accents of irresponsibility – in festal dress as for a day out, clutching death certificates like passports to a good time. There was the smell of cheap spirit – alc, as it was called – and Beatrice-Joanna saw the coarse skins and blear eyes of inveterate alc-drinkers. The day of the pawning of the flat-iron was over; the State condoned infanticide.

'Got sort of sufflicated in the bedclothes. Only three weeks old to the day he was, too.'

'Scalded, mine was. Pulled the kettle right on top of him.' The speaker smiled with a sort of pride, as though the child had done something clever.

'Fell out of the window, he did. Playing, he was.'

'Money comes in handy.'

'Oh, yes, it does that.'

A handsome Nigerian girl took the death certificate from Beatrice-Joanna and went off to a central cash-desk. 'God bless you, miss,' said a harridan who, from the look of her, seemed well past child-bearing age. She folded the notes the Euro-African clerk gave her. 'God bless you, miss.' Clumsily counting her coins, she waddled off happily. The clerk smiled at the old-fashioned locution; God was not much mentioned these days.

'Here you are, Mrs Foxe.' The handsome Nigerian had returned. 'Six guineas, three septs.' How this amount had been arrived at Beatrice-Joanna did not trouble to ask. With a flush of guilt she couldn't explain, she swept the money hurriedly into her bag. The three-shilling piece called a sept shone at her in triplicate, sliding into her coin-purse – King Charles VI as triplets, smiling quizzically to the left. The King and Queen were not subject to the same generative laws as ordinary people: three princesses had been killed last year, all in the same air crash; the succession had to be secured.

Don't have any More, said the poster. Beatrice-Joanna pushed her angry way out. She stood in the vestibule, feeling desperately lonely. White-coated workers rushed, busy and brisk as spermatozoa, into the department of Contraceptive Research. The lifts rose and fell, to and from the many floors of the Propaganda Department. Beatrice-Joanna waited. Men and half-men all about her, twittering and sibilating. Then she saw, as she had thought she might at this precise hour, her brother-in-law Derek, her furtive lover Derek, brief-case under his arm, talking animatedly with a flash of rings to a foppish colleague, making point after point on unfolding flashing fingers. Seeing the superb mime of orthodox homosexual behaviour (secondary or social aspects) she could not quell entirely the spark of contempt that arose in her loins. She could hear the snorting emphasis of his speech; his movements had a dancer's grace. Nobody knew, nobody except her, what a satyr lay couched behind the epicene exterior. He was, it was said by many, likely to rise very high in the hierarchy of the Ministry. If, she reflected with an instant's malice, if only his colleagues knew, if only his superiors knew. She could ruin him if she wanted to. Could she? Of course she couldn't. Derek was not the sort of man who would let himself be ruined.

She stood there, waiting, her hands folded in front of her. Derek Foxe said good-bye to his colleague ('Such a *very* good suggestion, my dear. I promise you, tomorrow we must really *hammer it out.*') and patted him in valedictory archness thrice on the left buttock. Then he saw Beatrice-Joanna, looked warily about him, and came over. His eyes gave nothing away. 'Hallo,' he said, writhing with grace. 'What news?'

'He died this morning. He's now –' She took a hold on herself '– now in the hands of the Ministry of Agriculture.'

'My dear.' That was spoken in a lover's tone, a man to a woman. He glanced furtively about him again, then whispered, 'We'd best not be seen together. Can I come round?' She hesitated, then nodded. 'What time does my dear brother get home today?' he asked.

'Not till seven.'

'I'll be along. I have to be careful.' He smiled queenlily at a passing colleague, a man with Disraeli-like ringlets. 'Some queer things are going on,' he said. 'I think I'm being watched.'

'You're always careful, aren't you?' she said, somewhat loudly. 'Always too damned careful.'

'Oh, do be quiet,' he whispered. 'Look,' he said, slightly agitated. 'Do you see that man there?'

'Which man?' The vestibule was thick with them.

'That little one with the moustache. Do you see him? That's Loosely. I'm sure he's watching me.' She saw who he meant: a small friendless-looking man with his wrist to his ear as though checking that his watch was going, actually listening to his microradio, standing aloof on the periphery of the crowd. 'You go off home, my dear,' said Derek Foxe. 'I'll be along in about an hour.'

'Say it,' commanded Beatrice-Joanna. 'Say it before I go.'

22

'I love you,' he mouthed, as through a window. Dirty words from a man to a woman in that place of anti-love. His face contorted as though he were chewing alum.

Six

'BUT,' went on Tristram, 'the Interphase cannot, of course, last for ever.' He contorted his face to a mask of shock. 'Shock,' he said. 'The governors become shocked at their own excesses. They find that they have been thinking in heretical terms – the sinfulness of man rather than his inherent goodness. They relax their sanctions and the result is complete chaos. But, by this time, disappointment cannot sink any deeper. Disappointment can no longer shock the state into repressive action, and a kind of philosophical pessimism supervenes. In other words, we drift into the Augustinian phase, the Gusphase. The orthodox view presents man as a sinful creature from whom no good at all may be expected. A different dream, gentlemen, a dream which, again, outstrips the reality. It eventually appears that human social behaviour is rather better than any Augustinian pessimist has a right to expect, and so a sort of optimism begins to emerge. And so Pelagianism is reinstated. We are back in the Pelphase again. The wheel has come full circle. Any questions?'

'What do they gouge eyes out with, sir?' asked Billy Chan.

Bells shrilled, gongs clanged, an artificial voice yelled

over the speakers, 'Change, change, all, all change. Fifty seconds to change. Count-down now begins. Fifty – forty-nine – forty-eight –' Tristram mouthed a good afternoon inaudible under the racket and walked out into the corridor. Boys dashed to lessons in concrete music, astrophysics, language control. The count-down went rhythmically on: 'Thirty-nine – thirty-eight –' Tristram walked to a staff lift and pressed the button. Lights showed that the cabin was already shooting down from the top floor (big-windowed art-rooms there; art-master Jordan quick, as always, off the mark). $43 - 42 - 41 - 40$, flashed the indicator. 'Nineteen – eighteen – seventeen –' The cretic rhythm of the count-down had changed to trochaic. The lift stopped and Tristram entered. Jordan was telling Mowbray, a colleague, about new movements in painting; names like Zvegintzoy, Abrahams, ·F. A. Cheel were dealt like dull cards. 'Plasmatical assonance,' intoned Jordan. In some things the world had not changed at all. 'Three – two – one – zero.' The voice had stopped, but each floor ($18 - 17 - 16 - 15$) that rose before the eyes of Tristram showed boys not yet in their new classrooms, some not even scurrying. The Pelphase. Nobody tried to enforce the rules. The work got done. More or less. $4 - 3 - 2 - 1$. Ground floor. Tristram left the lift.

Seven

BEATRICE-JOANNA entered the lift in Spurgin Building on

Rossiter Avenue. 1 – 2 – 3 – 4. She rose to the fortieth floor, where their tiny flat waited, empty of a son. In half an hour or so Derek would arrive, the comfort of whose arms she desperately needed. Was not Tristram then equipped to give of the same commodity? It was not the same, no. The flesh has its own peculiar logic. There had been a time when it had been pleasant, thrilling, ecstatically exciting, to be touched by Tristram. That had long gone – gone, to be precise, shortly after Roger's birth, as though Tristram's sole function had been to beget him. Love? She still, she thought, loved Tristram. He was kind, honest, gentle, generous, considerate, calm, witty sometimes. But it was Tristram in the living-room she loved, not Tristram in bed. Did she love Derek? She did not answer the question for a moment. 26 – 27 – 28. She thought it was strange that their flesh should be the same. But Tristram's had become carrion; that of his elder brother was fire and ice, paradisaical fruit, inexpressibly delicious and exciting. She was in love with Derek, she decided, but she did not think she loved him. 30 – 31 – 32. She loved, she decided, Tristram, but was not in love with him. So, so far hence in time, a woman contrived to think with (as it was in the beginning) her instincts, (is now) her complicated nerves, and (ever shall be) her inner organs (world without end) 39 – 40. (Amen.)

Courageously Beatrice-Joanna turned the key of the flatlet and walked in to the familiar smell of *Anaphro* (an air-freshener devised by chemists of the Ministry where her lover worked, piped throughout the block from an engine in the basement) and the hum of the refrigerator. Even though she had no real standards of comparison, she was always, on each entrance, struck afresh and aghast by the exiguity of the living-space (standard for people of their income-group) – the box of a bedroom, kitchen-coffin, bathroom almost to be worked into like a dress. Two fair strides would see her across the living-room, and the strides were only possible because all the furnishings hid in ceiling and walls, to be released, when wanted, at the touch of a switch. Beatrice-Joanna bade a chair come out, and an angular unlovely sit-unit grudgingly appeared. She was weary, she sat, sighing. The *Daily Newsdisc* still shone, like a black flat sun, on its wall-spindle. She conjured its artificial voice, sexless, expressionless. 'The strike at the National Synthelac Works continues. Appeals to the workers to return have proved of no avail. The strike-leaders are unwilling to compromise on their demand for a basic increase of one crown three tanners a day. Dock-workers at Southampton are, as a gesture of sympathy with the strikers, refusing to handle imported synthelac.' Beatrice-Joanna moved the needle on to the Woman's Band. A genuinely female voice – strident with a vinegar enthusiasm – spoke of the further reduction of the bust-line. She switched off. Her nerves still danced, her occiput still rocked from repeated hammer-cracks. She took off her clothes and bathed in the basin that was called a bath. She dusted her body with plain white scentless powder and donned a dressing-gown woven of some new long-chain synthetic polymeric amide. Then she went to the wall-panel of buttons and switches and made a pair of metal arms gently lower a plastic cupboard from a recess in the ceiling. She opened the cupboard and, from a brown bottle, shook out two tablets. She washed these down with water in a paper cup, thrust the empty cup into a hole in the wall. This launched it on a journey whose destination was the basement furnace. Then she waited.

Derek was late. She grew impatient. Her nerves zithered still, her head thumped. She began to have premonitions of death, doom; then, dragging in reason like some alien constrictive metal, she told herself that these premonitions were a hangover from events already past and irrevocable. She took two more tablets and sent another cup to fiery atomization. Then, at last, there came a knock at the door.

Eight

TRISTRAM knocked at the Principal's secretary's door, said that his name was Foxe and that the Principal wished to see him. Buttons were pressed; lights flashed over lintels; Tristram was bade enter. 'Come in, Brother Foxe,' cried Joscelyne. He looked rather like a fox himself, certainly not Franciscan. He was bald, twitched and had a good degree from the University of Pasadena. He himself, however, came from Sutton, West Virginia, and, though he was too foxily modest to talk much about it, was closely related to the High Commissioner for North American Territories. Nevertheless, he had obtained this post of Principal on sheer merit. That, and a life of blameless sexlessness. 'Sit down, Brother Foxe,' said Joscelyne. 'Sit right down. Have a caff.' He hospitably motioned towards the dish of caffeine tablets on his blotter. Tristram shook his head, smiling. 'Give you a lift when it's needed most,' said Joscelyne, taking two. Then he sat down at his desk. The afternoon sea-light shone on a long nose, a blue muzzle, the mouth large and mobile, the face prematurely lined. 'I tapped your lesson,' he said, nodding first towards the switchboard on the white wall, then to the ceiling-speaker. 'Do you think the kids take in much of that stuff?'

'They're not supposed to understand it too well,' said Tristram. 'Just a general impression, you know. It's in the syllabus but never comes up in the exam.'

'Yah, yah, I guess so.' Joscelyne was not really interested. He was fingering a grey-backed dossier, Tristram's: Tristram saw FOXE upside down on its cover. 'Poor old Newick,' said Joscelyne. 'He was pretty good. Now he's phosphorus pentoxide some place in Western Province. But I guess his soul goes marching on,' he said vaguely. And then, with speed, he added, 'Here in the school, I mean.'

'Yes, yes, of course. In the school.'

'Yah. Now,' said Joscelyne, 'you were all lined up to take his place. I've been reading through your dossier today –' *Were*. Tristram swallowed a bolus of surprise. *Were*, he said, *were*. '– Quite a book. You've done pretty good work here, I can see that. And you're senior in the department. You should have just walked into the job.' He leaned back, put thumb-tip to thumb-tip, then – little, ring, middle, index – let finger-tip meet finger-tip. He twitched meanwhile. 'You realize,' he said, 'that it's not up to me who fills these vacancies. It's up to the Board. All I can do is recommend. Yah, recommend.

Now, I know this sounds crazy, but what gets a man a job these days is not pry-merrily qualifications. No. It isn't how many degrees he's got or how good he is at whatever it is he does. It's – and I'm using the term in its most general sense – his family background. Yah.'

'But,' began Tristram, 'my family –'

Joscelyne held up a traffic-stopping hand. 'I don't mean whether your family was up in the world,' he said. 'I mean how much of it there is. Or was.' He twitched. 'It's a matter of arithmetic, not of eugenics or social status. Now I know as well as you do, Brother Foxe, that all this is absurd. But there it is.' His right hand suddenly took flight, hovered, then dropped to the desk like a paper-weight. 'The records,' he said, pronouncing the word 'wreckerds', 'the records here say – the records say – yah, here it is: they say you come of a family of four. You have a sister in China (she's on the Global Demographic Survey, right?) and a brother in, of all places, Springfield, Ohio. I know Springfield well. And then, of course, there's Derek Foxe here, homo and highly placed. Now you, Brother Foxe, are married. And you have one kid.' He looked up at Tristram sadly.

'Not any more. He died in hospital this morning.' Tristram's lower lip jutted, quivering.

'Dead, eh? Well.' Condolences nowadays were purely financial. 'Young, wasn't he? Very young. Not much P_2O_5 there. Well, his being dead doesn't alter the position as far as you're concerned.' Joscelyne clasped his hands tight as if about to pray away the fact of Tristram's fatherhood. 'One birth per family. Alive or dead. Singleton, twins, triplets. It makes no difference. Now,' he said, 'you've broken no law. You've not done a thing you theoretically shouldn't have. You're entitled to marry if you want to, you're entitled to one birth in the family, though, of course, the best people just don't. Just don't.'

'Damn it,' said Tristram, 'damn it all, somebody's got to keep the race going. There'd be no human race left if some of us didn't have children.' He was angry. 'And what do you mean by "the best people"?' he asked. 'People like my brother Derek? That power-struck little nancy, crawling, yes, literally crawling up the –'

'Calmo,' said Joscelyne, 'calmo.' He had only just returned from an educational conference in Rome, that popeless city. 'You were just going to say something very opprobrious then. "Nancy" is a very contemptuous term. The homos, remember, virtually run this country and, for that matter, the whole of the English-Speaking Union.' He lowered his eyebrows, gazing at Tristram with foxy sorrow. 'My uncle, the High Commissioner, he's homo. I was nearly homo myself once. Let's keep emotion out of this,' he said. 'It's unseemly, that's what it is, yah, unseemly. Just let's try to *parlare* about this *calmamente*, huh?' He smiled, trying to make the smile look homespun and cracker-barrel. 'You know as well as I do that the job of breeding's best left to the lower orders. Remember that the very term proletariat comes from Latin *proletarius*, meaning those that serve the State with their offspring or *proles*. You and me, we're supposed to be above that sort of thing, huh?' He sat back in his chair, smiling, tapping the desk with his ink-pencil – O, for some reason, in Morse. 'One birth per family, that's the rule or recommendation or whatever you like to call it, but the proletariat breaks that rule all the time. The race is in no danger of dying. Just the opposite, I'd say. I hear rumours from high places, but never mind, never mind. The fact is that your old man and your old lady broke the rule very nastily, very nastily indeed. Yah. He was what? – something in the Ministry of Agriculture, wasn't he? According to this dossier he was. Well, it was just a little bit cynical, I'd say, helping to increase the national food supply with one hand and getting four kids with the other.' He saw that this was rather a grotesque antithesis but he shrugged it off. 'And that's not forgotten, you know, Brother Foxe, not forgotten. The sins of the fathers, as they used to say.'

'We'll all help the Ministry of Agriculture some day,' sulked Tristram. 'Quite a nice lump of phosphorous pentoxide, the four of us.'

'Your wife, too,' said Joscelyne, rustling the many sheets of the dossier. 'She's got a sister in Northern Province. Married to an agricultural officer. Two children there.' He tutted. 'A kind of aura of fertility surrounds you, Brother Foxe. Anyway, as far as this post of departmental head is concerned, it's pretty evident that, all things being equal, the Board will want to appoint a candidate with a cleaner family wreckerd.' This pronunciation became a focus of irritation to Tristram. 'Let's see. Let's look at the other candidates.' Joscelyne leaned forward, elbows on the desk, and began to tick them off on his fingers. 'Wiltshire's homo. Cruttenden's unmarried. Cowell's married with one kid, so he's out. Crum-Ewing's gone the whole hog, he's a *castrato*, a pretty strong candidate. Fiddian's just nothing. Ralph's homo –'

'All right,' said Tristram. 'I accept my sentence. I just stay where I am and see somebody younger – it's bound to be somebody younger; it always is – promoted over my head. Just because of my *wreckerd*,' he added bitterly.

'Yah, that's it,' said Joscelyne. 'I'm glad you're taking it this way. You see how a lot of these top-brass are going to look at it. Heredity, that's the word, heredity. A family pattern of deliberate fertility, that's it. Yah. Like being a hereditary criminal. Things are very tricky these days. In confidence, fella, you watch your step. Watch your wife. Don't start having any more kids. Don't start getting irresponsible like the proletariat. One false step like that and you'd be out. Yah, out.' He made the gesture of cutting his own throat. 'Lots of promising young men coming up. Men with the right ideas. I'd hate to lose you, Brother Foxe.'

Nine

'Dearest one.'

'Darling, darling, darling.' They embraced hungrily, the door still open. 'Yumyumyumyumyum.' Derek disengaged himself and kicked it shut.

'Must be careful,' he said. 'I wouldn't put it past Loosley to follow me here.'

'Well, what's the harm?' said Beatrice-Joanna. 'You can visit your brother if you wish to, can't you?'

'Don't be silly. Loosley's thorough, I'll say that for the

little swine. He'll have found out what Tristram's working-hours are.' Derek went over to the window. He came back from it immediately, smiling at his own foolishness. So many storeys up, so many indistinguishable crawling ants on the deep street. 'Perhaps I'm getting a bit too nervy,' he said. 'It's only that – well, things are happening. I've got to see the Minister this evening. It looks as though I'm in for a big job.'

'What sort of job?'

'A job that means, I'm afraid, we shan't be seeing quite so much of each other. Not for a time, anyway. A job with a uniform. Tailors came in this morning, measuring. Big things are happening.' Derek had shed his public skin of dandified epicene. He looked male, tough.

'So,' said Beatrice-Joanna. 'You're getting a job that's going to be more important than seeing me. Is that it?' She had thought, on his entering the flat and taking her in his arms, of urging, in a mad instant, that they run away together, to live for ever on coconuts and love among the banyans. But then her woman's desire for the best of both worlds had supervened. 'I sometimes wonder,' she said, 'whether you really mean what you say. About love and so on.'

'Oh, darling, darling,' he said impatiently. 'But listen.' He was in no mood for dalliance. 'Some things are happening which are far more important than love. Matters of life and death.'

Just like a man. 'Nonsense,' she said promptly.

'Purges, if you know what those are. Changes in the Government. The unemployed being drafted into the police force. Oh, big things, big things.'

33

Beatrice-Joanna started to snivel, to make herself look very weak, defenceless, small. 'It's been such an awful day,' she said. 'I've been so miserable. I've been so lonely.'

'Dearest one. It's beastly of me.' He took her in his arms again. 'I'm so sorry. I think only of myself.' Content, she went on snivelling. He kissed her cheek, neck, brow, buried his lips in hair the colour of cider. She smelt of soap, he of all the perfumes of Arabia. Embraced, they four-legged their way clumsily into the bedroom, as in some blind dance undisciplined by music. The switch had long been touched which sent the bed swinging – in an arc like Tristram's chalked Pelphase – to the floor. Derek swiftly undressed, disclosing a spare body knobbed and striated with muscle, and then the dead eye of the television screen on the ceiling was able to watch the writhing of a male body – crust-brown, delicate russet – and a female – nacreous, touched subtly with blue and carmine – in the exordia of an act which was technically both adulterous and incestuous.

'Did you,' panted Derek, 'remember to –?' There was now no possible ideal observer who could think of Mrs Shandy and, thinking, grin.

'Yes, yes.' She had taken tablets; everything was quite safe. It was only when the point of no return had been reached that she remembered that the tablets she had swallowed were analgesic, not contraceptive. Routine let one down sometimes. Then it was too late and she didn't care.

Ten

'GET on with it,' said Tristram, frowning unwontedly. 'Read it up on your own.' The seventh stream of the Fourth Form offered him wide eyes and mouths. 'I'm going home,' he said. 'I've had enough for one day. To-morrow there will be a test on the matter contained between Pages 267 and 274 – inclusive – of your textbook. The Chronic Nuclear Scare and the Coming of Perpetual Peace. Dunlop,' he said sharply. 'Dunlop.' The boy had a rubbery face, but, in this age of total nationalization, his name was neither appropriate nor inappropriate. 'Nose-picking is an unseemly habit, Dunlop,' he said. The class tittered. 'Get on with it,' repeated Tristram at the door, 'and a very good day to you. Or early evening,' he amended, glancing out at the rose marine sky. Curious that the English tongue had never evolved a valedictory form fitting this time of day. [Malay A sort of Interphase. Pelagian day, Augustinian night. Tristram walked boldly out of the classroom, down the corridor to the lift, then sped down and out of the mammoth building itself. Nobody hindered his leaving. Teachers just did not desert their classes before the final bell; ergo, Tristram was still, in some mystical way, at work.

He swam strongly through the crowds on Earp Road (tides simultaneously flowing in and out) and then turned left into Dallas Street. And there, just by the turning into McGibbon Avenue, he saw something which, for no immediate reason he could assign to the

35

sensation, chilled him. On the road, blocking the sparse traffic, watched by crowds that kept their decent distance, was a company of men in the grey uniform of the police – three platoons with platoon commanders – standing at ease. Most of them grinned awkwardly, shuffled; recruits, Tristram divined, new recruits, but each already armed with a squat dull-shining carbine. Their trousers tapered to black elasticated bands which hugged the uppers of deep-soled boots; their waisted tunics were curiously archaic with their collars, brassy collar-dogs glinting on them, and with the collars went black ties. The men were capped in grey cheese-cutters; a police badge shone dead above the frontal lobes.

'Finding jobs for them,' said a man next to Tristram – an unshaven man in rusty black, a roll of fat on his chin though his body was meagre. 'The out-of-work, they are. Were,' he corrected himself. 'About time the Government did something about them. That's my brother-in-law there, see, second from the end of the first row.' He pointed, vicariously proud. 'Giving them jobs,' he repeated. He was evidently a lonely man, glad of the chance to talk to anybody.

'Why?' asked Tristram. 'What's it all about?' But he knew; this was the end of the Pelphase: people were going to be made to be good. He felt a certain panic on his own account. Perhaps he ought to be getting back to the school. Perhaps nobody would know anything about it if he went back right away. It was foolish of him, he'd never done anything like that before. Perhaps he ought to ring up Joscelyne and say he'd left before time because he wasn't feeling well –

'Keep some of them in order,' said the fat-chinned

thin man promptly. 'Too many of these young hooligans round the streets at night. Not strict enough with them, they're not. Teachers don't have any control over them any more.'

'Some of those young recruits,' said Tristram carefully, 'look suspiciously like young hooligans.'

'Are you calling my brother-in-law a hooligan? Best lad who ever breathed, he is, and been unemployed near fourteen months. He's no hooligan, mister.'

An officer now took post before the company. Smart, his pants moulded to his bottom, silver bars on his epaulettes agleam in the sun, a gun holstered in rich leather-substitute on his hip, he called in an unexpectedly manly voice: '*Campniiiiigh –*' The company stiffened, as if for a blow. '*Shn.*' The snarl was hurled like a pebble; the men came to attention raggedly. '*To your jewtahhhhz, diiiii –*' (The syllable wavered between two allophones) '*– zmiss.*' Some turned left, some right, some waited to see what the others were doing. Laughter and jeering claps from the crowd. And now the street was full of wandering knots of self-conscious policemen.

Tristram, feeling somewhat sick, made for Earnshaw Mansions. In a cellar under that thick dry tower was a drinking-shop called the Montague. The only intoxicant available these days was a pungent distillation from vegetable and fruit-peel. It was called alc, and only the lowest-class stomach could take it neat. Tristram put down a tosheroon on the counter and was served with a glass of this vicious viscous spirit, well diluted in orangeade. There was nothing else to drink: hop-fields, the ancient centres of viticulture – these had gone the way of the grazing-plains and the tobacco-lands of

37

Virginia and Turkey; all now supported more esculent crops. A near-vegetarian world, non-smoking, teetotal except for alc. Tristram gravely toasted it and, after another tosheroon's worth of orange fire, felt himself sufficiently reconciled to it. Promotion dead, Roger dead. To hell with Joscelyne. He panned his head almost genially round the close little drinking-hole. Homos, some of them bearded, twittered among themselves in the dark corner; the bar-drinkers were mostly hetero and gloomy. The greasy fat-bottomed barman waddled to a musicator in the wall, put a tanner in the slot, and let loose, like an animal, a grating kind of concrete music – spoons rattling in tin basins, a speech made by the Minister of Pisciculture, a lavatory cistern filling up, a revving engine: all recorded backwards, augmented or diminished, thoroughly mixed. The man next to Tristram said, 'Bloody awful.' He said this to the alc-casks, not moving his head and hardly moving his lips, as if, though the remark had had to be made, he did not want it to be picked up as a pretext for drawing him into conversation. One of the bearded homos now began to recite:

'My dead tree..Give me back my dead dead tree.
Rain, rain, go away. Let the earth be still
Dry. Kick the gods back into the cakey earth,
Making a hole, for that purpose, with a drill.'

'Bloody nonsense,' said the man, more loudly. Then he swung his head, slowly and warily, from side to side, examining Tristram on his right and the drinker on his left with care, as if one were a sculpture of the other and the likeness had to be checked. 'Know what I was?'

he said. Tristram wondered. A saturnine man with eyes in charcoal caves, reddish beak, sulky Stuart mouth. 'Give me another of those,' he said to the barman, plonking his money down. '*Thought* you wouldn't be able to tell,' he said in triumph, turning to Tristram. 'Well,' he said, and he downed raw alc with a smack and a sigh, 'I was a priest. Do you know what that is?'

'A sort of monk,' said Tristram. 'Something to do with religion.' He gave this man a mouthful of awe, as though he were Pelagius himself. 'But,' he objected, 'there aren't any priests any more. There haven't been priests for hundreds of years.'

The man held out his hands, fingers spread, as though testing himself for the shakes. 'These,' he said, 'have performed the daily miracle.' More reasonably, 'There've been a few,' he said. 'One or two pockets of resistance in the Provinces. People who don't hold with all this liberal muck. Pelagius,' he said, 'was a heretic. Man needs divine grace.' He returned to his hands, examining them clinically, as if for some minute spot which would announce the onset of disease. 'More of this stuff,' he told the barman, now using his hands to search in his pockets for money. 'Yes,' he told Tristram. 'There are priests still, though I'm no longer one of them. Thrown out,' he whispered. 'Unfrocked. Oh, God, God, God.' He became histrionic. One or two of the homos tittered, hearing the divine name. 'But they can never take away this power, never, never.'

'Cecil, you old cow!'

'Oh, my dear, just look what *she's* wearing!'

The heteros also turned to look, but with less enthusiasm. A trio of police recruits had come in, smiling wide. One of them performed a small step-dance, ending with a palsied salute. Another pretended to spray the room with his carbine. Remote, cold, abstract, the concrete music went on. The homos laughed, whinnied, embraced.

'It wasn't for that sort of thing I was unfrocked,' said the man. 'It was for real love, the real thing, not this blasphemous mockery.' He nodded gloomily in the direction of the gay group of police and civilians. 'She was very young, only seventeen. Oh, God, God. But,' he said strongly, 'they can't take away this divine power.' He again gazed at his hands, this time like Macbeth. 'Bread and wine,' he said, 'into the body and blood – But there's no wine any more. And the Pope,' he said 'an old, old, old man on St Helena. And me,' he said, without false modesty, 'a blasted clerk in the Ministry of Fuel and Power.'

One of the homo policemen had inserted a tanner in the musicator. A dance-tune plopped out suddenly, as though a bag of ripe plums had burst – a combo of abstract tape-noises with a slow gut-shaking beat deep beneath. One of the policemen began to dance with a bearded civilian. It was graceful, Tristram had to admit that, intricate and graceful. But the unfrocked priest was disgusted. 'Bloody exhibition,' he said, and, as one of the non-dancing homos turned up the volume of the music, he shouted loud and without warning, *'Shut that blasted row!'*

The homos gazed with mild interest, the dancers open-mouthed at him, still rocking gently in each other's arms. *'You* shut it,' said the barman. 'We don't want any trouble here.'

'Unnatural lot of bastards,' said the priest. Tristram admired the priestly language. 'The sin of Sodom. God ought to strike the lot of you dead.'

'You old spoilsport,' one snorted at him. 'Where's your manners?' And then the police were upon him. It was swift, balletic, laughing; not violence as Tristram had read of violence in the past; it seemed more tickling than hitting. But, in no more than a count-out of five, the unfrocked priest was leaning against the bar, trying to draw up breath from a great way down, blood all over his mouth. 'Are you his friend?' one of the police said to Tristram. Tristram was shocked to see that this one wore black lipstick to match his tie.

'No,' said Tristram. 'I've never seen him before. Never seen him before in my life. I was just going anyway.' He finished his alc-and-orange and started to leave.

'And then the cock crew,' grunted the unfrocked priest. 'This is my blood,' he said, wiping his mouth. He was too tipsy to have felt any pain.

Eleven

WHEN they lay panting more slowly, detumescence magically synchronically achieved, his arm under her relaxed body, she wondered if perhaps after all she hadn't meant that to happen. She said nothing to Derek; this was her own affair. She felt rather remote, detached from Derek, as a poet may feel – after a sonnet – detached from the pen that wrote it. The foreign word

Urmutter swam up from her unconscious, and she wondered what it meant.

He was the first to surface from the parachronic, asking, man being a chronic animal, lazily, 'What would the time be now?'

She didn't answer. 'I can't understand,' she said instead. 'All this hypocrisy and deceit. Why do people have to pretend they're something they're not? It's all a ghastly farce.' She spoke sharply but still as from some timeless state. 'You love love,' she said. 'You love love more than any man I've ever known. And yet you treat it as something to be ashamed of.'

He sighed profoundly. 'Dichotomy,' he said, throwing the word languidly at her, like a ball stuffed with duck's down. 'Remember the human dichotomy.'

'What about –' she yawned '– the human whatever-it-is?'

'The division. Contradictions. Instincts tell us one thing and reason tells us another. That could be tragic if we allowed it to be. But it's better to see it as comic. We were right,' he said elliptically, 'to throw God out and install Mr Livedog in his place. God's a tragic conception.'

'I don't know what you're talking about.'

'Never mind.' He caught her yawn belatedly, showing snowy plastic crowns. 'The conflicting claims of line and circle. You're all line, that's your trouble.'

'I'm circular. I'm globular. Look.'

'Physically, yes. Mentally, no. You're still a creature of instinct, after all these years of education and slogans and subliminal film propaganda. You don't give a damn about the state of the world, the state of the State. I do.'

'Why should I? I've got my own life to live.'

'You'd have no life at all to live if it weren't for people like me. The State is each of its members. Supposing,' he said seriously, 'nobody worried about the birth-rate. Supposing we didn't get concerned about the straight line travelling on and on and on. We'd literally starve. Dognose we've little enough to eat as it is. We've managed to achieve a sort of stasis, thanks to my department and similar government departments all over the world, but that can't last much longer, not the way things are going.'

'What do you mean?'

'It's the old story. Liberalism prevails, and liberalism means laxness. We leave it to education and propaganda and free contraceptives, abortion clinics and condolences. We encourage non-productive forms of sexual activity. We like to kid ourselves that people are good enough and wise enough to be aware of their responsibilities. But what happens? There was the case, only a few weeks ago, of a couple in Western Province who'd had six children. *Six.* I ask you. And all alive, too. A very old-fashioned couple – God-followers. They talked about fulfilling God's will and all that nonsense. One of our officials had a word with them, tried to make them see sense. Imagine – eight bodies in a flat smaller than this. But they wouldn't see sense. Apparently they had a copy of the Bible – Dognose where they'd got it from. Have you ever seen one of those?'

'No.'

'Well, it's an old religious book full of smut. The big sin is to waste your seed, and if God loves you He fills your house with kids. The language is very old-fashioned, too. Anyway, they kept appealing to this all the time, talking about fertility and barren fig trees getting cursed and so on.' Derek shuddered with genuine horror. 'They were quite a young couple, too.'

'What happened to them?'

'What *could* happen? They were told there was a law limiting offspring to one birth only, dead or alive, but they said it was a wicked law. If God didn't intend man to be fruitful, they said, why did He implant the instinct for increase in him? They were told that God was an outmoded concept, but they wouldn't take that. They were told they had a duty to their neighbours, and they conceded that, but they couldn't see how limitation of family constituted a duty. A very difficult case.'

'And nothing happened to them?'

'Nothing much. They were fined. They were warned against having any more kids. They were given contraceptive pills and ordered to attend the local birth-control clinic for instruction. But they seemed quite unrepentant. And there are a lot of people like that, all over the world – China, India, the East Indies. That's what's so frightening. That's why there's going to be a change. The world population figures are hair-raising. We're several millions on the wrong side. All through trusting people. You wait, you'll see our rations reduced in a day or so. What *is* the time?' he asked again. It was not an urgent question; he could, if he'd wanted, have removed his arm from under her warm lax body, leaned out to the far corner of the tiny room, and picked up his wrist micro-radio, which had a watch-face in its back. But he was too lazy to move.

'I should think it's about five-thirty,' said Beatrice-

Joanna. 'You can check with the telly, if you like.' His free arm was able, quite comfortably, to click the switch by the bedhead. A light curtain came down over the window, shutting out just enough of the day, and in a second or so synthetic music came gurgling and wailing gently from the ceiling. Unblown, unplucked, unbeaten music, like that heard distractedly by alc-drinking Tristram at that very moment. Here were oscillating valves, tap-water, ships' sirens, thunder, marching feet, vocalizations into a throat-mike – crabbed and inverted to create a brief symphony designed to please rather than excite. The screen above their heads glowed whitely, then erupted into a coloured stereoscopic image of the statue that crowned Government Building. The stone eyes, above a baroque beard, a nose strong to break the wind, glared out defiantly; clouds moved behind as if in a hurry; the sky was the colour of school ink.

'There he is,' said Derek, 'whoever he is – our patron saint. St Pelagius, St Augustine, or St Anonymous – which? We shall know tonight.'

The saint's image faded. Then bloomed an imposing ecclesiastical interior – venerable grey nave, ogee arches. From the altar marched down two plump male figures dressed snowily like hospital housemen. 'The Sacred Game,' announced a voice. 'Cheltenham Ladies against West Bromwich Males. Cheltenham Ladies have won the toss and elected to bat first.' The plump white figures came down to inspect the wicket in the nave. Derek switched off. The stereoscopic image lost a dimension, then died.

'It's just after six, then,' said Derek. 'I'd better be going.' He eased his numb arm from under his mistress's shoulder-blades, then swung himself off the bed.

'There's plenty of time,' yawned Beatrice-Joanna.

'Not any more.' Derek drew on his narrow trousers. He strapped his microradio to his wrist, glancing at the watch-face. 'Twenty past,' he said. Then, 'The Sacred Game, indeed. The last ritual of civilized Western Man.' He snorted. 'Look,' he said, 'we'd better not see each other for a week or so. Whatever you do, don't come looking for me in the Ministry. I'll get in touch with you somehow. Somehow,' he said vaguely, muffled by his shirt. 'Would you be an angel,' he said, putting on the homosexual mask with his jacket, 'and just peep out and see if there's anybody on the corridor? I don't want to be seen leaving.'

'All right.' Beatrice-Joanna sighed, got off the bed, put on her dressing-gown, and went to the door. She looked left and right, like a child practising kerb-drill, came back in and said, 'Nobody there.'

'Thank Dog for that.' He pronounced the final plosive too sibilantly, petulantly.

'There's no need to put on that homo act with me, Derek.'

'Every good actor,' he minced, 'starts acting in the wings.' He gave her a butterfly kiss on the left cheek. 'Good-bye, dearest.'

'Good-bye.' He undulated down the corridor towards the lift, the satyr in him put to sleep till next time, whenever that would be.

Twelve

STILL somewhat shaken, despite two more glasses of alc in a drinking-cellar nearer home, Tristram entered Spurgin Building. Even here, in the large vestibule, there were laughing grey uniforms. He didn't like it, he didn't like it one bit. Waiting at the lift-gates were neighbours of the fortieth floor – Wace, Durtnell and Visser; Mrs Hamper and young Jack Phoenix; Miss Wallis, Miss Runting, Arthur Spragg; Phipps, Walker-Meredith, Fred Hamp, the octogenarian Mr Earthrowl. The lift-indicators flashed yellow: 47 – 46 – 45. 'I saw a rather terrible thing,' said Tristram to old Mr Earthrowl. 'Eh?' said Mr Earthrowl. 38 – 37 – 36. 'A special emergency regulation,' said Phipps of the Ministry of Labour. 'They've all been ordered back to work.' Young Jack Phoenix yawned; Tristram noticed, for the first time, black hairs on his cheekbones. 22 – 21 – 20 – 19. 'Police on the docks,' Durtnell was saying. 'Only way to deal with the bastards. Rough stuff. Should have done it years ago.' He looked with approval at the grey police, black-tied as if in mourning for Pelagianism, light carbines under their arms. 12 – 11 – 10. In imagination Tristram punched a homo or castro on his sweet plump face. 3 – 2 – 1 – G. And there was the face, neither sweet nor plump, of his brother Derek. Both looked astonished at each other.

'What,' asked Tristram, 'in Dogsname are you doing here?'

'Oh, Tristram,' minced Derek, alveolizing the name

to an insincere caress. 'So there you are.'

'Yes. Have you been looking for me or something?'

'That's it, my dear. To tell you how terribly sorry I am. Poor, poor little boy.'

The lift was filling fast. 'Is this official commiseration? I always understood your department rejoiced over deaths.' He frowned, puzzled.

'This is me, your brother,' said Derek. '*Not* an official of the M of I.' He spoke rather stiffly. 'I came to offer my –' He nearly said 'condolences', but that, he realized in time, would have sounded cynical. 'A fraternal visit,' he said. 'I've seen your *wife*' (the slight pause before the word, the unnatural stressing – these made it rather obscene) 'and she told me you were still at work, so I – Anyhow, I'm terribly, terribly sorry. We must,' he valedicted vaguely, 'get together some evening. Dinner, or something. Now I must fly. An appointment with the Minister.' And he was off, his bottom wagging. Tristram crushed himself into the lift, hard against Spragg and Miss Wallis, still frowning. What was going on? The door slid to, the lift began to rise. Miss Wallis, a pallid dumpling with a nose that shone as if wet, breathed on Tristram a ghost of reconstituted dehydrated potatoes. Why had Derek deigned to pay their flat a visit? They disliked each other, and not solely because the State had always, as an aspect of the policy of discrediting the whole notion of family, encouraged fraternal enmity. There had always been jealousy, resentment of the preferential cosseting given to Tristram, his father's favourite – a warm place in his dad's bed on holiday mornings; the top of his breakfast egg; the superior toys on New Year's Day. The other brother and the sister

48

had shrugged good-humouredly at this, but not Derek. Derek had expressed his jealousy in sly kicks, lies, mud spattered on Tristram's Sunday space-suit, acts of vandalism on his toys. And the final channel between them had been dug in adolescence – Derek's sexual inversion and Tristram's undisguised nausea at this. Moreover, despite inferior educational chances, Derek had got on far, far better than his brother – snarls of envy, thumbed noses of triumph. So, what malevolent motive had brought him here today? Tristram instinctively associated the visit with the new régime, the opening of the Interphase. Perhaps there had been swift telephone messages to and from Joscelyne and the Ministry of Infertility (search his flat for heterodox lecture-notes; question his wife about his views on Population Control). Tristram, in slight panic, leafed through memories of lessons he had given – that ironic laudation of the Mormons in Utah; that eloquent digression on *The Golden Bough* (forbidden reading); a possible sneer at the homo hierarchy after a particularly bad school luncheon. It was most unfortunate that he should have chosen to leave the school premises without permission, he thought yet again, on this day of all days. And then the brave spirit rose within his stomach as the lift stopped at the fortieth floor. The alc cried, 'To hell with them!'

Tristram made for his flat. Outside the door he paused, wiping out the automatic expectation of a child's cry of greeting. He went in. Beatrice-Joanna sat in her dressing-gown, doing nothing. She got up quickly, very surprised, on seeing her husband home so early. Tristram noticed, the bedroom door being open, a crumpled bed, bed of a fever-patient.

'Have you had a visitor?' he asked.

'A visitor? What visitor?'

'I saw my dear brother down below. He said he'd been here, looking for me.'

'Oh, him.' She let out a good deal of breath. 'I thought you meant, you know – a visitor.'

Tristram sniffed through the all-pervading scent of Anaphro, as if after something fishy. 'What did he want?'

'Why are you home so early?' asked Beatrice-Joanna. 'Didn't you feel well or something?'

'What I was told made me very unwell. I don't get my promotion. My father's philoprogenitiveness disqualifies me. And my own heterosexuality.' He wandered, hands behind him, into the bedroom.

'I didn't have time to tidy up,' she said, coming in to straighten the bedclothes. 'I was at the hospital. I haven't been back long.'

'We seem to have had a disturbed night,' he said. He left the bedroom. 'Yes,' he continued. 'The job's going to some little homo squirt like Derek. I suppose I should have expected it.'

'We're going through a rotten period, aren't we?' she said. She stood limply an instant, forlorn-looking, holding the end of a rumpled sheet. 'No luck at all.'

'You still haven't told me what Derek was after.'

'It wasn't at all clear. He was looking for you.' A close squeak, she was thinking; a very narrow shave. 'It was a bit of a surprise, seeing him,' she improvised.

'The liar,' he said. 'I thought it wouldn't be just to commiserate with us. How would he know about Roger, anyway? How would he have found out? I bet he only knew because you told him.'

'He knew,' she invented. 'He'd seen it at the Ministry. The daily death figures, or something. Will you eat now? I'm not a bit hungry.' She left the bed, came into the living-room, and made the tiny refrigerator, like some Polar god, descend from the ceiling.

'He's after something,' said Tristram. 'That's certain. I'll have to watch my step.' And then, the alc helping, 'Why the hell should I? Blast the lot of them. People like Derek running the country.' He summoned a chair from the wall. Beatrice-Joanna capped this by making a table rise from the floor. 'I feel anti-social,' said Tristram, 'deliriously anti-social. Who are they to tell us how to run our lives? And, oh,' he said, 'I don't like what's happening at all. There are a lot of police about. Armed.' He neglected to tell her what had happened to the unfrocked priest in the bar. She didn't approve of his drinking.

Beatrice-Joanna served him with a cutlet of reconstituted vegetable dehydrate, cold. He ate with fair appetite. Then she gave him a slice of synthelac pudding. 'Have a nut?' she offered, when he'd finished. A nut was a nutrition-unit, creation of the Ministry of Synthetic Food. She leaned over him, reaching for these from a wall-cupboard, and he caught a glimpse of her rich nakedness under the dressing-gown. 'God damn and blast them all,' he said, 'and it's God I mean.' He got up and tried to take her in his arms.

'No, please, don't,' she begged. It was no good; she couldn't bear his touch. She struggled. 'I'm not feeling at all well,' she said. 'I'm upset.' She began to snivel. He desisted.

'Oh, well,' he said. 'Oh, very well.' He bit at his left little finger-nail with his plastic teeth, standing by the window, awkward. 'I'm sorry I did that. I just didn't think.' She gathered the paper plates from the table and shot them into the firehole in the wall. 'Ah, hell,' he said with sudden violence. 'They've turned normal decent sex into a crime. And you don't want it any more. Just as well, I suppose.' He sighed. 'I can see that I'll have to join the volunteer geldings if I even want to keep my job.'

At that moment Beatrice-Joanna had a sharp revisitation of a sensation that, just for a blinding second, had buffeted her cortex when lying under Derek on that crumpled fever-bed. A sort of eucharistic moment of high-pitched trumpets and a crack of light like that (so it is said) seen at the instant of severing the optic nerve. And a tiny voice, peculiarly penetrating, squealing, 'Yes yes yes.' If everybody was talking about being careful, perhaps she'd better be careful, too. Not all that careful, of course. Only careful enough for Tristram not to know. Contraceptive devices had been known to fail. She said: 'I'm sorry, darling. I didn't mean that.' She put her arms round his neck. 'Now, if you like.' If only it could be done under an anaesthetic. Still, it wouldn't last long.

Tristram kissed her hungrily. '*I'll* take the tablets,' he said, 'not you.' Ever since the birth of Roger – on the admittedly and blessedly few occasions of his seeking his conjugal rights – he had always insisted on taking the precautions himself. For he had not really wanted Roger. 'I'll take three,' he said. 'Just to be on the safe side.' The tiny voice within had a miniature chuckle at that.

Thirteen

BEATRICE-JOANNA and Tristram, preoccupied in their several ways, did not see and hear the Prime Minister's announcement on television. But in millions of other homes – generally on the bedroom ceiling, there being insufficient space elsewhere – the stereoscopic image of the pouched, bulbous, classical scholar's face of the Right Hon. Robert Starling glowed and scolded like a fretful lamp. It spoke of the desperate dangers that England, that the English-Speaking Union, that the great globe itself would soon be running into unless certain strong repressive measures were, albeit regretfully, taken. This was war. War against irresponsibility, against those elements that were sabotaging – and such sabotage was clearly intolerable – the engines of state, against the wholesale flouting of reasonable and liberal laws, especially that law which, for the community's good, sought to limit the growth of population. All over the planet, said the luminous face with gravity, the leaders of state would be speaking – tonight or tomorrow – in similar urgent terms to their various peoples; the whole world was declaring war on itself. The severest punishments for continued irresponsibility (hurting the punishers more than the punished, it was implied); planetary survival dependent on the balance of population and a scientifically calculated minimal food supply; tighten belts; win through; evil things they would be fighting; pull together; long live the King.

Beatrice-Joanna and Tristram also missed some exciting stereoscopic film-shots of the summary settling of the strike at the National Synthelac Works – the police, nicknamed greyboys, using truncheons and carbines, laughing the while; a splash of chromatic brains on the camera lens.

They also missed a later announcement about the formation of a corps called the Population Police, its proposed Metropolitan Commissioner well-known to them both – brother, betrayer, lover.

Part Two

One

An eight-hour shift system operated in all the State Utilities. But the schools and colleges split the day (every day, vacations being staggered) into four shifts of six hours each. Nearly two months after the opening of the Interphase, Tristram Foxe sat at midnight breakfast (shift starting at one) with a full summer moon slanting in. He was trying to eat a sort of paper cereal moistened with synthelac, and – though hungry at all hours these days, the rations having been cut considerably – he found it very difficult to spoon down the wet fibrous horror: it was somehow like having to eat one's words. As he munched an endless mouthful, the synthetic voice of the *Daily Newsdisc* (23.00 edition) squealed like a cartoon mouse, what time the organ itself wheeled slow and shiny black on the wall-spindle. '. . . Unprecedently low herring catches, explicable only in terms of inexplicable failure to breed, Ministry of Pisciculture reports –' Tristram reached out his left hand and switched off. Birth control among fish, eh? Tristram reeled an instant in a sudden race-memory – a sort of round flat fish overlapping the plate, crisp brown with a sharpish sauce. But all fish caught these days were crunched up by machines, converted into manure or mashed into the all-purpose nutrition-block (to be served as soup, cutlets, bread or pudding) which the Ministry of Natural Food issued as the main part of the weekly ration.

The living-room now being emptied of the manic voice and its ghastly journalese, Tristram could hear more clearly his wife being sick in the bathroom. Poor girl, she was regularly sick on rising these days. Perhaps it was the food. Enough to make anyone sick. He got up from the table and looked in on her. She was pale and tired-looking, limp as though the vomiting had wrung her out. 'I should go to the hospital if I were you,' he said kindly. 'See what's the matter.'

'I'm all right.'

'You don't seem all right to me.' He turned over his wrist microradio; the watch-face on the back said past twelve-thirty. 'I must fly.' He kissed her damp forehead. 'Look after yourself, dear. Do go and see somebody at the hospital.'

'It's nothing. Just a tummy upset.' And indeed she began, as if for his benefit, to look much better.

Tristram left (just a tummy upset) and joined the group waiting at the lift. Old Mr Earthrowl, Phipps, Arthur Spragg, Miss Runting – race-blocks like nutrition-blocks: Europe, Africa, Asia mashed together, salted by Polynesia – off to their jobs in the ministries and the national factories; Allsopp and the bearded Abazoff, Darking and Hamidun, Mrs Gow whose husband had been taken off three weeks before – ready for the shift that would end two hours later than Tristram's own. Mr Earthrowl was saying, in a wavering ancient voice, 'It's not right at all, the way I see it, having these coppers watching you all the time. Wasn't like that in my young days. If you wanted a smoke in the lavatory you went for a smoke, and no questions asked. But not now, oh, no. Breathing down your neck, these coppers are, all the time. Not right, way I look at it.' He continued his grumbling, the bearded Abazoff nodding the while, as they got into the lift – an old man, harmless and not very bright, driver of a large screw into the back of the television cabinet that, in endless multiplication, crawled towards and past him on a conveyor-belt. In the lift, Tristram said quietly to Mrs Gow:

'Any news?'

She looked up at him, a long-faced woman of forty-odd, her skin dry and smoked like that of a gipsy. 'Not a word. It's my belief that they've shot him. *Shot him,*' she suddenly cried aloud. Fellow-passengers pretended not to hear.

'Nonsense.' Tristram patted her thin arm. 'He didn't commit any real crime. He'll be back soon, you'll see.'

'It was his own fault,' said Mrs Gow. 'Drinking that there alc. Shooting his mouth off. I always told him he'd go too far one of these days.'

'There, there,' said Tristram, continuing to pat. The truth was that Gow hadn't technically shot his mouth off at all; he'd merely rasped a brief rude noise at a knot of policemen outside one of the rougher drinking-shops, somewhere off Guthrie Road. He'd been carted off amid great hilarity, and no more had been seen of him. It was best to keep off alc these days, best to leave alc to the greyboys.

4 – 3 – 2 – 1 – G. Tristram shuffled out of the lift. Moonshot plummy night waited outside in the packed street. And in the vestibule were members of the Poppol or Population Police – black uniform, cap with shiny

59

peak, badge and collar-dogs ashine with a bursting bomb which proved, on closer inspection, to be a breaking egg. Unarmed, less given to summary violence than the greyboys, smart, polite, they were mostly a credit to their commissioner. Tristram, joining the I-had-not-thought-death-had-undone-so-many workward crowd, uttered the word 'brother' aloud to the night-running Channel and its silver sky. The term had taken on purely pejorative connotations for him, which was not fair on poor inoffensive George, eldest of the three, hard at work on an agricultural station near Springfield, Ohio. George had recently sent one of his rare letters, dully factual about experiments with new fertilizers, puzzled about a strange wheat-blight seeping east through Iowa, Illinois and Indiana. Good solid old George.

Tristram entered the good solid old skyscraper which was the South London (Channel) Unitary School (Boys) Division Four. The Delta Shift was streaming out, and one of Joscelyne's three deputies, an open-mouthed grey-coxcombed man named Cory, stood in the great vestibule, watching. The Alpha Shift darted and needled into lifts, up stairs, down corridors. Tristram's first lesson was on the second floor – Elementary Historical Geography for the twentieth stream of the First Form. The artificial voice counted: '– Eighteen – seventeen –' Was it only his imagination, or was that creation of the National Syntheglot Corporation sterner, more iron-like, than it used to be?' '– Three – two – one.' He was late. He shot up in a staff-lift and panted into the class-room. One had to be careful these days.

Fifty-odd boys of various colour-mixtures greeted him

in a single polite 'Good morning'. Morning, eh? Night sat firmly on outside; the moon, great and frightening female symbol, sat over the night. Tristram said:

'Homework. Homework on your desks, please.' The tinkle of metal fasteners as the boys undid their satchels, then the flap of exercise-books, the rustle as they turned to the page where they had drawn their map of the world. Tristram strolled round, hands clasped behind, cursorily examining. The great crowded globe on Mercator's Projection, the two great empires – Enspun (English-Speaking Union) and Ruspun (Russian-Speaking Union) – crudely copied by lolling tonguetip-protruding boys. The Annexe Islands for population overflow, still building on the major oceans. A peaceful world that had forgotten the arts of self-destruction, peaceful and worried. 'Careless,' said Tristram, his forefinger on Cottam's drawing. 'You've put Australia too far south. You've forgotten to put in Ireland.' 'Sir,' said Cottam. And here was a boy – Hynard – who had not done his homework, a scared-looking boy, dark moons under his eyes. 'What,' asked Tristram, 'is the meaning of this?'

'I wasn't able to, sir,' said Hynard, his lower lip shaking. 'They moved me to the Hostel, sir. I hadn't time, sir.'

'Oh. The Hostel.' This was something new, an institution for orphans, temporary and permanent. 'What happened?'

'They took them away, sir, my dad and mum. They said they'd done wrong.'

'What had they done?'

The boy hung his head. An awareness of crime, not

taboo, kept him red and silent. Tristram said, kindly:

'Your mother has just had a baby, is that it?'

'Going to,' mumbled the boy. 'They took them away. They had to pack everything up. And then they took me to the Hostel.'

A great anger suffused Tristram. It was (and he realized this with shame) really a factitious anger, a pedantic anger. He saw himself in the Principal's office, ranting: 'The State regards the education of these children as important, which presumably means that they regard homework as important, and here the State comes sticking in its ugly hypocritical snout and stops one of my pupils from doing his homework. For Dog-sake let's know where we stand.' The weak fretfulness of a man invoking principle. He knew, of course, what the answer would be: first things first, the first thing being survival. He sighed, patted the boy's head, then went back to the front of the class. 'This morning,' he said, 'we're going to draw a map of the Sahara Reclamation Area. Take out your pencils.' Morning indeed. Night, that sea of school ink, flowed strongly away outside.

Two

BEATRICE-JOANNA sat writing a letter. She wrote in pencil, unhandily through desuetude, using the paper-saving logograms she had learned at school. Two months, and she had seen both nothing and too much of Derek. Too much of the public television image – Derek as black-uniformed reasonably exhorting Commissioner of the Population Police; nothing of Derek the lover, wearing a more becoming uniform of nakedness and desire. There was no censorship of letters, and she felt she could write freely. She wrote: 'Darling, I suppose I ought to be proud of the great name you're making for yourself, and you certainly look lovely in your new clothes. But I can't help wishing things were as they were before, when we could lie together loving each other, and not a care in the world except making sure that nobody knew what was going on between us. I refuse to believe that those lovely times are over. I miss you so much. I miss your arms around me and your lips on mine and –' She deleted this ampersand; some things were too precious to give to cold logograms. '– and your lips on mine. Oh, darling, sometimes I wake in the night or afternoon or morning or whenever it is we go to bed, according to the shift he's working, and want to cry out with desire for you.' She crammed her left fist in her mouth as if to stifle such a cry. 'Oh, dearest one, I love you, love you, love you. I long for your arms around me and your lips –' She saw that she had already said that, so she crossed it out; but the crossing-out made it appear that she had thought better of wanting his arms, lips and so on. She shrugged and went on. 'Couldn't you get in touch with me somehow? I know it's too risky for you to write to me, as Tristram would be sure to see the letter in the block letter-rack, but surely you could somehow give me a sign to show you still love me? And you do still love me, don't you, dearest?' He could send her a token. In the old days, the days of Shakespeare and steam radio, lovers had sent their mistresses flowers.

Now, of course, what flowers there were were all rendered esculent. He could send a packet of dehydrated cowslip broth, but that would mean cutting into his meagre rations. She longed for something romantic and daring, some big heretical gesture. In inspiration she wrote, 'When next you are on the telly please, if you love me still, bring in some special word, just for me. Bring in the word "love" or the word "desire". Then I'll know that you go on loving me as I go on loving you. There is no news, life goes on as it always does, very dull and dreary.' That was a lie: there was, she thought, a very definite item of news, but that had to be kept to herself. The straight line within her, the eternal and life-giving lance, wanted to say 'Rejoice', but the circle counselled caution; more than that, it span in a self-made breeze of apprehension. She refused to worry; things would work out all right. She signed the letter, 'Your eternally adoring Beatrice-Joanna.'

She addressed the letter to Commissioner D. Foxe, Population Police HQ, Infertility Building, Brighton, London, feeling a slight tremor as she wrote 'Infertility', that word which contained its opposite. She added in big bold logograms 'PRIVATE AND CONFIDENTIAL'. Then she went on the long vertical journey to the post-box by Earnshaw Mansions. It was a lovely July night, high moon riding, stars, earth-satellites wheeling, a night for love. Five young greyboys, lit by a streetlamp, were laughingly beating up a bewildered-looking old man who appeared, from his lack of response to the slaps and truncheonings, anaesthetized by alc. He seemed also, a Neronian Nazarene set upon by tittering lions, to be singing a hymn. 'You ought to be ashamed,' rebuked Beatrice-Joanna fiercely, 'downright ashamed. A poor old man like that.'

'You mind your own business,' said one of the grey policemen peevishly. '*Woman.*' he added with scorn. Their victim was allowed to crawl away, still singing. Very much a woman, minding her own business, socially and biologically, she shrugged and posted her letter.

Three

A LETTER for Tristram in the staff-room letter-rack, a letter from his sister Emma. It was four-thirty, hour of the half-hour luncheon break, but the bell had still to go. Dawn was coming up deliciously over the sea far beneath the staff-room window. Tristram fingered the letter with its garish Chinese stamp, its superscription *Air Mail* in ideograms and Cyrillic, smiling at yet another example of family telepathy. It was always happening like this – a letter from George in the West followed a day or so after by one from Emma in the East. Neither of them, significantly, ever wrote to Derek. Tristram read, still smiling, standing among his colleagues: '. . . The work goes on. I flew last week from Chengkiang to Hingi to Changchai to Tuyun to Shihtsien – exhausting. It's still almost standing room only here, but really frightening measures are being taken by the Central Government since the recent change in policy began. A mass execution of offenders against the Increase in Family laws took place in Chungking only ten days ago. This seemed to a lot of us to be going too far –' Typical of her, that understatement; Tristram caught an image of her prim forty-five-year-old face, the thin prim lips saying it. '– But it does seem to be having a salutary effect on some who, despite everything, still cherish as a life's ambition becoming an honourable ancestor to be worshipped by a milling mound of progeny. Such people are likely to become ancestors sooner than they expect. Curiously, ironically, there looks like being something of a famine in Fukien Province where the rice-crops – for some reason unknown – have failed . . .' Tristram frowned and wondered. George's report about the wheat-blight, the news about herring catches, now this. There awoke in him a faint nagging suspicion about something, he couldn't tell what.

'And how,' said a young mincing niggling voice, 'is our dear Tristram today?' It was Geoffrey Wiltshire, the new head of the Social Studies Department, literally a blue-eyed boy, so fair as almost to look white-headed. Tristram, who was trying not to hate him too much, gave a lemony smile and said, 'Well.'

'I tuned in to your Sixth Form lesson,' said Wiltshire. 'I know you won't mind my saying this, my dear dear Tristram.' He brought a whiff of perfume and two sets of twittering lashes close to his colleague. 'Saying that, in effect, you were teaching something you should *not* have been teaching.'

'I don't recollect.' Tristram tried to master his breathing.

'I, on the other hand, recollect rather perfectly. You said something like this: art, you said, cannot flourish in a society like ours, because, you seemed to say, art is

the product of – I think this is the term you used –
paternity lust. Wait,' he said, 'wait,' to Tristram's open
mouth. 'You also said that the materials of the arts were,
in effect, fertility symbols. Now, apart from the fact, my
still dear Tristram, apart from the fact that one is at a
complete loss to know how exactly this fits into the
syllabus, you were quite gratuitously – and you can't
deny this – quite gratuitously teaching something which
is, however you look at it, to say the least heretical.'
The bell rang for luncheon. Wiltshire put his arm
round Tristram as they all processed to the staff dining-
hall.

'But,' said Tristram, fighting his anger, 'damn it all,
it's true. All art is an aspect of sexuality –'

'Nobody, my dear Tristram, denies that that, to some
extent, is perfectly true.'

'But it goes deeper. Great art, the art of the past, is
a kind of glorification of increase. I mean, take even
drama for instance. I mean, tragedy and comedy had
their origin in fertility ceremonies. The sacrificial goat –
that's *tragos* in Greek – and the village Priapic festivals
which crystallized into comic drama. I mean – and,'
spluttered Tristram, 'take architecture –'

'We shall take no more.' Wiltshire stopped, dropped
his arm from around Tristram's shoulder, and wagged
a forefinger at Tristram's eyes, as though to disperse the
smoke in them. 'We shall have no more of that, shall
we, dear Tristram? Do, please, please, be careful. Everybody's really quite fond of you, you know.'

'I don't quite see what that has to do with anything –'

'It has a *lot* to do with *everything*. Now, just be a
good boy –' he was at least seven years younger than

Tristram '– and stick to the syllabus. You can't go very far wrong if you do that.'

Tristram said nothing, pushing the lid down hard on his boiling temper. But, entering the steamy dining-hall, he deliberately stalked away from Wiltshire, seeking a table where sat Visser, Adair, Butcher (a very ancient trade-name), Freathy and Haskell-Sprott. These were harmless men who taught harmless subjects – simple skills into which controversy could never enter. 'You look,' said Mongol-eyed Adair, 'pretty sick.'

'I feel pretty sick,' said Tristram. Haskell-Sprott, at the head of the mess, spooned out very thin vegetable stew, saying:

'This'll make you sicker.'

'– Little bastards have been better behaved since we've had a chance to be tough with them,' Visser was saying. He mimed violent boxing. 'Take young Mildred, for example – queer name, Mildred, a girl's name, though that's the lad's surname, of course – take him. Late again today, so what do I do? I let the toughs get at him –you know, Brisker and Couchman and that lot. They roughed him up something beautiful. Just two minutes of that, that's all. He couldn't get up from the floor.'

'You've got to have discipline,' agreed Butcher through a mouthful of stew.

'I say,' said Adair to Tristram, 'you *do* look pretty sick.'

'As long as he hasn't got morning sickness,' leered the joker Freathy.

Tristram put down his spoon. 'What did you say then?'

68

'A joke,' said Freathy. 'I meant no harm.'

'You said something about morning sickness.'

'Forget it. Just my fun.'

'But that's impossible,' said Tristram. 'That couldn't be possible.'

'If I were you,' said Adair, 'I should go and have a lie down. You don't look at all well.'

'Absolutely impossible,' said Tristram.

'If you don't want your stew,' said Freathy, dripping with greed, 'I'd be very much obliged –' And he slid Tristram's plate towards himself.

'That's not fair,' said Butcher. 'It should be shared out. That's sheer damned gutsiness.' They tugged, slopping the stew.

'I think I'd better go home,' said Tristram.

'You do that,' said Adair. 'You might be sickening for something. Something catching.' Tristram got up and tottered over to tell Wiltshire. Butcher had won the stew and was sucking it down in triumph.

'Gulosity,' said Haskell-Sprott tolerantly. 'That's the word.'

Four

'But how could it have happened?' cried Tristram. 'How? How? How?' Two paces to the window, two paces back to the wall, his hands agitatedly clasped behind him.

'Nothing's one hundred per cent sure,' said Beatrice-

Joanna, sitting placidly. 'There might have been sabotage at the Contraceptive Works.'

'Nonsense. Absolute and utter bloody nonsense. That's a frivolous sort of remark,' cried Tristram, turning on her. 'That's typical of your whole attitude.'

'Are you sure,' said Beatrice-Joanna, 'that you actually took your tablets on that memorable occasion?'

'Of course I'm sure. I wouldn't dream of taking a risk like that.'

'No, of course you wouldn't.' She swayed her head, reciting in sing-song: 'Take a tablet instead of a risk.' She smiled up at him. 'That would have made a good slogan, wouldn't it? But, of course, we don't have slogans to make us good any more. We have the big stick.'

'It's completely beyond my understanding,' said Tristram. 'Unless –' He beetled down at her. 'But you wouldn't do that, would you? You wouldn't be so wicked and evil and sinful as to do that.' Augustinian words. He grasped her by the wrist. 'Is there anybody else?' he asked. 'Tell me the truth. I promise not to be angry,' he said angrily.

'Oh, don't be stupid,' she said very quietly. 'Even if I wanted to be unfaithful, who could I be unfaithful with? We don't go anywhere, we don't know anyone. And,' she said with heat, 'I object strongly to your saying that. To your thinking that. I've been faithful to you ever since the day we got married, and a fat lot of thanks or appreciation I've ever had for my fidelity.'

'I must have taken the tablets,' said Tristram, thinking hard back. 'I remember when it was. It was the day when poor young Roger –'

'Yes, yes, yes.'

'– And I'd just had my dinner and, if I remember rightly, it was you who suggested –'

'Oh, no, Tristram. It wasn't me. It certainly wasn't me.'

'– And I have a distinct recollection that I pulled the medicine cupboard down from the ceiling and that I –'

'You'd been drinking, Tristram. You smelt *terribly* of alc.' Tristram hung his head an instant. 'Are you sure you took the *right* tablets? I didn't check that with you. You always know best, don't you dear?' Her natural teeth gleamed in sarcasm. 'Anyhow, there it is. Perhaps it was a sudden accession of *paternity lust.*'

'Where did you get that expression from?' he blazed at her. 'Who told you those words?'

'You did,' she said sighing. 'It's an expression you sometimes use.' He stared at her. 'There must,' she added, 'be quite a lot of the heretic in you. In your unconscious, anyway. You say things in your sleep, you know. You wake me up with your snoring and then, assured of an audience, you talk. You're quite as bad as I am, in your way.'

'Well.' He looked round vaguely for somewhere to sit down. Beatrice-Joanna made another chair come purring out of the wall. 'Thanks,' he said distractedly. 'However it happened,' he said, sitting, 'you'll have to get rid of it. You'll have to take something. You won't want to leave it till you have to go to the Abortion Centre. That'll be shameful. That'll be almost as bad as breaking the law. Carelessness,' he muttered. 'No self-control.'

'Oh, I don't know.' She was too cool about the whole thing. 'Things may not be as bad as you think. I mean, people have been having children in excess of the ration and nothing much has happened to them. I'm entitled to a child,' she said more warmly. 'The State killed Roger. The State let him die.'

'Ah, nonsense. We've been over all that before. What you don't seem to realize in your stupidity is that things have changed. *Things have changed.*' He emphasized this by punching her on the knee, once for each word. 'Look,' he said. 'The days of asking are over. The State doesn't ask any more. The State orders, the State compels. Do you realize that in China people have actually been put to death for disobeying the birth-control laws? Executed. Hanged or shot – I'm not sure which. It's in a letter I got from Emma.'

'This isn't China,' she said. 'We're more civilized here.'

'Ah, arrant bloody nonsense. It's going to be the same everywhere. The parents of one of my pupils were carted off by the Population Police – do you realize that? It happened only last night. And, as far as I can gather, they hadn't even had the baby yet. She just happened to be pregnant, as far as I can gather. Good Dog, woman, it won't be long before they'll be coming round with mice in a cage, testing urine for pregnancy.'

'How do they do that?' she asked, interested.

'You're incorrigible, that's what you are.' He got up again. Beatrice-Joanna let his chair whine back to the wall, giving him room to pace. 'Thanks. Now, look,' he said, 'just think of our position. If anybody found out we'd been careless, even without the results of the carelessness going any further, if anybody found out that –'

'How could anybody find out that?'

'Oh, I don't know. Somebody might hear you, in the morning, when you get up, that is,' he said delicately. 'There's Mrs Pettitt next door. There are spies around, you know. Where you have police you always have spies. Narks, they call them. Or you might say something to somebody – accidentally, I mean. I might as well tell you that I don't like the way things are going at the school. That little swine Wiltshire keeps plugging in on my lessons. Look,' he said, 'I'm going out now. I'm going to the chemist's. I'm going to get you some quinine tablets. And some castor oil.'

'I don't like them. I hate the taste of both of them. Give it a bit longer, will you? Just give it a bit longer. Everything may be all right.'

'There you go again. Let me try and get it into your thick skull,' said Tristram, 'that we're living in dangerous times. The Population Police have a lot of power. They can be very very nasty.'

'I don't think they'd ever do me any harm,' she said complacently.

'Why not? Why wouldn't they?'

'I've just got a feeling, that's all.' Careful, careful. 'I just have a sort of intuition about it, that's all.' Then, 'Oh,' she cried powerfully, 'I'm sick to death of the whole business. If God made us what we are, why should we have to worry about what the State tells us to do? God's stronger and wiser than the State, isn't He?'

'There is no God.' Tristram looked at her curiously. 'Where have you been getting these ideas from? Who's been talking to you?'

'Nobody's been talking to me. I see nobody, except when I go out to buy rations. When I talk, I talk to

73

myself. Or to the sea. Sometimes I talk to the sea.'

'What is all this? What exactly is going on? Do you feel all right?'

'Except for being hungry all the time,' said Beatrice-Joanna, 'I feel very well. Very well indeed.'

Tristram went to the window and gazed up at the patch of sky visible between topless towers. 'I wonder sometimes,' he said, 'if perhaps there is a God after all. Somebody up there,' he mumbled, musing, 'controlling everything. I wonder sometimes. But,' he said, turning in a small show of sudden panic, 'don't tell anybody I said that. I didn't say there *was* a God. I just said I wondered sometimes, that's all.'

'You don't trust me very much, do you?'

'I don't trust anyone. Forgive me, but I might as well be honest with you. I just daren't trust anybody at all. I don't seem able even to trust myself, do I?' Then he went out into the pearly morning to buy quinine in one State Druggist's, castor oil in another. In the first shop he talked loudly about malaria, even mentioning an educational trip he had once taken down the Amazon; in the second he simulated a convincing costive look.

Five

IF no God, there must be at least a pattern-making demiurge. So Tristram was later to think, when he had leisure and inclination for thinking. The next day (though only the calendar really accepted such a term, the shift-system cutting across natural time like a global air-journey) the next day Tristram knew he was being followed. A neat blob of black in the crowds behind him, keeping its distance, seen fully – as Tristram turned into Rostron Place – as a comely small man with a moustache, Poppol egg bursting in the sun on his cap-badge, three glinting stars on each epaulette. Tristram became aware of the gelatinous sensations of nightmare – limbs melting, shallow breath, hopelessness. But, when a lorry and trailer loaded with equipment for the Ministry of Synthetic Food timidly began to poke into Adkins Street from Rostron Place, Tristram had enough strength and will-to-survive to dash round to its off-side, so that many red tons of pipes and cauldrons interposed themselves between himself and his pursuer. Not that it made any difference, he realized, feeling hopeless and foolish; they would get him if they really wanted him. He took the second turning to the left – Hanania Street. There stretched, along the whole bottom storey of Reppel Building, the Metropole, haunt of high officials, no place for a humble schoolmaster unsure of his position. Clacking the few septs, tanners and tosheroons in his left-hand trouser-pocket, he entered.

Ring of glasses, broad backs and girlish shoulders in grey and black uniforms, voices of policy. ('RB stroke 371 is perfectly clear about it.') Tristram crawled to an empty table and awaited a waiter. ('Allocation of raw materials should be worked out in inter-departmental conference.') A waiter came, black as the ace of spades in a cream jacket. 'With what, sir?' he asked. 'With orange,' said Tristram, his eyes on the swinging doors. A couple of grey-uniformed exquisites entered, expiring with laughter; an eye-glassed stern bald gelding with his boy secretary; a mannish woman with a big useless bust. Then Tristram saw his pursuer enter, saw with a kind of relief. The officer took off his cap, disclosing short straight oiled rust-coloured hair, and looked into the throng of drinkers; Tristram nearly waved to show where he was. But the officer noticed him soon enough and, smiling, came over. 'Mr Foxe? Mr *Tristram* Foxe?'

'Yes, as you very well know. You'd better sit down. Unless, of course, you want to take me off right away.' The black waiter brought Tristram's drink.

'Take you off?' The officer laughed. 'Oh, I see. Look,' he said to the waiter, 'I'll have one of those. Yes,' he said to Tristram, 'you are quite like your brother. Your brother Derek, that is. In appearance. For the rest, of course, I just don't know.'

'Don't play with me,' said Tristram. 'If you want to prefer a charge, then prefer it.' He even thrust forward his wrists, as if in a mime of cycling.

The officer laughed louder. 'Take a tip from me, Mr Foxe,' he said. 'If you've done something indictable, wait till it's found out. We've enough to cope with without people volunteering, do you see.' He put both hands supine on the table, as if to show that they were free of blood, and smiled pleasantly at Tristram. He seemed a decent sort of man, about Tristram's own age.

'Well,' said Tristram, 'if I may ask –' The officer swivelled his head as though to see whether anybody, whether listening or not, would be able to hear. But Tristram had humbly chosen a remote and isolated table. The officer nodded slightly in satisfaction. He said:

'I won't tell you my name. My rank you can see – captain. I work in the organization of which your brother is Commissioner, do you see. It's about your brother that I wish to speak. I take it that you're not too fond of your brother.'

'I'm not, as a matter of fact,' said Tristram. 'But I don't see what that's got to do with anything or anybody.' The waiter brought the captain's alc, and Tristram ordered another. 'This is on me,' said the captain. 'Bring two more. Doubles, make them.' Tristram raised his eyebrows. He said:

'If your intention's to make me drunk so that I'll say things I shouldn't say –'

'Such balderdash,' laughed the captain. 'You're a very suspicious type of man I'd say, do you see. You know that, I suppose. You know that you're a very suspicious type of man, I should imagine.'

'I am,' said Tristram. 'Circumstances are making all of us suspicious.'

'I would say,' said the captain, 'that your brother Derek has done very well for himself, wouldn't you agree? That, of course, is in spite of a lot of things. In spite of his family background, for instance. But being homo, do you see, wipes out all other sins, the sins of the fathers, for instance, do you see.'

'He's got on very well,' said Tristram. 'Derek is now a very big man.'

'Oh, but I'd say his position is not impregnable, not impregnable at all. And as for being a *big* man – well, bigness is a very relative thing, isn't it? Yes,' the captain agreed with himself, 'it is.' He leaned closer to Tristram and said, with seeming irrelevance, 'My rank in the

Ministry rightly entitled me to a majority at least, do you see, in the new corps. You behold me, however, with but three captain's pips. A man called Dann, much my junior, wears the crowns. Have you ever experienced that sort of thing, Mr Foxe? Have you ever, do you see, had the humiliating experience of seeing a junior man promoted over your head?'

'Oh, yes,' said Tristram. 'Oh, yes, indeed. Oh, very much yes, indeed.' The waiter brought two double alcs. 'Run out of orange,' he said. 'This here is blackcurrant. Hope you gentlemen will not mind.'

'I thought,' nodded the captain, 'you would understand.'

'It's through not being homo, of course,' said Tristram.

'I do believe,' said the captain in massive understatement, 'that that has something to do with it. Your brother would certainly be the last to deny how much he owes, do you see, to his pretty inverted sexual ways. But now you must tell me, Mr Foxe, about these pretty inverted sexual ways of his, you having known him all your life. Would you say they were genuine?'

'Genuine?' Tristram frowned. 'All too horribly genuine, I'd say. He started to play about in that way before he was sixteen. He never showed any interest in girls.'

'Never? Well. We revert now to your admission that you're a suspicious man, Mr Foxe. Have you ever been suspicious of your wife?' He smiled. 'That's a hard question to ask any husband, but I ask it in all good faith.'

'I don't quite see –' said Tristram. And then, 'Good Dog, what are you implying?'

'You begin to see,' nodded the captain. 'You're quite

78

quick at this sort of thing. This, do you see, is a matter of very great delicacy.'

'Are you trying to tell me,' said Tristram, incredulous, 'are you trying to insinuate that my wife – that my wife and my brother Derek –'

'I've watched him for some time now,' said the captain. 'He's known that I've watched him, but he doesn't seem to have cared very much. Pretending to be homosexual must, for a normally sexed man, be a very great strain, rather like trying to smile all the time. That your brother Derek has met your wife on various occasions I can vouch for. I can give dates. He has been to your flat many times. All this, of course, may have meant nothing. He may have been giving your wife Russian lessons.'

'The bitch,' said Tristram. 'The bastard.' He didn't know which one to turn on more. 'She never said. She never said a word about his going to the flat. But it all ties up now. Yes, I begin to see. I met him coming out. About two months ago.'

'Ah.' The captain nodded again. 'There was never any real proof of anything, though, do you see. In a court of law, when there used to be courts of law, all this would not be real evidence of misconduct. Your brother may have visited your flat regularly because he was fond of his nephew. He would not, of course, visit when you were there, knowing you had no love for him, nor, for that matter, he for you. And your wife would not want to mention his visits, do you see, for fear of your becoming angry. And when your child died, two months ago if I remember rightly, these visits ceased. Of course, the visits may have ceased for a quite different reason, namely his elevation to the post he now holds.'

'You know a lot, don't you?' said Tristram bitterly.

'I have to know a lot,' said the captain. 'But, do you see, suspicion is not knowledge. Now I come to something important that I really know about your wife and your brother. Your wife has been writing to your brother. She has written what, in the old days, was known as a love-letter. Just one, no more, but, of course, very incriminating. She wrote the letter yesterday. In it she says how much she misses your brother and, inevitably, how much she loves him. There is a certain amount of erotic detail also – not too much, but a certain amount. It was foolish of her to write the letter, but it was even more foolish of your brother not to destroy the letter as soon as he'd read it.'

'So,' said Tristram growling, '*you* saw it, did you? The faithless bitch,' he added. And then, 'That explains everything. I knew I couldn't have made a mistake. I knew it. The deceiving treacherous little –' He meant both of them.

'Unfortunately,' said the captain, 'you only have my word for this business of the letter. Your wife will deny everything, I should imagine. But she will be waiting for your brother Derek's next little talk on the television, for in that next little talk she has requested a hidden message to herself. She has requested that he introduce somehow the word "love" or the word "desire". A pretty idea,' commented the captain. 'I take it, however, that you will not find it necessary to wait for that sort of confirmation. It may never occur, do you see. In any case, those two words, both or either, could occur quite naturally in a television talk of a patriotic nature (all television talks are patriotic now, are they not?). He could say something about love of country or everybody's desire, do you see, to do their bit to end the present emergency, such as it is. The point is, I take it, that you'll want to act almost at once.'

'Yes,' said Tristram. 'At once. She can leave. She can go. She can get out. I never want to see her again. She can have her child. She can have it wherever she likes. I shan't stop her.'

'You mean to say,' said the captain in awe, 'that your wife is pregnant?'

'It's not me,' said Tristram. 'I know that. I swear it's not me. It's Derek. The swine Derek.' He bashed the table and made the glasses dance to their own tune. 'Cuckolded,' he said, as in some sniggering Elizabethan play, 'by my own brother.'

The captain smoothed his rusty moustache with his left little finger, now one wing, now the other. 'I see,' he said. 'Officially, I have no knowledge of this. There is no proof, do you see, that you are not responsible. There is, as you yourself must admit, a possibility that the child – if the child is ever born, which, officially, of course, it must not be – that the child is yours. What I mean is, how, officially, does anybody know that you're telling the truth?'

Tristram looked narrowly at him. 'Do you believe me?'

'What I believe is neither here nor there,' said the captain. 'But you must admit that pinning this business on the Commissioner of the Population Police is going to be met with, do you see, incredulity. A liaison with a woman is a different matter. That is, for your high-placed brother, wickedness and foolishness. But to impregnate his *inamorata* – that would be a glorious kind of head-swimming idiocy too imbecilic to be true. Do you see? Do you see?' It was the first time he had used this tag as a genuine question.

'I'll get him,' vowed Tristram. 'Never fear, I'll get him, the swine.'

'We'll have another drink on that,' said the captain. The black waiter was near, banging his metal tray against his slightly flexed knee, humming tunelessly to the tinny drum-beat. The captain finger-snapped. 'Two more doubles,' he ordered.

'They're equally guilty,' said Tristram. 'What worse betrayal could there be than this? Betrayal by wife. Betrayal by brother. Oh, Dog, Dog, Dog.' He clapped his hands on his eyes and cheeks, shutting out the betraying world but letting his mouth tremble at it.

'He's the really guilty one,' said the captain. 'He's betrayed more than his brother. He's betrayed the State and his high position in the State. He's committed the foulest of crimes and the most stupid of crimes, do you see. Get him first, get him. Your wife has been merely a woman, and women haven't much sense of responsibility. He's the one, he. Get him.' The drinks came, funeral purple in colour.

'To think,' moaned Tristram, 'that I gave her love, trust – all that a man can give.' He sipped his alc and fruit-juice.

'To hell with that, do you see,' said the captain impatiently. 'You're the only one who can get him. What can I do, eh, in my position? Even if I'd kept that letter, even if I'd kept it, don't you think he would have known? Don't you think he'd get some of the thugs on to me? He's a dangerous man.'

'What can *I* do?' said Tristram tearfully. 'He's in a very high position.' This new glass was full of the stuff of snivelling. 'Taking advantage of his position, that's what he's been doing, to betray his own brother.' His mouth crumbling, wet oozed round his contact lenses. But, suddenly cracking his fist hard on the table, 'The bitch,' he exploded, showing his lower set. 'Wait till I see her, just wait.'

'Yes, yes, yes, that can indeed wait, do you see. Look, get him first, as I tell you. He's changed his flat, he's at 2095 Winthrop Mansions. Get him there, do him in, teach him a lesson. He lives alone, do you see.'

'Kill him, you mean?' said Tristram in wonder. 'Kill?'

'*Crime passionel*, they used to call it. Your wife can be made to confess, sooner or later, do you see. Get him, do him in.'

Tristram gleamed with unsteady suspicion. 'How far can I trust you?' he said. 'I'm not going to be used, I'm not going to be made to do somebody else's dirty work, do you see.' That tag was bound to infect him. 'You've said things about my wife. How do I know it's right, how do I know it's true? You've got no proof, you've shown me no proof.' He pushed his empty glass to the centre of the table. 'You keep your dirty drink, trying to make me drunk.' He started, with some small difficulty, to rise. 'I'm going home to have it out with my wife, that's what I'm going to do. Then we'll see. But I'm not doing any of your dirty work for you. I don't trust one of you, and that's flat. Plotting, that's what it is.'

'So you're still unconvinced,' said the captain. He began to feel in one of his tunic side-pockets.

'Yes, plotting. Struggle for power within the party – characteristic of the Interphase. Historian, that's what I am. I should have been Head of the Social Studies Department, if that homo swine hadn't –'

'All right, all right,' said the captain.

'Betrayed,' said Tristram dramatically. 'Betrayed by homos.'

'If you go on like this,' said the captain, 'you'll get yourself arrested.'

'That's all you people can do, arrest people. Arrested development, ha ha.' And then, 'Betrayed.'

'Very well,' said the captain. 'If you want proof, here it is.' And he took a letter out of his pocket and held it up.

'Give it me,' said Tristram, clawing. 'Let me see it.'

'No,' said the captain. 'If you don't trust me, why should I trust you?'

'So,' said Tristram. 'So she did write to him. A filthy love letter. Wait till I see her. Wait till I see both of them.' He clanked an uncounted handful of septs and florins on to the table and, unseeing and very unsteady, began to leave.

'Him first,' said the captain. But Tristram was weaving his way out, blindly firm of purpose. The captain made a tragi-comic face and put the letter back in his pocket. It was a letter from an old friend, one Dick Turnbull, on holiday in the Schwarzwald. People didn't look these days, didn't listen, didn't remember. Still, that other letter did exist. Captain Loosley had quite definitely seen it on the Metropolitan Commissioner's desk. And, unfortunately, the Metropolitan Commissioner had – before sweeping it and other private correspondence, some of it abusive, into the hellhole in the wall – seen that he'd seen it.

Six

SAND-HOPPERS, mermaids' purses, sea gooseberries, cuttle bones, wrasse, blenny and bullhead, tern, gannet and herring gull. Beatrice-Joanna took a last breath of the sea and then went to the State Provisions Store (Rossiter Avenue branch) at the foot of the mountain of Spurgin Building. The rations had been cut yet again with neither warning nor apology from the twin ministries responsible. Beatrice-Joanna received and paid for two blocks of brown vegetable dehydrate (legumin), a large white tin of synthelac, compressed sheets of cereal, a blue bottle of 'nuts' or nutrition units. Unlike the other women shoppers, however, Beatrice-Joanna did not indulge in whines and threats (though these were muffled, there having been a small quickly quelled shoppers' riot three days before, the door today flanked by greyboys); she felt full of the sea, as of some huge satisfying round dish of wobbly blue-green marbled meat. She wondered vaguely, leaving the shop, what meat had tasted like. Her mouth recollected only the salt of live human skin in a purely amatory context – lobes, fingers, lips. 'He's my meat,' sang the song about adorable Fred. That, she supposed, was what was meant by the term sublimation.

It was thus in a full street, engaged in an innocent housewife's task, that she was suddenly confronted with the loud accusations of her husband. 'There you are,' he called, swaying with alc. He semaphored wildly at her, his feet seemingly glued to the pavement outside the entrance to the flats which made up the greater part of Spurgin Building. 'Caught in the act, eh? Caught coming back from it.' Many passers-by became interested. 'Pretending to go and do the shopping, eh? I know all, so you needn't pretend.' He ignored her string-bag of meagre groceries. 'I've been told everything, the lot.' He teetered, with balancing arms, as though on a high window-ledge. The little life inside Beatrice-Joanna shuddered as if threatened. 'Tristram,' she began to scold bravely, 'you've been on the alc again. Now get inside at once and into that lift —' 'Betrayed,' wailed Tristram. 'Going to have a baby. By my own blasted brother. Bitch, bitch. Well, have it. Go on, get out and have it. They all know, everybody knows.' Some passers-by tutted. 'Tristram,' said Beatrice-Joanna with spread lips. 'Don't call me Tristram,' said Tristram, as though that were not his name. 'Deceiving bitch.' 'Get inside,' ordered Beatrice-Joanna. 'There's been a mistake. This is not a public matter.' 'Isn't it?' said Tristram. 'Isn't it just? Go on, get out.' The whole crowded street, the sky, had become his own betrayed home, a cell of suffering. Beatrice-Joanna firmly tried to enter Spurgin Building. Tristram tried to prevent her with arms weaving like cilia.

Then noise could be heard coming from Froude Place. It was a procession of rough-looking men in overalls, loud with confused cries of disaffection. 'You see,' said

Tristram triumphantly. 'Everybody knows.' They all wore the crown and the NSW of the National Synthefabrik Works. Some carried banners of grievance – pieces of synthetic cloth tacked on to broom-handles, hastily cut bits of card on slender laths. The only true inscription was the logogram STRK; for the rest, there were crude drawings of human skeletons. 'It's all over between us,' said Tristram. 'You stupid idiot,' said Beatrice-Joanna, 'get inside. We don't want to be involved in this.' A wild-eyed workers' leader stood on the plinth of a street lamp, hugging the pillar with his left arm. 'Brothers,' he called, 'brothers. If they want a fair day's work they've got to bloody well feed us proper.'

'Hang old Jackson,' wavered an elderly worker. 'String him up.'

'Shove him in a stewpot,' called a Mongol with comic strabismus.

'Don't be a fool,' said Beatrice-Joanna in disquiet. 'I'm getting out of this if you're not.' She pushed Tristram violently out of her way. Her provisions went flying and Tristram himself staggered and fell. He began to cry. 'How could you, *how could you*, with my own brother?' She went grimly into Spurgin Building, leaving him to his sonata of reproach. Tristram got up from the pavement with difficulty, clutching the tin of synthelac. 'You stop shoving,' said a woman. 'Nowt to do with me. I want to get home.'

'They can threaten,' said the leader, 'till they're bloody well blue in the face. We have our rights and they can't take them away, and the withholding of labour's a lawful right in case of just grievance, and they can't bloody well deny it.' Roars. Tristram found himself wound round, stirred into the crowd of workers. A schoolgirl, also caught in it, began to cry. 'You do well to do that,' nodded a youngish man with pimples and a bad shave. 'Starved, the bloody lot of us, that's about it.' The cross-eyed Mongol turned to give Tristram his full face. A fly had settled on his porous nose; his eyes were well set for looking at it. He watched it fly away, wondering, as though it symbolized liberation. 'My name,' he said to Tristram, 'is Joe Blacklock.' Then, satisfied, he turned back to listening to his leader. The leader called, himself unfortunately plump as a table bird, 'Let them listen to the crying-out of the empty guts of the workers.' Roars. 'Solidarity,' yelled this solid man. More roars. Tristram was crushed, pushed. Then two greyboys from the State Provisions Store (Rossiter Avenue branch) appeared, armed only with truncheons. Manly-looking, they began vigorously to belabour. There was a great cry of pain and anger as they jerked at the right arm of the lamp-clutching leader. The leader flailed and protested. One of the police went down, crunched under boots. Blood appeared from nowhere on somebody's face, an earnest of earnest. 'Aaaaargh,' gargled the man next to Tristram. 'Do the bastards in.' The schoolgirl shrieked. 'Let her get out,' cried soberer Tristram. 'For Dogsake clear a way there.' The crushing crowd came on. The still upright greyboy was now at bay against the freestone wall of Spurgin Building. He cracked, his panting mouth open, at skulls and faces. An upper set was spewed out by someone, a Cheshire Cat grin in the air for an instant. Then whistles shrilled hollowly. 'More of the bastards,' throated a voice in Tristram's neck-nape. 'Make a bloody dash for it.'

'Solidarity,' cried the lost leader from somewhere among fists. The sirens of police cars rose and fell in *glissandi* of dismal tritones. The crowd tongued out in all directions like fire or stone-dinged water. The schoolgirl needled across the street with spider-legs, escaped into an alley. Tristram was still clutching, like a baby, the white tin of synthelac. Greyboys now held the street, some tough and stupid, others sweetly prettily smiling, all with carbines at the ready. An officer with two bright bars on each shoulder strutted, whistle in mouth like a baby's dummy, hand on holster. At each end of the street were crowds, watching. Placards and banners shifted to and fro uncertainly above shoulders, already looking sheepish and forlorn. There were black vans waiting, side-doors open, lorries with tail-boards down. A sergeant yelped something. There was a jostling at one place, the vexillae advanced. The whistled shining inspector unholstered his pistol. He peeped one silver blast, and a carbine spat at the air. 'Get the sods,' called a worker in torn overalls. A tentative thrust of a phalanx of crushed men gained momentum speedily, and a greyboy went down shrieking. The whistle now pierced like toothache. Carbines opened out frankly, and shot whined like puppies from the walls. 'Hands up,' ordered the inspector, whistle out of his mouth. Some workers were down, gaping and bleeding in the sun. 'Get 'em all in,' yelped the sergeant. 'Room for everyone, the little beauties.' Tristram dropped his tin of synthelac. 'Watch that one there,' cried the officer. 'Home-made bomb.'

'I'm not one of these,' Tristram tried to explain, hands clasped over his head. 'I was just going home. I'm a teacher. I object strongly. Take your dirty hands off.'

'Right,' said a bulky greyboy obligingly, and carbine-butted him fairly in the gut. Tristram sent out a delicate fountain of the purple juice that had diluted the alc. 'In.' He was prodded to a black lorry, his nasopharynx smarting with the taste of the brief vomit. 'My brother,' he protested. 'Commissioner of the Pop-poppoppop –' He couldn't stop popping. 'My wife's in there, let me at least speak to my wife.' 'In.' He fell up the rungs of the swinging tail-board. 'Speeeeak tuh mah wahf,' mocked a worker's voice. 'Haw haw.' The lorry was full of sweat and desperate breathing, as though all inside had been kindly rescued from some killing cross-country run. The tail-board clinked up with merry music of chains, a tarpaulin curtain came down. The workers cheered at the total darkness, and one or two squeaked in girly voices, 'Stop it, I'll tell my ma' and 'Oh, you *are* awful, Arthur.' An earnest breathing bulk next to Tristram said, 'They don't take it seriously, that's the trouble with a lot of these here. Let the side down, that's what they do.' A hollow voice with slack Northern vowels ventured a pleasantry: 'Would anybody lahk a fried egg samwidge?' 'Look,' almost wept Tristram to the odorous dark, 'I was just going in to have it out with my wife, that's all. It was nothing to do with me. It's unfair.' The serious voice at his side said, 'Course it's unfair. They never have been fair to the working man.' Another, hostile to Tristram's accent, growled, 'Shut it, see. We know your type. Watching you, I am,' which was manifestly impossible. Meanwhile, they roared along in convoy, as they could tell, and there was a sense of streets full of happy unarrested people. Tristram wanted to blubber. 'I take it,' said a new voice, 'that you don't want to associate yourself with our struggle, is that it, friend? The intellectuals have never been on the side of the workers. Sometimes they've let on to be, but only for purposes of betrayal.' 'I'm the one who's been betrayed,' cried Tristram. 'Betray his arse,' said someone. 'Treason of clerks,' came a bored voice. A harmonica began to play.

At length the lorry stopped, and there was a grinding finality of brakes, an opening and slamming of the doors of the driver's cabin. A noise of unslotting, a chainy rattle, and then great daylight blew in like a wind. 'Out,' said a carbined corporal, pock-marked Micronesian. 'Look here,' said Tristram, getting out, 'I want to register the strongest possible protest about this. I demand that I be allowed to telephone Commissioner Foxe, my brother. There's been a ghastly mistake.' 'In,' said a constable, and Tristram was shoved with the rest through a doorway. Forty-odd storeys dove into heaven over their heads. 'You lot in here,' said a sergeant. 'Thirty-five to a cell. Plenty of room for all, you horrible great antisocial things, you.' 'I protest,' protested Tristram. 'I'm not going in there,' going in. 'Ah, shut it,' said a worker. 'With pleasure,' said the sergeant. Three bolts slammed in on them and, for good measure, a key ground round in a rusty ward.

Seven

BEATRICE-JOANNA packed one bag only, there not being

much to pack. This was no age of possessions. She said good-bye to the bedroom, her eyes moistening at her last sight of the tiny wall-cot that had been Roger's. Then, in the living-room, she told out all her cash: five guinea-notes, thirty crowns, odd septs, florins and tanners. Enough. There was no time to let her sister know, but Mavis had often said, often written, 'Now, come any time. But don't bring that husband of yours with you. You know Shonny can't stand him.' Beatrice-Joanna smiled at the thought of Shonny, then cried, then pulled herself together. She also pulled the main switch and the hum of the refrigerator ceased. It was a dead flat now. Guilty? Why should she feel guilty? Tristram had told her to get out, and she was getting out. She wondered again who had told him, how many knew. Perhaps she would never see Tristram again. The small life within her said, 'Act, don't think. Move. I'm all that counts.' She would, she thought, be safe in Northern Province; *it* would be safe. She could think of no other obligation than to this, the single inch of protest, weighing thirty-odd grains, the cells dividing again and again in protest, blasts of protest – epi, meso, hypo. Tiny life protesting at monolithic death. Away.

It was starting to rain, so she put on her waterproof, a thin skin like a mist. There was dried blood on the pavement, needles of rain pricking it to make it flow, if only down the gutter. The rain came from the sea and stood for life. She walked briskly into Froude Square. The red-lit underground station entrance milled with people, red-lit like devils of the old mythical hell, silent, chunnering, giggling, sped singly or in pairs down the grumbling escalator. Beatrice-Joanna bought her ticket

from a machine, dove down to the aseptic white catacombs where winds rushed out of tunnels, and boarded
a tube-train to Central London. It was a swift service
and would get her there in less than half an hour. Next
to her an old woman champed and champed, talking to
herself, her eyes closed, saying aloud at intervals, 'Doris
was a good girl, a good girl to her mother, but the other
one –' Preston, Patcham, Pangdean. Passengers left,
passengers boarded. Pyecombe. The old woman alighted,
mumbling, 'Doris.' 'A pie was what they used to eat,'
said a pale fat mother in powder-blue. Her child cried.
'Hungry, that's his trouble,' she said. And now the legs
of the journey grew longer. Albourne. Hickstead.
Bolney. Warninglid. At Warninglid a scholarly-looking
man with a stringy neck boarded, sitting next to
Beatrice-Joanna to read, puffing like a tortoise, *Dh Wks
v Wlym Shkspr*. He unwrapped a synthechoc bar and
began to chew, puffing. The child renewed his crying.
Handcross. Pease Pottage. 'Pease pottage was something
else they used to eat,' said the mother. Crawley, Horley,
Salfords. Nothing edible there. Redhill. At Redhill the
scholar alighted and three members of the Population
Police came aboard. They were young men, subalterns,
well set-up, their metal ashine and their black unmacu-
lated by hairs, scurf or food-droppings. They examined
the women passengers insolently, as with eyes expert at
burrowing to illegal pregnancies. Beatrice-Joanna
blushed, wishing the journey were over. Merstham,
Caterham, Coulsdon. It soon would be. She pressed her
hands over her belly as though its cellulating inmate
were already leaping with audible joy. Purley, Croydon,
Thornton Heath, Norwood. The police officers alighted.

And now the train went purring into the deep black heart of the immemorial city. Dulwich, Camberwell, Central London. And soon Beatrice-Joanna was on the local line to the North-West Terminus.

She was shocked at the number of grey and black police that infested the noisy station. She joined a queue in the booking-hall. Officers of both forces sat at long tables barring the way to the bank of booking-guichets. They were smart, pert, clipped.

'Identity-card, please.' She handed it over. 'Destination?'

'State Farm NW313, outside Preston.'

'Purpose of trip?'

She fell easily into the rhythm. 'Social visit.'

'Friends?'

'Sister.'

'I see. *Sister.*' A dirty word, that. 'Duration of visit?'

'I can't say. Look here, why do you want to know all this?'

'Duration of visit?'

'Oh, perhaps six months. Perhaps longer.' How much should she tell them? 'I'm leaving my husband, you see.'

'Hm. Hm. Check on this passenger, will you?' A constable-clerk copied from her identity-card on to a buff form, official. Meanwhile another young woman was in trouble. 'I tell you I'm *not* pregnant,' she kept saying. A gold-haired thin-lipped policewoman in black began to pull her to a door blazoned MEDICAL OFFICER. 'We'll soon see,' she said. 'We'll soon know all about that, shan't we, dear?'

'But I'm *not*,' cried the young woman. 'I tell you I'm *not.*'

'There,' said Beatrice-Joanna's interrogator, handing back her stamped carnet. He had a pleasant prefect's face on which grimness sat like a bogey-mask. 'Too many illeg pregs trying to escape to the provinces. *You* wouldn't be trying anything like that, would you? Your card says you've got one child, a son. Where is he now?'

'Dead.'

'I see. I see. Well, that's that then, isn't it? Off you go.' And Beatrice-Joanna went to book her single ticket to the north.

Police at the barriers, police patrolling the platform. A crowded train (nuclear-propelled). Beatrice-Joanna sat down, already exhausted, between a thin man so stiff that his skin seemed to be armour and a very small woman whose legs dangled like a very big doll's. Opposite was a check-suited man with a coarse comedian's face, sucking desperately at a false molar. A small girl, open-mouthed as with adenoid growths, surveyed Beatrice-Joanna from head to foot, foot to head, in a strict slow rhythm. A very fat young woman glowed like a deliberate lamp, her legs so tree-like that they seemed to be growing out of the floor of the compartment. Beatrice-Joanna closed her eyes. Almost at once a dream leaped on to her: a grey field under a thundery sky, cactus-like plants groaning and swaying, skeletal people collapsing with their black tongues hanging out, then herself involved – with some bulky male form that shut out the scene – in the act of copulation. Loud laughter broke out and she awoke fighting. The train was still in the station; her fellow-travellers stared at her with (except for the adenoidal girl) only a little curiosity. Then–as if that dream had been an obligatory rite before departure – they began to ease out, leaving the grey and black police behind.

Eight

'WHAT will they do to us?' asked Tristram. His eyes had grown used to the dark and could see that the man next to him was the cross-eyed Mongol who, ages ago in the rebellious street, had announced his name as Joe Blacklock. Of the other prisoners, some squatted like miners – there were no seats – and others propped up the walls. One old man, formerly phlegmatic, had become possessed of a fit of excitement and had gripped the bars, crying to the corridor, 'I left the stove on. Let me get home and turn it off. I'll come straight back, honest I will,' and now lay exhausted on the cold flags.

'Do to us?' said Joe Blacklock. 'There's nothing laid down, far as I know. Far as I know, they let some out and keep others in. That's right, isn't it, Frank?'

'Ringleaders gets what for,' said Frank, gaunt, tall, gormless. 'We all said to 'Arry it was waste of time. Shouldn't never have done it. Look where it's got us. Look where it'll get him.'

'Who?' asked Tristram. 'Where?'

'Strike-leader he calls himself. He'll do hard labour for a bit. Might be worse than that, what with things getting tougher all round.' He made a gun of his hand and levelled it at Tristram. 'As it might be yourself,' he said. 'Bang bang.'

'It was nothing to do with me,' said Tristram for the thirtieth time. 'I just got caught up in the crowd. It's all a mistake, I keep telling you.'

'That's right. You tell them that when they come for you.' Frank then went into the corner to micturate. The whole cell stank cosily of urine. A middle-aged man with grey chick-down on his dome, wild-looking like a lay-preacher, came over to Tristram and said:

'You'll convict yourself soon as you open your mouth, mister. Bless your heart and soul, they'll know you for an intellectual soon as you walk in there. I reckon you've been real brave in one way or another, sticking up for the workers. You'll get your reward when better times come, you mark my words.'

'But I wasn't,' almost wept Tristram. 'I didn't.'

'Ah,' said a voice in a corner, 'I heareth footsteps, verily I dost, methinks.' The corridor light was switched on, raw as an egg, and boots clomped towards the cell. From the floor the old man pleaded, 'I only want to turn it off. I won't be gone long.' The cell-bars, dead black against the new light, grinned frankly at them all. Two greyboys, young and thuggish, armed, grinned in between the grinning bars. The bolts shot out, the key ground round, the cell-door clanged open. 'Right,' said one of the greyboys, a lance-jack, shuffling a deck of identity cards. 'I'm giving these out, back, see? Them I give them to can skedaddle and are not to be naughty boys no more. Right. Aaron, Aldiss, Barber, Collins, Chung –' 'Now what the hell have *I* done wrong?' said Joe Blacklock. '– Davenport, Dilke, Mohamed Daud, Dodds, Endore, Evans –' The men came eagerly grabbing and were pushed out roughly to freedom. '– Fairbrother, Franklin, Gill, Hackney, Hamidin –' 'There must be some mistake,' cried Tristram. 'I'm an F.' '– Jones, Lindsay, Lowrie –' The cell was emptying fast. '– Mackintosh, Mayfield, Morgan, Norwood, O'Connor –' 'I'll be back,' said the old man, trembling, taking his card, 'as soon as I've turned it off. Thanks, lads.' '– Paget, Radzinowicz, Smith, Snyder, Taylor, Tucker, Ucuck, Vivian, Wilson, Wilson, Wilson. That's the lot. Who are you, chum?' asked the greyboy of Tristram. Tristram told him. 'Right, you're to stay here, you are.' 'I demand to see the man in charge,' demanded Tristram. 'I demand that I be allowed to contact my brother. Let me phone my wife. I shall write to the Home Secretary.' 'No harm in writing,' said the greyboy. 'Perhaps writing will keep you quiet. You do that, chum. You write.'

Nine

'WELL,' boomed Shonny, 'glory be to God in the highest, look who it is. My own little sister-in-law, God bless us and keep us, not looking a day older than when I saw her last, and that must be all of three years ago. Come in, come in, and highly welcome.' He peered suspiciously out, saying, 'I mean no harm to him, mind, but I hope you haven't brought that horrible man with you, seeing as there's something in the very look of the man that makes my hackles rise and sets my teeth on edge.' Beatrice-Joanna shook her head, smiling. Shonny was something out of the fabulous past – open, direct, honest, virile, with a burnt coarse humorous moon-face, surprised ice-blue eyes, a simian upper lip, a lower lip that drooped fleshily, big-bodied in sack-like farmer's garb. 'Mavis,' he called, 'Mavis,' and Mavis appeared in the tiny hallway – six years older than Beatrice-Joanna, with the same cider hair, speck-brown eyes and lavish limbs, bathycolpous.

'I didn't have time to let you know,' said Beatrice-Joanna, kissing her sister. 'I left in rather a hurry.'

'A good place to leave in a hurry,' said Shonny, picking up her bag, 'that great horrible metropolis, God send it bad dreams.'

'Poor little Roger,' said Mavis, her arm round her sister, leading her to the living-room. 'Such a shame.' The room was not much bigger than the one in the Foxe flat, but it seemed to breathe space and oxygen. Shonny said:

'Before we go any further, we'll have a drink of something.' He opened a trap-door to disclose a platoon of bottles. 'Something you'd never buy at twenty crowns the noggin in that benighted carcinoma you've left behind, God blast it.' He held up a bottle to the electric light. 'Plum wine of my own making,' he said. 'Wine-making's supposed to be forbiden like a lot of other wholesome and God-fearing things, but the hell with the lot of the little-souled law-making dung-beetles, Christ have mercy on them.' He poured. 'Take that in your right hand and say after me,' he ordered. They drank. 'Wait,' said Shonny. 'What is it we drink to?'

'A lot of things,' said Beatrice-Joanna. 'Life. Freedom. The sea. Us. Something I'll tell you about later.'

'We'll have a glass for each of those,' said Shonny. He beamed. 'Nice to have you with us,' he said.

Shonny was a Pancelt, one of the rare survivors of the Celtic Union that, in voluntary exodus, had left the British Isles and, wave after wave, settled in Armorica nearly a century before. In Shonny was a heartening stew of Manx, Glamorgan, Shetland, Ayrshire and County Cork, but this, as Shonny was hot in pointing out, could not be called miscegenation. Fergus, the Moses of the Union, had taught that the Celts were one people, their language one language, their religion fundamentally one. He had wrung the doctrine of the Messiah's second coming out of Catholicism, Calvinistic Methodism, Presbyterianism: church, kirk and chapel were one temple of the imminent Lord. Their mission was, in a world whose Pelagianism was really Indifferentism, to cherish the Christian flame, as once before in face of the Saxon hordes.

'We've been praying, you know,' said Shonny, pouring out more wine for the ladies, 'though, of course, that's illegal, too. They used to leave us alone in the old days, but now they've got these infernal police on the job, spying and arresting, just like in the ancient penal days of sacred memory. We've had mass here a couple of times. Father Shackel, God bless and help the poor man, was picked up in his own shop the other day by some of these simperers with guns and lipstick – Father Shackel's a seedsman by trade – and taken off we don't know where. And yet, and this the poor benighted imbeciles can't or won't realize, we've been offering the sacrifice for the State's own good. We're all going to starve, God bless us, if we don't pray for forgiveness for

our blasphemous ways. Sinning against the light, denying life. The way things are going is being sent as a
divine judgment on the lot of us.' He tossed off a beaker
of plum wine and smacked his great meaty lips.

'They've kept on cutting the rations,' said Beatrice-
Joanna. 'They don't say why. There've been demonstrations in the streets. Tristram got mixed up in one of
those. He was drunk at the time. I think the police
must have taken him off. I hope he's going to be all
right.'

'Well,' said Shonny, 'I don't wish him any real harm.
Drunk, was he? There may be some good in him after
all.'

'And how long do you propose to stay with us?' asked
Mavis.

'I suppose I might as well tell you now as later,' said
Beatrice-Joanna. 'I hope you're not going to be shocked
or anything. I'm pregnant.'

'Oh,' said Mavis.

'And,' said Beatrice-Joanna, 'I'm glad I'm pregnant.
I *want* to have the baby.'

'We'll certainly drink to that,' roared Shonny. 'Damn
the consequences, say I. A gesture, that's what it is, keeping the flame going, saying mass in the cellar. Good
girl.' He poured more wine.

'You want to have the baby here?' said Mavis. 'It's
dangerous. It's not something you can keep hidden for
long. It's something you ought to think about very carefully, things being as they are these days.'

'It's the will of God,' cried Shonny. 'Go forth and
multiply. So that little man of yours has still got some
life in him, eh?'

'Tristram doesn't want it,' said Beatrice-Joanna. 'He told me to get out.'

'Does anybody know you've come here?' asked Mavis.

'I had to tell the police at Euston. I said I was just coming on a visit. I don't think they'll do anything about it. There's nothing wrong with coming on a visit.'

'A pretty long visit,' said Mavis. 'And there's the question of room. The children are away at the moment, staying with Shonny's Aunt Gertie in Cumnock. But when they come back –'

'Now, Mavis,' said Beatrice-Joanna, 'if you don't want me to stay, tell me straight. I don't want to be a burden and a nuisance.'

'You won't be either,' said Shonny. 'We can fix you up, if need be, in one of the outhouses. A greater mother than you gave birth in a –'

'Oh, stop that sentimentality,' scolded Mavis. 'That's the sort of thing that turns me against religion sometimes. If you're determined,' she said to her sister, 'really determined, well, we must just go ahead and hope for better times soon. I know how you feel, don't think I don't. Our family's always been very strong on motherhood. We must just hope for more sensible times to come again, that's all.'

'Thank you, Mavis,' said Beatrice-Joanna. 'I know there'll be a lot of problems – registration and rations and so on. There's time enough to think of those things.'

'You've come to the right place,' said Shonny. 'My veterinary training will come in very handy, God bless you. Many's the litter I've helped to bring into the world.'

'Animals?' said Beatrice-Joanna. 'You don't mean to say you have animals?'

'Battery hens,' said Shonny gloomily, 'and our old sow Bessie. Jack Beare over at Blackburn has a boar which he hires out. It's all supposed to be illegal, may the Holy Trinity curse them, but we have managed to eke out our shameful diet with a bit of pig-meat. Everything's in a shocking state,' he said, 'and nobody seems able to understand it at all. This blight that seems to be sweeping the world, and the hens won't lay, and Bessie's last farrow so sickly with some queer internal growth, vomiting worms and all, I had to put them out of their misery. There's a curse settling on us, God forgive us all, with our blaspheming against life and love.'

'Talking about love,' said Mavis, 'is it all over between you and Tristram?'

'I don't know,' said Beatrice-Joanna. 'I've tried to worry about him, but somehow I can't. It seems I've got to concentrate all my love now on something that hasn't even been born. I feel as though I'm being taken over and *used*. But I don't feel unhappy about it. Rather the opposite.'

'I always felt you married the wrong man,' said Mavis.

Ten

DEREK FOXE read for a second time the scrawled two sheets of toilet paper signed by his brother; read smiling. 'I am illegally incarcerated here and I am not allowed to see anybody. I call upon you as my brother to bring your influence to bear and have me released. The whole thing is shameful and unjust. If this simple brotherly appeal fails to move you, perhaps the following intimation will: to wit, I know now that you and my wife have been conducting a protracted liaison and that she is now carrying your child. How could you – you, my brother? Get me out of here at once, it is the least you can do and you owe it to me. You have my solemn assurance that I will not let this go any further if you give me the help I ask. If you do not, however, I shall be compelled to divulge *all* to the appropriate authorities. *Get me out of here.* Tristram.'

The letter was rubber-stamped all over like a passport: '*Seen*, Commandant Franklyn Road Temporary Detention Centre'; '*Seen*, Officer Commanding Brighton Police District'; '*Seen*, Officer Commanding 121 Police Circle'; '*Opened*, Poppol Central Registry'. Derek Foxe smiled, leaning back in his leather-substitute chair, smiled at the huge idiot moon of a clock on the wall opposite, at the bank of telephones, at the back of his flavicomous male secretary. Poor Tristram. Poor not-very-bright Tristram. Poor moronic Tristram who had, by the mere act of writing, already divulged all to all available authorities, appropriate and inappropriate. And it didn't, of course, matter. Unsupported libels and slanders whizzed all day long through the offices of the great, a sort of gnat-fritinancy, disregarded. Still, Tristram at large might be a nuisance. Tristram, horn-mad, with a gang of schoolboy thugs. Tristram with a sly knife waiting in the shadows. Tristram alc-demented with a pistol. It was better that Tristram remain caged for a while; it was a bore to have to contemplate being on guard against one's brother.

How about her? That was altogether different. Wait, wait – the next phase might not be too long coming. And poor stupid Captain Loosley? Leave him alone for the time being, idiot. Derek Foxe rang through to Police Headquarters and requested that Tristram Foxe be, on grounds of suspicion, kept indefinitely out of circulation. Then he went on with the draft of the television talk (five minutes after the 23.00 news on Sunday), warning and appealing to the women of Greater London. 'Love of country,' he wrote, 'is one of the purest kinds of love. Desire for one's country's welfare is a holy desire.' This sort of thing came easily to him.

Part Three

One

A WET August and a parched September, but the sickness of the world's grain crops seemed to ride, like an aircraft, above the weather. It was a blight never known before, its configuration under the microscope not cognate with any other pattern of disease, and it proved resistant to all the poisons the Global Agricultural Authority could devise. But it was not only rice, maize, barley, oats and wheat that were affected: fruit fell off the trees and the hedges, stricken with a sort of gangrene; potatoes and other roots became messes of black and blue mud. And then there was the animal world: worms, coccidiosis, scaly leg, marble bone disease, fowl cholera, prolapse of the oviduct, vent gleet, curled toe paralysis, slipped hock disease – these were just a few of the maladies that struck the hen batteries and turned them into feathery morgues. Shoals of rotting fish corpses were washed ashore on the north-east coast during early October; the rivers stank.

The Right Hon. Robert Starling, Prime Minister, lay awake in an October night, tossing alone in his double bed, his catamite having been banished from it. His head was full of voices – voices of the experts who said they didn't know, they just didn't know; voices of the fanciful who blamed stowaway viruses in returned moon-rockets; panicky fruity voices of the last Enspun Premiers' Conference saying, 'We can get through this year, we can just about get through this year, but wait till next –' And one very privy voice whispered statistics and showed, against the blackness of the bedroom, horrific lantern slides. 'Here we see the last food riot in Cooch Behar, dealt with most summarily, four thousand shovelled into a common grave, plenty of phosphorus pentoxide there, eh? And now we have highly coloured famine in Gulbarga, Bangalore and Rajura: look closely, admire those rib-cages. We turn now to Nyasaland: starvation in Livingstonia and Mpika. Mogadishu in Somalia – that was great fun for the vultures. And now we cross the Atlantic –'

'No! No! No!' The Right Hon. Robert Starling shouted so loud that he awoke his little friend Abdul Wahab, a brown boy who slept on a truckle-bed in the Right Hon. Robert Starling's dressing-room. Abdul Wahab came running in, knotting a sarong round his middle. He switched on the light.

'What is it? What's the matter, Bobby?' The melting brown eyes were full of concern.

'Oh, nothing. Nothing we can do anything about. Go back to bed. I'm sorry I woke you.'

Abdul Wahab sat on the edge of the bouncy mattress and stroked the Prime Minister's forehead. 'There,' he said. 'There, there, there.'

'They all seem to think,' said the Prime Minister, 'that we're in this game for our own ends. They think I'm in love with power.' He closed his eyes gratefully to the cool stroking. 'They don't know, they just don't know the first thing about it.'

'Of course they don't.'

'It's all for their own good, everything we do is for their own good.'

'Of course it is.'

'How would they like to be in my position? How would they like to have the responsibility and the heartbreak?'

'They wouldn't stand it for one minute.' Wahab went on soothing with his cool brown hand.

'You're a good boy, Wahab.'

'Oh, not really.' He simpered.

'Yes, you're a good boy. What are we going to do, Wahab, what are we going to do?'

'Everything will be all right, Bobby. You'll see.'

'No, everything won't be all right. I'm a liberal, I believe in man's ability to control the world about him. We don't just leave things to chance. The whole planet is dying, and you say everything will be all right.'

Abdul Wahab changed hands; his master was lying at a very awkward angle. 'I'm not very clever,' he said. 'I don't understand politics. But I always thought that the big trouble was having too many people in the world.'

'Yes, yes. That is our great problem.'

'But not now, surely? The population is being very quickly reduced, isn't that so? People are dying of not having enough to eat, aren't they?'

'You foolish boy. You very nice but very foolish boy. Don't you see, you foolish boy, that we could, if we wanted, kill off three-quarters of the world's population like that –' He snapped finger and thumb. '– Just like that? But government is not concerned with killing but with keeping people alive. We outlawed war, we made war a terrible dream of the past; we learned to predict earthquakes and conquer floods; we irrigated desert places and made the ice-caps blossom like a rose. That is progress, that is the fulfilment of part of our liberal aspirations. Do you understand what I'm saying, you foolish boy?'

Abdul Wahab tried to yawn with his mouth closed, smiling tight-lipped.

'We removed all the old natural checks on population,' said the Prime Minister. '*Natural checks* – what a cynical and sinister term. The history of man is the history of his control over his environment. True, we have often been let down. The greater part of mankind is not yet ready for the Pelagian ideal, but soon perhaps they may be. Perhaps very soon. Perhaps already they are learning. Learning through pain and privation. Ah, what a wicked world, a foolish world.' He sighed deeply. 'But what are we going to do? The shadow of famine stalks the world and we are caught in its clutches.' He frowned at that metaphor but let it pass. 'All our scientific knowledge and skill are set at nought by this menace.'

'I'm not very clever,' said Wahab again. 'My people used to do not very clever things when they thought the harvest might be bad or the fish fail to bite. They did perhaps very foolish things. One thing they used to do was to pray.'

'Pray?' said the Prime Minister. 'When we pray we admit defeat. There is no place for prayer in a liberal society. Moreover, there is nothing to pray to.'

'My people,' said stroking Wahab eagerly, 'had many

things to pray to. But mostly they prayed to what they called Allah.' He pronounced the name in the strict Arabic way, with a great curled l and a harsh snore at the end.

'Another name for God,' said the Prime Minister. 'God is the enemy. We have conquered God and tamed him into a comic cartoon character for children to laugh at. Mr Livedog. God was a dangerous idea in people's minds. We have rid the civilized world of that idea. Do go on stroking, you lazy boy.'

'And,' said Wahab, 'if praying was no good, then they used to kill something. That was meant to be a sort of present, you see. They used to call it *madzbuh*. If you wanted a really big favour then you offered up something very big, very important. You made a present of an important man, such as the Prime Minister.'

'If that is meant to be funny I don't consider it to be very funny,' huffed the Right Hon. Robert Starling. 'You can be a very facetious boy sometimes.'

'Or the King,' said Wahab, 'if you happened to have one.'

The Prime Minister thought about that. Then he said, 'You're full of the silliest ideas, you silly boy. And you're forgetting that, even if we did want to sacrifice the King, there's nothing to sacrifice him to.'

'Perhaps,' suggested Wahab, 'this thing has a sort of understanding. This thing, I mean, that's stalking the earth like a shadow with claws. You could pray to that.'

'That,' said the Prime Minister, huffily again, 'was a rather inept personification on my part. Inept figures of speech are the very stuff of political oratory.'

'What,' asked Wahab, 'is personification?'

'You pretend that something has life when it really hasn't. A kind of animism. Do you know that word, you ignorant boy?'

Wahab smiled. 'I'm very stupid,' he said, 'and I know very few words. Years and years ago my people used to pray to trees and rivers, pretending that these things could hear and understand. You would regard them as very foolish, being a great man and a Prime Minister, but I have heard you pray to the rain.'

'Nonsense.'

'I've heard you say, "Rain, rain, go away, come again another day." That was when you and I and Reginald and Gaveston Murphy were to go walking in Northern Province.'

'That was just a joke, just a bit of superstition. It didn't mean anything.'

'Nevertheless, you wanted it to stop raining. And now you want this thing to stop. Perhaps you ought to try a bit of superstition, as you call it. You certainly ought to try a bit of something. But,' added Wahab, 'don't listen to me. I'm just an ignorant boy and a foolish boy and a facetious boy.'

'Also a nice boy,' smiled the Prime Minister. 'I think I'll try and get some sleep now.'

'You don't want me to stay?'

'No, I want to sleep. Perhaps I'll dream of the solution to all our problems.'

'You're a great one for dreams,' said Abdul Wahab acutely. He kissed his finger-tips and shut his master's eyes with them. Then, before leaving the chamber, he put out the light and his tongue.

In the darkness the lantern-lecture began again.

'Here,' said the voice, 'we see a fine specimen of a diet riot, all the way from yellow Mozambique. The rice-store at Chovica was raided, with what results you here see. Black man's blood, red as your own. And now comes starvation in Northern Rhodesia, broken men at Broken Hill, Kabulwebulwe a lament in itself. Finally, for a *bonne bouche*, cannibalism in – guess where? You'll never guess, so I'll tell you. In Banff, Alberta. Incredible, isn't it? A very small carcase, as you see, a boy's rabbit-body. A few good stews out of that, though, and there's one lad who'll never go hungry again.'

Two

TRISTRAM was much thinner and he had a beard, very wiry. He had long been transferred from the Franklyn Road Temporary Detention Centre to the formidable Metropolitan Institute of Correction (Male) at Penton-ville, growing there – with his beard – daily more trucu-lent, frequently gorilla-shaking the bars of his cage, sullenly scratching scabrous graffiti on the walls, snarl-ing at the warders, a changed man. He wished Joscelyne were there and also that pretty boy Wiltshire: he would give them what for and think nothing of it. And as for Derek – A delirium of gouged-out eyeballs, castration with a bread-knife and other pretty fancies passed much of Tristram's waking time. Tristram's cell-mate was a veteran criminal of about sixty – pickpocket, forger, peterman – a man of grey dignity who smelled musty.

'If,' he said to Tristram this October dawn, 'if I'd had the benefit of book-learning like yourself, there's no knowing to what heights I mightn't have reached.' Tristram shook the bars and snarled. His cell-mate placidly went on mending his upper denture with a bit of putty he had swiped from one of the workshops. 'Well,' he said, 'despite the pleasure of your company this month and more, I can't say as how I shall be sorry to leave, especially as the weather looks to be keeping up a bit longer. Though without a doubt I shall be renewing the privilege of your acquaintance in the not too distant future.'

'Look, Mr Nesbit,' said Tristram, turning from the bars. 'For the last time. Please. It would be a service not only to me but to the entire community. Get him. Do him in. You've got his address.'

'Speaking for the last time myself, Mr Foxe, on this particular matter, I repeat again that I am in the criminal profession for gain and not for the pleasure of private vendettas or the like. In murder of the revengeful kind there is no money. Much as I'd like to oblige a friend, which I presume to consider that you are, it would go very much against my principles.'

'That's your last word?'

'Regretfully, Mr Foxe, as I have to say it, I have to definitely say it.'

'Well, then, Mr Nesbit, you're an unfeeling bastard.'

'Tut, Mr Foxe, such words is unseemly. You're a young man and still have your way to make so you won't resent a last bit of advice from an old codger like myself. Which is, to keep self-control. Without self-control you will achieve nothing. With self-control and keeping all personal feeling out of things allied to your book-learning, that way you should go far.' He thumbed the putty which wedded teeth to plastic palate and, seemingly satisfied, inserted the denture in his mouth. 'Better,' he said. 'That should serve. Always keep a smart appearance is my advice to young aspirants. As it might be yourself.'

The clanking of keys approached. A hatchet-faced pigeon-chested warder in worn blue opened the cell door. 'Right,' he said to Mr Nesbit, 'out, you.' Mr Nesbit got up from his plank-bunk, sighing.

'Where's bloody breakfast?' snarled Tristram. 'Breakfast is bloody late.'

'Breakfast is done away with,' said the warder, 'as from this morning.'

'That's bloody unfair,' shouted Tristram. 'That's bloody monstrous. I demand to see the bloody Governor.'

'I've told you before,' said the warder sternly. 'Keep a clean tongue in your head or things'll be made really hot for you, they will that.'

'Well,' said Mr Nesbit, extending a courtly hand, 'I take my leave, hoping for a resumption of a very pleasant acquaintanceship.'

'He talks proper, he does,' said the warder. 'You and your type'd do better to take example by him than go on blinding and bloodying all the time.' And he led Mr Nesbit out, clanging the door shut afterwards, grinding the key like a rebuke. Tristram took his iron spoon and savagely hacked a filthy word on the wall.

Just as he was finishing the oblique down-stroke of the last letter, the warder returned with a clank and grind. 'Here,' he said, 'is a new pal for you. One of *your*

sort, not a gentleman like the last one you had. In, you.'
It was a saturnine-looking man with eyes deep in charcoal caves, a vermilion beak, a small sulky Stuart mouth. The loose grey sack-garment of shame suited him, seeming to suggest the habit of a monk.

'Here,' said Tristram, 'I think we've met before.'

'Nice, isn't it?' said the warder. 'An old pals' reunion.' He left the cell, locked the door and grinned sardonically through the bars. Then he clanked off.

'We met,' said Tristram, 'in the Montague. The police beat you up a bit.'

'Did they? Did we?' said the man vaguely. 'So many things, so many people, so many affronts and buffetings. As to my Master, so to me.' He surveyed the cell with very dark eyes, nodding. Then he said, conversationally, 'If I forget thee, O Jerusalem, let my right hand lose her cunning, let my tongue cleave to the roof of my mouth if I remember not Jerusalem above my chief joy.'

'What are you in for?' asked Tristram.

'They caught me saying mass,' said the man. 'Unfrocked as I am, I still have the power. There has been a demand lately, a growing demand. Fear breeds faith, never doubt that. Quite a fair congregation can be assembled, believe me, these days.'

'Where?'

'It is a return to the catacombs,' said the man with satisfaction. 'Disused underground tunnels. Underground platforms. Even underground trains. Mass in motion, I call that. Yes,' he said, 'the fear is growing. Famine, that dread horseman, rides abroad. God asks an acceptable sacrifice, a placation of His anger. And, under one kind, wine being outlawed, it is offered to

Him. Ah,' he said, squinting at Tristram's graffiti, 'lapidary inscriptions, eh? Something to pass the time.' He was a very different man from the one Tristram remembered from that brief violent occasion in the Montague. He was tranquil, measured of speech, and he examined Tristram's carved obscenities as if they were in an unknown tongue. But 'Interesting,' he said. 'I see that you have inscribed the name of your Maker several times. You mark my words, everybody is coming back to God. You will see, we shall all see.'

'I used the word,' said Tristram brutally, 'as a gesture of defiance. It's just a dirty word, that's all.'

'Exactly,' said the unfrocked with quiet joy. 'All dirty words are fundamentally religious. They are all concerned with fertility and the processes of fertility and the organs of fertility. God, we are taught, is love.'

As if in derision of that statement, the big loudspeakers, set like doomsday trumpets at the imagined corners of each round tiered gallery, blasted a noise of eructation that fell into the empty belly of the well. 'Attention,' they said, and the word ('Attention -tension-ension-shun') bounced like a ball, the call of the farthest speakers overlapping the call of the nearest. 'Pay great attention. This is the Governor speaking.' It was the tired refined voice of ancient royalty. 'I am instructed by the Home Secretary to read out the following, which is being read out also at this moment in the schools, hospitals, offices and factories of the kingdom. It is a prayer devised by the Ministry of Propaganda.'

'Do you hear that?' danced the unfrocked priest in awed jubilation. 'God be praised, things are going our way. Alleluia.'

'Here it is,' said the tired voice. It coughed and then went into a hypnotic singsong. ' "It is conceivable that the forces of death which at present are ravaging the esculent life of this planet have intelligence, in which case we beseech them to leave off. If we have done wrong – allowing in our blindness natural impulse to overcome reason – we are, of course, heartily sorry. But we submit that we have already suffered sufficiently for this wrong and we firmly resolve never to sin again. Amen." ' The voice of the Governor collapsed into loud coughing and, before crackling out, muttered, 'Lot of damned nonsense.' The mutterings were at once taken up all around the gallery of cells.

Tristram's cell-mate looked ashen. 'God forgive us all,' he said, deeply shocked, crossing himself, 'they're going the other way. They're praying to the powers of evil, God help us.'

But Tristram was elated. 'Don't you see what this means?' he cried. 'It means the Interphase is coming to an end. The shortest on record. The State's reached the limit of despair. Sin, they're talking about sin. We'll be out soon, any day now.' He rubbed his hands. 'Oh, Derek, Derek,' he growled. 'I can hardly wait.'

Three

AUTUMN passed into winter, and that prayer, of course, was not answered. Nobody, of course, had ever seriously, of course, thought that it would be. As far as H.M.

Government was concerned, it was a mere sop to the irrational: nobody could now possibly say that H.M. Government had not tried everything.

'It all shows you, though,' said Shonny in December, 'how everything leads back to the Almighty.' He was far more optimistic than Tristram's cell-companion. 'Liberalism means conquest of environment and conquest of environment means science and science means a heliocentric outlook and a heliocentric outlook means an open mind about there being forms of intelligence other than human and –' He took a deep breath and swigged some plum wine '– and, well, you see, if you accept the possibility of that, then you concede the possibility of superhuman intelligence and so you get back to God.' He beamed at his sister-in-law. In the kitchen his wife was trying to make sense of the pitiful rations.

'Superhuman intelligence might be evil, though,' objected Beatrice-Joanna. 'That wouldn't be God, would it?'

'If you have evil,' said Shonny, 'you've got to have good.' He was unshakable. Beatrice-Joanna smiled her confidence in him. In another two months she would be relying on Shonny a great deal. The life inside her kicked; she was swollen but very well. There were many worries, though she was happy enough. Guilt about Tristram pricked her, she was exercised by the problems of keeping her long secret. When visitors came or farmworkers looked in, she had to dart to the lavatory, as fast as her bulk would allow. She had to take exercise furtively, after dark, walking with Mavis between ruined hedgerows, by fields of blasted wheat and barley. The children were good, long conditioned to not talking in school or out of it about the dangerous blasphemies of their parents; quiet about God, they were also quiet about their aunt's pregnancy. They were sensible handsome country-looking children, though thinner than was right, Dymphna seven and Llewelyn nine. They sat today, Christmas a day or two off, cutting bits of cardboard into silhouettes of holly leaves, all the natural holly being stricken by the blight. 'We'll do our best for Christmas again,' said Shonny. 'I've plum wine still and a sufficiency of alc. And there are those four poor old hens sitting in the icebox. Time enough to contemplate the uncontemplatable future when Christmas has come and gone.'

Dymphna, steering her scissors, her tongue-tip out with concentration, said, 'Dad.'

'Yes, my dear?'

'What's Christmas really about?' They were as much the children of the State as of their parents.

'You know what it's about. You know as well as I do what it's *all* about. Llewelyn, you tell her what it's about.'

'Oh,' said Llewelyn, cutting, 'this chap was born, you see. Then he was killed by being hung up on a tree, and then he was eaten.'

'Now, for a start,' said Shonny, 'He wasn't a chap.'

'A man, then,' said Llewelyn. 'But a man's a chap.'

'The Son of God,' said Shonny, banging the table. 'God and man. And He wasn't eaten when He was killed. He went straight up to heaven. Now, you're half-right about the eating, God bless your heart, but it's ourselves that do the eating. When we have mass we eat His body and drink His blood. But they're disguised – do you see, are you listening to what I'm telling you? – as bread and wine.'

'When He comes again,' said Llewelyn, snipping, 'will He be eaten properly?'

'What, now,' asked Shonny, 'would you be meaning by that strange statement?'

'Eaten,' said Llewelyn, 'like Jim Whittle was eaten.' He started cutting out a new leaf, intent on it. 'Will it be like that, Dad?'

'What's all this?' said Shonny, agitated. 'What's all this you're saying about somebody being eaten? Come on now, speak up, child.' He shook the boy's shoulder, but Llewelyn went on cutting calmly.

'He didn't come to school,' he said. 'His mother and dad cut him up and ate him.'

'How do you know this? Where did you get that outrageous story from? Who's been telling you these wicked things?'

'It's true, Dad,' said Dymphna. 'Is that all right?' she asked, showing her cardboard leaf.

'Never mind about that,' said her father impatiently. 'Tell me about this, come on now. Who's been telling this horrible tale to you?'

'It's not a horrible tale,' pouted Llewelyn. 'It's true. A lot of us went by their house coming home from school and it was true. They had a big pan sort of thing on the stove and it was bubbling away like anything. Some of the other kids went in and they saw.' Dymphna giggled.

'God forgive everybody,' said Shonny. 'This is a shocking and terrible thing, and all you can do is laugh about it. Tell me –' He shook both his children. '– Are you speaking the truth, now? Because, by the Holy Name,

123

if you're just making a joke out of a horrible thing like that I promise you, by the Lord Jesus Christ, I'll give both of you the father and mother of a beating.'

'It's true,' wailed Llewelyn. 'We saw, we both did. She had a big spoon and she was putting it on two plates and it was all steaming hot and some of the other kids asked for some because they were hungry, but Dymphna and me were frightened because they said that Jim Whittle's father and mother are not right in the head, so we ran home quick but we were told to say nothing about it.'

'Who told you to say nothing about it?'

'They did. Some of the big boys did. Frank Bamber said he'd hit us if we told.'

'If you told what?'

Llewelyn hung his head. 'What Frank Bamber did.'

'What did he do?'

'He had a big piece in his hand, but he said he was hungry. But we were hungry too, but we didn't have any. We just ran home.' Dymphna giggled. Shonny let his hands drop. He said:

'God Almighty.'

'Because it was stealing, see, Dad,' said Llewelyn. 'Frank Bamber grabbed it in his hand and ran out and they shouted at him.'

Shonny looked green, Beatrice-Joanna felt it. 'What a horrible, horrible thing,' she panted.

'But if you eat this chap who's God,' said Llewelyn stoutly, 'how can it be horrible? If it's all right to eat God why is it horrible to eat Jim Whittle?'

'Because,' said Dymphna reasonably, 'if you eat God there's always plenty left. You can't eat God up because

God just goes on and on and on and God can't ever be finished. You silly clot,' she added and then went on cutting holly leaves.

Four

'A VISITOR for you,' said the warder to Tristram. 'But if you curse and blind at him as you have done at me, then you're really for it and no error, Mister Foulmouth. This way, sir,' he said to the corridor. A black-uniformed figure marched up, eggs bursting on its lapels. 'Neither of these will do you any harm, sir, so there's no call to be nervous. I'll come back in about ten minutes, sir.' And the warder went off.

'Look, I know you,' said Tristram, thin, weak, well-bearded.

The captain smiled. He took off his cap, disclosing short straight oiled rust-coloured hair and, still smiling, smoothed one wing of his moustache. 'You *should* know me,' he smiled. 'We had a very pleasant but, I fear, as it turned out, not very profitable drinking session together, do you see, at the Metropole, do you see, a couple of months ago.'

'Yes, I know you all right,' said Tristram fiercely. 'I never forget a face. That's where being a teacher comes in. Well, have you got an order for my release? Are the times of trial over at last?'

The unfrocked priest, who lately had insisted on being called the Blessed Ambrose Bayley, looked up light-headedly and said, 'Come, there's a mile of penitents out-side. Kneel down quickly and make your confession.' The captain grinned foolishly.

'I've merely come to tell you,' he said, 'where your wife is.'

Tristram looked sullen and blockish. 'Haven't got a wife,' he muttered. 'I put her away.'

'Nonsense, do you see,' said the captain. 'You most certainly have a wife, and at the moment, do you see, she's staying with her sister and brother-in-law near Preston. State Farm NW313 is the address.'

'So,' said Tristram evilly. 'So that's where the bitch is.'

'Yes,' said the captain, 'your wife is there, awaiting her illegal though legitimate, do you see, child.'

The unfrocked priest, weary of waiting for the cap-tain to kneel down and begin, was now hearing, with much head-rolling and groaning, the confession of some-one unseen and unknown. 'A foul sin,' he said, 'fornica-tion. How many times?'

'At least,' said the captain, 'one presumes that. She has been left alone, do you see, she has remained un-molested by any of our people in that corner of Northern Province. I received the information of her whereabouts from our Travel Control Branch. Now,' he said, 'you may be wondering, do you see, why we do not pounce. Perhaps you have been wondering that.'

'Ah, bloody nonsense,' snarled Tristram. 'I don't wonder anything because I don't know anything. Stuck in here starving, no news of the outside world, no letters. Nobody comes to see me.' He was ready to revert to the old Tristram, to start to snivel, but he took a grip on himself and growled, 'I don't care, damn you. I don't care for any of the damned lot of you, get it?'

'Very well,' said the captain. 'Time is short, do you see. I want to know when, by your computation, she will be having the child.'

'What child? Who said anything about a child?' growled Tristram.

'Go in peace and God bless you,' said the Blessed Ambrose Bayley. And then, 'I forgive my tormentors. Through the light of these consuming flames I see the everlasting light of the hereafter.'

'Oh, come on now, do you see,' said the captain impatiently. 'You said she was to have a child. We can check easily enough, of course, do you see, that she's pregnant. What I want to know is, when is she to have the child? When did she, by your calculation, conceive?'

'No idea.' Tristram shook his head in gloom and apathy. 'No idea at all.'

The captain took from one of his tunic pockets something in rustling yellow paper. 'Perhaps you're hungry,' he said. 'Perhaps a little synthechoc would help.' He unwrapped the bar and held it out. The Blessed Ambrose Bayley was quicker than Tristram; he darted like a ray and snatched the bar, drooling. Tristram was on to him, and the two snarled, clawed, tore. Finally each got about half. Three seconds were enough to wolf the brown sticky stuff down. 'Come on now,' said the captain sharply. 'When was it?'

'En oz ot?' Tristram was licking round his palate and sucking his fingers. 'Oh, that,' he said at last. 'It must have been in May. I know when it was. It was at the beginning of the Interphase. Have you any more of that stuff?'

'What do you mean?' asked the captain patiently. 'What is the Interphase?'

'Of course,' said Tristram, 'you're not a historian, are you? Of the science of historiography you know nothing. You're just a hired thug with pockets crammed tight with synthechoc.' He belched and then looked sick. 'When all you hired thugs began to swagger through the streets. Give me more of that, blast you.' He then turned savagely on his cell-mate. 'That was mine and you ate it. It was meant for me, blast you.' He weakly belaboured the Blessed Ambrose Bayley who, hands joined and eyes swooning upwards, said, 'Father, forgive them, for they know not what they do.' Tristram gave up, panting.

'Good,' said the captain. 'Well, then, we know when to take action. You can look forward, do you see, to the final disgracing of your brother and the punishment of your wife.'

'What do you mean? What are you talking about? Punishment? What punishment? If it's my wife you're going to go for, you leave that bitch alone, do you hear? She's my wife, not yours. I'll deal with my wife in my own way.' He sank without shame into snivelling. 'Oh, Beattie, Beattie,' he whined, 'why don't you get me out of here?'

'You realize, of course,' said the captain, 'that you're in here because of your brother?'

'Less talk from you,' sneered Tristram, 'and more synthechoc, you gutsy hypocrite. Come on, hand over.'

'Sustenance, for the love of heaven,' fluted the Blessed

128

Ambrose Bayley. 'Do not forget the servitors of the Lord in the days of your fatness.' He fell on to his knees and clung to the captain's shins, nearly bringing him over.

'Warder!' called the captain.

'And,' said Tristram, 'you leave my child alone. It's *my* child, you infanticidal maniac.' He started. with feeble fists, to hammer on the captain like a door. '*My* child, you swine. My protest, my dirty word to the dirty world, you robber.' He began to frisk the captain for synthechoc with the quick long hands of a monkey.

'Warder!' called the captain, fighting him off.

The Blessed Ambrose Bayley relaxed his hold and crawled, dispirited, back to his bench-bunk. 'Five Our Fathers and five Hail Marys,' he said perfunctorily, 'today and tomorrow in honour of the Little Flower. Go in peace and God bless you.'

The warder came, saying cheerfully, 'Not given you any trouble, have they, sir? That's right.' Tristram's arms, too weak for further frisking, had dropped to his sides. 'Him,' pointed the warder. 'A proper little terror he was, when he first came here. Couldn't get no sense out of him, one of the real criminal class. Much tamer now, he is,' he said, with a touch of pride. Tristram slumped in his corner, muttering, '*My* child, *my* child, *my* child.' With those spondees in his ears, the captain, grinning nervously, left.

Five

Late December, in Bridgwater, Somerset, Western Province, a middle-aged man named Thomas Wharton, going home from work shortly after midnight, was set upon by youths. These knifed him, stripped him spitted him, basted him, carved him, served him – all openly and without shame in one of the squares of the town. A hungry crowd clamoured for hunks and slices, kept back – that the King's Peace might not be broken – by munching and dripping greyboys. In Thirsk, North Riding, three lads – Alfred Pickles, David Ogden and Jackie Priestley – were struck dead with a hammer in a dark ginnel and dragged into a terraced house by way of the backyard. The street was gay for two nights with the smoke of barbecues. In Stoke-on-Trent the carcase of a woman (later identified as Maria Bennett, spinster, aged twenty-eight) grinned up suddenly – several good clean cuttings off her – from under a bank of snow. In Gillingham, Kent, Greater London, a shady back-street eating-shop opened, grilling nightly, and members of both police forces seemed to patronize it. In certain unregenerate places on the Suffolk coast there were rumours of big crackling Christmas dinners.

In Glasgow, on Hogmanay, a bearded sect professing worship of Njal offered a multiple human sacrifice, reserving the entrails for the deified burnt advocate, the flesh for themselves. Kirkcaldy, less subtle, saw a number of private ceilidhs with meat sandwiches. The New Year commenced with stories of timid anthropophagy from

Maryport, Runcorn, Burslem, West Bromwich and Kidderminster. Then the metropolis flashed its own sudden canines: a man called Amis suffered savage amputation of an arm off Kingsway; S. R. Coke, journalist, was boiled in an old copper near Shepherd's Bush; Miss Joan Waine, a teacher, was fried in segments.

Those were the stories, anyway. There was no real way of checking the truth of them; they might well have been the delirious fantasies of extreme hunger. One story in particular was so incredible that it cast doubt on the others. It was reported from Brodick on the Isle of Arran that a vast communal nocturnal gorge of man-flesh had been followed by a heterosexual orgy in the ruddy light of the fat-spitting fires and that, the morning after, the root known as salsify was seen sprouting from the pressed earth. That could not, by any manner of means or stretch of the organ of credulity, possibly be believed.

Six

BEATRICE-JOANNA'S pains were starting.

'Poor old girl,' said Shonny. 'Poor, poor old lady.' He and his wife and sister-in-law were standing, this bright snappy forenoon in February, by the sty of Bessie, the ailing sow. Bessie, all the slack grey deadweight of her, lay snorting feebly, a great ruin of flesh, on her side. Her uppermost flank, curiously mottled, heaved as in a dream of hunting. Shonny's Panceltic eyes filled with tears. 'Worms a yard long,' he grieved, 'horrible live worms. Why should a worm have life and she none? Poor, poor, poor old lady.'

'Oh, stop it, Shonny,' Mavis sniffed. 'We've got to make ourselves hard-hearted. She's only a pig, after all.'

'Only a pig? *Only* a pig?' Shonny was indignant. 'She's grown up with the children, God bless the old girl. She's been a member of the family. She's given her piglings unstintingly that we might be decently fed. She shall, the Lord keep her soul, be given a Christian burial.'

Beatrice-Joanna could sympathize with his tears; she was, in many ways, closer to Shonny than Mavis was. But she had other things on her mind now. The pains had started. A fair balance today: death of a pig, birth of a man. She was not afraid, she had confidence in Shonny and Mavis, especially Shonny; her pregnancy had run a healthy conventional course, subject only to certain frustrations: a strong desire for pickled gherkins had had to go unsatisfied, an urge to rearrange the furniture of the farmhouse had been stamped on by Mavis. Sometimes in the night an overwhelming longing for the comforting arms not, strangely, of Derek but of –

Aaaargh.

'That makes two in twenty minutes,' said Mavis. 'You'd better come inside.'

'It's the contractions,' said Shonny with something like glee. 'It'll be some time tonight, praise the Lord.'

'A bit of a twinge,' said Beatrice-Joanna. 'Not much. Just a bit, that's all.'

'Right,' bubbled Shonny eagerly. 'The first thing you've got to have is an enema. Soap and water. You'll see to that, will you, Mavis? And she'd better have a good warm bath. Right. Thank the Lord we've plenty of hot water.' He rushed them into the house, leaving Bessie to suffer in loneliness, and started opening and slamming drawers. 'The ligatures,' he cried. 'I've got to make the ligatures.'

'There's plenty of time,' said Mavis. 'She's a human being, you know, not a beast of the field.'

'That's why I've got to make the ligatures,' blustered Shonny. 'Good God, woman, do you want her just to bite it off, like a she-cat?' He found linen thread and, singing a hymn in Panceltic, twisted ten-inch lengths for tying the umbilical cord, knotting them at the ends. Meanwhile Beatrice-Joanna was taken upstairs to the bathroom, and the hot-water pipes of the house sang full-throatedly, creaking and straining like a ship under way.

The pains grew more frequent. Shonny prepared the bed in the heated outhouse, spreading brown paper across its middle and smoothing a drawsheet over, singing all the time. The crops had failed and a faithful sow was dying, but a new life was preparing to thumb its nose – in the gesture once known as 'fat bacon' – at the forces of sterility. Suddenly, unbidden, two strange names – bearded names they seemed somehow – came into Shonny's head: Zondek and Aschheim. Who were they now? He remembered: they were the ancient devisers of a pregnancy test. A few drops of pregnant woman's urine would send a baby mouse speeding to sexual maturity. He had read that, reading up the duties which he was now beginning to perform. His heart, for some reason, lifted in tremendous elation. Of course, *there* was the big secret – all life was one, all life was one. But no time to think about that now.

Dymphna and Llewelyn came home from school. 'What's the matter, Dad? What's going on, Dad? What are you doing, Dad?'

'Your aunt's time is come. Don't bother me now. Go and play somewhere. No, wait, go and stay with poor old Bessie. Hold her trotter, poor old girl.'

Beatrice-Joanna now wanted to lie down. The amnion had ruptured in a rush, the amniotic waters had escaped. 'On your left side, girl,' ordered Shonny. 'Is it hurting? Poor old lady.' The pains were, in fact, growing much worse; Beatrice-Joanna began to hold her breath and to bear down strenuously. Shonny knotted a long towel to the bed-head, urging, 'Pull on that, girl. Pull hard. God bless you, it won't be long now.' Beatrice-Joanna pulled, groaning. 'Mavis,' said Shonny, 'this is going to be a longish job. Fetch me in a couple of bottles of plum wine and a glass.'

'There are only a couple of bottles left.'

'Fetch them in just the same like a good girl. There, there, my beauty,' he said to Beatrice-Joanna. 'You pull away there, bless you.' He checked that the old-fashioned swaddling clothes – knitted by the two sisters in the long winter evenings – were warming on the radiator. He had sterilized his ligatures; a pair of scissors was boiling in a pan; a tin bath shone on the floor; cotton wool waited to be teased into pledgets; there was a bolster-slip for a binder – all, in fact, was ready. 'God bless you, my dear,' he said to his wife as she reappeared with the bottles. 'This is going to be a great day.'

It was certainly a long day. For nearly two hours

Beatrice-Joanna struggled muscularly. She cried with the pains, and Shonny, swigging his plum wine and shouting encouragement, watched and waited, sweating as much as she. 'If only,' he muttered, 'we had an anaesthetic of some kind or another. Here, girl,' he said boldly, 'drink some of this,' and he proffered his bottle. But Mavis dragged his hand back.

'Look,' she cried. 'It's coming!'

Beatrice-Joanna shrieked. The head was being born: it had finished its difficult journey at last, leaving behind the bony tunnel of the pelvic girdle, pushing through the sheath to the air of a world that, now indifferent, would soon be hostile. After a brief pause the child's body pushed itself out. 'Perfect,' said Shonny, his eyes shining, wiping the child's shut eyes with a moist pledget, delicate and loving in his movements. The newborn yelled to greet the world. 'Lovely,' said Shonny. Then, when the pulse in the umbilical cord began to stop, he took two of his ligatures and skilfully made his ties, tight, tighter, tightest, forming two frontiers with a no-man's-land in the middle. Here, careful with his sterilized scissors, he snipped. The new bit of life, full of savagely gulped air, was now on its own. 'A boy,' said Mavis.

'A boy? So it is,' said Shonny. Free of its mother, it had ceased to be merely a thing. Shonny turned to watch for the thrust of the placenta while Mavis wrapped the child in a shawl and laid it, him, in a box by the radiator; the bath could come later. 'Good God,' said Shonny, watching. Beatrice-Joanna cried out, but not so loud as before. 'Another one,' called Shonny in awe. 'Twins, by God. A litter, by the Lord Jesus.'

Seven

'Out, you,' said the warder.

'And about time,' blustered Tristram, getting up from his bunk. 'About bloody time, you nasty thing. Give me something to eat, blast you, before I go.'

'Not you,' said the warder with relish. 'Him.' He pointed. 'You'll be with us a long time yet, Mister Dirty. It's him as has got to be released.'

The Blessed Ambrose Bayley, shaken by the warder, blinked and goggled his way out of the perpetual presence of God that had set in at the end of January. He was very weak.

'Traitor,' snarled Tristram. 'Stool-pigeon. Telling lies about me, that's what you've been doing. Buying your shameful freedom with lies.' To the warder he said, hopefully, his eyes fierce and large, 'Are you sure you haven't made a mistake? Are you quite sure it isn't me?'

'Him,' pointed the warder. 'Not you. Him. You're not a –' He squinted at the paper in his hand. '– Not a minister of the cloth, whatever that means, are you now? All them have to be released. But foul-mouths like you have to go on being here. Right?'

'It's flagrant bloody injustice,' yelled Tristram, 'that's what it is.' He fell on his knees before the warder, clasping his hands in prayer and hunching his shoulders as if he had just broken his neck. 'Please let me out instead of him. He's past it. He thinks he's dead already, burnt at the stake. He thinks he's well on the road to canonization. He just doesn't know what's going on. *Please.*'

'Him,' pointed the warder. 'His name's on this bit of paper. See – A. T. Bayley. You, Mister Swearer, have got to stay here. We'll find another pal for you, don't worry. Come on, old man,' he said gently to the Blessed Ambrose. 'You've got to get out there and report for orders to some bloke in Lambeth who's going to tell you what to do. Come on, now.' And he shook him somewhat roughly.

'Let me have his rations,' begged Tristram, still on his knees. 'That's the least you can do, damn and blast your eyes. I'm bloody starving, blast it, man.'

'We're all starving,' snarled the warder, 'and some of us have to work and not just lounge about all day. We're all trying to live on these here nuts and a couple of drops of this here synthelac, and they reckon those can't last much longer, things being the way they are. Do come on,' he said, shaking away at the Blessed Ambrose. But the Blessed Ambrose lay bright-eyed in a holy trance, hardly moving.

'Food,' grumbled Tristram, getting up with difficulty. 'Food, food, food.'

'I'll give you food,' scolded the warder, not meaning that at all. 'I'll send in one of these man-eaters as have been picked up, that's what I'll do. That's who your new cell-pal will be, one of those. He'll have your liver out, that he will, and cook it and eat it.'

'Cooked or raw,' moaned Tristram, 'makes no difference. Give it me, give it me.'

'Aaargh, you,' sneered the warder in disgust. 'Come on now, old man,' he said to the Blessed Ambrose in growing disquiet. 'Get up now, like a good fellow. You're going out. Out, out, out,' he went like a dog.

The Blessed Ambrose rose very shakily, leaning on the warder. '*Quia peccavi nimis*,' he wavered in a senile voice. Then he collapsed clumsily. The warder said, 'You look to me to be in a pretty bad way, you do that.' He hunkered, frowning over him as if he were a stopped-up drain. '*Quoniam adhuc*,' mumbled out of the Blessed Ambrose, supine on the flags.

Tristram, thinking he saw his chance, fell on to the warder, like, as he thought, a tower. The two rolled and panted all over the Blessed Ambrose. 'You would, would you, Mister Nasty?' growled the warder. The Blessed Ambrose Bayley moaned as the Blessed Margaret Clitheroe must, pressed by hundredweights, have, at York in 1586, moaned. 'You've done for yourself good and proper now,' gasped the warder, kneeling on Tristram and pounding him with his two fists. 'You've asked for this, you have, Mister Treacherous. You'll never get out of here alive, that you won't.' He cracked him on the mouth viciously, breaking his dentures. 'You've had this coming a long time, you have.' Tristram lay still, breathing desperately. The warder began, still panting, to drag the Blessed Ambrose Bayley to freedom. '*Mea culpa, mea culpa, mea maxima culpa*,' went this unfrocked man, banging his own chest thrice.

Eight

'GLORY be to God,' ejaculated Shonny. 'Mavis, come and see who's here. Llewelyn, Dymphna. Quick, quick, the lot of you.' For who should have walked into the house but Father Shackel, seedsman by trade who, many months before, had been taken off by lipsticked brutal greyboys. Father Shackel was in his early forties, with a very round cropped head, pronounced exophthalmia, and chronic rhinitis caused by a one-sided bulge on the septum. His ever-open mouth and wide eyes gave him a look of William Blake seeing fairies. He raised his right hand now in blessing.

'You're very thin,' said Mavis.

'Did you get tortured?' asked Llewelyn and Dymphna.

'When did they let you out?' cried Shonny.

'What I'd like most of all,' said Father Shackel, 'is a drink of something.' His speech was muffled and de-nasalized, as with an everlasting cold.

'There's a tiny drop of plum wine,' said Shonny, 'left over from the labour and the celebration of the end of the labour.' He rushed to get it.

'Labour? What labour is he talking about?' asked Father Shackel, sitting down.

'My sister,' said Mavis. 'She had twins the other day. You have a christening job to do, Father.'

'Thank you, Shonny.' Father Shackel took the half-filled glass. 'Well,' he said, having sipped, 'there are some queer things going on, aren't there?'

'When did they let you out?' Shonny asked again.

'Three days ago. Since then I've been in Liverpool. Incredible, but the whole hierarchy's at large – arch-bishops, bishops, the lot. We can drop the disguise now. We can even wear clerical dress if we wish to.'

'We don't seem to get any news,' said Mavis. 'Just talk, talk, talk these days – exhortation, propaganda –

but we hear rumours, don't we, Shonny?'

'Cannibalism,' said Shonny. 'Human sacrifice. We hear about those things.'

'This is very good wine,' said Father Shackel. 'I suppose one of these days we'll be seeing the ban taken off viticulture.'

'What's viticulture, Dad?' asked Llewelyn. 'Is it the same as human sacrifice?'

'You two,' said Shonny, 'can go back to holding poor old Bessie's trotter. Kiss Father Shackel's hands before you go.'

'Father Shackel's trotters,' giggled Dymphna.

'Enough of that now,' warned Shonny, 'or you'll be receiving a clout on the earhole for yourself.'

'Bessie's a long time dying,' grumbled Llewelyn with youth's heartlessness. 'Come on, Dymph.' They kissed Father Shackel's hands and went chattering out.

'The position isn't at all clear yet,' said Father Shackel. 'All we know is that everybody's getting very scared. You can always tell. The Pope, apparently, is back in Rome. I saw the Archbishop of Liverpool with my own eyes. He's been working, you know, poor man, as a bricklayer. Anyway, we kept the light going through the dark times. That's what's meant by a Church. It's something to be proud of.'

'And now what's going to happen?' asked Mavis.

'We're to return to our priestly duties. We're to celebrate mass again – openly, legally.'

'Glory be to God,' said Shonny.

'Oh, don't think the State's at all concerned with the glory of God,' said Father Shackel. 'The State's scared of forces it doesn't understand, that's all. The leaders

of the State are suffering from an accession of superstitious fear, that's what it is. They've done no good
with their police, so now it's the priests they call on.
There aren't any churches now, so we have to go up
and down our allotted areas, feeding them all God instead of the law. Oh, it's all very clever. I suppose
sublimation is the big word: don't eat your neighbour,
eat God instead. We're being used, that's what it is. But
in another sense, of course, we're using. We're right
down to essential function now – the sacramental function. That's one thing we've learnt: the Church can take
in any heresy or unorthodoxy – including your harmless
belief in the Second Coming – so long as it holds fast to
essential function.' He chuckled. 'A surprising number
of policemen are being eaten, I gather. God works in a
mysterious way. Epicene flesh seems to have the greater
succulence.'

'How horrible,' grimaced Mavis.

'Oh yes, it's horrible,' grinned Father Shackel. 'Look,
I haven't much time: I've got to get to Accrington tonight and I may have to walk: the buses don't seem to
be running. Have you got the communion wafers?'

'Some of them,' said Shonny. 'The kids, God forgive
them, found the packet and started eating them, blasphemous little heathens. They'd have wolfed the lot if
I hadn't caught them.'

'A little job of baptism before you go,' said Mavis.

'Oh, yes.' Father Shackel was led to the outhouse
where Beatrice-Joanna lay with her twins. She looked
thin but rosy. The twins slept. Shonny said:

'And after the rites for the new-born, how about the
rites for the dying?'

'This,' said Mavis, introducing, 'is Father Shackel.'

'I'm not dying, am I?' said Beatrice-Joanna in alarm. 'I feel fine. Hungry, though.'

'It's poor old Bessie that's dying, poor old lady,' said Shonny. 'I claim the same rights for her as for any Christian soul.'

'A pig doesn't have a soul,' said Mavis.

'Twins, eh?' said Father Shackel. 'Congratulations. Both are boys, are they? And what names have you chosen for them?'

'Tristram for one,' said Beatrice-Joanna promptly. 'And Derek for the other.'

'Can you give me water?' asked Father Shackel of Mavis. 'And also a little salt?'

Llewelyn and Dymphna came panting in. 'Dad,' cried Llewelyn, 'Dad. It's about Bessie.'

'Gone at last, has she?' said Shonny. 'Poor faithful old girl. Uncomforted by the last rites, God have mercy on her.'

'She's not dead,' cried Dymphna. 'She's eating.'

'Eating?' Shonny stared.

'She's standing up and eating,' said Llewelyn. 'We found some eggs in the henhouse and gave her those.'

'Eggs? *Eggs?* Is everybody going mad, including myself?'

'And those biscuits,' said Dymphna. 'Those round white ones in the cupboard. We couldn't find anything else.'

Father Shackel laughed. He sat on the edge of Beatrice-Joanna's bed in order to have his laugh out. He laughed at the mixture of feelings on Shonny's face. 'Never mind,' he said at last, grinning imbecilically. 'I'll

find some bread on the road to Accrington. There's
bound to be bread somewhere.'

Nine

TRISTRAM's new cell-mate was a massive Nigerian called
Charlie Linklater. He was a friendly talkative man,
with a mouth so large that it was a wonder he was able
to attain any precision in his enunciation of the English
vowel-sounds. Tristram tried frequently to count his
teeth, which were his own and flashed often as in pride
of the fact, and the total he arrived at seemed always
in excess of the statutory thirty-two. This worried him.
Charlie Linklater was serving an indefinite sentence for
an indefinite crime that, as far as Tristram could make
out, involved multiple progeniture along with beating-
up of greyboys, flavoured with committing a nuisance
in the vestibule of Government Building and eating
meat when drunk. 'A nice little rest in here,' he said,
'won't do me no harm.' His voice was rich crimson-
purple. Tristram felt thinner and weaker than ever in
this polished blue-black meaty presence. 'They talk
about meat-eating,' said Charlie Linklater in his lazy
way, relaxed on his bunk, 'but they don't know the first
thing about it, boy. Why, a good ten years ago I was
keeping company with the wife of a man from Kaduna,
same as myself. His name was George Daniel, and he
was a meter-reader by trade. Well, he comes back unexpected and catches us at it. What could we do but

give him the old hatchet? You'd do the same, boy. Well, there we have this body – a good thirteen stone if he was a pound. What could we do but get the old stew-pot going? Took us a week, that did, eating all the time. We buried the bones and nobody one bit the wiser. That was a big meal, brother, and a real good eat.' He sighed, smacked his huge lips, and even belched in appreciative recollection.

'I've got to get out of here,' said Tristram. 'There's food in the outside world, isn't there? Food.' He drooled, shaking the bars but feebly. 'I've got to eat, got to.'

'Well,' said Charlie Linklater, 'for myself there's no hurry right away to get out. One or two people are looking for me with the old hatchet and I reckon I'm as well off here as anywhere. For a little while, anyhow. But I'd be happy to oblige in any way I could to get you out of here. Not that I don't like your company, you being a well-behaved and educated man and with good manners. But if it would oblige you to get out, then I'm the boy to assist you, boy.'

When the warder came along to shove the midday nutrition tablets and water between the bars, Tristram was interested to see that he carried a truncheon. 'Any nonsense from you,' said the warder, 'and you'll get a fine big crack with this gentleman'– he brandished it – 'on the soft part of your skull, Mister Bloody-minded. So watch out, that's what I say.'

'That black stick of his will come in very nice,' said Charlie Linklater. 'The way he speaks to you is not very good-mannered,' he added. Then he devised a simple plan for securing Tristram's release. It involved some punitive danger to himself, but he was a man of big heart. Having consumed about nine stone of meter-reader in seven days, he was evidently also a man of steadiness and persistence. Now, in the first simple phase of his simple plan, he built up a show of enmity towards his cell-mate so that there should be no danger of the suspicion of complicity when the time came for the second phase. From now on, whenever the warder looked in through the bars, he would howl out loud at Tristram:

'You stop getting on to me, boy. You keep them dirty words to yourself. I'm not used to being treated like that, nohow.'

'At it again, is he?' nodded the grim warder. 'We'll break his spirit, you just wait and see. We'll have him grovelling before we're through with him.'

Tristram, sunken-jawed because his dentures were broken, opened his mouth in a sort of fish-snarl. The warder snarled back, dentate, and went off. Charlie Linklater winked. Three days of this.

On the fourth day Tristram lay much as the Blessed Ambrose Bayley had lain – out, still, his eyes up to heaven. Charlie Linklater agitated the bars. 'He's dying. Come quick there. This boy here's snuffing it. Come along now.' The warder câme grumbling. He saw the prostrate Tristram and ground open the cell-door.

'Right,' said Charlie Linklater, fifteen seconds after. 'You just climb into his clothes, boy. Nice little job, this is,' he said, swinging the truncheon by its leather-substitute loop. 'Just you get into that man's uniform, you two being much of a size.' Between them they stripped the dead-out warder. 'Pimply sort of a back he's got,' commented Charlie Linklater. Tenderly he lifted him on to Tristram's bunk and covered him with Tristram's blanket. Meanwhile, breathing hard with excitement, Tristram buttoned himself into worn warder's blue. 'Don't forget his keys,' said Charlie Linklater, 'and more than that, boy, don't forget his truncheon. That'll really get you places, that will, the little beauty. Now, I reckon he'll be well out for another half an hour, so just take your time and act natural. Pull that cap well down over your eyes, boy. Pity about that beard.'

'I'm grateful,' said Tristram, his heart pumping like mad. 'I really am.'

'Don't think nothing of it,' said Charlie Linklater. 'Now, just give me one little crack on the back of the head with that truncheon, so as it'll look more natural. No need to lock the cell-door, because nobody's going to try and get out, but don't forget to keep them keys jingling, so as to be nice and natural. Go on, now. Hit.' Tristram tapped weakly, as at a breakfast egg, on the oaken skull. 'You can do better than that,' said Charlie Linklater. Tristram, his lips tight, cracked him a beauty. 'Something like, that is,' said Charlie Linklater, showing the whites of his eyes. His bulk crashed to the flags, making the tin mugs rattle on their shelf.

Outside on the corridor Tristram looked both ways with care. At the far end of the gallery two warders leaned gloomily on the well-rails, chatting, gazing down as into the sea. At this end the way was clear: four cells only to the stairhead. Tristram was worried about being a bearded warder. He found a handkerchief in the pocket of the stiff alien trousers and, with a fully stretched hand, he spread this over his muzzle. Toothache or jaw-ache or something. He decided against Charlie Linklater's advice: looking unnatural, he must behave unnaturally. A jangle of keys and clomp of boots, he danced clumsily down the iron stairs. On the landing he met another warder going up. 'What's the matter with you?' this one asked. 'Burk crawk workers-gate,' mumbled Tristram. The other nodded, satisfied, and continued to climb.

Tristram clattered on down. He held his breath. This looked as if it were going to be too easy. Flight after flight of ringing iron, row after endless row of cells, a yellowing card of close print on each landing: *H.M. Prisons. Regulations.* Then at last came the ground floor and the feeling that he was balancing these tiers of cells on his own delirious head. A beef-faced warder, stiff as if artificially braced, collided with him head-on as he turned a random corner. 'Here, here,' he said. 'You all right? New here, aren't you?' 'Humgoil,' chumbled Tristram. 'Gert webbing. Gort foresight.' 'If it's the sick-bay you're after,' said the warder, 'it's straight down there. Can't miss it.' He pointed. 'Inch of bellrope,' chewed Tristram. 'That's all right, mate,' said the warder. Tristram hurried on. Now it was all institutional corridors, the walls buff with nigger-brown dadoes, a strong smell of disinfectant, OFFICERS' SICKBAY said a blue box over a lintel, a light inside it. Tristram walked boldly into a place of cubicles, youths in white coats, the stench of spirit. From the nearest door came the splashing and churning of bath-water, the grunting of a male bather. Tristram found the door open and entered. Blue tiles, steam, the bather lathering his head with eyes tight shut as in direst agony. Forgot

147

to shave,' shouted Tristram. 'Eh?' the bather shouted
back. To his minor elation Tristram found an electric
shaver clamped to a bracket in the wall. He switched on
and started to carve his beard like so much meat. 'Here,'
said the bather, his sight restored, 'what's going on?
Who let you in?' 'Shaving,' said Tristram, seeing with
shock his lantern jaws emerge in the mirror as the
swathes fell, with horror the fierce mistrustfulness of his
eyes. 'Won't be a minute,' he said. 'Nothing's private
these days,' grumbled the bather. 'Not even when you
have a bath is it private.' He stirred the water fretfully,
saying, 'You might have the decency to take your hat
off when you come barging in disturbing a bloke's bath.'
'Shan't be more than two seconds,' said Tristram. He
left a moustache to save time. 'You might clear up all
that mess on the floor,' said the bather. 'Why should I
have to tread in my bare feet on another bloke's
whiskers?' And then, 'Here, what's going on? Who are
you, anyway? You've got a beard, leastways you had
one, and that's not right. Warders don't have beards,
not in this prison they don't.' He tried to get out of
the bath, a rabbit-bodied man with a black pelt from
sternum to pubes. Tristram pushed him back in again,
very soapy, and dashed to the door. There was, he was
glad to see, a key in it, and this he transferred to the
outside. The bather, all suds, tried again to lift himself
out. Clean-shaven Tristram mouthed good-bye fishily,
went out, then locked the door. 'Here,' the bather could
be heard calling, sploshing. In the corridor Tristram
calmly said to a white-coated youth, 'I'm new here and
seem to have got lost. How do I get out of this place?'
The youth led him, smiling, from the sickbay and gave

directions. 'Down there, dear,' he said, 'then turn sharp left, then straight on, you can't miss it, dear.' 'Thank you very much,' said Tristram, smiling with his black hole for a mouth. Everybody had been, really and truly, most obliging.

In the wide high gloomy hall there were several warders apparently coming off duty, handing their keys over to a chief officer, his blue new and smart, very thin, his height nearer seven feet than six. 'Right,' he kept saying with little interest, 'Right,' checking the key-numbers with a list, ticking, 'Right,' passing the keys to an assistant who hung them on a wall-board. 'Right,' he said to Tristram. There was a small open port in the massy left-hand metal door of the prison. The warders went out that way. It was as easy as that. Tristram stood on the steps an instant, inhaling freedom, gazing up, astonished at the height of the sky. 'Careful, careful, don't give yourself away,' he counselled his shaking heart. He walked off slowly, try-ing to whistle. But his mouth was still too dry for that.

Ten

SEED-TIME, eggs trickling in from the battery, Bessie the sow almost frisky, the twins thriving. Beatrice-Joanna and her sister sat together in the living-room, knitting a sort of wool-surrogate into warm baby-coats. In a double cradle hammered together by Shonny, Tristram and Derek Foxe slept in amity. Mavis said:

'Far be it from me to propose that you go out into the night with your double bundle, but I'm only thinking of what's best for you. Obviously, you yourself wouldn't want to stay here for ever, apart from there not really being room. And then there's the danger for all of us. I mean, you've got to make up your mind about the future, haven't you?'

'Oh, yes,' agreed Beatrice-Joanna dispiritedly. 'I see that. You've been very kind. I see all that.'

'So,' asked Mavis, 'what have you in mind?'

'What can I have in mind?' said Beatrice-Joanna. 'I've written three letters to Tristram, care of the Home Office, and all of them have come bouncing back. He may be dead. They may have shot him.' She sniffed two or three times. 'Our flat will have been pounced on by the Housing Department. I've nowhere to go and nobody to go to. It's not a very pleasant situation, is it?' She blew her nose. 'I've no money. All I've got in the world is these twins. You can throw me out if you want to, but I've literally nowhere to go.'

'Nobody's suggesting throwing you out,' said Mavis sharply. 'You're my sister, and these are my nephews, and if you have to stay here, well, I suppose that's all there is to it.'

'Perhaps I could get a job in Preston or somewhere,' said Beatrice-Joanna with very small hope. 'That would help a little, perhaps.'

'There aren't any jobs,' said Mavis. 'And money's the least of anybody's worries. It's the danger I'm thinking about. I'm thinking about Llewelyn and Dymphna and what would happen to them if we were arrested. Because we would be, you know, if they found out, for harbouring a what's-its-name.'

'A multipara is the term. I'm a multipara. You don't see me as your sister, then. You just see me as something dangerous, a multipara.' Mavis, her lips a line, bent to her knitting. 'Shonny,' said Beatrice-Joanna, 'doesn't think that way. It's only you who think I'm a nuisance and a danger.'

Mavis looked up. 'That's a very unkind and unsisterly thing to say. That's completely heartless and selfish. You ought to realize that the time's come now for being sensible. We took chances before the babies were born, a lot of chances. Now you're blaming me for putting my own children before yours. And as for Shonny – he's too good-hearted to live. So good-hearted that he's stupid, going on as he does about God protecting us. I get sick of hearing the name of God sometimes, if you want to know the truth. One of these days Shonny will get us all into trouble. He'll land us all properly in the soup one of these days.'

'Shonny's sane enough and sensible enough.'

'He may be sane, but sanity's a handicap and a liability if you're living in a mad world. He's certainly not sensible. Put out of your head any notion that Shonny is sensible. He's just lucky, that's all. He talks too much and says the wrong things. One of these days, you mark my words, his luck's going to change, and then God help the lot of us.'

'So,' said Beatrice-Joanna after a pause, 'what do you want me to do?'

'You must do whatever you think's best for yourself. Stay here if you have to, stay as long as you think fit. But try and remember sometimes –'

'Remember what?'

'Well, that some people have put themselves out for you and have even run into danger. I'll say it now and I won't say it again. That's an end of it. But I'd just like you to remember sometimes, that's all.'

'I do remember,' said Beatrice-Joanna, her voice tightening, 'and I'm very grateful. I've said that about three times a day every day since I've been here. Except, of course, on the day that I was actually giving birth. I would have done so then, but I had other things to think about. If you like, I'll say it now to make up for it. I'm very grateful, I'm very grateful, I'm very grateful.'

'Now there's no need to be like that,' said Mavis. 'Let's drop the subject, shall we?'

'Yes,' said Beatrice-Joanna, rising. 'Let's drop the subject. Remembering, of course, that it was you who raised it.'

'There's no call to speak in that manner,' said Mavis.

'Oh, to hell,' said Beatrice-Joanna. 'It's time for their feed.' She lifted the twins. There was too much of this, too much of this altogether; she would be glad when Shonny came home from his seed-drills. One woman was enough in a house, she saw that, but what could she do? 'I think I'll keep to my room,' she said to her sister, 'for the rest of the day. If you can call it a room, that is.' Having said this, she could have bitten her tongue out. 'Sorry,' she said. 'I didn't mean that.'

'Do what you like,' said Mavis acidly. 'Go exactly where you want to go. You always have, ever since I can remember.'

'Oh, to hell,' said Beatrice-Joanna, and she bounced out with her pink twins.

'Stupid,' she thought later, lying in the outhouse. 'No way to behave.' She had to reconcile herself to the fact that this was the only place where she could live, the only place until she knew what precisely was going on in the world, where – if above ground, otherwise it didn't matter –Tristram was, how to fit Derek into the scheme. The twins were awake, Derek (the one with the D sewn on his tucker) burbling with a bubble of mother's milk on his mouth, both kicking. Bless their little cotton-substitute socks, the darlings. She had to endure much for their sake, endurance was one of her duties. Sighing, she left the outhouse and went back to the living-room. 'I'm sorry,' she said to Mavis, wondering what precisely she was saying she was sorry for.

'That's all right,' said Mavis. She had laid aside her knitting and was viciously manicuring.

'Would you like me,' said Beatrice-Joanna, 'to do something about getting a meal ready?'

'You can if you want to. I'm not particularly hungry.'

'How about Shonny?'

'Shonny's taken hard-boiled eggs with him. Cook something if you want to.'

'I'm not all that hungry myself.'

'That's all right then.'

Beatrice-Joanna sat down, distractedly rocking the empty cradle. Should she lift the twins from their cot, bring them in? Poor little intruders, let them stay where they were. Brightly she said to Mavis, 'Giving your talons a bit of a sharpening?' She could have bitten her tongue out, etc.

Mavis looked up. 'If,' she snapped, 'you've just come back in here to be insulting –'

'I'm sorry, I'm sorry, I really am. Just a joke, that's all. I just didn't think.'

'No, that's one of your characteristics. You just don't think.'

'Oh, to hell,' said Beatrice-Joanna. Then, 'Sorry, sorry sorry.'

'There's no point at all in your keeping on saying you're sorry if you don't mean it.'

'Look,' said Beatrice-Joanna desperately, 'what do you really want me to do?'

'I've told you already. You must do exactly what you think best for yourself and your *children*.' Her enunciation of this last word made it ring with a dissonant cluster of overtones, suggesting that the only genuine children in that household were Mavis's and that Beatrice-Joanna's were, being illegal, spurious.

'Oh,' said Beatrice-Joanna, snuffing up her tears, 'I'm so unhappy.' She ran back to her gurgling, not at all unhappy twins. Mavis, tight-lipped, went on manicuring her talons.

Eleven

IT was a good deal later in the day that Captain Loosley of the Population Police arrived in his black van. 'Here it is,' he said to young Oxenford, the driver. 'State Farm NW313. It's been a long journey.'

'A disgusting journey,' said Sergeant Image, with the strongly alveolated sibilants of his type. They had seen things in the ploughed fields, horrible things. 'Disgusting,' he repeated. 'We should have filled their buttocks with bullets.'

'Not enough ammo on board, Sarge,' said Oxenford, a literal young man.

'And not our job,' said Captain Loosley. 'Public indecency is the concern of the regular police.'

'Those of them that have not yet been eaten,' said Sergeant Image. 'Go on, Oxenford,' he said with petulance. 'Get out and open that gate.'

'That's not fair, Sarge. I'm driving.'

'Oh, all right, then.' And Sergeant Image extruded his long snaky body to open up. 'Children,' he said. 'Children playing. Pretty children. All right,' he said to Oxenford, 'you drive up to the homestead. I'll walk.' The children ran.

In the house, breathlessly, 'Dad,' Llewelyn cried, 'there are men coming in a black van. Policemen, I think.'

'Black, you say?' Shonny rose to peer out of the window. 'So,' he said. 'We've been expecting them a long time, God forgive them, and they haven't been. And now, when we're lulled asleep, they come lolloping along in their jackboots. Where's your sister?' he asked Mavis sharply. 'Is she away in the outhouse?' Mavis nodded. 'Tell her to lock herself in and keep quiet.' Mavis nodded but hesitated before going. 'Go on, then,' urged Shonny. 'They'll be here in a second.'

'We come first,' said Mavis. 'Remember that. You and me and the children.'

'All right, all right, go on now.' Mavis went to the outhouse. The van drew up and Captain Loosley alighted stretching. Young Oxenford revved up then switched off. Sergeant Image walked up to join his chief. Young Oxenford took off his cap, disclosing a red band on his brow like the mark of Cain, wiped with a spotted handkerchief, then set his cap on again. Shonny opened the door. All was ready.

'Good afternoon,' said Captain Loosley. 'This is State Farm NW313, and you are – I'm afraid I can't pronounce your name, do you see. But that doesn't matter. You have a Mrs Foxe staying with you, haven't you? Are these your children? Delightful, delightful. May we come in?'

'It's not for me to say yes or no,' said Shonny. 'I suppose you must have a warrant.'

'Oh, yes,' said Captain Loosley, 'we have a warrant, do you see.'

'Why does he say that, Dad?' asked Llewelyn. 'Why does he say "Do you see"?'

'It's just his nerves, God have mercy on him,' said Shonny. 'Some people twitch, others say, "Do you see". Come on in then, Mister –'

'Captain,' said Sergeant Image. 'Captain Loosley.' They all came in, keeping their caps on.

'Now,' said Shonny, 'what precisely is it you're looking for?' ?

'This is interesting,' said Sergeant Image, rocking the rough cradle with his foot. 'When the bough breaks the cradle will fall. Down will come baby –'

'Yes,' said Captain Loosley. 'We have reason to believe, do you see, that Mrs Foxe has been living here for the whole period of her illicit pregnancy. "Baby" is the operative word.' Mavis came into the room. 'This,' said Captain Loosley, 'is not Mrs Foxe.' He spoke peevishly, as though they were trying to fob him off. 'She is like Mrs Foxe but she isn't Mrs Foxe.' He bowed to her as in ironic congratulation on a reasonable attempt at deception. 'I want Mrs Foxe.'

'That cradle there,' said Shonny, 'was for pigs. The runt of the litter usually needs special looking after.'

'Shall I,' asked Sergeant Image, 'tell young Oxenford to beat him up a little?'

'Let him try,' said Shonny. Swift red suffused his face as though through the operation of dimmers. 'Nobody beats me up. I've a good mind to ask the lot of you to leave.'

'You can't do that,' said Captain Loosley. 'We're doing our duty, do you see. We want Mrs Foxe and her illegal offspring.'

'Illegal offspring,' parroted Llewelyn. 'Illegal offspring,' delighted with the phrase.

'Supposing I were to tell you that Mrs Foxe isn't here,' said Shonny. 'She paid us a visit just before Christmas and then moved on. Where to I don't know.'

'What is Christmas?' asked Sergeant Image.

'That's irrelevant,' snapped Captain Loosley. 'If Mrs Foxe isn't here, I take it you'll have no objection to our confirming that for ourselves. I have here,' he fumbled in his tunic side-pocket, 'a sort of all-purposes warrant. It covers search, do you see, and everything else.'

'Including beating-up,' said Mavis.

'Exactly.'

'Get out,' said Shonny, 'the lot of you. I'll not have State hirelings rummaging through my house.'

'You're a State hireling, too,' said Captain Loosley evenly. 'We're all servants of the State. Come now, do please be reasonable, do you see. We don't want any nastiness.' He smiled wanly. 'We've all got to do our duty, when all's said and done.'

'Do you see,' added Dymphna and then giggled.

'Come here, little girl,' said Sergeant Image ingratiatingly. 'You're a nice little girl, aren't you?' He crouched, rocking on his hunkers, and puss-pussed her, snapping his fingers.

'You stay here,' said Mavis, drawing both children to her.

'Aaargh.' Sergeant Image snarled briefly at Mavis and then, rising, put on a mask of idiotic sweetness. 'There's a little baby in this house, isn't there?' he said wheedlingly to Dymphna. 'A wee sweet little baby, that's right, isn't it?' Dymphna giggled. Llewelyn said stoutly:

'No.'

'And that's the truth, too,' said Shonny. 'The boy spoke no less than the truth. Now will you all get out and stop wasting your time as well as mine? I'm a busy man.'

'It's not my intention,' sighed Captain Loosley, 'to prefer charges against either you or your wife. Produce Mrs Foxe and her offspring and you'll hear no more about it. You have my word for that.'

'Do I have to throw you out?' cried Shonny. 'Because, by the Lord Jesus, I've a mind to set on the lot of you.'

'Bash him a little, Oxenford,' said Sergeant Image. 'It's all a lot of nonsense.'

'We're going to start searching,' said Captain Loosley. 'I'm sorry you're being so unco-operative, do you see.'

'Get upstairs, Mavis,' said Shonny, 'you and the

children. You leave all this to me.' He tried to push his wife out.

'The children stay here,' said Sergeant Image. 'The children will be made to squeal a little. I like to hear children squeal.'

'You unholy Godless bastard,' cried Shonny. He threw himself at Sergeant Image, but young Oxenford was quick to interpose himself. Young Oxenford punched Shonny lightly in the groin. Shonny cried in pain and then began to flail wildly.

'All right,' said a voice from the kitchen doorway. 'I don't want to cause any more trouble.' Shonny dropped his fists.

'*This* is Mrs Foxe,' said Captain Loosley. '*This* is the genuine article.' He showed restrained delight.

Beatrice-Joanna was dressed for outdoors. 'What,' she said, 'will you do to my children?'

'You shouldn't have done it,' wailed Shonny. 'You should have stayed where you were. Everything would have been all right, God forgive you.'

'You have my assurance,' said Captain Loosley, 'that no harm will come either to you or to your children.' He suddenly started. 'Children? Children? Oh, I see. More than one. I hadn't considered that possibility. All the better, of course, do you see, all the better.'

'You can punish me as much as you like,' said Beatrice-Joanna, 'but the children have done no harm.'

'Of course not,' said Captain Loosley. 'No harm at all. We intend harm only to the father. My intention is merely to confront the Metropolitan Commissioner with the fruits of his crime. Nothing more than that, do you see.'

'What is this?' cried Shonny. 'What's going on?'

'It's a long story,' said Beatrice-Joanna. 'It's too late to tell it now. Well,' she said to her sister, 'it looks as though the future's taken care of. It seems that I've found somewhere to go.'

Part Four

Part Four

One

Tristram was ready to begin his anabasis. He yearned,
like a compass-needle, towards his wife in the north, the
prospect of repentance and reconciliation like the prospect of sore labour's bath. He wanted comfort, her arms,
her warm body, their mingled tears, rest. He did not
now particularly want revenge.

There was chaos in the metropolis, and that chaos
seemed at first like a projection of his own new freedom.
Chaos whooped like a big laughing Bacchante and told
him, not very far from Pentonville, to club a harmless
man with his truncheon and steal his clothes. This was
in an alley, after dark, in the hinterland of public cook-
ing-fires and flares spluttering with human fat. Electricity, like other public utilities, seemed to have failed.
Here was jungle night, broken glass crackling under
one's feet like an undergrowth. Tristram wondered at
the maintenance of civilized order in that jail he had
left; how much longer could it last? Then, wondering,
he saw a man leaning by the mouth of the alley, singing to himself, drunk on something. Tristram raised his
club and the man went down at once, obligingly, as
if this was what he had been waiting for, and his clothes
– a round-necked shirt, a cardigan, a checked suit – came
off without effort. Tristram turned swiftly into a free

civilian but decided to keep his warder's truncheon. Dressed for dinner, he went off looking for food.

Jungle noises, black skyscraper forest, starred sky dizzily high, the ruddiness of fires. In Claremont Square he came upon people eating. They sat, men and women alike, round a barbecue, about thirty of them. Metal grills of roughly reticulated telegraph wire – these rested on plinths of heaped bricks; beneath were glowing coals. A man with a white cap forked and turned spitting steaks. 'No room, no room,' fluted a thin donnish person as Tristram shyly approached. 'This is a dining club, not a public restaurant.'

'I,' said Tristram, brandishing his truncheon, 'also have a club.' Everybody laughed at this puny threat. 'I've only just got out of prison,' wailed Tristram plaintively. 'I've been starved.'

'Fall to,' said the donnish person. 'Though this may prove, at first, too rich for your stomach. These days,' he epigrammatized, 'your criminal is your only moral man.' He reached over to the nearest grill and picked up, with a pair of tongs, a long hot metal skewer spitted with chunks of meat. 'A kebab,' he said. Then, squinting at Tristram in the firelight, 'You've no teeth. You'll have to get some teeth somewhere. Wait. We have some very nourishing broth over here.' And, most hospitably, he fussed round searching for a bowl, a spoon. 'Try this,' he said, ladling from a metal pot, 'and heartily welcome.' Tristram, like an animal, carried this gift trembling to a corner away from the others. He sucked in a steaming spoonful. Rich, rich, an oily liquid in which were suspended gobbets of smoking pliant rubbery stuff. Meat. He had read about meat. Ancient literature was full of meat-guzzling – Homer, Dickens, Priestley, Rabelais, A. J. Cronin. He swallowed the spoonful, retched, lost it. 'Slowly, slowly,' said the donnish man, coming up to him kindly. 'You will find it delicious fairly soon. Think of it not as what it is but as one of the pulpy fruits of the tree of life. All life is one. Why did they put you in prison?'

'I suppose,' said Tristram, still retching, 'because,' recovering, 'I was against the Government.'

'Which government? At the moment we don't seem to have a government.'

'So,' said Tristram, 'the Gusphase has not yet begun.'

'You seem to be something of a scholar. In prison you must have had leisure to think. Tell me, what do you make of the present times?'

'You can't think without data,' said Tristram. He tried the broth again; it went down much better. 'So this is meat,' he said.

'Man is a carnivore, just as man is a breeder. The two are cognate and the two have been long suppressed. Put the two together and you have no rational cause for suppression. As far as information is concerned, we have no information because we have no information services. However, we can take it that the Starling Government has fallen and that the Praesidium is full of snarling dogs. We shall have a government soon, I don't doubt. Meantime, we band ourselves into little dining clubs for self-protection. Let me warn you, who are just out of prison and hence new to this new world, not to go out alone. I will, if you like, put you up for this club of ours.'

'That's very kind,' said Tristram, 'but I have to find

my wife. She's in Northern Province, just outside Preston.'

'You'll have some difficulty,' said this kind man. 'The trains have stopped running, of course, and there's little road transport. It's a very long walk. Don't go unvictualled. Go armed. Don't sleep in the open. It worries me,' he said, squinting again at Tristram's sunken jaws, 'that you have no teeth.'

Tristram took from his pocket the twice-transferred halves of dental plate. He turned them over and over ruefully. 'A brutal prison warder,' he said unjustly.

'I think,' said the donnish man, 'we may have a dental mechanic among our members.' He went over to the group and Tristram finished his broth. It was heartening, no doubt about that. A memory of an ancient Pelagian poem – or rather one of the author's own notes to it – steamed into his mind. *Queen Mab.* Shelley. 'Comparative anatomy teaches us that man resembles frugivorous animals in everything, and carnivorous in nothing; he has neither claws wherewith to seize his prey, nor distinct and pointed teeth to tear the living fibre.' And again, 'Man resembles no carnivorous animal. There is no exception, unless man be one, to the rule of herbivorous animals having cellulated colons.' That was, perhaps, after all, all bloody nonsense.

'Your teeth can be mended,' said the kindly donnish man, returning, 'and we can fill a scrip for you with cold meat for the journey. I shouldn't, if I were you, think of starting before daylight. You're very welcome to spend the night with me.'

'You're genuinely very kind,' said Tristram genuinely. 'I've never before, I honestly think, met such kindness.'

His eyes began to fill with tears; it had been an exhausting day.

'Think nothing of it. When the State withers, humanity flowers. There are some very nice people about these days. Still, hang on to that weapon of yours.'

Tristram retired that night with his teeth in. Lying on the floor in the donnish man's flat, he champed again and again at the darkness as at so much airy meat. His host, who had given his name as Sinclair, had lighted them both to rest with a wick floating in fat; it had smelled delicious. The homely flame had shown a small untidy room crammed with books. Sinclair, however, had disclaimed any pretensions to being what he called a 'reading man'; he had been, before the electricity failed, an electronic composer, specializing in atmospheric music for television documentaries. Again, before the electricity failed and the elevators were grounded, his flat had been a good thirty storeys higher than this one; today, apparently, the weakest rose and the strongest fell. This new flat of his had belonged to a real reading man, a professor of Chinese, whose flesh had proved, despite his great age, not unsucculent. Sinclair slept innocently on his wall-bed, snoring gently, only occasionally talking in his sleep. Most of his utterances were gnomic, some were plain nonsense. Tristram listened.

'The cat's way is only exceeded by its perpenderosity.'

'I love potatoes. I love pork. I love man.'

'Eucharistic ingestion is our answer.'

That dark term – eucharistic ingestion – became a sort of key to sleep. As though it were indeed an answer, Tristram passed, content and comforted, into oblivion.

Sinking out of time, he rose into it again to see Sinclair, humming and dressing, blinking down at him amiably. It seemed to be a fine spring morning. 'Well,' said Sinclair, 'we must set you on your way, mustn't we? First, however, a good breakfast is essential.' Sinclair washed quickly (the public water supply still seemed in order) and shaved with an antique cut-throat. 'Well-named,' he smiled, naming it, lending it to Tristram. 'It has cut throats enow.' Tristram found no cause to disbelieve him.

The barbecue fires were, it seemed, never allowed to go out. Templar, thought Tristram, Olympic, flashing a modest smile at the members of the dining club, four of whom had guarded and tended the flames through the night. 'Bacon?' said Sinclair, and he heaped a singing tin plate high for Tristram. All ate heartily, with many a merry quip, and drank water by the quart. Then these kind people filled a postman's sack with cold joints and, with several expressions of good will, loaded their guest and sped him on his way.

'Never,' declared Tristram, 'have I met such generosity.'

'Go with God,' said Sinclair, replete and ripe for solemnity. 'May you find her well. May you find her happy.' He frowned and amended that. 'Happy to see you, that is, of course.'

Two

TRISTRAM walked all the way to Finchley. There would

not be, he knew, any sense in taking the road until well past, say, Nuneaton. It was a long long plodding of a town street, between skyscraper dwelling-blocks and factories with smashed windows. He passed jolly or somnolent dining clubs, corpses, bones, but was not himself molested. The endless city had a smell of roasting flesh and stopped-up drains. Once or twice, to his embarrassment, he saw open and unashamed copulation. I love potatoes. I love pork. I love woman. No, that was wrong. Something like that, though. He saw no police; they all seemed absorbed or digested into the generality. At a street-corner near Tufnell Park mass was being said before a small but fairly devout congregation. Tristram knew all about mass from the Blessed Ambrose Bayley and so was surprised to see the priest – a grey-coxcombed boyish man with a roughly painted surplice (the cross, IHS) – doling out what looked like rounds of meat. *'Hoc est enim Corpus. Hic est enim calix sanguinis.'* Some new Council of somewhere or other must be, in this shortage of the orthodox accidents, countenancing that sort of improvisation.

It was a fine spring day.

Just beyond Finchley Tristram sat down to rest in a shop doorway in a safe back-street and drew food from his scrip. He was footsore. He ate carefully and slowly, his stomach – as was evident from a bout of dyspepsia after breakfast –still having much to learn, and, having eaten, sought water. Queen Mab whispered to him about thirst being the necessary concomitant of a flesh diet, great thirst. In the rear living-quarters of the rifled shop Tristram found a tap in working order and, laying his mouth beneath it, drank as if he would drink for ever.

The water tasted faintly foul, faintly corrupt, and he thought: 'Here is where future trouble lies.' He rested a while longer, sitting in the doorway, clutching his truncheon, watching the passers-by. They all kept to the middle of the road, an interesting characteristic of the later part of the Interphase. He sat idly reviewing the thoughts and feelings it seemed to him he ought to have. It surprised him that he now felt so little desire to smash in the face of his brother. Perhaps it had all been a malicious lie of that ambitious and aggrieved captain; one needed proof, one needed definite and incontrovertible evidence. The meat growled in his stomach; he belched an utterance that sounded like 'paternity lust'.

Would the child, if there was to be a child, be born yet? He had lost track of time somehow. He felt that Beatrice-Joanna would, in all this chaos, be safer than before. She must still be up north (if that man had told the truth); she had nowhere else, anyway, to go. He himself, he was sure, was doing the only possible thing. He too had nowhere else to go. How he detested his brother-in-law, however: the bluff bluster, pious shouts apt for tug-of-war teams always on his lips. This time he would bluster back and out-God him; he was not going to be bullied by anyone any more.

Keeping to the pavement, he made Barnet by mid-afternoon. Hesitating between the roads to, respectively, Hatfield and St Albans, he was surprised to see a motor-van come coughing slowly up, north-bound like himself. It was painted a sort of earth-colour and the ghost of its provenance – *Ministry of Infertility* – showed faintly under the single coat. Tristram, hesitating between roads, hesitated before gesturing for a lift. A nerve in his sore left foot decided for him and, by-passing his brain, shot up its reflex message to his thumb.

'I'm only going as far as Aylesbury,' said the driver. 'You might pick up something else there. If we get to Aylesbury, that is.' The car shuddered agreement. 'You're making a long trip,' he said, glancing curiously at Tristram. 'There's not much travelling done these days.' Tristram explained. The driver was a lean man in a strange uniform: greyboy's tunic and civilian trousers dyed the earth-colour of the van itself, an earth-coloured cheese-cutter on his knees, white bands looped through his shoulder-straps. When Tristram spoke of his escape from prison he laughed in a brief snort. 'If you'd waited till this morning,' he said, 'you would have been bowed off the premises. They opened up their gates, apparently, because of the failure of the food supply. At least, that's what they told me at Ealing.'

Tristram also barked a short laugh. All Charlie Linklater's work for nothing. He said, 'You can understand that I'm very much out of touch. I just don't know what's going on.'

'Oh,' said the man. 'Well, there's not a lot I can tell you. There doesn't seem to be a central government at the moment, but we're trying to improvise some kind of regional law and order. A sort of martial law you could call it. You behold in me one of the resuscitated military. I'm a soldier.' He snorted another laugh.

'Armies,' said Tristram. 'Regiments. Battalions. Platoons.' He had read of such things.

'We can't have all this,' said the man. 'Indiscriminate cannibalism and the drains out of order. We've got our wives and children to think of. We've got something started in Aylesbury, anyway. We've even got people doing a bit of work again.'

'What do you eat?' asked Tristram.

The soldier laughed very loud. 'It's officially called tinned pork,' he said. 'We've got to eat something. Waste not want not. We've had to do a fair amount of shooting, you see, in the name of law and order,' he said seriously. 'Meat and water. It's a bit too much of a tiger's diet, perhaps, but the canning makes it seem civilized. And we have hopes, you know, we have hopes that things will start growing again. And, believe it or not, I actually did some fishing last week-end.'

'Much of a catch?'

'Chub,' said the soldier. He laughed again. 'Measly little chub.'

'And,' said Tristram, 'if I may ask, what's been the purpose of your journey?'

'This journey? Oh, we'd had a report of a police ammunition dump along the road from Ealing to Finchley. Some swine had got there first, though. One of these gangs. They knocked off my corporal. He wasn't a very good corporal, but they shouldn't have knocked him off. Probably eating him now, blasted cannibals.' He spoke quite calmly.

'It would seem,' said Tristram, 'that we're all cannibals.'

'Yes, but, damn it all, we in Aylesbury are at least civilized cannibals. It makes all the difference if you get it out of a tin.'

Three

WEST of Hinckley Tristram saw his first ploughed fields.
He had done well on the whole: a night in barracks in
civilized Aylesbury; a walk in weather continuing fair
along the Bicester road with a lift in an army truck five
miles out of Aylesbury as far as Blackthorn; lunch in
armed but kindly Bicester and even a shave and hair-
cut there; a walk up the railway line to Ardley and
there a surprise – an ancient steam train run on wood
as far as Banbury. Tristram had only the few septs and
tanners and tosheroons he had found in the pockets of
the man he had truncheoned, but the amateurs who
manned the three-coach train were archaeologists vague
about fares. Tristram spent the night in a cobwebbed
cellar on the Warwick Road and reached Warwick, with
the aid of a lift on a truck musical with small arms,
well before lunch-time the next day. At Warwick, which
was sullen under martial law, he was told to beware of
Kenilworth, this town apparently being ruled by a sort
of Fifth Monarchy fanatics who preached a doctrine of
rigid exophagy; Coventry, he was assured, was safe
enough to the stranger. So Tristram plodded the secondary road through Leamington, the journey eased by a
pillion lift on a cheerful dispatch-rider's motor-cycle.
Coventry seemed almost a normal city except for its
flavour of the garrison: communal messes, roll-calls outside factories, a curfew at nightfall. Tristram was asked
eagerly for news at the city-frontier, but of course he
had none to give. Still, he was made welcome and given

the freedom of the Engineers' Sergeants' Mess. A couple
of tins of meat were crammed into his pockets when he
left at dawn and, for the first time in many years, he
actually felt like singing as he marched, in this miraculous
weather, towards Nuneaton. He was near the
northern limit of Greater London now; he fancied he
could snuff country air. At Bedworth he was picked up
in a staff car (a Falstaffian colonel and his adjutant, red-
faced on alc) and was taken through Nuneaton on to the
Shrewsbury road. Here at last was country indeed: the
flatness of ploughed fields, hardly a building in sight,
the sky no longer challenged by proud monoliths. He
lay down behind a gate and took a nap in the smell of
earth. Thanked be Almighty God.

When he awoke he thought he was dreaming. He
thought he heard a flute playing breathily and voices
singing more breathily still. The words of the song
seemed to resolve themselves into a statement so direct
and final that it was as though he was hearing 'Eucharistic
Ingestion' all over again. The words were something
like 'Apples be ripe and nuts be brown, petticoats
up and trousers down', and the simple tune went round
and round, an endless *da capo*. And he saw, he saw, he
saw men and women in the furrows – a pair here and
a pair there – making, with ritual seriousness, beast
after beast after beast with two backs. Petticoats up and
trousers down in the spring sun, in the sown furrows,
ripe apples and brown nuts, country copulatives. Six
men, five men, four men, three men, two men, one man
and his, and their – Why did the song say 'dog'? Sow-
ing, not mowing, a meadow. But they would mow in
due time, they would quite certainly mow. All life was

174

one. That blight had been man's refusal to breed.

Four

'COME on, now,' called the leader crossly. He had the
look of a morris-dance organizer, stringy and sniffly,
red-nosed and blue-cheeked. 'Listen, please, everybody,'
he said plaintively. 'The following partners have been
drawn.' He read from the list in his hand. 'Mr Lipset
with Miss Kemeny. Mr Minrath with Mrs Graham. Mr
Evans with Mrs Evans. Mr Hilliard with Miss Ethel
Duffus.' He read on. Tristram, blinking in the warm
sun, sat outside the inn at Atherstone, watching benevolently as the men and women paired. 'Mr Finlay with
Miss Rachel Duffus. Mr Mayo with Miss Lowrie.' As
for country dancing, those called did a stand-and-face-
your-lover line-up, giggling, blushing, bold-faced, bash-
ful, game, ready. 'Very well,' said the leader, tiredly.
'Into the fields.' And off, hand in hand, they went. The
leader saw Tristram and, shaking his head resignedly,
came over and sat next to him on the bench. 'These are
strange times we're living in,' he said. 'Are you just
passing through?'

'On my way to Preston,' said Tristram. 'Why, if I
may ask, do you have all this organizing?'

'Oh, the usual thing,' said the leader. 'Greed, selfishness. Some people getting all the plums. That man
Hilliard, for instance. And poor Belinda Lowrie left out
in the cold all the time. I wonder if it really does any

good,' he wondered gloomily. 'I wonder if it's really anything more than sheer self-indulgence.'

'It's an affirmation,' said Tristram. 'It's a way of showing that reason is only one instrument for running our lives. A return to magic, that's what it is. It seems very healthy to me.'

'I foresee danger,' said the leader. 'Jealousy, fights, possessiveness, the breaking-up of marriages.' He was determined to look on the black side.

'Things will sort themselves out,' soothed Tristram. 'You'll see. A recapitulation of whole aeons of free love, and then the Christian values will be reasserted. Nothing to worry about at all.'

The leader gloomed at the sun, at the clouds gently and seriously propelled across the blue acres. 'I suppose you're normal,' he said at length. 'I suppose you're one of those like that man Hilliard. A real told-you-so, born and bred, that man. He was always saying that things couldn't go on as they were for ever. They laughed at me when I did what I did. Hilliard laughed louder than anybody. I could kill Hilliard,' he said, clenching his fists with the thumbs inside.

'Kill?' said Tristram. 'Kill in these days of,' he said, 'love?'

'It was when I was working at the Lichfield Housing Office,' bubbled the leader, 'that this thing happened. There was the question of a vacancy and me getting up-graded. I was senior, you see.' If not days of love, these were certainly days of open and frank confiding. 'Mr Consett, who was in charge, told me it was a toss-up between me and a man called Maugham, very much my junior Maugham was, but Maugham was homo.

Well, I thought about that a good deal. I was never that
way inclined myself but, of course, there was something
I could do. I thought about it a good deal before taking
action, because it was, after all, a pretty momentous
step to take. Anyway, after a good deal of thought and
lying in bed, tossing and turning, worrying about it, I
made up my mind and went to see Dr Manchip. Dr
Manchip said it was quite an easy job, no danger at all,
and he did it. He said a general anaesthetic wasn't necessary. I watched him do it.'

'I see,' said Tristram. 'I wondered about your
voice –'

'That's right. And look at me now.' He extended his
arms. 'What's done can't be undone. How do I fit into
this new world? I should have been warned, somebody
should have told me. How was I to know that that sort
of world wasn't going to go on for ever?' He lowered his
voice. 'You know what that man Hilliard's been calling
me lately? He's been calling me a *capon*. And he smacks
his lips, joking of course, but it's not in very good taste.'

'I see,' said Tristram.

'I don't like it at all. I don't like it one little bit.'

'Sit tight and wait,' counselled Tristram. 'History is
a wheel. This sort of world can't go on for ever, either.
One of these days we're bound to go back to liberalism
and Pelagianism and sexual inversion and, and – well,
your sort of thing. We're obviously bound to, because
of all this.' He waved his hand in the direction of the
ploughed fields, whence came muffled noises of intense
concentration. 'Because,' he clarified, 'of the biological
purpose of all this.'

'But in the meantime,' said the leader sadly, 'I've

people like Hilliard to contend with.' He shuddered.
'Calling me a capon, indeed.'

Five

TRISTRAM, being still young and not ill-looking, was
kindly received by the ladies of Shenstone. He excused
himself courteously, pleading that he must reach Lichfield by nightfall. He was sped on his way with kisses.

Lichfield burst on him like a bomb. Here some kind
of carnival was in progress (though it was no farewell
to flesh, far from it) and Tristram's eyes were confused
by a torch-procession and by banners and streamers
dancing aloft: *Lichfield Fecundity Guild* and *South
Staffs Love Group*. Tristram mingled with the crowd on
the pavement to watch the parade go by. First marched
a band of pre-electronic instruments booming and shrill-
ing what sounded like that thin flute-tune of the fields
outside Hinckley, but the tune was now, in all its brass,
beefy, blood-red, confident. The crowd cheered. Next
came two clowns buffeting and falling at the head of a
comic squad in boots, long tunics, but no trousers. A
woman behind Tristram screamed, 'Eeeee, there's our
Arthur, Ethel.' The tunics and caps of this leering,
waving, shouting, staggering bare-legged phalanx had
evidently been stolen from the Poppol (where were they
now, where were they?) and a card on a stick was held
high, lettered neatly COPULATION POLICE. They
belaboured each other with truncheons of stuffed sack-

ing or thrust at the air with them in ithyphallic rhythms. 'What's that word mean, Ethel?' cried the woman behind Tristram. 'Real jaw-breaker, that is.' A small man with a hat on told her in one brief Lawrentian term. 'Eeeeeee,' she screamed.

Next toddled little boys and girls in green, sweet and pretty, soaring multicoloured sausage balloons moored to their fingers. 'Awwww,' went a droop-mouthed lank-haired girl next to Tristram. 'Em's nice, ennem?' The balloons jostled high in the torchlit air, an airy languid pillow-fight. After the children leaped and staggered more buffoons, men in antique billowing female skirts, enormously and unevenly breasted, others in skintight motley with Panurgian codpieces. Dancing clumsily, they engaged in brief spasmodic parodies of the claw-buttock act. 'Eeeeeee,' yelled the woman behind Tristram, 'I shall fair pass out of laughing, that I shall.' Then, to a hush of admiration followed by sincere cheers, there trundled up a white-decked float of paper flowers with, high on a throne, a buxom lass in blue, paper-flower-crowned, a staff in her grip, clustered about by all her starry fays, smiling and waving nubility, Lichfield's, so it would appear, festal queen. 'Real lovely she is,' said another woman. 'Joe Treadwell's daughter.' The float was pulled – crackling flower-twined ropes – by young men in white shirts and red leggings, hand-some and muscular. After this float there walked sedate members of the clergy, bearing, in embroidered silk-surrogate, the motto *God Is Love*. The local army marched behind, terrible with banners: *General Hapgood's Boys* and *We Saved Lichfield*. The crowd cheered full-throatedly. And then, at the end, young girls trod daintily (not one of them more than fifteen), each with a streamer and each streamer attached to the top of a high thick pole, the Priapic emblem which evoked redoubled cheers, borne in the arms of a long-robed comely matron, a blown rose in this garden of callow cowslips. The procession moved on to the town's outskirts and the crowd jostled, thumped, pushed on to the road to follow it. From the unseen head of the parade the jaunty six-eight tune – mulberry bush, nuts and may, apples be ripe – blasted and thumped brassily on, clearing the way through the spring night. Tristram was caught in the crowd, borne irresistibly, apples be ripe, through the town, home of a swan, and nuts be brown, and a lexicographer, petticoats up, *Lich* meaning a corpse in Middle English, and trousers down, how inappropriately named – Lichfield – tonight. Men and women, youths and girls, thrust, elbowed, laughed, in the procession's wake, the high white wooden phallus gleaming ahead, swaying, the focus of pretty ribbons, old men bent but game, middle-aged women solidly eager, young lusty boys, girls shy but ready, faces like moons, hatchets, flat-irons, flowers, eggs, mulberries, all the noses of the world (haughty Italian, crushed Oriental, snub, splayed, spurred, bulbous, crested, tilted, flared), corn-hair, rust-hair, Eskimo-straight, crinkled, undulant, receding, gone, tonsures and bald spots, cheeks warmed to ripe-apple and nut-brown in the flares and fires and enthusiasm, the swish of petticoats, on to the sown furrows of the fields, and trousers.

Down, somewhere, had gone Tristram's near-empty food-sack; his truncheon had disappeared. His arms were free for dancing and embracing. On the green at the town's end the band had settled, squat on benches, blasting, cracking, clashing, skirling away. The Priapic pole was being plunged into a hole already dug in the centre of the green, the streamers flapping and entwining the men who pushed it down and tamped the soil at its base. The local army was smartly fallen out and started to pile arms. There were flares and a bonfire, there were glowing and spitting barbecues. *Lichfield Sausages*, said a notice. Tristram joined hungry wolfers of these, doled out free on skewers, and chewed the salty meat, ho', 'ery ho', his mouth smoking.

Dancing began round the Priapic pole, youths and putative maidens. On the periphery of the green (a euphemistic term for the brown near-bald half-acre) their elders twirled and clodhopped lustily. A warm dark woman in her thirties came up to Tristram and said, 'How about you and me, duck?' 'Gladly,' said Tristram. 'You look proper sad,' she said, 'as if you was pining away after somebody. Am I right?' 'Another couple of days, with a bit of luck,' said Tristram, 'and I'll be with her. In the meantime –' They rolled into the dance. The band played their rollicking six-eight tune over and over. Soon Tristram and his partner rolled into the furrows. Many were rolling into the furrows. It was a warm night for the time of year.

At midnight, the revellers breathing hard, unbuttoned about the fires, the contest for the male festal crown was fanfared. The queen sat aloof on her float, her dishevelled and rosy retinue settling their skirts, with many a giggle, at her feet. Below the float, at a rough table, passing from hand to wrinkled hand a flask of alc, sat the judges, elders of the town. There was a short list of five competitors in a trial of physical strength and agility. Desmond Seward bent a poker – teeth gritted, thews bursting – and walked forty yards on his hands. Jollyboy Adams turned innumerable somersaults and then leapt over a fire. Gerald Toynbee held his breath for five minutes and performed a frog-dance. Jimmy Quair walked on all fours, supinated, a little boy (his brother, as it turned out) striking an Eros-pose upon his, Jimmy Quair's, stomach. This, for its novelty and aesthetic appeal, drew much applause. But the crown went to Melvin Johnson (illustrious surname) who, balanced on his head, feet high in the air, recited loudly a triolet of his own composition. It was strange to see the upside-down mouth, hear the right-way-up words:

> This lovely queen, if I should win her,
> Shall have my heart for a medallion.
> She'll never lack a hearty dinner,
> This lovely queen, if I should win her.
> My fire shall rouse the fire that's in her,
> She'll ride my sea, a golden galleon,
> This lovely queen. If I should win her,
> She'll have my heart for a medallion.

In vain for the captious to grumble that the rules of the contest said nothing about facility in versifying and how, anyway, had this competitor shown strength and agility? He would show it soon enough, laughed some. There were roars of approval at the judges' unanimous decision. Melvin Johnson was crowned with castellar tinfoil and borne, amid cheers, on strong shoulders to meet his queen. Then the royal pair, hand in hand, youths and maidens singing behind them an old nuptial song whose words Tristram could not catch, proceeded majestically to the field for the consummation of their love. At a decent distance the common sort followed after.

There they all were under the moon, seed busy above seed busy below: Charlie Aaron with Gladys Woodward, Dan Abel with Monica Wilson, Howard Wilson with Clara Hoskyns-Abrahall, Freddie Adler with Diana-Gertrude Williams, Bill Agar with Mary Westcott, Harold Auld with Louisa Wertheimer, Jim Weeks with Pam Asimov, Ford Wolverton Avery with Lucy Vivian, Denis Brodrick with Dorothy Hodge, John Halberstram with Jessie Greenidge, Tristram Foxe with Ann Onymous, Ron Heinlein with Agnes Gelber, Sherman Feyler with Margaret Evans, George Fisher with Lily Ross, Alf Meldrum with Joanie Crump, Elvis Fenwick with Brenda Fenwick, John-James De Ropp with Asmara Jones, Tommy Eliot with Kitty Elphick – and scores more. With the sinking of the moon and the rising of the wind they sought the fires, sleeping till dawn in a red crackling haze of fulfilment.

Tristram woke at dawn to hear bird-twitterings; he rubbed his eyes at the cool distant bass flute of a cuckoo. A priest appeared with his field-altar and a yawning cross boy-servitor. '*Introibo ad altare Dei.*' 'To God Who giveth joy to my youth.' The consecration of the roasted meat (bread and wine would doubtless be back soon), the donation of a eucharistic breakfast. Washed but un-shaven, Tristram kissed his new friends good-bye and took the north-west road to Rugeley. The fine morning weather might well hold all day.

Six

THERE were Dionysian revels at Sandon, Meaford and the cross-roads near Whitmore, but at Nantwich there was the sophistication of a fair. Tristram was interested to see a brisk flow of small money at the stalls (rifle-range, aunt sally, try-your-strength, roll-a-coin-on-to-a-lucky-square): people must be working and earning again. Food (he noticed small spitted birds among the kebabs and sausages) was being sold, not given away. Barkers urged lubricious males to pay a tosheroon to see Lola and Carmenita in their sensational seven-veils speciality. It seemed that, in one town at least, the novelty of free flesh had begun to pall.

But, in its lowliest form, an art had been revived. How long was it since anybody in England had seen a live play? For generations people had lain on their backs in the darkness of their bedrooms, their eyes on the blue watery square on the ceiling: mechanical stories about good people not having children and bad people having them, homos in love with each other, Origen-like heroes castrating themselves for the sake of global stability. Here in Nantwich customers queued outside a big tent to see *The Unfortunate Father: A Comedy*. Tristram shrugged over his small handful of coin and counted out the price of admission: one and a half septs. His feet were weary; it would be somewhere to rest.

This, he thought, crammed on a bench, was what the first Greek comedy must have been like. On a creaking platform, lighted by two uncertain floods, a narrator wearing a large false phallus introduced, and commented coarsely on, a simple story of bawdry. A bald impotent husband (impotence symbolized by a flaccid codpiece) had a flighty wife, regularly impregnated by lusty lovers, and, in consequence, a house full of children. The poor man, reviled and ridiculed and taunted, eventually in a blazing temper tackled a pair of these cuckolders in the street and was cracked soundly on the pate for his pains. But, lo, a miracle. The bash on the head did strange things to his nervous system: the codpiece swelled and rose: he was no longer impotent. Cunningly feigning, however, to be as he had been, he found his way easily into the homes of those of his wife's lovers who had womenfolk, swiving them while the man of the house was at work. Uproarious. Finally, he sent his own wife packing and turned his house into a seraglio, the comedy ending with a phallic song and dance. Well, thought Tristram, leaving the tent at twilight, soon men would be dressing up as goats and presenting the first neo-tragedy. Perhaps in a year or two there would be mystery plays.

By one of the smoking food-stalls a little man was selling single sheets of paper, quarto, and doing a brisk trade. '*Nantwich Echo*,' he called. 'One tanner only.' Many were standing, reading, open-mouthed. Tristram, trembling a little, spent one of his last coins and took off his paper to a corner, as furtive as when, a few days before, he had carried off his first meat-meal. This – a newspaper – was almost as archaic as a comedy. There were two sides of blurred print, under the name NNTWTSH EKO the legend 'Put out by Min of Inf microwave transmitter picked up 1.25 p.m. G. Hawtrey Publisher.' Private enterprise: beginning of the Gusphase. Tristram gobbled the news without chewing. Mr Ockham invited by His Majesty to form a government, names of cabinet members to be announced tomorrow. Emergency national martial law, immediate establishment of central control of regional (irregular) armed forces, regional commanders to report forthwith for instructions to provincial headquarters as listed below. Regular communications and information services expected to be resumed within forty-eight hours. Return to work in twenty-four hours ordered, dire penalties (unspecified) for refusal.

Return to work, eh? Tristram thought about that, looking up from his paper. The men and women that stood around, reading with their lips or skimming, openmouthed, puzzled and wondered. There was no throwing of hats in the air or huzzaing to celebrate this news of the reimposition of stability. Return to work. Officially he must still be workless, a committal to jail automatically depriving a government servant of his post. He would push on to State Farm NW313. Surely one's wife and children came first? (Children? One of them was dead.) Officially, anyway, he had received no information.

He would try to reach Chester tonight. He bought himself the viaticum of a large sausage for a tanner and sought the Chester road munching. His marching feet teased out from deep memory the rhythm of a gnomic quatrain written by some forgotten poet:

> The northern winds send icy peace,
> The southern gales blow balmy.
> Pelagius is fond of police;
> Augustine loves an army.

Seven

CAPTAIN LOOSLEY devoured crackling morsels of the news received on the dashboard microwave radio. 'There,' he said with nasty satisfaction, 'that'll teach them, do you see. There'll be a bit more respect for law and order.' As Tristram Foxe had so rudely told him that day in jail, he had no knowledge of historiography, no sense of the cycle. Young Oxenford, driving, nodded without much conviction. He was fed up; it had been a rotten journey. The police rations had been meagre and his stomach growled. The nuclear motor of the Poppol van had misbehaved several times, and Oxenford was no nuclear mechanic. Coming out of Chester he had mistaken the road and gone blithely west (this being at night and he no astro-navigator either), only at Dol-gelley discovering his error (signposts had been uprooted for fuel). At Mallwyd, on the Welshpool road, men and women with lilting speech and magicians' faces had halted them. These people had been charmed by Beatrice-Joanna's twins ('There's pretty') but antagonized by the haughty demeanour and trembling gun of Sergeant Image. 'Queer the poor bugger is,' they said, taking his weapon with gentle fingers. 'Boil up lovely he will,' they had nodded, fingering his soft joints as they undressed him. They had also taken the uniforms of Captain Loosley and young Oxenford, saying, 'Come in nice these will for the army. Proper, these are.' Seeing the two shivering in their underclothes they had said, 'There's pity now. Who knows for some brown paper to cwtch their chests?' Nobody did. 'Treating you kind we are, see,' they said finally, 'because of her in the back. Fair play.' And they had sped them on to Welshpool with waves, Sergeant Image protesting loudly at treachery, writhing in the grip of strong butchers.

Taking their uniforms, the people of Mallwyd had perhaps saved their lives, but Captain Loosley was too stupid to see it. As for Beatrice-Joanna, her sole anxiety was for her babies. She feared these towns and villages with their fires and hearty meat-eating faces, faces that looked in on her sleeping pair and grinned amiably. The smiles and words of admiration seemed to her to be equivocal: cooing might soon turn to lip-smacking. Whatever official fate waited in the capital, it would, surely, not stoop to teknophagy? Anxious for her babies, Beatrice-Joanna forgot to feel hungry, but malnutrition spoke loud in the quality and quantity of her milk. Involuntarily she occasionally yearned towards the smell of roasting or simmering as they sped through a town; whenever the van was stopped by held-up meaty hands and curious eyes examined the pair in their underwear, herself with the twins at her breasts, she would feel sick at the thought of what was being roasted and boiled.

But why? Sense was primal, and sense was not revolted; it was always the great traitor *thought* that threw its shoe into the works.

'Things look almost back to normal, do you see,' said Captain Loosley as, at last, they took the Brighton road. 'Too many smashed windows, though, and look at that twisted metal in the road, do you see. Overturned vehicles. Barbarous, barbarous. Martial law. Poor Sergeant Image. We should have taken the names, do you see, of those responsible. Then they could be summarily punished.'

'Don't talk so bloody wet,' said young Oxenford. 'The way you go on makes me proper bloody sick sometimes.'

'Oxenford,' cried Captain Loosley, shocked. 'I don't think you quite know what you're saying. Just because we haven't our uniforms on, do you see, is no excuse for forgetting the deference due to, due to –'

'Aw, shut it. It's all over. Haven't you got the bloody sense to see it's all over? How the hell you got where you have got bloody well beats me.' They were now coming into Haywards Heath. 'First thing I do when I get back and get some clothes on is to join the bloody army. I'm finished with this lot because this lot is finished anyway.' They were coming out of Haywards Heath.

'This lot is *not* finished, do you see,' said Captain Loosley. 'There must always be an organization for keeping the population down, whether by force, do you see, or by propaganda. I forgive you, Oxenford,' he added generously. 'The fate of Sergeant Image must have unnerved you as, I confess, it's unnerved me, do you see, a little. But don't let it happen again. Remember, please, the difference in our ranks.'

'Aw, shut it,' said Oxenford again. 'I'm bloody freezing cold and I'm bloody hungry and I've a bloody good mind to stop the van and leave you to get on with it while I go and join that lot there.' He gestured roughly with his head towards a gipsy-like company at the roadside who were placidly eating round a fire.

'The army will get them,' said Captain Loosley calmly. 'They'll be picked up, never fear.'

'Aaaaarch,' suddenly sneezed Oxenford. And again, 'Aaaaah Chag. Blast it and damn it, I've got a cold, a real beauty. Blast your eyes, Loosley. Aaaaaaah Shok.'

'The Metropolitan Commissioner will have something to say about this, do you see,' warned Captain Loosley. 'Sheer unmitigated insubordination.'

'I thought,' said Oxenford sarcastically, 'that the purpose of the exercise was to get the Metropolitan Commissioner given the sack. I thought that was the idea.'

'That's where you're stupid, Oxenford. There will be another Metropolitan Commissioner,' said Captain Loosley loftily. 'He'll know how to deal with insubordination.'

'Aaaarch,' went young Oxenford, and then, 'Chow,' nearly running into a lamp-standard. 'It won't be you, anyway,' he said rudely. 'It won't be you who'll get the bloody job, and that's a fact. And, anyhow, I'll be in the army tomorrow or the next day. A man's life that'll be. Howrashyouare. Dog damn and blast it. Not running after poor defenceless women and kids, same as we've been doing.'

'I've heard quite enough, do you see,' said Captain Loosley. 'That will do very well, Oxenford.'

'Raaaaaarch. Blast it.'

Soon they were running into Brighton. Sunlight was merry on the sea, on the coloured dresses of the women and children, on the drab suits of the men. There seemed to be fewer people about; you couldn't have your cake and eat it too. Now they came to the lofty Government offices. 'Here we are,' said Captain Loosley. 'Drive straight in there, Oxenford, where it says *In*. Strange, I can't remember that *In* being there, do you see, when we left.'

Oxenford laughed raucously. 'You poor silly bloody clot,' he said. 'Can't you see where that *In* has come from? Can't you, you daft fool?'

Captain Loosley stared at the façade. 'Oh,' he said. 'Oh, dear.' For the great sprawling sign – *Ministry of Infertility* – had changed; its last word had lost its negative prefix.

'Ha ha,' went young Oxenford. 'Ha ha ha.' And then, 'Raaaaaaarch! Damn and blast it.'

Eight

'AND as far as possible,' said the television face of the Right Honourable George Ockham, Prime Minister, 'to pursue the good life with a minimum of State interference.' It was the face of a business tycoon – fat-jowled with firm but self-indulgent lips, hard-bargain-driving eyes behind hexagonal glasses. It could be seen only intermittently because of a transmission fault: it alternated with rapid ripples or itself dissolved into geometrical tropes and fancies; it wobbled, wambled; it split itself into autonomous grimaces; it flew pentecostally up out of the screen and, in frame after rising frame, chased its own flight. But the firm calm steady business voice remained undistorted. It spoke long, though – in the true Augustinian manner – it had little to say. Difficult times might well still lie before them, but, thanks to the spirit of hard-headed British compromise that had weathered so many crises in the past, the nation would undoubtedly win through to happier days. Confidence was the thing; Mr Ockham asked for confidence. He had confidence in the British people; let them have confidence in him. His image nodded itself to extinction and television darkness.

Tristram himself nodded, picking his teeth in the eleemosynary eating-centre which had been set up by the Chester Ladies' Fecundity Association on the north bank of the Dee. He had just consumed, listening to Mr Ockham, a fair meat-meal served by rosy bantering Cheshire girls in pleasant though austere surroundings, daffodils in jars spouting to the ceiling. Many men in his position were, and had been, eating there, though mostly, it seemed, provincial men: men let, bewildered, out of prison, now on the road to find families evacuated from the towns during diet-riots and the first dining-club atrocities; jobless men tramping to newly re-opened factories; men (but there ought to be *women*, too; where were the women?) evicted from their low-storey flats by the strong and ruthless – all tannerless.

Tannerless. Money was a problem. Tristram had found a bank open that afternoon, a branch of the State 3 in which his few guineas were deposited, doing brisk business again after the long moratorium. He had been told politely by a teller that he must draw at his own branch though, and Tristram had a grim smile at this, he was very welcome to pay in money if he wished. Banks. Perhaps those who mistrusted them were not so foolish. A man at Tarporley, so he had heard, had sewn three thousand guinea-notes into his mattress and been able to open up a general store while the banks were still closed. The small capitalists were crawling out of their holes, rats of the Pelphase but Augustine's lions.

'– Cordially invited,' a woman's voice was calling over a loudspeaker, 'to attend. Eight o'clock. A light barbecue supper will be served. Partners,' and this sounded sinister, 'for everyone.' The voice clicked out. More of an order than an invitation. A bonfire dance by the river, not in the fields. Did they hope that Dee salmon would soon start leaping again? Two things idly struck Tristram this fine, but chill, spring evening: the toughness of women; the fact that everything, however small, had to be paid for. Sighing, he rose from the table; he would take a stroll through Chester's streets. At the door an eager woman said, 'You won't forget, will you? Eight o'clock sharp. I'll be watching out for you, you greedy boy.' She giggled, a plump woman, more easily thought of as an aunt than a mistress. Greedy? In what way had he shown himself greedy? Was the term facetiously proleptic, in no wise a food-referent? Tristram combined a smirk and a grunt and went out.

Had Chester smelled like this in the days of Roman occupation – smelled of soldiery? *Army of the West – GHQ*, cried the sign-board; noble, thrilling the sound of that, Arthurian almost. As, in the days of Caesar's legionaries, the town must have smoked with the breath of slithering horses, so now the exhausts of motor-cycles gushed and plumed caerulean – dispatch-riders arriving with top-secret messages in nests of envelopes, leaving – gloved and helmeted – with such letters, kicking their machines afire to burn up one of the tentacle-roads that roared out of the city-camp, camp-city. Cryptic sign-posts pointed to *Director of Ordnance Supplies, Director of Medical Supplies, Office of Quartermaster-General.* There were lorries clattering out their freights of lumpish soldiers in their improvised uniforms; a work-ing squad – with brooms for rifles – was dismissed in a side-street; a couple of chaplains were learning shyly to salute. Cans were being unloaded into the guarded food-store.

By what hypocritical gesture of the head were the supplies being maintained? Civilian contracts with no questions asked; the troops called the anonymous tinned meat 'bully', and there was no such animal as that; the keeping of law and order was not incompatible with tolerance of the quiet work of the slaughter-house. Martial law was the only way, Tristram supposed. An army being primarily an organization set up for mass murder, morality could never be its concern. Clear the road-arteries for traffic, the country's blood; watch the water-supply; keep the main streets well-lighted, the alleys and back-lanes can look after themselves. Theirs not to reason why. I'm a simple soldier-man, sir, damn your eyes, not one of your flaming politicians: leave the dirty work to them.

The *Daily Newsdisc* was functioning once more. Tristram heard the metal voice booming from the

Garrison Officers' Mess (dim lights, a white-coated orderly, cutlery ringing silverily) and stopped to listen. The cult of Quetzlcoatl revived in Mexico: love-feasts and human sacrifice reported from Chihuahua, Moctezuma, Chilpanzingo. Meat-eating and the salting-down of meat all along Chile's long thin strip. Vigorous canning in Uruguay. Free love in Utah. Riots in the Panama Canal Zone, a loose-loving loose-feeding people unsubmissive to the newly-raised militia. In Suiyuan Province, Northern China, a local magnate with a pronounced limp had been mactated with due ceremony. 'Rice babies' had been moulded in the East Indies and drowned in the paddies. Good news of grain crops in Queensland.

Tristram walked on, seeing troops off duty laughing, their arms round local girls. He heard a band tuning up for a dance, fairy lights delicate on the buds of the riverside trees. He began to formicate all over with the languor of one digesting meat. This was the world, acquiesce in it: the mutter of love-making and the mass, the grinding of meat and the wheels of the military. Life. No, damn it, no. He pulled himself together. He was on the last stage of his journey now. With luck and lifts he might even reach Preston by morning. He had been long enough on the road; he must look forward to one known and loved pair of arms, a languor consecrated by love and private darkness, away from the fires and the gay feasts. He tramped briskly to the mouth of the road leading north and stood, jerking his raised thumb, under a signpost pointing to Warrington. He was not perhaps showing due gratitude to the duennas of the Chester Ladies' Fecundity Association, but never mind.

Fecundity ought to be a fruit of the Holy Ghost reserved to the married, anyway. Too much fornication going on.

After six or seven unheeded thumb-jerks, just as he was about to start walking, an army lorry squeal-ground to a halt by him. 'Wigan,' said the soldier-driver, 'with this here lot behind.' He gave his head a savage jolt towards the rear in indication. Tristram's heart bounded. Twenty miles north of Wigan lay Preston. Three miles west of Preston, on the Blackpool road, lay State Farm NW313. He climbed aboard, full of thanks. 'Well,' said the driver, his hands gripping the big wheel at a diameter's span, 'I reckon it won't be all that long now then, mister.'

'No,' agreed Tristram fervently.

'Tell me, then, mister,' said the driver. 'Who do you think it's going to be?' He sucked loudly at a natural pre-molar, a youngish fattish fair man with a greasy cap.

'Eh?' said Tristram. 'I'm afraid I didn't – I was thinking of something else, I'm afraid.'

'*Afraid,*' repeated the driver in satisfaction. 'That's just about it, isn't it? That's the word. There's a lot going to be afraid before long, mister, you among them, I dare say. But it stands to reason you've got to have a war. Not because anybody wants it, of course, but because there's an army. An army here and an army there and armies all over the shop. Armies is for wars and wars is for armies. That's only plain common sense.'

'War's finished,' said Tristram. 'War's outlawed. There hasn't been any war for years and years and years.'

'All the more reason why there's got to be a war,' said the driver, 'if we've been such a long time without one.'

'But,' said Tristram, agitated, 'you've no conception what war was like. I've read books about the old wars. They were terrible, terrible. There were poison gases that turned your blood to water and bacteria that killed the seed of whole nations and bombs that smashed cities in a split second. All that's over. It's got to be over. We can't have all that again. I've seen photographs,' he shivered. 'Films, too. Those old wars were ghastly. Rape, looting, torture, arson, syphilis. Unthinkable. No, no, never again. Don't say things like that.'

The driver, tilting his wheel gently, his shoulders jigging like a bad dancer's, sucked hard. 'I didn't mean that sort, mister. I meant, you know, fighting. Armies. One lot having a bash at another lot, if you see what I mean. One army facing another army, like it might be two teams. And then one lot shoots at another lot, and they go on shooting till somebody blows the whistle and they say, "This lot's won and this lot's lost." Then they dish out leave and medals and the tarts are all lined up waiting at the station. That's the sort of war I mean, mister.'

'But who,' asked Tristram, 'would go to war with whom?'

'Well,' said the driver, 'that would have to be sorted out, wouldn't it? Arrangements would sort of have to be made, wouldn't they? But, you mark my words, it's got to come.' The cargo behind him danced tinnily, jauntily, as they went over a hump bridge. 'A hero's death,' said the soldier suddenly with a sort of complacency. The battalion of tinned meat jingled applause, like some giant chestful of medals.

Nine

TRISTRAM got a lift in a Military Police van from Wigan to Standish, then the road was suddenly empty of traffic. He walked slowly and with some difficulty through the plenilunar night, his left foot giving him trouble – a thick seg and the shoe-sole worn to a neat hole. Still, he shogged along bravely, with quiet excitement trotting in front of him, its tongue out, and the night shogged with him towards morning. His feet suggested a rest at Leyland, but his heart would have none of that. On to dawn in Preston: a breather there, perhaps an eleemosynary breakfast, then on to his goal, three miles west. Morning and the town approached stealthily.

What was that ringing noise? Frowning, Tristram poked his little fingers into his ears, agitating the wax with a deafening rumble. He automatically sniffed at the waxy finger-tip (the only pleasant odour of all that the body secreted), listening. That bell-noise came from the world, not his head: it clanged out of the town itself. Bells to welcome the pilgrim in? Nonsense. It was not bells, either: it was an electronic fabrication of bells – slow-pulsing from shaking loudspeakers, throwing up a metallic spray of harmonics, demented silver. Wondering, Tristram approached. He entered Preston in full morning and was swallowed by crowds and the jubilant clanging, crying to the strangers who surrounded him, 'What is all this? What's going on?' They laughed in answer, deaf, dumb, mouthing in the mad swirl of auricular metal. A shuddering bronze lid, which miraculously seemed to let in more light, had come down in silver over the township. People were moving towards the source of the mad angelic din; Tristram followed. It was like entering the very heart of noise, noise as ultimate reality.

A grey freestone anonymous building – provincial architecture, no more than ten storeys – and loudspeakers flaring down from its roof. Tristram entered, jostled, out of the lemon sunlight, and inside the building opened his mouth at the vast cubic hollowness. Never in his life had he seen an interior so large. It could not be called a room – a hall, meeting-place, place of assembly; there must be a special word and he searched for it. It was an improvisation: the cells of the old block (flats or offices) had been shelled out; room-walls had been knocked down, as jagged brick buttresses showed; the floor-ceilings of several storeys cleared, stripped, so that the eyes were shocked at the height. Tristram recognized an altar on a rostrum at the far end; rows of rough benches, people sitting waiting, kneeling praying. The appropriate terms began to creak back from his reading, as *platoon, battalion* had come back before in a context that, for some reason, seemed similar. *Church. Congregation.* 'You're oldin oop traffic, lad,' said a genial voice behind. Tristram took a, took a – what was the word? Took a *pew*.

Priests, a plurality of them, marched burlily in with big fat candles, a platoon (no, a section) of boy-servitors. *'Introibo ad altare Dei –'* Mixed voices, a whole storey up, in a gallery at the rear of the building, replied in song: *'Ad Deum Qui laetificat juventutem meam.'* This was some very special occasion. This was like playing chess with carved ivory horses and elephants, not with bits of shaped prison soap. "*Alleluia*" kept crashing into the liturgy. Tristram waited patiently for the Consecration, the eucharistic breakfast, but the grace before meat was very long.

A heavy-lipped bull of a priest turned from the altar to the congregation, standing at the rostrum's edge, blessing the air. 'Brethren,' he said. A speech, an oration, an address, a *sermon*. 'This is Easter Day. This morning we celebrate the resurrection or rising-from-the-dead of Our Lord Jesus Christ. Crucified for preaching the kingdom of God and brotherhood of man, His dead weight dragged down from the cross and stamped in the earth – as weed is stamped or fire-ash – He yet rose on the third day in raiment glorious as the sun and moon and all the fires of the firmament. He rose to bear witness to the world that there is no death, that death is but appearance and not reality, that the seeming forces of death are but shadows and their prevalence but a prevalence of shadows.' The priest belched gently on a fasting stomach. 'He rose to extol life everlasting, not a white-lipped ghost-life in some tenebrose noosphere –' ('Ee,' said a woman behind Tristram) '– but a totality or unity of life in which the planets dance with the amœbæ, the great unknown macrobes with the microbes that swirl in our bodies and the bodies of the beasts our fellows, all flesh is one and flesh is also corn, grass, barley. He is the sign, the eternal symbol, the perpetual recurrence made flesh; He is man, beast, corn, God. His blood also becomes our blood through its act of refreshing our sluggish warm red, coiling along its palpitating channels. His blood is not only the blood of man, beast, bird,

fish; it is also the rain, the river, the sea. It is the ecstatically pumped seed of men and it is the flowing richness
of the milk of the mothers of men. In Him we become
one with all things, and He is one with all things and
with us.

'Today in England, today throughout the English-
Speaking Union, we joyfully celebrate, with sackbut and
psaltery and loud alleluias, the resurrection of the Prince
of Life. Today, too, in far lands which in the barren
past rejected the flesh and the blood of the Eternal Life-
giver, this His rising from the tomb is hailed with a joy
like to our own, though under figures and names of out-
landish meaning and heathenish sound.' The man to
Tristram's right frowned at that sentence. 'For, though
we call Him Jesus and the veritable Christ, yet is He
beyond all names and above them, so that Christ re-arisen
will hear Himself addressed in joy and worship as
Thammuz or Adonis or Attis or Balder or Hiawatha,
and to Him all is one as all names are one, as all words
are one, as all life is one.' The preacher was silent for a
space; spring coughs hacked out from the congregation.
Then, with the irrelevance proper to a religious dis-
course, he cried with a main voice, 'Therefore, fear not.
In the midst of death we are in life.'

'Aaaargh, bloody nonsense!' called a voice from the
rear. 'You can't bring the dead back, blast you, for all
your fine talk!' Heads swivelled gratefully; there was
a scuffle; arms flailed; Tristram could not see very well.

'I think,' said the preacher, unperturbed, 'it would be
better if my interrupter left. If he will not leave voluntarily perhaps he could be assisted to leave.'

'Bloody nonsense! Whoring after false gods, God forgive your black heart!' And now Tristram could see who it was. He knew that moon-face, red with generous anger. 'My own children,' it yelled, 'sacrificed on the altar of Baal that you worship as the true God, God forgive you!' The big body, in its sack farmer's garments, was being pulled out fighting by struggling panting men, leaving the presence correctly backwards, its arms pinned painfully behind it. 'God forgive the lot of you, for I never shall!'

'Excuse me,' murmured Tristram, pushing out of his pew. Somebody had placed a gagging hand over his brother-in-law's retreating mouth. 'Bob,' came the muffled protest. 'Bob blasp be bop ob boo.' Shonny and his rough hard-breathing escort were already through the doorway. Tristram walked fast up the aisle. 'To resume,' the preacher resumed.

Ten

'So,' said Tristram hopelessly, 'they just took her away.'

'And then,' said Shonny dully, 'we waited and waited, but they didn't come home. And then the next day we knew what had happened. Oh, God, God.' He made a big red plate of his hands and plopped the pudding of his head on to it, sobbing.

'Yes, yes, terrible,' said Tristram. 'Did they say where they were taking her to? Did they say they were going back to London?'

'I blame myself,' said Shonny's hidden head. 'I trusted

God. It was the wrong God I was trusting, all these long years. No God who was good could let that happen, God forgive Him.'

'All for nothing,' sighed Tristram. 'All that journey wasted.' His hand trembled round his glass. They were seated in a small shop that sold water barely touched by alc.

'Mavis has been wonderful,' said Shonny, looking up, dripping with tears. 'Mavis took it like a saint or an angel. But I'll never be the same again, never. I tried telling myself that God knew why it had happened, that there was a divine reason for everything. I even came to mass this morning, ready to be like Job and to praise the Lord in the transport of my miseries. And then I saw. I saw it in that priest's fat face; I heard it in his fat voice. A false God has taken possession of them all.' He breathed in hard with a curious rattling noise like sea-dragged shingle. The few other drinkers (men in old clothes, not celebrating Easter) looked up.

'You can have other children,' said Tristram. 'You still have your wife, your home, your work, your health. But what am I to do? Where can I go, who can I turn to?'

Shonny glared at him evilly. There was scum round his lips and his chin was ill-shaven. 'Don't talk to me,' he said. 'You with your children that I've protected all these months at the risk of the lives of my whole family. You and your sly twins.'

'Twins?' Tristram stared. 'Twins, did you say?'

'With these hands,' said Shonny, and he presented them to the world, huge and hooked, 'I brought your twins to birth. And now I say: Better if I hadn't. Better if I'd let them shift for themselves, like little wild animals. Better if I'd strangled them and given them to your false greedy God with His lips dripping with blood, picking His teeth after His favourite accursed meal of little children. Then, perhaps, He would have left mine alone. Then, perhaps, He would have permitted them to come home from school unmolested, as on any other day, and let them live. Live,' he shouted. 'Live, live, live.'

'I'm sorry,' said Tristram. 'You know I'm sorry.' He paused. 'Twins,' he said in wonder. And then, vigorously, 'Where did they say they were going? Did they say they were going back to my brother in London?'

'Yes, yes, yes, I suppose so. I suppose they said something like that. It doesn't matter, anyway. Nothing matters any more.' He sucked at his glass without relish. 'My whole world's shattered,' he said. 'I have to build it up again, searching for a God I can believe in.'

'Oh,' cried Tristram in sudden irritation, 'don't be so sorry for yourself. It's people like you who've made the kind of world you say you no longer believe in. We were all safe enough in that old liberal society.' He was talking of less than a year back. 'Hungry, but safe. Once you kill the liberal society you create a vacuum for God to rush into, and then you unleash murder and fornication and cannibalism. And,' said Tristram, his heart suddenly sinking, 'you believe it's right for man to go on sinning for ever, because that way you justify your belief in Jesus Christ,' for he saw that whatever government was in power he would always be against it.

'That's not right,' said Shonny, with surprising reasonableness. 'Not it at all. There are two Gods, you see.

They get mixed up, and it's hard for us to find the right one. Like,' he said, 'those twins, Derek and Tristram she called them. She got them mixed up when they were naked. But it's better to have it that way than to have no God at all.'

'Then what the hell are you complaining about?' snarled Tristram. The best of both worlds, as always; women always got the best of both worlds.

'I'm not complaining,' said Shonny, with frightening meekness. 'I'm going to put my trust in the real God. He'll avenge my poor dead children.' Then he clamped the two half-masks of his hands, dirty hands, over his fresh sobbing. 'You can keep your other God, your other filthy God.'

'I don't believe in either,' Tristram found himself saying. 'I'm a liberal.' Shocked, he said, 'I don't really mean that, of course. What I mean is –'

'Leave me to my misery,' cried Shonny. 'Get out and leave me alone.'

Embarrassed, Tristram mumbled, 'I'm going. I'd better start my return journey. They say there are trains running now. They say the State airlines are functioning again. So,' he said, 'she called them Tristram and Derek, did she? That was very clever.'

'You have two children,' said Shonny, removing his hands from his blear eyes. 'I have none. Go on, get to them.'

'The fact is,' said Tristram, 'the fact is that I've no money. Not a solitary tanner. If you could lend me, say, five guineas or twenty crowns or something like that –'

'You'll get no money from me.'

'A loan, that's all. I'll repay it as soon as I get a job.

It won't be long, I promise.'

'Nothing,' said Shonny, making an ugly mouth like a child. 'I've done enough for you, haven't I? Haven't I done enough?'

'Well,' said Tristram, puzzled, 'I don't know. I suppose you must have, if you say so. I'm grateful, anyway, very grateful. But you can see, surely, that I've got to get back to London and it's too much to ask me, surely, to return as I came, walking and cadging lifts. Look at this left shoe. I want to get there quickly.' He feebly banged the table with both fists. 'I want to be with my wife. Can't you see that?'

'All my life,' said Shonny sombrely, 'I've been giving, giving, giving. People have put upon me. People have taken and then laughed behind my back. I've given too much in my time. Time and work and money and love. And what have I ever got in return? Oh, God, God.' He choked.

'Be reasonable. Just a loan. Two or three crowns, say. I am, after all, your brother-in-law.'

'You're nothing to me. You're just the husband of my wife's sister, that's all. And a damned bad lot you've turned out to be, God forgive you.'

'Look here, I don't like that. You've no call to say that sort of thing.'

Shonny folded his arms, as if ordered to by a teacher, and shut his lips tight. Then, 'Nothing from me,' he said. 'Go somewhere else for your money. I've never cared for you or for your type of person. You and your Godless liberalism. And cheating, too. Having children on the sly. She should never have married you. I always said that, and Mavis said the same. Go on, get out of my sight.'

'You're a mean bastard,' said Tristram.

'I am what I am,' said Shonny, 'as God is what He is. You'll get no help from me.'

'You're a damned hypocrite,' said Tristram with something like glee, 'with your false "Lord have mercy on us" and "Glory be to God in the highest". High-sounding blasted religious phrases and not a scrap of real religion in you.'

'Get out,' said Shonny. 'Go quietly.' The bald waiter by the bar was biting his nails anxiously. 'I don't want to throw you out.'

'Anybody would think you owned the damned place,' said Tristram. 'I hope you remember this some day. I hope you remember that you refused help when it was desperately needed.'

'Go on, go. Go and find your twins.'

'I'm going,' said Tristram. He got up and plastered his rage with a grin. 'You'll have to pay for the alc, anyway,' he said. 'That's one thing you'll have to pay for.' He made a vulgar schoolboy's noise and went out in tearing anger. He stood on the pavement for a moment, hesitant, then, deciding to turn right, he caught, trudging on his way, through the smeared window of the cheap shop, a last glimpse of poor Shonny with his pudding head shaking in his hands.

Eleven

TRISTRAM walked hungry and wondering what to do,

rage still quaking inside, through the sunny Easter Preston streets. Should he stand in the gutter and beg, sing with his hand out? He was dirty and ragged enough for a beggar, he knew, gaunt, bearded, his hair a crinkly tangle. Someone out of ancient history or myth had been that not too unhappy teacher of Social Studies of less than a year ago, groomed, neat, eloquent, home to eat synthelac pudding prepared by a personable wife, the shiny black news spinning sedately on its wall-spindle. Things had not been too bad, really: just enough food, stability, a sufficiency of money, stereoscopic television on the bedroom ceiling. He choked back a dry sob.

Not far from a bus-terminal – red single-deckers filling up with passengers for Bamber Bridge and Chorley – Tristram's nostrils dilated at a briskly wind-borne smell of stew. It was a coarse charity kind of aroma – greasy metal and meat-fat mitigated by herbs – but he slavered lavishly, sucking the saliva back in as he followed his nose. In a side-street the smell blew out richly at him, heartening as low comedy, and he saw both men and women queueing outside a double-fronted shop whose windows had been rendered opaque with whitewash whorls like amateur reproductions of Brancusi's portrait of James Joyce. A metal plaque above the door said, white on scarlet, *WD North-West District Communal Feeding Centre*. God bless the army. Tristram joined the line of vagrants like himself – dusty-haired, clothes creased with sleep, fish-eyed with disappointment. One jockey of a wretched man kept doubling up as though punched in the guts, complaining monotonously of the belly-warch. A very thin woman with filthy grey hair stood upright in pathetic dignity, above these people, above begging except absent-mindedly. A quite young man sucked with desperate force at his mouth without teeth. Tristram was suddenly nudged by a jocular male bag of rags, smelling powerfully of old dog. 'What fettle?' he asked of Tristram. And then he said, nodding towards the greasy stew-aroma, 'Oo's getten chip-pan on.' Nobody else smiled. A young shapeless woman with hair like teased wool said to a bowed and sunken Oriental, 'Ad to ditch kid on't way, like. Couldn't carry im no more.' Wretched wanderers.

A ginger man in uniform, capless, arms akimbo but bent painfully forward the better to show his three chevrons of rank, now stood in the doorway and said, surveying the queue compassionately, 'The scum of the earth, the dregs of humanity,' and then, 'Right. In you come. No pushing and shoving. Plenty for everybody if you can call it a body. In, then.' The queue pushed and shoved. Inside, on the left, three men in dirty cooks' white stood with ladles over steaming drums of stew. On the right a private soldier, his tunic far too large, clattered out dull-gleaming pannikins and spoons. The hungrier members of the queue barked at each other, drooling as their doles were ladled out, clapping dirty paws over their portions, protective lids, as they staggered with them over to the rows of tables. Tristram had eaten the day before, but the morning's anger had made him ravenous. The room, whitewashed, coarsely functional, was full of the noise of sucking, the splash and tremulous clatter of spoons. Tristram, maddened by the odorous steam, supped up his stew in seconds. Hunger was now greater than before. The man next to him was licking his empty bowl. Somebody, eating too greedily, had been sick on the floor. 'Waste,' said somebody else, 'sheer bloody waste.' There seemed to be no second helpings. Nor was it possible to sneak out and re-join the queue: the akimbo sergeant was watchful at the door. It did not, as a matter of fact, seem possible to get out at all.

A door diagonally opposite to the entrance now opened and a uniformed man in early middle age marched in. He was capped, polished, brushed, pressed, holstered, and carried the three stars of a captain. His steel-rimmed army-issue spectacles gleamed benevolently. Behind him stood a stocky two-striped man, clipboard under his arm. Tristram, with wonder and hope, saw that the captain carried, in addition to his stars, a grey bag that chinked discreetly as he walked. Money? God bless the army. God very much bless the army. The captain stalked around the tables, surveying, weighing, and the corporal toddled after. At Tristram's table, 'You,' said the captain – his accent was cultured – to an old champing man with wild hair, 'could use, perhaps, a tosheroon or so.' He dug into the bag and, half-contemptuously, tossed a bright coin on to the table. The old man made the ancient gesture of touching his forelock. 'You,' said the captain to a young hungry man who was, ironically, very fat, 'could probably make use of a loan. Government money, no interest charged, repayable within six months. Shall we say two guineas?' The corporal presented his clipboard, saying, 'Sign here.' The young man, with shame, confessed that he could not write. 'A cross, then,' comforted the corporal, 'then out through that door.' He nudged towards it, the door he and the officer had entered by. 'Ah,' said the captain to Tristram, 'tell me all about yourself.' His face was remarkably unlined, as though the army possessed some secret face-iron; he smelled curiously spicy. Tristram told him. 'A schoolmaster, eh? Well, you shouldn't have anything to worry about. How much shall we say? Four guineas? Perhaps you can be persuaded to settle for three.' He rustled the notes out of the bag. The corporal pushed his clipboard forward and seemed ready to stick an inkpencil in Tristram's eye. 'Sign here,' he said. Tristram signed, shaky, the notes clutched in the same hand. 'Now out through that door,' nudged the corporal.

The doorway seemed not to be a way out. It led into a long wide kind of hallway, whitewashed and smelling of size, and a number of ragged people were being indignant with a young and unhappy-looking sergeant. 'It's no good going on at me about it,' he said in a Northern voice pitched tight and high. 'Day after day we get them in here going on at me as if it was my fault, and I have to tell them it's nowt to do with me. Nothing,' he translated, looking at Tristram. 'Nobody made you,' he told everybody reasonably, 'do what you've just done now, did they? Some – that is to say, the old ones – got a little present. You got a loan. That'll be taken out of your pay, so much per week. Now, you needn't have taken the King's money if you didn't want to, and you needn't have signed. It was all quite voluntary.' He pronounced this last word to rhyme with 'hairy'. Tristram's heart lunged down deep then up again into his throat, as if it were on elastic.

'What is all this?' he said. 'What's going on?' To his surprise he saw the dirty-grey lady there, ramrod with *grande dame* hauteur. 'This creature,' she said, 'has the impertinence to say that we've joined the army. I never heard such nonsense. *Me* in the army. A woman of my age and position.'

'I daresay you'll do all right,' said the sergeant. 'They like them a bit younger as a rule, but you'll as like as not get a nice job looking after the auxiliaries. Women soldiers,' he explained courteously to Tristram, as though Tristram were the most ignorant one there, 'are called auxiliaries, you see.'

'Is this true?' asked Tristram, fighting for calm. The sergeant, who seemed a decent young man, nodded gloomily. He said:

'I always tell people never to sign anything till they've read it. That thing that Corporal Newlands has out there says at the top that you've volunteered to serve with the colours for twelve months. It's in pretty small printing, but you could have read it if you'd wanted.'

'He had his thumb over it,' said Tristram.

'I can't read,' said the young fat man.

'Well, then, that's your funeral, isn't it?' said the sergeant. 'They'll teach you to read, never fear.'

'This,' said the grey lady, 'is preposterous. This is an utter scandal and a disgrace. I shall go back there at once and give them back their filthy money and tell them precisely what I think of them.'

'That's the way,' said the sergeant admiringly. 'I can just see you in the orderly room, giving them what for. You'll do pretty well, you will. You'll be what they call a real old battle-axe.'

'Disgraceful.' And she made, a real old battle-axe, for the door.

'What's done can't be undone,' said the sergeant philosophically. 'What's been signed can't be unsigned. Fair means or foul, they've got you. But twelve months isn't much, now, is it? They talked me into signing on for seven years. A right twit, I was. A mug,' he translated for Tristram. 'Between you and me, though,' he confided to all, 'there's a lot more chance of promotion if you're a volunteer. Eee, she's at it,' he said, cocking an ear. From the dining-hall the raised voice of the grey woman could be clearly heard. 'Do well, she will.' Then, 'They'll be having what they call Con Scrip Shun before long, so Captain Taylor says. A volunteer will be in a different position altogether from one of those. That stands to reason.'

Tristram began to laugh. There was a chair just inside the doorway and he sat on it the better to laugh. 'Private Foxe,' he said and laughed, crying.

'That's the way,' said the sergeant approvingly. 'That's the real army spirit. Keep smiling is what I say, it's better to laugh than do the other thing. Well,' he said, standing at ease, nodding as other pressed vagrants came in, 'you're in the army now. You might as well make the best of it.' Tristram continued to laugh. 'Just like he's doing.'

Part Five

One

'It sy bitsy booful,' went Derek Foxe, first to one drib-
bling chuckling twin, then to the other. 'Boo boo boo
boop a doop,' he booed to his little namesake and then,
scrupulously fair, that identical phatic utterance to tiny
Tristram. He was never anything but scrupulously fair,
as his subordinates at the Ministry of Fertility could
testify; even Loosley, demoted to rather junior executive rank could – though he was now trying to prove
Derek a homosexual – hardly prate of injustice. 'Worple
worple worple,' chortled Derek in serial duplicate, typing
the twins with two fingers. These meanwhile, bubbling
like fish, secure in their play-pen, podgily clutched the
rails and performed a treadmill action. Tiny Tristram
alone said, like Upanishadian thunder, 'Da da da.' 'Ah,'
said Derek seriously, 'we ought to have more, lots, lots
more.'

'So they can be put in the army and shot at?' said
Beatrice-Joanna. 'Not likely.'

'Oh, that –' Derek, hands clasped behind, did a brief
quarterdeck-pacing act round the drawing-room. He
then drank off his coffee. It was a spacious drawing-room;
all the rooms of the seaward-looking flat were spacious.
There was space nowadays for men of Derek's rank, for
their wives or pseudo-wives, their children. 'Everybody's

got to take his chance,' he said. 'Her chance, too. That's why we ought to have lots more.'

'Nonsense,' said Beatrice-Joanna. She was stretched on a deep-piled chunky couch that was eight feet long and claret-coloured. She was leafing through the latest issue of *Sheek*, a fashion magazine which was all pictures. Bustles, her eye noted, were decreed by Paris for day-wear; daring décolletages were *de rigueur* for evening; Hongkong cheongsams were lascivious with fourfold slits. Sex. War and sex. Babies and bullets. 'In the old days,' she mused, 'I'd have been told that I've already exceeded my ration. And now your Ministry tells me that I've not fulfilled my quota. Mad.'

'When we're married,' said Derek, 'properly married, that is, you may feel differently about it.' He padded round to the rear of the couch and kissed her nape, its broth of goldish flue delicate in the weak sun. One of the twins, perhaps tiny Tristram, made, as on a satirical sound-track, a synchronic farting lip-noise. 'Then,' said Derek jocularly, 'I can *really* start talking about wifely duties.'

'How long now?'

'About six months. That will make it a full two years since you last saw him.' He kissed her delicious nape once more. 'The statutory period for desertion.'

'I keep thinking about him,' said Beatrice-Joanna. 'I can't help it. I had a dream a couple of nights ago. I saw Tristram quite clearly, wandering through the streets, crying out for me.'

'Dreams don't mean anything.'

'And I've been thinking about that business of Shonny saying he'd seen him. In Preston.'

'Just before they put the poor man away.'

'Poor, poor Shonny.' Beatrice-Joanna gave the twins a glance of desperate fondness. Shonny's brain turned by the loss of his children, the defection of his God, he now recited long liturgies of his own composition – in a cell in Winwick Hospital, near Warrington, Lancs. – trying to munch consecrated bedclothes. 'I can't help feeling that. That he's been wandering everywhere, all over the country, looking for me.'

'There were ways and means,' said Derek. 'Were you honestly expected to live off air, you and the two children? I've said often, and I say again now, that the most charitable thing is to think of Tristram long dead and long eaten. Tristram is ended, over. Now it's you and me. The future.' He looked, bending over her, masterfully smiling, groomed and smooth, very much like the future. 'Heavens,' he said, without anxiety. 'The time.' A clock on the far wall meekly showed it him – a stylized golden sun of a clock, fiery rays like hair-locks set all round it. 'I must fly,' he said, without hurry. And then, with even less hurry, into her ear, 'You wouldn't really like things to be any different, would you? You're happy with me, aren't you? Say you're happy.'

'Oh, I'm happy.' But her smile was wan. 'It's just that I – that I like things to be right, that's all.'

'Things are right. Very much right.' He kissed her fully on the mouth with a relish that smacked nothing of valediction. But he said, 'Now I really must fly. I've a busy afternoon ahead of me. I'll be home about six.' He did not forget the twins, kissing each on its flossy pate and blowing final phatic vocables at them. Waving, smiling, brief-case under arm, he left: the Ministry car would be waiting below.

After about three minutes Beatrice-Joanna glanced round the room somewhat furtively, then tiptoed over to the switch which operated the *Daily Newsdisc*, shiny-black as a liquorice pancake on its wall-spindle. She could not altogether explain to herself this sensation of small guilt at wanting to hear the day's news again: after all, the *Daily Newsdisc* – now one of a number of free-enterprise organs, auditory, audio-visual, even (the *Weekly Feel*) tactile – was there for anybody's re-listening. What itched in Beatrice-Joanna's brain-stem was a hint that there was something disingenuous about the news these days, something crafty and implausible which Derek and people like him knew all about (laughing up their sleeves at it) but didn't want people like her to know all about. She wanted to see if she could find a crack in the too-smooth plaster which now –

'– Secession of China from Ruspun and the declaration of China's intention – made by Premier Poh Soo Jin in Peking – to establish an independent association of states to be known in Kuo-Yü as Ta Chung-kuo, anglicized as Chinspun. Indications are already reported of aggressive intentions towards both Ruspun and Enspun, as witness raids on Kultuk and Boryza and massing of infantry in Southern Canton. There is every sign, says our Midway Island observer, of an intended annexation of Japan. With the laying bare of the western flank of Enspun –' Beatrice-Joanna clicked off the manic synthetic voice. Sheer damned nonsense. If the world were really considering starting a real war, surely there should be talk of soaring planes and plunging warships as well as trudging armies with simple portable weapons; there should, surely, be threats of the resurrection of one of those ancient but efficacious province-blasting nuclear devices. But there wasn't. That British Army improvised last year and now superseded – for the maintenance of civil order – by reasonable blue-clad bobbies, was pure infantry with minimal support of specialist corps; in the magazines and on the news-reels one saw the soldiers climbing the ramps of troopers – off for training, it was said, on the Annexe Islands or for police work in dissident corridors – up-thumbing at the cameras with a partially dentate leer, the best of British luck and pluck.

Beatrice-Joanna had almost convinced herself that she had been convinced, one evening before the stereo-telly in this very flat, that she had seen in penumbral background to the close-up of an up-thumbing cheerful Tommy a face she knew. 'Nonsense,' of course, from Derek, stretched in his purple dressing-gown. 'If Tristram were in the army Army Records would have his name. You sometimes forget I'm his brother and I have a certain duty. I consulted Army Records and they know nothing. I've said before, and I say again now, the most charitable thing is to think of Tristram long dead and long eaten.' Still –

She pressed an electric buzzer on a wall-panel of switches and buzzers; almost at once a cheerful (cheer-ful as a Tommy) brown girl glided in, bowing in spasms, dressed in servant's black silk-substitute. She was a pretty little orchestra of races and her name was Jane. 'Jane,' said Beatrice-Joanna, 'please get the twins ready for their afternoon outing.' 'Yes, yes, madam,' said Jane, and she wheeled the castered play-pen across the sea-green fitted carpet, clucking and creasing her face at the two treadmilling infants.

Beatrice-Joanna went to her bedroom to make herself ready for the afternoon's walk. Her dressing-table carried, in neat order, a whole pharmacy of creams and unguents; her wall-fitted wardrobes were full of gowns and costumes. She had servants, children, a handsome and successful pseudo-husband (co-ordinating sub-minister at the Ministry of Fertility, soon, it was said, to be Minister), all that love could give and money could buy. But she did not think she was really happy. A dim film in some basement projection-room of her mind occasionally flickered a sequence of things as they had been. Often called a flower by Derek (and, previously, by Tristram), had she really been a flower she would have belonged to the class Diandria. She needed two men in her life, her day to be salted by infidelity.

She now unlocked a carved camphorwood box and took from it a letter she had written the day before; it smelled deliciously of mingled camphor and sandalwood. She read through it for the seventh or eighth time before definitely making up her mind to send it. It said:

'Dearest dearest Tristram, there have been such changes in this mad world, so many strange things have been happening since we parted so unhappily, that there is nothing I can say here that will make much sense to either of us except that I miss you and love you and long for you. I'm living with Derek now, but don't think badly of me for that: I have to keep a home going for your two sons (yes, I do honestly believe they are really yours). Perhaps you have already tried to write to me, perhaps – and I firmly believe this – you have tried to get in touch with me, but I know how difficult life has been. Your brother has been most kind to me and I think he genuinely loves me, but I don't think any letter you write c/o him would ever reach me. He has his precious career to think of, a man with children standing a better chance of promotion to Minister of Fertility than a man with none, or so he says. You will remember how every day when we were together I used to take my walk by the sea, not far from Government Building. Every afternoon I still do that, wheeling my two sons in their pram, from three to four. Looking out to sea I now pray daily that the sea will send you back to me. This is my hope. I love you and if I ever hurt you I am sorry. Come back to your always loving Beattie.'

She refolded this and placed it in a fine-quality subtle-smelling envelope. Then she took her dainty ink-pencil and addressed the envelope in her bold mannish hand to Tristram Foxe, Esq., B.A., British Army. There was just a chance; it was the only way, anyway. As for Army Records – Derek must either be most influential or a great liar; she herself, one furtive afternoon after seeing that television newsreel, had telephoned the War Office (the house telephone was an extension of the Ministry switchboard) and, after endless shuttling from department to department, had finally contacted a little Scots voice which admitted to being Army Records but said coldly that private individuals could not be informed of troop locations. Something to do with security. But she was not, said Beatrice-Joanna, concerned primarily with anything so sophisticated as location; her enquiry was more fundamental, more ontological. The voice had clicked itself sternly off.

Derek had come home smiling at six and wanted to know, smiling, why she had been telephoning Army Records. Didn't she believe him, her pseudo-husband, didn't she trust him? That was the whole point: she didn't. One could forgive mendacity and untrustworthiness in a lover but hardly in a husband, even pseudo. She didn't tell him this, however. Still, his love seemed to be an unscrupulous sort of love, and that was flattering, but she preferred that sort of love in a lover.

So she went out with the twins in a pram in the winter marine sunshine, the little black-clad nurse clucking and moon-smiling at the two bubbling little men in their warm woollies, and she posted the letter in a pillarbox whose top had been whitened by seagull-droppings. It was like launching a letter in a bottle on the sea, that great unpunctual deliverer.

Two

'SAH,' snarled R.S.M. Backhouse, with a terrifying jaw-twist. '7388026 Sergeant Foxe T. Sah.' Tristram marched in in a sort of lope and saluted without grace. Lieutenant-Colonel Williams looked up sadly from his desk; his swarthy adjutant, standing behind, gave a grin of pain.

'Sergeant Foxe, eh?' said Lieutenant-Colonel Williams.

He was a handsome tired greying man wearing, at the moment, clumsy reading-spectacles. The aura of long service which beat from him was, of course, illusory: all the soldiers of all the new armies were rookies. But Lieutenant-Colonel Williams, like all the senior officers, came out of that old liberal police force almost entirely superseded by the greyboys; he had been a scholarly superintendent of the Special Branch. 'Foxe with an "e", I see,' he said now, 'like the *Book of Martyrs* man.'

'Sir,' said Tristram.

'Well,' said Lieutenant-Colonel Williams, 'there's this question of your terms of reference as a sergeant-instructor.'

'Sir.'

'Your duties are, I think, straightforward enough. You have, according to Q.M.S.I. Bartlett, fulfilled them adequately. You have done good work in the class for illiterates, for example. You have, in addition, taught elementary arithmetic, report-writing, use of the telephone, military geography and current affairs.'

'Sir.'

'And it's these current affairs that have been causing the trouble. That right, Willoughby?' He peered up at his adjutant who, picking his nose, stopped picking his nose and nodded eagerly. 'Now, let me see. You seem to have been holding certain discussions with the men. Something about Who Is The Enemy? and What's All The Fighting About? You admit that, I take it.'

'Yes, sir. In my opinion, the men have a perfect right to discuss why they're in the army and what –'

'A soldier,' said Lieutenant-Colonel Williams wearily, 'has no right to opinions. That is laid down, rightly or

225

wrongly. Rightly, I suppose, as it's laid down.'

'But, sir,' said Tristram, 'surely we have to know what we're involved in. We're told that there's a war on. Some of the men, sir, refuse to believe it. I'm inclined to agree with them, sir.'

'Indeed?' said Lieutenant-Colonel Williams coldly. 'Well, be enlightened, Foxe. There is fighting, so there must be war. There is not perhaps a war in the ancient sense, but war and fighting are, I should have supposed, in the organized sense, in the sense of armies being involved, as good as synonymous.'

'But, sir –'

'I hadn't finished, Foxe, had I? As far as these two questions of who and why are concerned, those are – and you must take it from me apodictically – no business of soldiers. The enemy is the enemy. The enemy is the people we're fighting. We must leave it to our rulers to decide which particular body of people that shall be. It's nothing to do with you or with me or with Private Snooks or Lancejack Dogsbody. Is that quite clear?'

'But, sir –'

'Why are we fighting? We're fighting because we're soldiers. That's simple enough, isn't it? For what cause are we fighting? Simple again. We're fighting to protect our country and, in a wider sense, the whole of the English-Speaking Union. From whom? No concern of ours. Where? Wherever we're sent. Now, Foxe, I trust all this is perfectly clear.'

'Well, sir, what I –'

'It's very wrong of you, Foxe, to disturb the men by starting them thinking and making them ask questions.'

He examined the sheet in front of him, droning. 'Very interested, Foxe, I take it you are, in the enemy and fighting and so forth?'

'Well, sir, in my view –'

'We're going to give you an opportunity for closer contact. Good idea, Willoughby? You approve, Sergeant-major? I'm taking you, Foxe, off instructional duties w.e.f. today, 1200 hours. You'll be posted from HQ Company to one of the rifle companies. It's B Company, I believe, Willoughby, that's short of a platoon sergeant. Right, Foxe. It will do you a lot of good, lad.'

'But, sir –'

'Salute!' cried R.S.M. Backhouse, formerly a sergeant of police. 'About turn! Quick march!' Tristram left-right-left-right-lefted out, furious and apprehensive. 'Better report now,' said the R.S.M., in the more brotherly tones of the mess.

'What did he mean,' asked Tristram, 'when he talked about closer contact? What was he getting at?'

'I reckon he meant what he said,' said the R.S.M. 'I reckon some will be on the move before long. Won't be no time for teaching them their ABC and their once times table then, there won't. Right, Sarnt, off you go.'

Tristram, no very soldierly figure, tramped to B Company Office, his boots ringing and sparking on the metal deck. This – Annexe Island B6 – was an artifact of limited area anchored in the East Atlantic, intended originally to accommodate population overflow, now compactly holding a brigade. All that could be seen of the natural world was a bitter winter sky and, railed off all round, the grey acid sea. This endless dual ambient made one glad to turn inward, to the empty discipline, the childish training, the warm fug of barrack-room and company office. Tristram entered B Company lines, reported to the C.S.M. – a slack-mouthed stupid Nordic giant – and then was admitted to the presence of Captain Behrens, O.C. B Company. 'Good,' said Captain Behrens, a fat white man with very black hair and moustache. 'That makes the company about up to strength. You'd better cut along and report to Mr Dollimore – he's your platoon commander.' Tristram saluted, nearly fell over executing his about-turn, and cut along. He found Lieutenant Dollimore, an amiable young man with idiot spectacles and mild acne rosacea, giving his platoon a lesson in the naming of parts of the rifle. Rifles – there had been, Tristram knew, rifles in those ancient pre-atomic wars; the organization, nomenclature, procedure, armament of this new British Army all seemed to have come out of old books, old films. Rifles, indeed. 'Cocking piece,' pointed Mr Dollimore. 'No, sorry, that's the firing pin. Bolt, striker – What's this one called, Corporal?'

'Sear spring, sir.' A squat middle-aged two-striper looked on, standing to attention, prompting, helping, as now.

'Sergeant Foxe reporting, sir.'

Mr Dollimore gazed with mild interest at Tristram's idiosyncratic salute and snapped it with a bizarre allomorph of his own – a briefly fluttering coxcomb of fingers at his brow. 'Good,' he said, 'good, good.' A wash of vapid relief animated his face. 'Naming of parts,' he said. 'You can take over.'

Tristram looked at the platoon in bewilderment. Thirty men were squatting in the lee of a sleeping-hut, grinning or gawping up. He knew most of them; most of them had had to come to him for rudimentary educational instruction; most of them were still analphabetic. The other ranks of this entire brigade (East Atlantic) were pressed thugs, corner-boys, sexual perverts, gibberers, morons. Still, as far as the naming of the rifle's parts was concerned, he and they were much on a level of ability. 'Very good, sir,' said Tristram and, cunning, 'Corporal.'

'Sarnt?'

'You can take over.' Tristram shuffled into step with Mr Dollimore, who was walking in the direction of his mess. 'What do you actually do with them, sir?'

'Do with them? Well, there's not very much one *can* do, is there?' Mr Dollimore opened his mouth suspiciously at Tristram. 'I mean, all that's laid down is that they learn how to fire that gun of theirs, isn't that it? Oh, and to keep themselves clean, of course, as far as they can.'

'What's going on, sir?' said Tristram somewhat sharply.

'What do you mean – what's going on? That's all that's going on, that that I told you.' They marched metallically, sparkily, across the open winter Atlantic deck of the barren man-made island.

'What I meant was,' said Tristram, with more patience, 'have you heard anything about our going into action?'

'Action? Action against whom?' Mr Dollimore paused in his march the better to stare at Tristram.

'Against the enemy.'

'Oh, I see.' Mr Dollimore used a tone implying that there were hosts other than the enemy that one could go into action against. Tristram crawled all over with a ghastly intimation that Mr Dollimore must be regarded as expendable; if he was expendable, then so was his platoon sergeant. And then, it being just noon, a scratchy record hissed from the loudspeakers, a synthetic bugle blared its angelus, and Mr Dollimore said, 'I just hadn't thought of that. I thought *this* was meant to be a sort of action, really. I thought we were sort of doing a sort of protection job.'

'We'd better go and look at Battalion Orders,' said Tristram. An orderly-room orderly was pinning them up – flapping desolate surrender flags in the Atlantic wind – as they approached the prefabricated huts (ringing with typewriter-bells) of Battalion Headquarters. Tristram nodded, grim, reading faster than his officer. 'That's it, then,' he said. Mr Dollimore, mouth open at it, said, 'Oh, oh, I see. What's that word? Oh, oh, I see.' It was all there, crisp and cold as a lettuce though less digestible. A movement order from Brigade: a draft of six hundred officers and men – two hundred from each battalion – to parade for embarkation at 0630 hours the following day. 'Yes, yes,' said Mr Dollimore eagerly, 'we're in it, you see.' He pointed with joy as though he had his name in the papers. 'There – 2nd Battalion: B Company.' And then, surprisingly, he stood to awkward attention and said, 'Now God be thanked Who has matched us with His hour.'

'I beg your pardon?' said Tristram.

'If I should die, think only this of me,' said Mr Dollimore. It was as if part of his school reading had been an index of first lines. ' "Ye have robbed, said he," ' said he, ' "ye have slaughtered and made an end." '

'That's more like it,' said Tristram, though his head reeled. 'That's a good deal more like it.'

Three

THEY could hear sea transport hooting in at midnight. The men had been sent to bed at ten, stuffed with cocoa and bully, having suffered an inspection of rifles and feet, had deficiencies of clothing and equipment made up, and been issued with many rounds of live ammunition. After three other ranks had been shot accidentally dead and the C.S.M. of HQ Company sustained a flesh wound in the buttock, this issue was withdrawn as premature: the troops would be given their bullets – strictly for the enemy – at the base camp at the port of disembarkation.

'But who is this damned enemy?' asked Sergeant Lightbody for the thousandth time. He lay in the bunk above Tristram, on his back, head resting on folded hands, a handsome sardonic young man with a Dracula jaw. Tristram was writing a letter to his wife, sitting up with blankets round his knees. He was sure she would not receive it, as he was sure she had not received the thirty-odd others he had written, but writing to her was like launching a prayer, a prayer for better times, normality, the decent ordinary comforts of home and love. '– Moving off into action tomorrow. Where, God knows. Be assured that you will be in my thoughts as always. We shall be together again soon, perhaps sooner than we think. Your loving Tristram.' He wrote her name on a cheap canteen envelope and sealed the letter in; he then scribbled his invariable covering note: 'Swine who call yourself my brother, give this to my wife, you unloving hypocritical bastard. All everlasting hate from T.F.' He addressed his outer envelope to D. Foxe, Government Building, Brighton, Greater London, being quite sure that Derek was of that type who would have power, in his trimmer's Vicar-of-Bray way, whatever party reigned. Derek was quite probably behind this war, if there was a war. The C.O.'s definition of 'enemy' was wrong. 'You know what I think?' said Sergeant Lightbody, when Tristram had answered that first question to himself and his own satisfaction but not aloud at all. 'I think there is no enemy. I think that as soon as we get aboard that trooper they'll just sink it. I think they'll drop a few bombs on it and smash us all to smithereens. That's what I think.'

'There aren't any bombing planes,' said Tristram. 'Bombing planes don't exist any more. They went out a long time ago.'

'I've seen them on the films,' said Sergeant Lightbody.

'Very ancient films. Films of the twentieth-century wars. Those ancient wars were very complex and elaborate.'

'They'll split us with torpedoes.'

'Another obsolete technique,' said Tristram. 'No warships, remember.'

'All right,' said Sergeant Lightbody. 'Poison gas, then. They'll get us somehow. We won't have a chance to fire a single shot.'

'Possible,' conceded Tristram. 'They wouldn't want to damage our uniforms or equipment or the ship itself.'

He shook himself, asking, 'Who the hell do we mean when we talk about "they"?'

'Obvious, I should have thought,' said Sergeant Lightbody. 'By "they" we mean the people who get fat through making ships and uniforms and rifles. Make them and destroy them and make them again. Go on doing it for ever and ever. They're the people who make the wars. Patriotism, honour, glory, defence of freedom – a load of balls, that's what it is. The end of war is the means of war. And *we* are the enemy.'

'Whose enemy?'

'Our own. You mark my words. We shan't be alive to see it, but we're in now for an era of endless war – endless because the civilian population won't be involved, because the war will be conveniently far away from civilization. Civilians love war.'

'Only,' said Tristram, 'presumably, so long as they can go on being civilians.'

'Some of them will be able to – those who govern and those who make the money. And their women, of course. Not like the poor bitches we'll be fighting side by side with – if they kindly allow us to live, that is, till we get to the other shore.'

'I've not,' said Tristram, 'clapped eyes on one single auxiliary since I joined.'

'Auxiliaries? That's a load of balls, too. Battalions of women, that's what they've got, whole damned regiments of them. I ought to know – my sister got conscripted into one. She writes now and again.'

'I didn't know that,' said Tristram.

'According to her, they seem to do pretty well what we do. Damn all, in other words, except practising how to shoot. Marking time till they drop a bomb on the poor bitches.'

'Do you,' asked Tristram, 'very much mind the prospect of being killed?'

'Not all that much. It's best to be caught by surprise. I shouldn't like to lie in bed, waiting for it. When you come to think of it,' said Sergeant Lightbody, settling himself snug as in his coffin, 'that business about "Let me like a soldier fall" has a lot in its favour. Life's only choosing when to die. Life's a big postponement because the choice is so difficult. It's a tremendous relief not to have to choose.' In the distance the sea transport bellowed, as in derision of these trite aphorisms.

'I intend to live,' said Tristram. 'I have so much to live for.' The sea transport bellowed again. It did not waken the four other sergeants in the billet; they were rough men, inclined to jeer at Tristram because of his accent and pretensions to polite learning, now snoring after a heavy mess-night on alc. Sergeant Lightbody said nothing more and was soon lightly asleep himself, neatly asleep, as if he had carved himself a dainty helping of oblivion. But Tristram was in a strange bed in a strange barrack-room, the bed of Sergeant Day (discharged dead of a botulism) whom he was now replacing. All night long the sea transport roared as if hungry for its freight of expendables, unwilling to wait till breakfast-time, and Tristram, tossing in dirty blankets, listened to it. Endless war. He wondered. He did not think that possible, not if the law of the historical cycle was a valid law. Perhaps, all these years, the historiographers had been unwilling to recognize history as a spiral, perhaps because a spiral was so difficult to describe. Easier to photograph the spiral from the top, easier to flatten the spring into a coil. Was war, then, the big solution after all? Were those crude early theorists right? War the great aphrodisiac, the great source of world adrenalin, the solvent of ennui, *Angst*, melancholia, accidia, spleen? War itself a massive sexual act, culminating in a detumescence which was not mere metaphorical dying? War, finally, the controller, the trimmer and excisor, the justifier of fertility?

'War,' bawled the trooper in the metal bay. And, turning over in his heavy sleep, 'War,' imploded snoring Sergeant Bellamy. All over the world, at this very moment, infants by the million were fighting into the outer air bellowing 'War'. Tristram yawned, and his yawn was 'War'. He was desperately weary but could not sleep, despite the lullaby ('War' on so many instruments) around him. The night, however, was not very long; it became arbitrary morning at 0400 hours, and Tristram was thankful not to have to undergo the agony of his fellow-sergeants, groaning back to the world, cursing to be dead again as the synthetic bugle bounced reveille all over the camp.

Four

SPARKS on the morning-night road outside its barrack-room as No. 1 Platoon fell in, coughs, hawks, curses five feet above the sparks. Corporal Haskell syringed light from a thin torch on to the nominal roll held by his

sergeant. Tristram, in steel helmet and a raglan greatcoat of ancient design, called the names into the wind:

'Christie.'

'Sarnt.'

'Crump.'

'Boogger off.'

'Gashen. Howell. Mackay. Muir. Talbot.' Several men
answered, some obscenely. 'Better count them,' said
Tristram. Corporal Haskell took his thin-rayed torch to
each trio of faces, disclosing serially decollated masks,
horrible apparitions in the Atlantic blackness. 'Twenty-
nine, Sarnt,' said Corporal Haskell. 'O'Shaughnessy got
hisself shot last night.'

'Platoon shun,' suggested Tristram. 'Move to the
right in threes. By the left quick march.' This total order
was roughly obeyed. The platoon sparked off, left-wheel-
ing, right-wheeling, halting on the wrong foot at the
company lines. The other platoons came shambling up
severally, fire at their heels, barked at, and the platoon
commanders came out to take posts. Captain Behrens
eventually appeared, a milk-white ghost in an officer's
raincoat, to march the company off to the battalion
parade-ground. Here, arc-lamped like a tattoo, mass was
said by the Battalion chaplain, yawning and shivering
as he made his obeisances at the canopied altar. There
was bread to be transubstantiated (a bumper harvest
last year) but still no wine: blackcurrant-flavoured alc
went into the chalice. The chaplain, a long unhappy-
looking man, blessed the troops and their cause; some of
the troops ironically blessed him back.

Breakfast and, above the champing and sucking, the
C.O. gave his valedictory speech over the loudspeakers.

'You will be fighting an evil and unscrupulous enemy in the defence of a noble cause. I know you will cover yourselves in glo in glo in glo in glo craaaaaark come back alive and therefore I say godspeed and all the luck in the world go with you.' A pity, thought Tristram, drinking tea-substitute in the sergeants' mess, a pity that a cracked record should make that perhaps sincere man sound so cynical. A sergeant from Swansea, Western Province, got up from the table singing in a fine tenor, 'Cover yourselves in glow, in glow, in glo-o-ow.'

At 0600 hours the battalion's share of the draft, having drawn the unexpired portion of the day's rations, marched – packed, strapped, water-bottled, helmeted, rifled, all cartridge-pouches (except for those of the officers and N.C.O.s) safely empty – down to the quay. Their transport waited, sparsely lighted but its name covered in glow: T3 (ATL) *W. G. Robinson London*. The smell of sea, oil, unclean galleys, merchant seamen in turtle jerseys spitting from the top deck; the sudden appearance of a bawling scullion emptying swill over the side; the plaintive pointless hoot of the siren. Tristram took in the scene as they were fallen out to wait – the drama of hard shadow, bales, gantries, the scurrying RTO men, the troops already unwrapping their rations (bully between doorsteps) as they stood or squatted. Mr Dollimore, withdrawn from his fellow-subalterns, gaped ever and anon up at the black sky as at a source of eventual glory. The tripartite draft completed itself – more troops marching on to lip-farts, cheers and up-your-pipe V-signs. The brigade major appeared, dressed as for a riding-lesson, saluted and saluting. Breath rose from speaking mouths like cartoon-dialogue. Oil was steadily pumped in by pipe, the nozzle asp-like at the ship's breast. A C.S.M. from another battalion took off his helmet to scratch a head obscenely bald. Two privates punched each other in yelping gleeful play-fight. A tall captain irritably rubbed his crotch. The ship's siren booed. A lance-corporal's nose bled. Like a Christmas tree the covered gangway suddenly lit up with pretty lights. Some troops groaned. 'Attedtiod,' called a loudspeaker voice, muffled and denasalized. 'Attedtiod. The ebbarkatiod will dow cobbedce. Ebbark id order of codstituedt battaliods, duberically.' Officers called and pleaded, taking post with the rocking ship for background. Tristram beckoned Corporal Haskell. Between them they ranged their platoon, blaspheming and chortling, at right angles to the ship's side. Mr Dollimore, recalled from dreams of England far and honour a name, counted with mouth and fingers. The six platoons from 1st Battalion went aboard first; one man's rifle fell over the side to everyone's joy; a clumsy near-imbecile tripped, nearly collapsing the men ahead like a cardpack. But, on the whole, it was a smooth embarkation. 2nd Battalion, No. 1 Platoon leading it up. Tristram saw his men into a troop-deck with hammock-hooks (hammocks to be drawn later, and fixed mess-tables; cold air hummed in, but the bulkheads sweated. 'Not sleepin in one of them buggers,' said Talbot, told about hammocks. 'Doss down on the floor like, that's about it.' Tristram went off to find his own quarters.

'There's one thing I'll bet,' said Sergeant Lightbody, easing his pack off, 'and that's that they'll batten down the hatches or whatever the nautical term is. You'll see. They won't let us up on deck. Rats in a trap, by God or

Dog.' He lay down, as though highly satisfied, on the shallow tray of a lower bunk. From the thigh-pocket of his antique battle-dress he drew out a scarred volume. 'Rabelais,' he said. 'Do you know of this old writer? *"Je m'en vais chercher un grand peut-être."* That's what he said on his death-bed. "I go to seek a great perhaps." Me too. All of us. "Ring down the curtain, the farce is finished." That's something else he said.'

'That's French, isn't it?'

'French. One of the dead languages.'

Sighing, Tristram heaved himself on to the upper bunk. Other sergeants – tougher, stupider perhaps – were already starting card-games; one group was even quarrelling over an alleged mis-deal. *'Vogue la galère!'* called Sergeant Lightbody's voice. The ship did not obey at once but, after about half an hour, they heard the clank of casting-off and, soon after that, the steady engine throbbing like a sixty-four-foot organ-stop. As Sergeant Lightbody had prophesied, no one was allowed on deck.

Five

'WHEN'S grub up, Sarge?'

'There'll be no grub up, today,' said Tristram patiently. 'You drew rations, remember. But you're supposed to send someone to the galley for cocoa.'

'I ate it,' said Howell. 'I ate me dinner when we was waiting to get on board. Bloody imposition I call it. Bloody half-starved and bloody f – ed about and being bloody sent to be bloody shot at.'

'We're being sent to fight the enemy,' said Tristram. 'We'll have our chance to shoot, never fear.' He had spent much of the battened-down morning cleaning his pistol, a rather beautifully made weapon which, thinking to serve out his time as a pacific instructor, he had never expected to have to use. He imagined the surprised expression of somebody toppling, shot dead by it; he imagined a face exploding in a riot of plum-jam, the mashing of the lineaments of surprise or any other emotion; he imagined himself, dentures and contact-lenses and all, suddenly become a man, performing the man's act of killing a man. He closed his eyes and felt the finger on the trigger of the pistol in his mind gently squeeze; the surprised face before him was the face of Derek; Derek, in the single smart crack, became jam pudding perched on a stylish jacket. Tristram, opening his eyes, was at once aware of how he must look to his troops – fierce, with slit eyes and a killer's grin, an example to them all.

But the men were restless, peevish, bored, inclined to reverie, in no mood for dreaming of blood. They sat about, chins in palms, elbows on knees, their eyes glassy with visions. They passed round snapshots while somebody played – most melancholy of instruments – a mouth-organ. They sang:

> We'll be coming home,
> Coming, coming home.
> Some day soon,
> January or June,
> Evening, morning or afternoon –

Tristram, back on his bunk, brooding, felt a shiver break over him as he listened to the sad little song. It seemed to him that he had been suddenly transported to a time and place he had never visited before, a world out of books and films, ineffably ancient. Kitchener, napoo, Bottomley, heavies, archies, zeppelins, Bing Boys – the words, fragrant and agonisingly evocative, sang over the song like a descant.

> – So just you stand and wait
> By the garden gate
> Till my ship comes bouncing o'er the foam.
> We'll be together
> For ever and ever,
> Never more to roam –

He lay transfixed, breathing hard. This was no operation of what the old SF writers called a 'time-warp': this was really a film, really a story, and they had all been caught in it. The whole thing was fictitious, they were all characters in somebody's dream.

> – He'll be coming,
> We'll be coming,
> I'll be coming home.

He vaulted from his bunk. He shook Sergeant Lightbody. 'We've got to get out of here,' he panted. 'There's something wrong, something evil.'

'Just what I've been trying to tell you all along,' said Sergeant Lightbody calmly. 'But we can't do anything about it.'

'Oh, pipe down for Christ's sake,' called a sergeant trying – for all sea-time was one – to sleep.

'You don't understand,' said Tristram urgently, still shaking. 'It's evil because it's unnecessary. If they want to kill us why don't they just get on with it, here and now? Why didn't they kill us over on B6? But they don't want that. They want us to go through an illusion –'

'An illusion of choice,' said Sergeant Lightbody. 'I'm inclined to agree with you now. I think it's going to be a rather prolonged illusion. Not too prolonged, I hope.'

'But why, why?'

'Perhaps because we've a government that believes in everybody having the illusion of free will.'

'Do you think this ship's really moving?' Tristram listened. The ship's engines organ-stopped on, comforting to the belly as a warm poultice, but it was impossible to tell whether –

'I don't know. I don't care.'

The ship's Orderly Sergeant came in, a boily young man with horse-teeth and a neck like twisted cables. He wore a cap and an arm-band – SOS. 'What's going on up there?' asked Tristram.

'How should I know? Bleeding fed up I am, copping this lot.' He dove into his thigh-pocket. 'Ought to be a post corporal,' he said. He shuffled letters. Letters? 'Got enough to flipping do. The O.C. Troops is a right bastard. Here,' he said, throwing the bundle in the middle of a card-game 'Roll on, Death, and let's have a go at the angels.'

'Where did you get those?' frowned Sergeant Lightbody, puzzled.

'From the Ship's Orderly Room. They reckon they got them dropped by helicopter.' There was a scramble. One of the card-players whined, 'Just as I got a decent effin hand, too.'

One for him, one for Tristram. His first, his very first, his literally the absolutely bloody first since joining. Was this ominous, part of the film? He knew the writing; it made his heart dance. He lay on his bunk, very weak and trembling, to slice it open with a delirious finger, sweating. Yes, yes, yes, yes. It was her, she, his loving – sandalwood and camphorwood. Dearest dearest Tristram, changes in mad world, strange happening parted so unhappily, nothing can say here except miss you, love you, long for – He read it four times, then seemed to faint. Coming to, he found he was still clutching it. – Pray daily sea will send you back to me. Love you and if ever hurt you sorry. Come back to your – Yes, yes, yes, yes. He would live. He would. They wouldn't get him. He trembled down from his bunk to the deck, squeezing the letter like his week's pay. Then he unashamedly knelt down, closed eyes, joined hands. Sergeant Lightbody gaped at that. One of the card-players said, 'Bugger there having a word with the C.O.' and dealt swiftly and with skill.

Six

THREE more days in the ship's womb, perpetual electric light, beating of the engines, sweating of the bulkheads, hum of the ventilators. Hard-boiled eggs for breakfast, slabs of bread and bully for lunch, cake for tea, cocoa and cheese for supper, constipation (a new day-long preoccupation) at the troops' heads. And then, one sleepy afterlunch, hooting from above and counter-hooting, very distant, later a heavy grating unwinding of a mile of anchor-chain, the voice of the Ship's R.S.M. over the Tannoy: 'Disembarkation at 1700 hours, tea-meal at 1600 hours, parade on troop-decks in F.S.M.O. at 1630 hours.'

'Can you hear that noise?' asked Sergeant Lightbody, frowning hard in the direction of his cocked left ear.

'Guns?'

'That's what it sounds like.'

'Yes.' Bits of old song spiralled through Tristram's brain, fuming up from some forgotten source: '– We were up at Loos When you were on the booze, The booze that no one here knows.' (Where was Loos and what were they doing there?) 'Take me back to dear old Blighty, Put me on the train to –' (Blighty was a wound that got you repatriated, wasn't it? The wound glowed desirably, so did England; England and the wound became one. How tragic man's lot.) Drearily, members of his platoon were droning in sentimental reprise:

> We'll be together
> For ever and ever,
> Never more to roam –

Tristram chewed and chewed at the dry seedcake they were given for tea; he almost had to push the bolus down with his finger. After tea he put on the greatcoat which, with its row of metal buttons straight down the front, gave him the look of a child's drawing of a man, and the shallow steel helmet like an inverted bird-bath. He heaved on his back-pack and hung his side-pack; he clipped on his ammunition-pouches and dryly clicked his pistol. Soon, an upright soldier, he was ready for his platoon and Mr Dollimore. When he entered their mess-deck he found Mr Dollimore already there, saying, 'This old country we love so well. We'll do our best for her, won't we, chaps?' His eyes shone through their glasses, his forehead was as moist as the bulkheads. The platoon averted their eyes, embarrassed. Tristram suddenly felt a great love for them.

Sea-air blew in icily: the hatches were open. Over the Tannoy the Ship's R.S.M. began, indifferently, to call out the order of disembarkation. Tristram had time to clomp out on deck. Darkness, rare lamps, ropes, hawsers, spitting jerseyed seamen, razor cold, thumps and crashes from the land, explosive flashes. 'Where are we?' Tristram asked a sailor with a flat face. The sailor shook his head and said that he didn't speak English: *'Ying kuo hua, wo pu tung.'* Chinese. The sea hissed and whooshed, the language of a foreign sea. Foreign? He wondered.

Platoon after platoon minced down the steep ramp in their great boots. A dark quay reeked of oil. Lamps were few, as if some modified black-out regulation prevailed. RTO men loped round with clipboards. MPs strolled in pairs. A red-tabbed major with a false patrician accent haw-hawed, slapping his flank with a leather-bound baton. Mr Dollimore was summoned, with other subalterns, to a brief conference near some sheds. Inland the crumps of heavies and squeals of shells, sheet lightning, all part of the war film. An unknown captain with corniculate moustaches spoke to open-mouthed Mr Dollimore and his fellows, gesticulating much. Where were the brigade's own captains? Tristram, uneasy, could see no officer of the brigade higher than lieutenant. So. Captain Behrens had merely escorted his company to the ship. Only lieutenants and below, then, considered expendable. Mr Dollimore came back, rather breathily saying that they had to march to the base camp, a mile inland.

They marched off, led by the strange captain, platoon after platoon. The troops sang softly, nocturnally:

> We'll be coming home,
> Coming, coming home.
> Some day soon,
> January or June,
> Evening, morning or afternoon –

Moonless the early evening. The flashes showed pruned trees like stage cut-outs on either side of the metalled road. Hedgeless, farmless country. But Corporal Haskell said, 'I know this place. I swear I do. There's something in the air. Soft. Kerry or Clare or Galway. I travelled this whole west coast in peacetime,' he said almost apologetic-ally. 'Buying and selling, you know. I know this part of Ireland like the back of my hand. A rainy softness,' he said, 'if you catch my meaning. So it's the Micks we're going to fight. Well. Devils for a scrap they are. No hard feelings after, though. Cut your head and plaster it.'

Approaching the base camp they marched to attention. Barbed-wire perimeter, concrete gate-posts, an unsteady gate skirred open by the sentry. Huts with lights. Little activity. A man walking singing, balancing cakes on top of mugs of tea. The doleful hollow clatter of table-laying in a hovel lettered SERGEANTS' MESS, the smell of frying in fat not hot enough. The draft was halted; the men were told off, platoon after platoon, to follow to their allotted barrack-rooms conducting C3 lance-corporals in plimsolls (smug with the smugness of depot staff); the sergeants were led to quarters without comfort – one bare transit-camp red bulb in the ceiling, dusty kapok-oozing biscuits to lie on, no bedsteads, no extra blankets, a dirty stove unlighted. A gaunt C.Q.M.S. was their conductor. 'Where are we?' asked Tristram. 'Base Camp 222.' 'Yes, we know that, but where?' He sucked his teeth in answer and went off.

'Listen,' said Sergeant Lightbody, standing, their kit dumped, by the door with Tristram. 'Do you notice anything queer about that crumping noise?'

'There are so many noises.'

'I know, but just listen. It's coming from over there. Dada *rump*, dada *rump*, dada *rump*. Can you pick it out?'

'I think so.'

'Dada *rump*. Dada *rump*. What does it remind you of?'

'It's a very regular sort of rhythm, isn't it? I see what you mean: *too* regular.'

'*Exactly*. Doesn't it remind you a bit of the C.O.'s farewell speech?'

'Good God,' said Tristram, freshly shocked. 'A

cracked gramophone record. Would that be possible?'

'Very much possible. Loud amplifiers. Magnesium flashes. Electronic war, gramophony war. And the enemy, poor devils, are seeing and hearing it too.'

'We've got to get out of here,' trembled Tristram.

'Nonsense. You're as trapped here as you were on that ship. An electrified perimeter, a sentry told to shoot without asking questions. We've got to see it through.'

But they walked together to the twelve-feet-high wire fence. It was a sturdy piece of knitting. Tristram sprayed the damp ground with the platoon torch. 'There,' he said. In the tiny spotlight lay a sparrow's corpse, charred as from a grill. Then a rabbity lance-corporal approached them, capless, tunic collar undone, swinging an empty tea-mug. 'Keep away from there, mate,' he said, with depot staff insolence. 'Electric, that is. A lot of volts. Burn you to buggery.'

'Where exactly are we?' asked Sergeant Lightbody.

'Base Camp 222.'

'Oh, for God's sake,' cried Tristram. *'Where?'*

'That doesn't apply,' said the lance-corporal with a sagacity worthy of his stripe. *'Where* doesn't mean anything. It's just a bit of land, that's all.' They could hear motor noises in crescendo on the road outside the camp. A three-ton lorry bounced by with full lights, travelling to the coast, then another, another, a convoy of ten. The lance-corporal stood to attention till the last tail-light had passed. 'The dead,' he said, with quiet satisfaction. 'Lorry-loads of corpses. And just to think, only two nights ago some of that lot were in here, taking a stroll before supper as you are, talking to me as it might be yourselves.' He shook his head in factitious grief. The distant gramophone record went Dada *rump*, dada *rump*.

Seven

NEXT morning, shortly after mass, they were told that they would be going up to the front that very evening, a 'show' of some sort being imminent. Mr Dollimore shone with joy at the prospect. 'Blow out, you bugles, over the rich dead!' he quoted, tactless, to his platoon.

'You seem to have the death-urge pretty strongly,' said Tristram, cleaning his pistol.

'Eh? Eh?' Mr Dollimore recalled himself from his index of first lines. 'We shall survive,' he said. 'The Boche will get what's coming to him.'

'The Boche?'

'The enemy. Another name for the enemy. During my officers' training course,' said Mr Dollimore, 'we had films every evening. It was always the Boche. No, I'm telling a lie. Sometimes it was Fritz. And Jerry, sometimes.'

'I see. And you also had war poetry?'

'On Saturday mornings. After break. For our morale, Captain Auden-Isherwood said. That was one of my favourite lessons.'

'I see.'

A cold dry day with a dusty wind. Barbed wire of high voltage, WD signboards, blasted-looking country beyond the perimeter, dispiriting as that bilious Atlantic had been, all round B6. There were still distant crashes and bumps – a twenty-four-hour performance, probably with three shifts of lance-corporal disc-jockeys – but no fire in the sky. At noon an ancient aircraft – strings, struts, an open cockpit and waving goggled aeronaut – lurched over the camp and away again. 'One of ours,' Mr Dollimore told his platoon. 'The gallant R.F.C.' Luncheon of bully and dehydrated greens reconstituted; a couple of hours on the charpoy; a tea-meal of fish-paste and Arbuckle's Individual Fruit Pies. Then, with the sun's wreck seaward – a celestial panful of broken eggs – came the drawing of ammunition from the quarter-master's stores, also a tin of bully per man and a grey hunk of cornbread. The bully-tin had a Chinese label whose key-words were:

Tristram grinned at that; any fool could read the bifurcated second word (the essence of man, then, to the Chinese, was bifurcation?) if he had a sister who worked in China. What, incidentally, had happened to her? What to his brother in America? He had received one letter in eleven months, one only, from one person dear to him, but that person most dear. He patted his breast-pocket where it lay safe. *Shou Jên*, eh? The Romanized transliteration was clear at the bottom of the label. Ripe, soft, properly cooked man.

Twilight, and they paraded in marching order, water-bottles filled, bayonets fixed, steel helmets covered with steel-helmet covers. Mr Salter of one of the other battalions appeared to take the parade, newly promoted to

Captain Salter and self-conscious about it. He seemed to have directions written out for him on a bit of paper; there was no guide. He told them, squeaking a little, to move to the right in threes, and Tristram, moving, wondered for the first time at that anachronism. Surely, in that prototypical war, they had formed fours? But the essence of modern war seemed to be eclectic simplicity: let us not be too pedantic. They marched to attention out of camp. Nobody waved them good-bye except the sentry who should, by rights, have saluted with his rifle. They left-wheeled and, after a quarter-mile, marched at ease. Nobody sang, though. The fixed bayonets looked like a Birnam Wood of spikes. Between crumps, bumps, thumps – more widely spaced than before and, surely, that cracked record had been discarded – one could hear the glug of bouncing water in water-bottles. There were flashes of sky-fire; on either side of the road the black cut-out tree-corpses stood out bleakly in the sudden light.

They marched through a hamlet, a contrived Gothic mess of ruins, and a few hundred yards outside it were given the order to halt. 'You will now micturate,' ordered Captain Salter. 'Fall out.' They fell out; the duller men found out quickly what that long word meant: the road was cosy with the comfortable warm noise of hissing. They were fallen in again. 'We are very near the front line now,' said Captain Salter, 'and subject to enemy shelling.' ('Nonsense,' thought Tristram.) 'We will march in file, hugging the left of the road.' From *tre corde* to *una corda*, like a piano damped. The draft was attenuated into a single long string, and the march was resumed. After another mile they came, on the left, to what seemed to be a ruined country house.

Captain Salter consulted his scrap of paper in a sky-flash, as if to see whether this was the right number. Seemingly satisfied, he marched boldly in by the front door. The long stream followed. Tristram was interested to find that they had entered a trench. 'Queer sort of 'ouse this is,' grumbled a man, as if he had genuinely thought they had been invited to supper there. It was a mere shell, like something from a film-set. Tristram flashed the platoon torch down at the earth – holes, a tangle of wires, the sudden scurry of a small beast with a long tail – and immediately heard 'Put that bloody light out.' He obeyed; the voice sounded authoritative. Warnings were passed down the endless line – 'Hole – 'ole – 'owl; wire – wayer – wah' – like specimens of English sound changes. Tristram stumbled on at the head of No. 1 Section of his platoon, seeing the whole montage clearly as the sky flashed with fireworks (that's what they were, that's what they *must* be). Surely there should be a reserve line, a support line, sentries on fire-steps, smoke and stink from dug-outs? The whole labyrinth seemed quite deserted, nobody to welcome them in. Suddenly they turned right. Ahead men were stumbling, cursing softly, being crammed into dug-outs.

'The enemy,' whispered Mr Dollimore with awe, 'is only about a hundred yards away. Over there.' He pointed, lit up finely by a great flash, in the direction of no-man's-land or whatever it was called. 'We must post sentries. One every forty or fifty yards.'

'Look,' said Tristram, 'who's in charge. What are we? Who do we belong to?'

'Dear me, what a lot of questions.' He gazed mildly, in a new firework flash, on Tristram.

'What I mean,' said Tristram, 'is – we are reinforcements for some troops or other already in the line, or
are we –? *What* are we? Where are our orders coming
from? What orders have we got?'

'Now, Sergeant,' said Mr Dollimore paternally, 'don't
worry about all these big issues. Those will be taken
care of, never fear. Just make sure the men get settled in
properly. Then arrange about sentries, will you?' Meanwhile, the harmless racket continued: the record-players
banged away at their simulacra of passionate war: the
loudspeakers must be very close. Lights of exquisite
intensity spewed, like fancy oil, out of the ground.
'Woonderful,' said a man from Northern Province, peep-
ing out of his dug-out.

'What,' said Tristram, persistent, 'is the point of posting sentries? There's no enemy over there. The whole
thing's a fake. Very shortly this trench will blow up and
the blowing-up will be done by remote control, by some
bloody big spider sitting at base. Don't you see? This is
the new way, the modern way, of dealing with excess
population. The noises are fakes. The flashes are fakes.
Where's our artillery? Did you see any artillery behind
the lines? Of course you didn't. Have you seen any
shells or shrapnel? Stick your head over that parapet
and what do you think will happen?' Tristram clam-
bered up some bags filled with earth, a neat pattern,
obviously bricklayers' work, and looked out. He saw,
momentarily lighted by a firework, a flat stretch of
country with a distant vista of trees, hills beyond.
'There,' he said, stepping down.

'I've a good mind,' said Mr Dollimore, shaking, 'to
put you under arrest. I've a good mind to strip you right

down. I've a good mind –'

'You can't.' Tristram shook his head. 'You're only a lieutenant. Your Temporary Acting Captain Salter can't do it, either. And that's another thing you can tell me – where are the senior officers? There's not one officer of field rank anywhere to be found. Where's Battalion HQ, for instance? I come back to my former question – who's giving the orders?'

'This is insubordination,' shook Mr Dollimore. 'This is also treason.'

'Oh, come, nonsense. Look,' said Tristram, 'it's your duty to tell these men what's going on. It's your duty to march them back to the Base Camp to stop them getting officially slaughtered. It's your duty to start asking a few questions.'

'Don't tell me my duty.' Mr Dollimore, surprisingly, unholstered his pistol. 'I've a good mind to shoot you,' he said. 'I'm entitled to. Spreading alarm and despondency.' It was as though he had acute dengue: the pistol rocked violently.

'You've got the safety-catch on,' said Tristram. 'Such bloody nonsense. You wouldn't have the guts. I'm getting out of here.' He about-turned.

'Oh, no, you're not.' And to Tristram's extreme astonishment, Mr Dollimore, safety-catch evidently off, fired. Crack, and the bullet whined well off target, bedding itself safe in an earth-bag. Some of the troops peeped out, chewing or, chewing suspended, gaping at the noise of a real weapon.

'All right,' sighed Tristram. 'But just wait, that's all. You'll see that I'm right, you idiot.'

Eight

But Tristram was not entirely right. His own common sense ought to have told him that there was a flaw in his violent supposition. Mr Dollimore shook off to whatever pathetic headquarters A/T/Captain Salter had contrived. Tristram looked in on his platoon. Corporal Haskell said, 'Know what I found, Sarge? A bit of shamrock. That proves where we are pretty well, doesn't it?'

'Can you think why we should be here?' asked Tristram.

Corporal Haskell made a frog-face and said, 'Fighting the Micks, as I said. Though why we should be fighting them, God alone knows. Still, we don't know half of what goes on, do we? From what I heard on the news a couple of weeks ago, I should have thought it would have been the Chinese. Perhaps the Irish and the Chinese are all tied up together.'

Tristram wondered whether he ought to enlighten Corporal Haskell, a good decent family man by the look of him. *They'd never believe me.* A callow officer-voice was singing that some yards up the trench. A session of ancient war-songs, then, on these officers' training courses? Tristram wondered whether he could risk now making his quiet get-away. But, seeing the whole thing as a trap, a contrivance, he knew that there was no way back, behind the lines. If there was any way at all, it lay ahead, over the top and the best of luck. He said to Corporal Haskell, 'Are you quite certain this is the west coast of Ireland?'

'As certain as I'm certain of anything.'

'But you couldn't say exactly where?'

'No,' said Corporal Haskell, 'but I'd say we definitely weren't as far north as Connaught. That means it must be Galway or Clare or Kerry.'

'I see. And how would one set about getting to the other coast?'

'You'd have to pick up the railway, wouldn't you? All old steam trains they have here in Ireland, or used to have when I was doing my travelling. Let me see. If this is Kerry, then you could get from Killarney to Dungarvan. Or further north it might be from Listowel across Limerick and Tipperary and Kilkenny to Wexford. Or, supposing we're in County Clare –'

'Thank you, Corporal.'

'Couldn't be done, of course, not if we're at war with the Micks. They'd cut your throat as soon as they heard the way you speak.'

'I see. Thanks, anyway.'

'You weren't thinking of doing a bunk, were you, Sarge?'

'No, no, of course not.' Tristram left the close stinking dug-out, full of lolling men, and went to have a word with the nearest sentry. The sentry, a spotty lad called Burden, said:

'They've been moving in over there, Sarge.'

'Where? Who?'

'Over there.' He bowed his steel helmet towards the opposed trenches. Tristram listened. Chinese? There was a murmuring of rather high-pitched voices. The recorded noises of battle had slackened a great deal. So.

His heart sank. He had been wrong, quite wrong. There *was* an enemy. He listened more closely. 'Been moving in real quick, they have, quiet too. Seem to be a very well behaved lot.'

'It won't be long now, then,' said Tristram.

As if to confirm that statement, Mr Dollimore came stumbling along the trench. He saw Tristram and said, 'You, is it? Captain Salter says you ought to be put under close arrest. But he also says it's too late now. We attack at 2200 hours. Synchronize watches.'

'Attack? How attack?'

'There you are again, asking your foolish questions. We go over the top at 2200 hours sharp. It is now –' he checked '– exactly 2134. Fixed bayonets. Our orders are to take that enemy trench.' He was bright and feverish.

'Who gave the orders?'

'Never you mind who gave the orders. Alert the platoon. All rifles loaded, not forgetting one up the spout.' Mr Dollimore stood upright, looking important. 'England,' he suddenly said, and his nose filled with tears. Tristram, having nothing further to say in the circumstances, saluted.

At 2140 hours there was sudden silence like a smack in the face. 'Cor,' said the men, missing the cosy noise. Lights ceased to flash. In this unfamiliar hushed dark the enemy could more clearly be heard, coughing, whispering, in the light tones of small-boned Orientals. At 2145 men stood, breathing hard through their mouths, all along the trench. Mr Dollimore, pistol trembling, eyes never leaving his wrist-watch, was ready to lead his thirty over (some corner of a foreign field) in brave assault, owing God a death (that is for ever England). 2150 and all hearts were all but audible. Tristram knew his own part in this impending suicide: if Mr Dollimore's office was to pull the men over, his own was to push them: 'Get up and out there, you scabs, or I shoot every cowardly one of you.' 2155. 'O God of battles,' Mr Dollimore was whispering, 'steel my soldier's heart.' 2156. 'I want my mum,' mock-sobbed a Cockney humorist. 2157. 'Or,' said Corporal Haskell, 'if we were far south enough you could get from Bantry to Cork.' 2158. The bayonets trembled. Somebody started hiccoughs and kept saying, 'Pardon.' 2159. 'Ah,' said Mr Dollimore, and he watched his second-hand as if it were an act in a flea circus. 'We're coming up now to, we're coming up now to –'

2200. Whistles skirled shrilled deadly silver all along the line, and the phonographic bombardment clamoured out at once dementedly. In mean spasmodic flashes Mr Dollimore could be seen, clambering over, waving his pistol, his mouth stretched in some inaudible OCTU battle-cry. 'Go on, you lot,' shouted Tristram, prodding with his own gun, pushing, threatening, kicking. The troops mounted, some with fair agility. 'No, no,' panicked one small gnarled man, 'for Christ's sake don't make me.' 'Over you go, blast you,' snarled Tristram's dentures. Corporal Haskell yelled, from above, 'Jesus, they're coming for us!' Rifles bitterly cracked and spattered, filling the sharp air with the sharper smoked-bacon tang of a thousand struck matches. Bullets dismally whinged. There were deep bloody curses, there were screams. Tristram, his head above the parapet, saw etched black cut-out bodies facing each other in hand-to-hand, clumsy, falling, firing, jabbing, in some old film about soldiers. He distinctly observed Mr Dollimore falling back (always this element of the absurd: as if he were in a dance and were trying to keep to his feet to go on dancing) and then crashing with his mouth open. Corporal Haskell was caught savagely in the leg; firing as he fell he opened his mouth (as for the host) for a bullet and his face disintegrated. Tristram, one knee on the topmost earth-bag, emptied his pistol wildly at the staggering advance. It was slaughter, it was mutual massacre, it was impossible to miss. Tristram reloaded, now belatedly infected with poor dead Dollimore's ague, scrambling backwards into the trench, his booted toes digging into the interstices of the earth-bags, his helmeted head, eyes and shooting hand above the parapet. And he saw the enemy. A strange race, small, bulky at chest and hips, high-screaming like women. They were all going down, the air full of tasty smoke, still zinging with bullets. And, seeing, a cold reserved chamber of his brain fitting everything into place, all this foreshadowed by that Sacred Game of Pelagian times, he retched and then vomited a whole sour gutful of chewed meat. One of his own men turned back to the trench, clawing air, having dropped his rifle, choking, 'Oh, bloody Christ.' And then a groan from behind his sternum as bullets entered his back. He toppled like a tumbler over, taking Tristram with him, all arms and legs, essence of man, bifurcation. Tristram, smashed hard against the rocking duckboards, struggled with the dead-weight incubus that snored out the last of its life, then heard from the flanks, as from stage-wings, the dry rain of machine-

gun fire, manifestly a live noise against the sham cacophony of bombardment. 'Finishing them off,' he
thought, 'finishing them off.'

Then all the big noise ceased, nor were there any
specifically human sounds, only animal gasps of those
late in dying. One last flash showed him his watch:
2203. Three minutes from start to finish. With great
difficulty he heaved the corpse off his stomach on to the
trench-floor; it groaned, collapsing. Fearful, he crawled
away sorely to whimper alone, the smell of the
monstrous smoked-bacon breakfast still swirling above.
His sobs started up irrepressibly; soon he was howling
with despair and horror, seeing, as if the darkness were
a mirror, his own wretched screwed face, tongue licking
the tears, the lower lip thrust out quivering with anger
and hopelessness.

When this ghastly transport had spent itself, he
fancied he heard the renewal of battle above him. But
it was only single cracks of pistol-shot, irregularly
spaced. Looking up in terror he saw torch-beams searching, as if for something lost in the shambles of bodies.
He stiffened in great fear. 'The old coop de gracy,' said a
coarse voice. 'Poor little bitch.' Then a couple of cracked
peremptory shots. A torch searched, searched, over the
trench-lip, searching for him. He lay, his face bunched
anew, like one who had met violent death. 'Poor old
bugger,' said the coarse voice and a resonant bullet
seemed to meet bone. 'Sergeant here,' said another voice.
'He's had it all right.' 'Better make sure,' said the first.
'Oh, hell,' said the other, 'I'm sick of this job. Real sick.
It's dirty, it's filthy.' Tristram felt the torch-beam travel
over his shut eyes, then pass on. 'All right,' said the

first. 'Pack it in. If they'll let you. You,' to someone more distant. 'Leave all pockets alone. No looting. Have some respect for the dead, blast you.' The boots crunched on over the field; more odd shots. Tristram lay on in dead stiffness, not budging even when some small animal ran over him busily, sniffing and twitching whiskers on his face. Human silence returned, but he lay on for an age longer, frozen.

Nine

AT last, in that dead but safe stillness, Tristram torch-lighted his way into the dug-out where Corporal Haskell had taught him the geography of Ireland, where the first section of his platoon had awaited, singing, lolling, fidgeting, action. It was still, sealed by its blanket-door, foul-smelling, odorous of life. Packs and water-bottles lay about, perhaps including his own, for he had dumped these impedimenta with one of the sections on moving into the trench. The battery-fed dug-out lantern had been doused before the attack and he did not re-light it. His torch showed a pile of money on the table – guineas, septs, tosheroons, crowns, tanners, quids, florins; this, he knew, was the pooled cash of the platoon, useless to the dead but a prize for the survivors – an ancient tradition. Tristram, sole survivor, bowed his head as he fed the money into his pockets. He then filled a random pack with tinned meat, strapped a full water-bottle on to his belt, and loaded his pistol. He sighed, facing another anabasis.

He stumbled out of the trench, tripping over the corpses in the tiny no-man's-land, not daring to use his torch yet in the open. He felt his way into and out of the opposed trench, a very shallow one, and then marched, wincing at the pain of that fall from parapet to duckboards so long ago, fearful of possible lurking gunmen. Bare ground stretched under faint starlight. After what he judged to be a mile's walking he saw lights ahead on the horizon, dim, widely spaced. Cautious, his pistol out, he trudged on. The lights glowed bigger, more like fruit than seeds. Soon he saw, fear beating hard in him, a high wire fence stretching on either hand indefinitely, a pattern of illuminated and penumbral close steel weaving. Probably electrified, like the Base Camp perimeter. There was nothing for it but to walk parallel to it (there was no cover of trees or bushes) and seek, ready with bluff, threats, force, some legitimate way through, if any.

At length he saw, and carefully approached, a sort of gateway let into the endless fence, the gate itself a firm metal frame garnished with barbed wire. Beyond was a wooden shack with a single dim-lighted window and, outside the door of this shack, stood a greatcoated, helmeted sentry nearly asleep on his feet. Hut, gate, wire, dark, sentry – nothing else. The sentry came alive with a startled jerk, seeing Tristram, and pointed his rifle. 'Open up,' ordered Tristram.

'Where've you come from?' His rather dim-witted face was uneasy.

'I've got a rank, haven't I?' blustered Tristram. 'Let me through. Take me to the N.C.O. in charge.'

'Sorry, Sergeant. It was a bit of a shock, like. First

time I've seen anybody coming through from that side.'
This was going to be easy. The sentry opened the gate,
which whirred along the ground on casters, and said,
'This way.' There was evidently no other way. 'Sergeant.' He led Tristram to the shack of a guard-room,
opened the door, showed him in. A bulb of low wattage
glowed like an orange from the ceiling; on the wall were
framed standing orders and a map. Corporal Haskell's
nose had been astonishingly accurate: it was a map of
Ireland. At a table, cleaning his nails, his feet on a
chair, sat a corporal not unlike Charles Baudelaire in
hair and expression. Tristram rapped, 'Stand up, Corporal.' The corporal knocked the chair over in his haste,
responding to Tristram's officer-accent more than his
stripes. 'All right,' said Tristram, 'sit down again. Are
you in charge here?'

'Sergeant Forester's asleep, Sarnt. I'd better wake him
up.'

'Don't trouble.' He decided to swell his bluff to skin-
bursting. 'What I'm after is transport. Where can I get
transport?'

The corporal stared as Charles Baudelaire stares from
his daguerreotype. 'Nearest M.T. park's at Dingle.
Depends where you want to get to.'

'I've got to report about this last show,' said Tristram.
'May I see that map?' He walked over to the fubsy
multi-coloured beast that was Ireland. Dingle was, of
course, on Dingle Bay; Dingle Bay and Tralee Bay had
carved a peninsula out of County Kerry. He saw everything now: various islands and teats on the west coast
were marked with WD flags, leased presumably for
ostensible training purposes by the Government of All

263

Ireland to the British War Department. 'I see, I see,' said Tristram.

'Where would it be,' said the corporal, 'that you'd be wanting to get to?'

'You should know better than to ask that question,' reproved Tristram. 'There *is* such a thing as security, you know.'

'Sorry, Sarnt. Sarnt,' asked the corporal shyly, 'what *really* goes on in there, Sarnt?' He pointed in the direction of the huge enclosed battleground.

'You mean to say you don't know?'

'Nobody's allowed in, Sarnt. Nobody's ever let in there. We just hear the noises, that's all. A very real kind of training it is, from the sound of it. But nobody's ever allowed through to see it, Sarnt. That's in the standing orders.'

'And how about letting people out?'

'Well, there's nothing about that, you see. Nobody ever comes out this way, that's why, I suppose. You're the first I've ever seen, and I've been on this job nine months. Hardly worth while having a gate here, is it?'

'Oh, I don't know,' said Tristram. 'It's served its purpose tonight, hasn't it?'

'That's true,' said the corporal, in a kind of awe as at the provisions of all-providing providence. 'That's very true.' And then, helpfully, 'Of course, you could always get a train to wherever it is you've got to go to, couldn't you, Sarnt?'

'The station?'

'Oh, only a mile or two down that road. Branch-line to Tralee. There's a train takes shift-workers to Killarney about two in the morning. You'd easily get that if that's any good to you.'

To think, just to think: it was still the same night and yet it seemed a whole slab of time somehow outside time since the blasting of those whistles. Sergeant Lightbody, he suddenly remembered, had talked about going to find a great perhaps: queer to think that he had already long found it. No longer a perhaps, of course. Tristram shivered.

'You don't look all that good, Sarnt. Are you sure you can make it?'

'I can make it,' said Tristram. 'I've got to make it.'

Epilogue

One

TRALEE to Killarney, Killarney to Mallow. Tristram had
bad dreams most of the way, slumped, greatcoat-collar
up, in a corner seat. A high-pitched voice seemed to be
keeping the score over the steam-train's noise: 'Say
twelve hundred seen off tonight, say ten stone average,
women being lighter than men, say twelve thousand
stone deadweight. Multiply by one thousand, making
twelve million stone – on the bone, on the hoof – for one
night's (convert to tons at leisure) good global work.' His
platoon paraded, pointing sadly at him because he was
still alive. Coming into Mallow he awoke fighting. An
Irish labourer held him down, calming him, saying,
'Dere y'are, fella.' He travelled by day from Mallow to
Rosslare. He spent the night in a hotel in Rosslare and
in the morning, having seen Military Police prowling
around, bought a ready-made suit, raincoat, shirt, pair
of shoes. He stuffed his army clothes into his pack – first
having given away his tins of meat to a poor whining
crone who said, 'May Jesus, Mary and Joseph bless ya,
acushla.' His pistol in his pocket, he boarded the packet
for Fishguard as a civilian.

It was a rough February crossing, St George's Channel
rearing and snorting like a dragon. He felt ill at Fishguard and spent the night there. The next day, in

chilled sunshine like hock, he travelled south-east to Brighton. At least, the ticket he bought was for Brighton. After Salisbury he yielded to a compulsive desire to count and re-count his money, the platoon's money: it came consistently to thirty-nine guineas, three septs, one tanner. He shivered perpetually, so that the other occupants of his compartment gave him curious stares. As they drew in to Southampton he decided he was really ill but probably had enough strength to alight at Southampton and find accommodation there to have the illness out. There were plenty of good reasons for not arriving, staggering and collapsing, in obvious need of help, everything beyond his control, at Brighton.

Near Southampton Central Station he found an Army hostel – the five bottom storeys of a skyscraper. He went in, showed his paybook, and paid for five nights' accommodation. He was taken by an old man in a faded blue servant's jacket to a small cold room, monastic, but with plenty of blankets on the bed. 'You all right?' said the old man. 'All right,' said Tristram. When the old man had left, he locked the door, undressed quickly and crept into bed. There he relaxed his hold and let the fever, like some devil or lover, take complete possession of him.

The endless shivering and sweating ate up time, place, sensation. He calculated, by the natural alternation of dark and light, that he lay in his bed for thirty-six hours, the sickness worrying and gnawing his body like a dog with a bone, the sweating so intense that his bladder was given a holiday, feeling himself grow palpably thinner and lighter, ridden at the crisis by a conviction that his body had become transparent, that each several inner organ shone phosphorescent in the dark, so that it seemed a scandalous waste no sister-tutor could bring her anatomy students to view him. Then he fell into a trench of sleep so deep that no dream or hallucination could reach him. He woke to morning, feeling he must have slept, like a bear or tortoise, a whole season away, for the sun in the room was like a spring sun. He yanked time painfully out of its hiding-place and computed that it must still be February, still winter.

Intense thirst drew him out of bed. He staggered to the wash-basin, took his chilled dentures out of their glass, then filled this again and again with the hard southern chalky water, glugging it down till finally he had to lie on his bed gasping. He had stopped shaking, but he still felt paper-thin. He rolled himself in his blankets and slept again. His brimming bladder woke him next time and, a little secret, he voided it in the wash-basin. Now he felt able to walk though very cold. That was because he had not eaten. The sun was setting, a chill evening closing in. He dressed without washing or shaving and went downstairs to the canteen. Soldiers sat about, drinking tea, moaning and bragging, their numbers not yet dry. Tristram asked for boiled hen-eggs and natural milk. Meat he did not dare even think of. He ate very slowly and felt a sort of promise of strength returning. He was intrigued to see that an ancient custom (its introduction to England attributed to a mythical seaman named John Player) had been revived: a few soldiers were choking over rolled paper tubes, the ends aglow. Cover yourselves in glow, in glow, dada *rump*. Tears burst audibly. He had better get back to bed.

He slept solid for another uncomputed slab of dark and light. When he woke, and this was suddenly, he found himself transferred to a region of great mental clarity. 'What do you propose?' asked the foot of the bed. 'Not to get caught,' answered Tristram aloud. He had been pressed into the army on 27 March, Easter Day of the previous year, and was due for demobilization exactly one year later. Till that date – over a month off – he could do nothing safely. He had failed to die: the War Department would probably chase him till he had made good that dereliction of duty. Would they, though, really care? He thought they would: they would be unhappy brooding over a nominal roll with a query instead of a tick against one name, a paybook missing. Perhaps even here, in this Army Hostel, he would not be safe. He felt, he thought, well enough to leave.

He washed and shaved thoroughly and then dressed with care as a civilian. He almost floated down the stairs, light as a shorn sheep: that illness had done him some good, purged him of gross humours. There were no military policemen in the vestibule. He had expected to walk out into morning but found, fully launched into the maritime city, that afternoon was well advanced. He ate fried fish in a back-street restaurant, then found, not too far from it, a dirty-looking lodging-block which would suit him well. No questions, no curiosity. He paid a week's rent in advance. His money would just about, he thought, last.

TWO

TRISTRAM spent the following four weeks fairly profitably. He recollected his function – that of a teacher of history and related subjects – and so, financed by his poor dead platoon, he treated himself to a brief course of rehabilitation. He sat all day in the Central Library, reading the great historians and historiographers of his age – Stott's *Twentieth-Century Ideological Struggles*; Zuckmayer and Feldwebel's *Principien der Rassens-geschichte*; Stebbing-Brown's *History of Nuclear War-fare*; Ang Siong-Joo's *Kung-Ch'an Chu I*; Sparrow's *Religious Substitutes in the Prototechnic Age*; Radzino-wicz on *The Doctrine of the Cycle*. They were all thin books in logogrammatic form, that clipped orthography designed to save space. But now there seemed to be enough space. For evening relaxation he read the new poets and novelists. The writers of the Pelphase seemed discredited, he noticed: one could not perhaps, after all, and it was a pity, make art out of that gentle old liberalism. The new books were full of sex and death, perhaps the only materials for a writer.

On 27 March, a Monday, in fine spring weather, Tristram travelled by rail to London. The War Office was situated in Fulham. He found it to be a block of offices in a skyscraper of moderate height (thirty storeys) called Juniper Building. A commissionaire said, 'You can't come in here, sir.'

'Why not?'

'Not without an appointment.'

Tristram snarled, 'Out of my way. You don't seem to know who I am,' and he pushed the commissionaire aside and strode into the first office he came to. Here a number of fattish blonde women in uniform were clacking at electric speech-machines. 'I want to see someone in charge,' said Tristram.

'You can't see anyone without an appointment,' said one of the young women. Tristram strode through this office and opened a door with a glazed upper half. A lieutenant sat, busily thinking, between two empty correspondence-trays. He said:

'Who let you in?' He had spectacles with big black frames, a sweet-eater's complexion, close-bitten nails, a patch of nap on his neck where he had shaved ill. Tristram said:

'That's a pointless sort of question, isn't it? My name's Sergeant Foxe, T. I'm reporting as the sole survivor of one of those pleasantly contrived miniature massacres on the West Coast of Ireland. I should prefer to talk to someone more important than you.'

'Survivor?' The lieutenant looked startled. 'You'd better come and report to Major Berkeley.' He rose from his desk, disclosing a desk-worker's paunch, then went out by a door opposite to the one by which Tristram had entered. A knock at this latter was answered by Tristram himself. It was the commissionaire. 'Sorry I let him get past me, sir,' he began to say. And then, 'Oh,' for Tristram had his pistol out: if they wanted to play at soldiers, let them. 'Barmy,' said the commissionaire and slammed the door quickly; his fast-retreating shadow could be seen through the glaze. The lieutenant returned. 'This way,' he said. Tristram followed him down

271

a corridor illuminated only by the light from other glazed doors; he pocketed his pistol.

'Sergeant Foxe, sir,' said the lieutenant, opening up on an officer pretending to be desperately engaged in the composition of an urgent despatch. He was a red-tabbed major with very fine auburn hair; he presented, writing, to Tristram a bald spot of the size and roundness of a communion host. On the walls were group photographs of dull-looking people mostly in shorts. 'Just one moment,' said the major severely, writing hard.

'Oh, come off it,' said Tristram.

'I beg your pardon?' The major glared up; his eyes were weak and oyster-coloured. 'Why aren't you in uniform?'

'Because, according to the terms of contract listed in my paybook, my engagement terminated today at 1200 hours precisely.'

'I see. You'd better leave us, Ralph,' said the major to the lieutenant. The lieutenant bowed like a waiter and left. 'Now,' said the major to Tristram, 'what's all this about your being the only survivor?' He did not seem to expect an immediate answer, for he followed up with, 'Let me see your paybook.' Tristram handed it over. He had not been asked to sit down, so he sat down. 'Hm,' said the major, opening, reading. He clicked a switch and spoke into a microphone: '7388026 Sergeant Foxe, T. File immediately, please.' And then, to Tristram, 'What have you come to see us about?'

'To register protest,' said Tristram. 'To warn you that I'm going to blow the bloody gaff.'

The major looked puzzled. He had a long nose which he now rubbed, puzzled. A buff file shot from a wall-slit into a wire basket; the major opened this file and read attentively. 'Ah,' he said, 'I see. Everybody's been looking for you, it seems. By rights you should be dead, shouldn't you? Dead, with the rest of your comrades. You must have made a very quick getaway. I could still have you arrested as a deserter, you know. Retrospectively.'

'Oh, nonsense,' said Tristram. 'As the sole survivor I was the head of that unfortunate murdered lot. It was up to me to make the decisions. I decided to send myself on a month's leave. I was also ill, and no wonder.'

'That's irregular, you know.'

'Let's not hear anything from you or your bloody murdering organization about irregularity,' said Tristram. 'A lot of murdering swine, that's what you are.'

'I see,' said the major. 'And you dissociate yourself from us, do you? I should imagine,' smoothly, 'you've done more killing than, say, I have. You've actually taken part in an E.S.'

'What's an E.S.?'

'Extermination Session. That's what the new battles are called, you know. I should imagine you did your share of – well, shall we call it self-defence? Otherwise, I can't see how you managed to survive.'

'We were given certain orders.'

'Of course you were. Orders to shoot. That's only reasonable, isn't it, when you're being shot at?'

'It was still murder,' said Tristram violently. 'Those poor, wretched, defenceless –'

'Oh, come, they weren't exactly defenceless, were they? Beware of clichés, Foxe. One cliché leads on to another, you know, and the final term of the series is

273

always absurd. They were well trained and well armed and they died gloriously, believing they were dying in a great cause. And, you know, they really were. And you survived, of course, for the most inglorious reason. You survived because you didn't believe in what we're fighting for, what we'll always be fighting for. Of course, you got dragged in at the beginning when the system was most imperfect. Our conscription system's very selective now. We don't call up suspicious people like you any more.'

'You just take advantage of the poor devils who don't know any better – is that it?'

'Of course. We're better off without the morons and the enthusiasts. Which means also the corner-boys and the criminals. And, as far as the women are concerned, the cretinous over-producers. That's genetically very sound, you know.'

'Oh God, God,' moaned Tristram, 'it's all sheer bloody madness.'

'Hardly. Look, you acted under orders. We all act under orders. The orders of the War Department come ultimately from the G.P.L.A.'

'Murderers, whoever they are.'

'Oh, no. The Global Population Limitation Authority. They don't, of course, actually give orders in the military sense. They merely report on population in relation to food supply – always with an eye to the future, of course. And their idea of a food supply is not the old primitive minimal notion – they're concerned with a high standard involving margins. I'm not an economist, incidentally, so don't ask me what margins are.'

'I know all about that,' said Tristram. 'I'm a historian.'

'Yes? Well, as I say, you should either have been kept on instructional duties – and somebody's going to get a rocket sooner or later over transferring you to combatant duties – or, what was I saying? Yes, you shouldn't have been called up at all.'

'I can see why you say that,' said Tristram. 'I know too much now, don't I? And I propose to write and talk and teach about your cynical murderous organization. This is no longer a police state. There are no spies, there's no censorship. I'll tell the bloody truth. I'll get the Government to act.'

The major was unperturbed. He stroked his nose in slow rhythm. 'Despite its name,' he said, 'the War Department is not really a branch of government at all. It's a corporation. The term "War Department" is merely a link with the past. A corporation with a charter. The charter comes up for renewal every three years, I think it is. I don't think there's any likelihood of its not being renewed. You see, what other way is there of keeping the population down? The birth-rate rose phenomenally last year and it's still rising. Not, of course, that there's anything wrong in that. Contraception is cruel and unnatural: everybody has a right to be born. But, similarly, everybody's got to die sooner or later. Our age-groups for call-up will get progressively older – as far, of course, as the healthy and mentally normal sections of the population are concerned; the trash can go shortly after puberty. Everybody must die, and history seems to show (you're a historian, so you'll agree with me here), history seems to show that the soldier's death is the best death. Facing fearful odds, as the poet says. Ashes of his fathers, temples of his gods, and so on. I don't think

275

you'd find anybody against the present system. The War Department is a bit like prostitution: it cleanses the community. If we didn't exist, a great deal of nastiness would bubble up in the State. We're the mother-of-pearl, you see. The ruffians, the perverts, the death-wishers: you don't want those in the civil community. So long as there's an army there'll never be a police state, no more greyboys or rubber truncheons or thumbscrews or rifle squads at inconveniently early hours. The final problems of the body politic have been solved. Now we have a free state – order without organization, which means order without violence. A safe and spacious community. A clean house full of happy people. But every house, of course, has to have a drainage system. We're that.'

'It's all wrong,' said Tristram. 'All, all wrong.'

'Yes? Well, when you can think out something better come and tell us all about it.'

With a tiny itch of hope, Tristram said, 'Do you think people are fundamentally good?'

'Well,' said the major, 'they now have a chance to be good.'

'Exactly,' said Tristram. 'Which means that it won't be long before the return of liberalism. I don't think a Pelagian State would renew your charter.'

'No?' The major was not very interested.

'You're signing your own death warrant just by existing.'

'That's a bit too epigrammatical for me,' said the major. 'Look, I've enjoyed this talk, but I really am rather busy. You should by rights, you know, go through the proper channels as far as your demobilization is concerned. But I'll sign your discharge, if you like, and

276

give you a chitty for the cashier's department.' He began to write. 'A gratuity of twenty guineas for each month of service. A month's *official* demobilization leave on full pay. Right. They'll work out the details for you. They'll pay you cash, seeing that you're such a suspicious sort of man.' He smiled. 'And,' he added, 'don't forget to hand that pistol in.' Tristram found, shocked, that he had been pointing it at the major. 'You'd better give it to me. We don't like violence all that much, you know. Shooting is for the army, and you're out of the army now, *Mister* Foxe.' Tristram meekly placed the pistol on the major's desk. He saw now that it would, after all, be wrong to shoot Derek. 'Any more questions?' said the major.

'Just one. What happens to the dead?'

'The dead? Oh, I see what you mean. When a soldier is discharged dead the soldier's paybook is collected and a letter of condolence sent to his – or her, of course – next-of-kin. After that the War Department has no further responsibility. Civilian contractors take over. We've learned something, you know, from the past: waste not, want not. What the civilian contractors do is their own affair. But the money comes in handy. The money keeps this corporation going. We're completely independent, you see, of the Treasury. I think that's something to be proud of. Any more questions?'

Tristram was silent.

'Good. Well, the best of luck, old man. Now I suppose you'll have to start looking for a job. You shouldn't have much difficulty with your qualifications.'

'And experience,' added Tristram.

'As you say.' Smiling cordially, he stood up to shake hands.

Three

TRISTRAM took the next tube-train to Brighton, saying to himself in time with the train's beat: 'Patience, patience, patience, patience.' The word summed up so much: patience of different lengths and weights, different lengths of waiting. When Brighton towered all around him his brain shuddered with memories, with expectations. Patience. Keep away from the sea, just for a little while. Do things properly.

He found the Education Department where it had always been: in Adkins Street, just off Rostron Place. Frank Gosport was in the Appointments Section, as he'd been before. He even recognized Tristram. 'You're looking well,' he said, 'really well. Just like somebody who's taken a long holiday. What can we do for you?' He was a pleasant round man, beaming, with fluffy hair like duck-down.

'A job,' said Tristram. 'A good job.'

'Hm. History, wasn't it? Civics and so on?'

'You've got a good memory,' said Tristram.

'Not all that good,' said Gosport. 'I can't recall your first name. Derek, isn't it? No, stupid of me, it can't be Derek. Derek Foxe is the Co-ordinating Secretary of the Ministry of Fertility. Of course, of course, he's your brother. It's all coming back to me. Your name begins with a T.' He pressed buttons on the wall; on the wall opposite, in letters of mild flame, details of vacancies appeared, frame after frame of mildly flaming letters. 'See anything you fancy?'

'South London (Channel) Unitary School (Boys) Division Four,' said Tristram. 'Who's Principal there now?'

'Same as before. Joscelyne. He got married, you know, to a real old battle-axe. Clever man, that. He swung with the tide, you know.'

'Like my brother Derek.'

'I suppose so. Fancy anything there?'

'Not really. Too many bad memories. I like the look of that lectureship at the Technical College. History of War. I think I could do that.'

'It's something new. Hardly any applicants. Shall I put you down for it?'

'I think so.'

'You could start at the beginning of the summer term. Do you know anything about war? My son's just had his calling-up papers.'

'Is he glad about it?'

'He's a young lout. The army ought to knock some sense into him. Good. You'd better go and look at the College sometime. It's a very nice building, I believe. The Principal's all right. Name of Mather. I think you'll get on all right.'

'Fine. Thanks.'

In Rostron Place Tristram found a house-and-flat agent's office. He was offered a very respectable apartment in Winthrop Mansions – two bedrooms, living-dining-room, fair-sized kitchen, fitted with refrigerator, stereotelly, and wall-spindle for the *Daily Newsdisc* or any of its auditory rivals. Having seen it, he took it, signing the usual form of agreement and paying a month's rent in advance. Then he did some shopping: kitchen utensils, provisions (a very fair variety in the new free-enterprise shops) and some underclothes, pyjamas and a dressing-gown.

And now. And now. And now. His heart pounding and fluttering like a bird in a paper-bag, he walked, trying to walk slowly, down to the sea-front. Crowds of people in the spring sun, encircled by fresh marine air, gulls cackling like heckelphones, the stony majesty of the offices of the Government. The Ministry of Fertility – bas-relief of an egg cracking open to display new-born wings – with a plaque saying: *Incorporating Departments of Food, Agriculture, Fecundity Research, Religion, Ritual and Popular Culture. Motto:* ALL LIFE IS ONE. And, looking, smiling nervously, Tristram decided that he didn't finally want to go in there after all, that there was nothing he could profitably say or do to his brother. He swung down in his swing for the last time, braking with his feet dug in the ground. For the victory was his, Tristram's, as this afternoon would show. What was most dearly his, Tristram's, he, Tristram, would, before ninety minutes or less were up, have regained. Finally. Utterly. That was the only kind of victory he needed.

High above Government Building the bronze robed figure with the baroque beard, baroque robe-folds, glared at the sun in this windless day, hair and clothes stirred by the baroque wind of the sculptor's fancy. Who was it? Augustine? Pelagius? Christ? Satan? Tristram fancied he caught the shine of tiny horns in the stirred mass of stone hair. He would have to wait, they would all have to wait. But he was very nearly confident that the cycle would start again, that figure preach to the sun and sea-clouds about man's ability to organize the good life, his lack of need for grace, the godhead implicit in him. Pelagius, Morgan, Old Man of the Sea.

He waited.

Four

'SEA,' whispered Beatrice-Joanna, 'teach us all sense.' She stood by the promenade rails, the gurgling woolly rosy twins belabouring each other softly in their perambulator. There it stretched all before her, endowed with delirium, panther-skin, mantle pierced with thousands upon thousands of the sun's idols, hydra absolute, drunk with its own blue flesh, biting its scintillating tail in a tumult like silence. 'Sea, sea, sea.'

Beyond the sea Robert Starling, late Prime Minister of Great Britain and Chairman of the Council of Prime Ministers of the English-Speaking Union, in a Mediterranean villa, surrounded by his sweet boys, eating delicately, sipping fruit-juice, reading the classics with his feet up, delicately calculated the end of his exile. On other shores of the sea the thalassographers prepared their attempts on the unplumbed green riches with new engines, cunning meters. Untouched life lurked, miles down, leagues down.

'Sea, sea.' And she prayed for someone, and the prayer was at once answered, but the answer did not come from the sea. It came from the warmer land behind her. A gentle hand on her arm. She turned, startled. Then, after her moment of wordless shock, she still had no words, only tears. She clung to him, the huge air, the life-giving sea, man's future history in the depths, the present towered town, the bearded man at the pinnacle, all shut out from the warmth of his presence, the closeness of his embrace. He became sea, sun, tower. The twins gurgled. There were still no words.

The wind rises . . . we must try to live. The immense air opens and closes my book. The wave, pulverized, dares to gush and spatter from the rocks. Fly away, dazzled, blinded pages. Break, waves. Break with joyful waters. . . .

1985

TO LIANA

CONTENTS

$2 + 2 = 5$

a notice put up in Moscow during the first Five Year Plan, indicating the possibility of getting the job done in four years, if workers put their backs into it

Part One

1984

Catechism

When did the twentieth-century nightmare begin?
In 1945, when, for many people, it seemed to have
ended.

How did it begin?
With the first use of atomic bombs, developed with
urgency to finish speedily a war that had gone on too long.
But with the end of the conflict between the fascist States
and the free world (which was not all free, because a great
part of it was totalitarian), the stage was cleared for the
enactment of the basic encounter of the century. The
communist powers faced the capitalist powers, and both
sides had unlimited nuclear weapons.

So that – ?
So that what had been used to end one war was now
employed to start another.

*What was the outcome of the Great Nuclear War of the
1950s?*
Countless atomic bombs were dropped on the industrial
centres of western Europe, the Americas and the Soviet
Empire. The devastation was so terrible that the ruling
élites of the world came to realize that nuclear warfare, in
destroying organized society, destroyed their own capacity for maintaining power.

So that – ?
By common consent the nuclear age was brought to an
end. Wars henceforth would be waged with conventional
weapons of the kind developed during the Second World
War. That wars should continue to be fought, and on a
global scale, was taken for granted.

*What was the disposition of the nations at the end of the
Great Nuclear War?*

The end of that war saw the world divided into three large power-units or superstates. Nations did not exist any more. Oceania was the name given to the empire comprising the United States, Latin America and the former British Commonwealth. The centre of authority was probably, but not certainly, North America, though the ideology that united the territories of the superstate had been developed by British intellectuals and was known as English Socialism or Ingsoc. The old geographical nomenclatures had ceased to have much meaning: indeed, their association with small national loyalties and traditional cultures was regarded as harmful to the new orthodoxy.

What happened to Great Britain, for instance?

Britain was renamed Airstrip One – a neutral designation not intended to be contemptuous.

The other superstates?

The two other superstates were Eurasia and Eastasia. Eurasia had been formed by the absorption of the whole of continental Europe into the Soviet Union. Eastasia was made up of China, Japan and the south-east Asian mainland, together with portions of Manchuria, Mongolia and Tibet that, bordering on the territories of Eurasia, fluctuated in imposed loyalty according to the progress of the war.

War?

War between the superstates started in 1959, and it has been going on ever since.

War with conventional weapons, then?

True. Limited armament and professional troops. Armies are, by the standards of earlier modern wars, comparatively small. The combatants are unable to destroy each other: if they could, the war would end, and the war must not end.

Why must it not end?

War is peace, meaning war is a way of life to the new age as peace was a way of life to the old. A way of life and an aspect of political philosophy.

But what is the war about?

Let me say first what the war is *not* about. There is no material cause for fighting. There is no ideological incompatibility. Oceania, Eurasia and Eastasia all accept the common principle of a single ruling party and a total suppression of individual freedom. The war has nothing to do with opposed world-views or, strictly, with territorial expansion.

But it has to do with – ?

The ostensible reason for waging war is to gain possession of a rough quadrilateral of territory whose corners are Tangier, Brazzaville, Darwin and Hong Kong. Here there is a bottomless reserve of cheap coolie labour, with hundreds of millions of men and women inured to hard work and starvation wages. The contest for this prize is conducted in equatorial Africa, the Middle East, southern India, and the Malay archipelago, and it does not move much outside the area of dispute. There is also a measure of fighting around the northern icecap, where valuable mineral deposits are believed to lie.

Ostensible. The real aim?

To use up the products of the industrial machine, to keep the wheels turning but the standard of living low. For the well-fed, physically contented citizen, with a wide range of goods for consumption and the money to buy them, is a bad subject for an oligarchical state. A man filled with meat turns his back on the dry bones of political doctrine. Fanatical devotion to the ruling party comes more readily from the materially deprived. Moreover, loyalty and what used to be called patriotism are best sustained when the enemy seems to be at the gates.

What enemy?

A good question. I said perpetual war, but it is not, to be strictly accurate, always the same war. Oceania is sometimes in alliance with Eurasia against Eastasia, sometimes with Eastasia against Eurasia. Sometimes she faces an alliance of the other two. The shifts in alignment occur with great rapidity and require correspondingly rapid readjustments of policy. But it is essential that the war be officially presented as always the same war, and it follows that the enemy must always be one and the same. The enemy at any given point in time must be the eternal enemy, the enemy past and future.

Impossible.

Impossible? The ruling party has total control of the collective memory and, by the alteration, or strictly rectification, of records, can easily bring the past into line with the present. What is true now must always have been true. Truth is actuality. Actuality is now. There is another

293

reason for requiring an eternal enemy, but consideration of that had best be deferred.

Until – ?

Until you properly understand the true aim of Ingsoc.

Describe Oceanian society.

It is very simply stratified. Eighty-five per cent of the population is proletarian. The proles, as they are officially called, are despicable, being uneducated, apolitical, grumbling but inert. They perform the most menial tasks and are satisfied with the most brutish diversions. The remaining fifteen per cent consists of the Party – Inner and Outer. The Inner Party is an elective aristocracy, dedicated to the implementation of the Ingsoc metaphysic. The Outer Party is made up of functionaries, a kind of lower civil service whose members are employed in the four main departments of government – the Ministries of Love, Plenty, Truth and Peace.

Peace?

Really war. But war is peace.

Who is the head of the Party?

A personage called Big Brother who, never having been born, can never die. Big Brother is God. He must be obeyed, but he must also be loved.

Is that possible?

It is essential.

But can one be made to love to order?

There are ways and means. The elimination of marital love, of love between parents and children, the destruction of joy in sex and in begetting help to direct what may be regarded as an emotional need towards its proper object. The existence of the traitor Emmanuel Goldstein, always in league with the enemy, who hates Big Brother and wishes to destroy Oceania, ensures a perpetual diffusion of fear and loathing among the population, with a compensatory devotion to him who alone can protect and save.

What is the Ingsoc metaphysic?

Ultimate reality, like the first cause or causes, has no existence outside the mind that observes it. Sense-data and ideas alike are mere subjective phantoms. The mind is not, however, an individual mind but a collective one. Big Brother's mind contains all others. His vision of reality is the true one, and all others are false, heretical, a danger to the State. The individual must learn to accept without question, without even hesitation, the vision of the Party, using a technique known as doublethink to reconcile what appear to be contradictions. Outward conformity of belief is not enough. There must be total and sincere allegiance. If the individual memory of the past conflicts with Party history, the device of instantaneous memory control must be employed. Any contradiction can be resolved, and must be. Doublethink – wholly instinctive, sincere, unqualified – is an essential instrument of orthodoxy.

What, apart from metaphysical idealism and the perfection of its diffusion through the body of the Party, is the true aim of Ingsoc?

If you expect demagogic hypocrisy, you will not get it. Rule is not directed towards the welfare of the ruled. Rule is for power. The Party desires total control of everything outside itself, ingesting all of exterior reality into its organism, but it is deliberately reluctant to absorb its enemies. The war with Eastasia or Eurasia or both will never end, the treacherous Goldstein will never die, because Ingsoc needs enemies as a nutcracker needs nuts. Only over an enemy can power be satisfactorily exercised. The future is a boot perpetually crushing the face of a victim. All other pleasures will in time be subordinated to the pleasure of power – food, art, nature and, above all, sex.

May nobody revolt against this monstrous denial of human freedom?

Nobody. Except, of course, the occasional madman. It is the loving concern of Big Brother to restore such a deviate to sanity. And then to vaporize him as a flaw in the pattern, to convert him into an unperson. Rebellion belongs to the old way. And what is this *human freedom*? Freedom from what? Freedom to do what? A man may be free of illness as a dog may be free of fleas, but freedom as an absolute is freedom in a void. The watchwords of old revolutions were always nonsense. Liberty. Equality. Fraternity. The pursuit of happiness. Virtue. Knowledge. Power is different. Power makes sense. God is power. Power is for ever....

Intentions

There are many who, not knowing Orwell's novel *Nineteen Eighty-Four*, nevertheless know such terms as doublethink and Newspeak and Big Brother, and, above all, associate the cipher 1984 with a situation in which the individual has lost all his rights of moral choice (this is what *freedom* means) and is subject to the arbitrary power of some ruling body – not necessarily the State. That the year 1984 may come and go without the realization of the nightmare – with, indeed, an augmentation of personal freedom and a decay of corporate power – will not necessarily invalidate the horrible identification. Doublethink, which the art of fiction can abet, enables us to reconcile the most blatant disparities. In the film Stanley Kramer made of Nevil Shute's novel *On The Beach*, the world comes to an end in 1962. Seeing the film in a television old-movie slot, we in the seventies can still shudder at what is going to happen in the sixties. In an idyllic 1984, the 1984 of Orwell's vision will still serve as a symbol of humanity's worst fears.

1984 is used as a somewhat vague metaphor of social tyranny, and one has to regret the vagueness. American college students have said, 'Like 1984, man,' when asked not to smoke pot in the classroom or advised gently to do a little reading. By extension, the term Orwellian is made to apply to anything from a computer print-out to the functional coldness of a new airport. There are no computers on Airstrip One, and most of the buildings we hear of are decaying Victorian. Present-day Leningrad, with its façades in need of a lick of paint, its carious warehouses, is closer to the look of Big Brother's London than is, say, Dallas International. For Orwellian read Wellsian – specifically the décor of the 1936 film *Things to Come*. The whole point of the urban scene in *Nineteen Eighty-Four* is that it doesn't matter what it looks like, since reality is all in the mind. And there is nothing 'Orwellian' about particular deprivations – like a ban on copulation in trams: it is the total and absolute, planned, philosophically consistent subordination of the individual to the collective that Orwell is projecting into a future that, though it is set in 1984, could be any time between now and 1962, when Nevil Shute brings the world to an end.

We have the following tasks. To understand the waking origins of Orwell's bad dream – in himself and in the phase of history that helped to make him. To see where he went wrong and where he seems likely to have been right. To contrive an alternative picture – using his own fictional technique – of the condition to which the seventies seem to be moving and which may well subsist in a real 1984 – or, to avoid plagiarism, 1985. Orwell's story was set in England, and so will be mine. Americans may reflect, before deploring this author's inverted chauvinism, that Britain has usually, with the absent-mindedness that acquired her an empire, blazed the major trails of social change. Change for the worse, as well as the better.

The French are cleverer than the British. They are skilful at the intellectual work of getting new constitutions on to paper, but the forms of new order have to emerge in Britain first. Montesquieu's *The Spirit of the Laws*, which had such an influence on the American Constitution, could not have been written if there had not been an existing social contract in Britain – one that Montesquieu did not thoroughly understand. The British do not well understand their political systems either, but they make no claim to be clever. It was Walter Bagehot who described the British as stupid. They lack the collective intelligence on which the French pride themselves, but they do not noticeably suffer for this deficiency. French intellectuality may have had something to do with the French surrender of 1940; British stupidity counselled resistance to Nazi Germany. Out of stupidity, which may be glossed as intuition, came the seventeenth-century revolution and the settlement of 1688, complete with limitation of the power of the executive and Bill of Rights. Out of the muddle and mess of contemporary Britain the pattern of the future of the West may well be emerging. It is a pattern which many of us must deplore, but only Ingsoc and Big Brother will prove capable of breaking it.

1948: an old man interviewed

Orwell's book is essentially a comic book.

A WHAT?

Consider. My bookshelves are disorganized. Wishing to reread *Nineteen Eighty-Four*, I could find at first only the Italian edition. This, for the moment, would have to do. But there was something wrong with that first sentence. *'Era una bella e fredda mattina d'aprile e gli orologi batterono l'una.'* It was a bright cold day in April and the clocks struck one. It ought to be *'battevano tredici colpi'*: they were striking thirteen. Latin logic, you see. The translator couldn't believe that clocks would strike thirteen, even in 1984, since no reasonable ear could ever take in more than twelve. So Italian readers were forced to miss a signal of the comic. Here's the original: 'It was a bright cold day in April, and the clocks were striking thirteen.' You laugh, or smile.

Or shudder?

Or shudder pleasurably. As at the beginning of the best kind of ogre story – one in which strange and terrible and unbelievable things are imposed on a familiar world. The world of English April weather, to begin with. A liverish wind mocking the sun. Swirls of dust at street corners. Grit in your eye. A run-down weary city at the end of a long war. Apartment blocks collapsing, a smell of boiled cabbage and old rag mats in the hallway.

COMIC, *for God's sake?*

Comic in the way of the old music halls. The comedy of the all-too-recognizable. You have to remember what it was like in 1948 to appreciate *Nineteen Eighty-Four*. Somebody in 1949 told me – that was the year the book came out – that Orwell had wanted to call it *Nineteen Forty-Eight*. But they wouldn't let him.

You remember the first reviews?

Yes. For the most part, tepidly laudatory. Only Bertrand Russell saw that this was that rare thing, a philosophical novel. The others said that Mr Orwell was more convincing with his boiled cabbage and rag mats than with his totalitarianism. Some truth there. Orwell was known as a kind of comic poet of the run-down and seedy. *Down and Out in Paris and London. The Road to Wigan Pier*. Wigan Pier – that was always a great music-hall joke. Orwell was good at things like working-class kitchens, nice cups of tea so strong as to be mahogany coloured, the latest murder in the *News of the World*, fish and chips, stopped-up drains. He got the feel of 1948 all right. Physical grittiness. Weariness and privation. Those weren't tragic. All the tragedy then was reserved for the Nazi death-camps. And the Russian ones too, but you weren't supposed to think of those. Ergo, our own troubles were comic.

You mean: if a thing isn't tragic it has to be comic?

In art, if not in real life. Let me tell you more about 1949, when I was reading Orwell's book about 1948. The war had been over four years, and we missed the dangers – buzz-bombs, for instance. You can put up with privations when you have the luxury of danger. But now we had worse privations than during the war, and they seemed to get worse every week. The meat ration was down to a couple of slices of fatty corned beef. One egg a month, and the egg was usually bad. I seem to remember you could get cabbages easily enough. Boiled cabbage was a redolent staple of the British diet. You couldn't get cigarettes. Razor blades had disappeared from the market. I remember a short story that began, 'It was the fifty-fourth day of the new razor blade' – there's comedy for you. You saw the effects of German bombing everywhere, with London pride and loosestrife growing brilliantly in the craters. It's all in Orwell.

What you seem to be saying is that Nineteen Eighty-Four *is no more than a comic transcription of the London of the end of the Second World War.*

Well, yes. Big Brother, for instance. We all knew about Big Brother. The advertisements of the Bennett Correspondence College were a feature of the pre-war press. You had a picture of Bennett *père*, a nice old man, shrewd but benevolent, saying, 'Let me be your father.' Then

Bennett *fils* came along, taking over the business, a very brutal-looking individual, saying: 'LET ME BE YOUR BIG BROTHER.' Then you get this business of the Hate Week. The hero of the book, Winston Smith, can't take the lift to his flat because the electricity's been cut off – we were all used to that. But the 1984 juice has been cut as part of an economy drive in preparation for Hate Week – typical government *non sequitur*. Now we knew all about organized hate. When I was in the army I was sent on a course at a Hate School. It was run by a suspiciously young lieutenant-colonel – boy friend of which influential sadist, eh? We were taught Hatred of the Enemy. 'Come on, you chaps, hate, for God's sake. Look at those pictures of Hun atrocities. Surely you want to slit the throats of the bastards. Spit on the swine, put the boot in.' A lot of damned nonsense.

And I suppose the contradiction of that section of the book is meant to be comic too?

Contradiction?

The electricity has been cut off, but the telescreen is braying statistics to an empty apartment. It's hard to accept the notion of two distinct power supplies.

I hadn't thought of that. I don't think anybody thinks of it. But there you are – a necessary suspension of disbelief, appropriate to a kind of comic fairy tale. And the television screen that looks at you – Orwell had lifted that from Chaplin's *Modern Times*. But it's prophetic, too. We're in the supermarket age already, with a notice saying, 'Smile – you're on TV!'

Did England have television in those days?

Are you mad? We'd had television back in the 1930s. The Baird system, what James Joyce called the 'bairdbombardmentboard' or something. Logie Baird, his name dimly echoing in Yogi Bear. I saw the very first BBC television play – Pirandello, *The Man with a Flower in His Mouth*. You got vision from your Baird screen and sound from your radio. Aldous Huxley transferred that system to his *Brave New World* – 1932, as I remember. Mind you, it's never been necessary actually to have television in order to appreciate its potentialities. The Queen in *Snow White* has a TV screen that puts out just one commercial. In England, Robert Greene has a TV screen or magic mirror for spying in *Friar Bacon and Friar Bungay*. That was about 1592. The word existed before the thing. In 1948 the thing was back, I think. It was evident then it was going to be a part of everybody's life. Among the ingenuous there was a feeling that the faces that spoke at you were really looking. The TV was intrusive. The first post-war programmes were more didactic than diverting. The screen was for big faces, not for the tiny figures of old movies. The adjustment of vision we take for granted now wasn't easy at first – I mean the ability to take in a Napoleonic battle on a pocket set. The TV set in the corner of the living-room was an eye, and it might really be looking at you. It was a member of the household, but it was also the agent of a great corporation. I remember a lot of people were shy of undressing in front of it.

You think this is comic? Listen –

> *There was of course no way of knowing whether you were being watched at any given moment. How often, or on what system, the Thought Police plugged in on any individual wire was guesswork. It was even conceivable that they watched everybody all the time. But at any rate they could plug in on your wire whenever they wanted to. You had to live – did live, from habit that became instinct – in the assumption that every sound you made was overheard, and, except in darkness, every movement scrutinized.*

No, not comic, but not as frightening as all that. It's the *possibility* of being caught out by the electronic eye that constitutes the real intrusion. Winston Smith isn't pursued to either the kitchen or the toilet – not, anyway, in Victory Mansions – by Big Brother. (Incidentally, it seems to me all wrong that he should be allowed to live alone in a flat. Wouldn't it be a matter of dormitories with a police thug in the end bed?) There can be plenty of subversive thought in bed, in the dark. The telescreen is perhaps no real menace – any more than bugging is to those who know it is going on. It's a metaphor of the death of privacy. The important thing is that it can't be switched off. It's like muzak, a perpetual reminder of the presence of the big corporation, the State, the anti-self.

But Winston is actually watched. He's rebuked from the screen by the morning physical-jerks instructress.

Yes, but the occasion's comic. We're not far from the Billy Butlin Holiday Camps, so popular in the post-war days. You were awakened in the morning with jocular cries from tannoys. You were cajoled into before-breakfast exercises to loud music.

Did Orwell know about these camps?

No, he died before they got going. And they didn't know about him. But the interesting thing is that they were immensely popular for a time, and that was when the term *camp* and the thought of even harmless regimentation ought to have sickened the average Briton. Of course, they were comparatively cheap. But that wasn't enough to recommend them. Men came out of the army to spend a summer fortnight with wife and family in an ambience which had a great deal of the army about it – reveille, cookhouses, dining-halls, organized diversions, physical jerks (an aspect of army life which most soldiers hated worse than going into battle). There were uniformed camp officers called redcoats – a name uncomfortably close to redcaps, which was what the Military Police were called. And there was always this loud big-brotherly voice from the loudspeakers, exhorting everybody to be happy. Late drinkers-up in the canteen at closing-time were danced off in a cunning conga-line by the female redcoats. The Butlin Holiday Camps proved that the British proletariat was not really averse to discipline. The working man opposed to army life not civilian freedom so much as the infusion of geniality into regimentation. The post-war proletariat accepted the Holiday Camps as readily as they accepted American Army units in English villages, endless shopping lines, the insolence of petty bureaucrats.

And that proves what?

I refuse to draw a moral. The moral that Orwell draws from what he saw of the British working man is terrible and excessive. I insist on looking for comedy.

And for an identification of 1984 with 1948?

Yes, which is part of the comedy, comedy a bit grim at times, positively black. And a touch of pathos. One wants to weep over Winston Smith, so recognizable as an Englishman of the forties bred out of the working class – 'a smallish, frail figure ... his skin roughened by coarse soap and blunt razor blades and the cold of the winter that had just ended'. Inured to cold weather and privation, undersized through a tradition of poverty and bad feeding. He looks out on London 'with a sort of vague distaste.... Were there always those vistas of rotting nineteenth-century houses, their sides shored up with baulks of timber, their windows patched with cardboard and their roofs with corrugated iron, their crazy garden walls sagging in all directions?' The answer is – not always. This is the London of war-time or just after. It's certainly not a London of prophetic vision.

It is, surely. How about the Ministry of Love, of Truth and so on?

Well, the Ministry of Truth may certainly be accepted as the Broadcasting House where Orwell worked during the war. Headquarters of the BBC. The other ministries merely have to look like this prototype. In the Ministry of Love there's that terrible room where the worst thing in the world happens – Room 101. Room 101, in the basement of Broadcasting House, was where Orwell used to broadcast propaganda to India. Not far from Broadcasting House was, and still is, a pub called the George, popular with BBC employees. Sir Thomas Beecham christened it the Gluepot, because his musicians got stuck in it. The name itself has stuck. Now, in *Nineteen Eighty-Four* you have this place with a bad aura, the Chestnut Tree Café, where Winston Smith ends up with his clove-flavoured gin, waiting for the bullet. They're one and the same place, though the Chestnut Tree Café has a touch of the Mandrake Club about it, a place where you drank gin of mysterious provenance and played chess. Strangely, the bad aura of the George began after Orwell's death. It was the pub where you had a drink with Dylan Thomas, Louis MacNeice or Roy Campbell and, on your next visit, learned they were dead. Notice what the song is that Winston hears coming out of the telescreen as he drinks his gin and puzzles over a chess problem:

Underneath the spreading chestnut tree,
I sold you and you sold me. . . .

We always associated that – not with those unpleasant words, of course – with King George VI in his scoutmaster capacity. The song was even turned into a dance, like the Lambeth Walk, and was terribly and bucolically innocent. Orwell really poisons the past when he puts in the sneering yellow note. Not funny. Not comic at all.

But, otherwise, you'd say that the book was an exaggerated picture of a bad time, no more?

Oh, much more, but I have to establish that Orwell wasn't really forecasting the future. Novels are made out of sense data, not ideas, and it's the sensuous impact of this novel that counts to me. I mean the gin – giving off 'a sickly oily smell, as of Chinese rice-spirit' (how could Winston know that? That's the author himself, late of the Burma police, getting in the way.) The shortage of cigarettes, and the only cigarettes on the ration are called Victory, the very brand that was issued to us overseas British troops during the war – sporadically. The cheating of the senses with shoddy food, drink and tobacco, the rough clothes, coarse soap, blunt razor blades, the feeling of being unkempt and unclean – it was all there for fictional transference. It was a bad time for the body. One asked for the bread of minimal comfort and was offered instead the stone of progress.

Progress. That brings us to Ingsoc, doesn't it?

Yes. The torn poster on the street, flapped by the wind, with the single word INGSOC on it. English Socialism. I remember English Socialism coming to power in 1945, a landslide victory for the Left. They sang *The Red Flag* at the opening session of Parliament. It drowned *God Save the King* and *Rule Britannia* and *Land of Hope and Glory*. Winston Churchill, war leader and head of the Conservative Party, was first astonished that the country should reject him, the man who had led it through the valley of the shadow to the sunlit uplands of a qualified triumph, and later he spoke of betrayal. The justification of his rejection lay in that very astonishment: he just didn't seem to understand what had been going on.

Why is Winston Smith so called?

We'll come to that. We've some tricky waters to navigate now. Is English Socialism the same as Ingsoc? Did Orwell think it was? And yet he wanted Socialism. We all did. They say that English Socialism prevailed in 1945 because of the services vote. An elaborate apparatus was set up in ships and camps all over the world to enable British servicemen to exercise their citizen's right of suffrage. Very few abstained from voting. A great many – even those who, like myself, had been brought up in a Conservative tradition and were later to return to it – voted Labour without hesitation.

Why?

Oh, Winston Churchill himself had something to do with it. The senior officers liked him, but he wasn't all that popular with the troops. He'd many of the qualities that make a people's hero – eccentric colourfulness, a gift for obscenity and coarse wit, a mode of speech that sounded more demotic than that of certain of the Labour leaders – though it was really the aristocratic twang of an earlier age. He had a large capacity for brandy and cigars. But it was unwise of him to smoke these when visiting the troops. Some of us at times would have given our souls for a puff at a Victory cigarette.

What, apart from the cigars, was the matter with him?

He was too fond of war. Many of us, by the time of the 1945 election, had been in uniform for nearly six years. We wanted to get out and resume – or begin, most of us – our real lives. Churchill orated about the dangers of a too-hasty disbanding of the citizen army. An iron curtain had come down in Eastern Europe; the Russian ally had returned to his old role of the Bolshevik menace. We knew nothing, we simple soldiers, of the new processes of international politics – the sudden shifts of policy. We'd thought Russia was our great fellow-fighter against fascist tyranny, and now she'd become the enemy. We were naïve enough to imagine that to great statesmen, as to us, war was a necessary but painful interlude. We didn't know that great statesmen consider war to be an aspect of a continuing policy. We'd had enough of Churchill. He wept when we rejected him.

But Orwell obviously admired him. He wouldn't have named his hero for him otherwise.

No, no, no. It seemed to many of the first American readers of *Nineteen Eighty-Four* that Winston Smith's name was a symbol of a noble free tradition lost for ever. But it was nothing of the kind. It was comedy again. The name Winston Smith is comic: it gets a laugh from British readers. It also suggests something vaguely shameful, a political amateurism that never stood a chance against the new professionals.

The rejection of Churchill must surely have represented a very small part of the reason for turning to Socialism in 1945. Wasn't there compulsory instruction in civics during the war? Didn't that lead servicemen to a wish for a change of government?

To some extent. The greater part of the British population had never been much interested in politics, but there was indeed a measure of compulsory civic education during the war, especially in the army, with weekly discussions led by platoon commanders on topical material supplied by the Army Bureau of Current Affairs – ABCA, a whiff of the new age, the pregnant acronym. There was even a stirring song that nobody sang:

ABCA –
Sing it or say it –
Leading the way
To a brave new world.
Till over Europe, freed from her chains,
Liberty's flag is again unfurled,
We'll keep aflame
Democracy's torchlight,
Scorching the wings
Of this night of shame –
Freedom to all,
To act and to utter:
ABCA is calling
In freedom's name.

God help us. There were also lectures by education officers or sergeants on what was called the British Way and Purpose. There was, in fact, a self-avowed attempt to revive the idea of a well-informed citizen army on the lines of Cromwell's Roundheads, who are said to have known what they were fighting for. There were also frank borrowings from the Soviet Army, with its wall-newspapers and political commissars or polkoms.

What, on a point of historical interest, were or was the British Way and Purpose?

I'm not sure. It seems to have been divided, even schizophrenic. Or perhaps the Way and the Purpose were not easily compatible. Much of the material provided was embarrassingly diehard, with its glorification of a colonial system already in process of being dismantled, but articulate members of service audiences were at liberty, during the weekly session, to denounce imperialism and influence comrades who had hardly known that a British Empire existed. Other material was about the building of the Welfare State, with a unified national insurance scheme borrowed from Bismarck's Germany by Lord Beveridge, the Liberal, and known as the Beveridge Plan. I think the British Way was democratic and the British Purpose to establish a sort of cautious egalitarianism wherever possible. I don't know. I do know that some reactionary colonels refused to allow either ABCA or BWP sessions in their battalions, saying that it was all 'socialism'.

Were there any revolutionary colonels?

Not in the British Army. There were plenty of revolutionaries in the rank and file, though, and the odd lieutenant from the London School of Economics. Generally speaking, however, the British class system found its most grotesque expression in the British Army. The professional officers of high rank imposed traditional modes of speech and social behaviour: an officer had to be a gentleman, whatever a gentleman was. Certainly there was, to say the least, a general antipathy on the part of the troops towards their officers, a great gulf of manners, speech, social values, a chasm between those who had to lead and those who did not want to be led. Thirty-odd years after demobilization, there are many former other ranks who enjoy a dream of avenging old insults, injustices, nuances of upper-class disdain. There remains something still in the memory of the 'officer voice' – the reedy vowels of Field-Marshal Lord Montgomery, for instance – which arouses a hopeless fury. The structure of the army was a kind of gross parody of the structure of pre-war civilian society. If a man entered the army as a mild radical, he approached the 1945 election as a raging one. A Welsh sergeant summed it up for me: 'When I joined up I was red. Now I'm bloody purple.' If the British Communist Party had fielded more candidates, the make-up of that first post-War Parliament might have been very interesting indeed.

And this was all it was? The British troops put the Labour Party in because they didn't like Churchill and didn't like the way the services were run?

No, there was much more than that. Along with the radical emotions there was a kind of utopianism necessary to fighting men. They had to believe they were struggling for something more than the mere defeat of an enemy. They weren't defending a good cause against a bad but a bad cause against a worse. Modern war disrupts civilian society and makes it easier to rebuild than to reconstitute. Rebuilding from scratch to secure long-delayed social justice – that had been a dream of the 1914–18 war, with its slogan, 'A country fit for heroes to live in,' but the dream

307

had not been fulfilled. Discharged soldiers in slums or casualty wards, jobless and hopeless, wished they'd been killed on the Somme. It was not to happen again, the British said, and in fact it did not. In 1945, perhaps for the first time in history, the ordinary British people got what they asked for.

Did Orwell get what he asked for?

Orwell was a good Socialist and was delighted to see a Socialist government in power at last.

But his response was to write a terrifying novel in which English Socialism is far worse than either the Nazi or the Russian variety. Why? What went wrong?

I don't know. The English Socialism that came to power in 1945 had nothing of Ingsoc about it. There was power-seeking there, of course, as well as corruption, inefficiency, a love of control for its own sake, a dour pleasure in prolonging 'austerity'. British radicalism has never been able to rid itself of its Puritan origins, and perhaps it hasn't wished to. A typical figure of the post-War Socialist Government was Sir Stafford Cripps, the Chancellor of the Exchequer. He was a sour devotee of progress without pleasure, of whom Winston Churchill once said: 'There but for the grace of God goes God.' He was treated by the common people as something of a joke. Potato crisps were metathesized in his honour, and men in pubs would ask for a packet of 'Sir Staffs'. But he was no joke, and British Puritanism has been too obdurate a strain to laugh off. The Puritanism of 1984, which goes to the limit – not even Sir Stafford Cripps could abolish sex – owes a lot to 1948. Along with the austerity went an insolent bureaucracy, as I've said, and it was the more insolent the closer it was to the ordinary citizen, as in the local Food Office, but there was no Big Brother. Among the first readers in America of Orwell's book there were many who assumed that here was a bitter satire on Labour Britain; even a few of the stupider British Tories rubbed their hands gleefully at what Orwell seemed to be doing for the Tory vote. None of these seemed to know, what was available for the knowing, that Orwell was a committed Socialist and was to remain so till his death. The paradox of an English Socialism appalled by English Socialism remains to be resolved, and the resolution is an intricate business.

I think I can resolve it.

How?

Listen to this extract from **The Road to Wigan Pier.** *Orwell was looking from the window of a train into the backyard of a Northern slum:*

> A young woman was kneeling on the stones, poking a stick up the leaden waste-pipe. I had time to see everything about her – her sacking apron, her clumsy clogs, her arms reddened by the cold. She looked up as the train passed, and I was almost near enough to catch her eye. She had a round pale face ... and it wore, for the second in which I saw it, the most desolate, hopeless expression I have ever seen.... What I saw in her face was not the ignorant suffering of an animal. She knew well enough what was happening to her – understood as well as I did how dreadful a destiny it was to be kneeling there in the bitter cold ... poking a stick up a foul drain-pipe.

The same image comes in Nineteen Eighty-Four, *you remember. Mrs Parsons, in the first part of the book. Her wastepipe's blocked up and Winston Smith unblocks it for her. It's a kind of Sisyphus image. The hopelessness of the working-woman's lot. Orwell saw that the allegiance of a good Socialist was to the woman struggling with the wastepipe, not to the big men of the Party. And yet how could you help her without putting the Party in power? The Party's in power, but the waste-pipe remains clogged. It's the disparity between the reality of life and the abstraction of Party doctrine – that's what sickened Orwell.*

That's part of it. But put it another way. One of the troubles with political commitment is that no political party can tell the whole truth about man's needs in society. If it could, it wouldn't be a political party. And yet the honest man who wants to work for the improvement of his country has to belong to a party, which means – somewhat hopelessly – accepting what amounts to a merely partial truth. Only the vicious or stupid can accord total loyalty to a party. Orwell was a Socialist because he could see no future in a continuance of traditional *laissez faire.* But it's very difficult to sustain a kind of wobbly liberal idiosyncratic socialism of your own in the face of the *real* Socialists – those who want to push Socialism, with impeccable logic, to the utter limit.

You mean Orwell's Socialism was pragmatic rather than doctrinaire?

Look at it this way. When he worked for the left-wing paper *Tribune,* he had to withstand the rebukes of more orthodox readers who didn't like his writing about litera-

ture that seemed to hinder rather than help the 'cause' –
the poems of the Royalist Anglican Tory T. S. Eliot, for
instance, or the in-grown verbal experiments of James
Joyce. He almost had to apologize for bidding his readers
go and look at the first daffodils in the park instead of
spending yet another Saturday distributing left-wing
pamphlets. He knew what Marxism was about. He'd
fought alongside Marxists in Spain, but he wasn't, like the
redder British Socialists, prepared to blind himself to what
Russia was doing in the name of Marxism. His radicalism
was of a nineteenth-century kind, with a strong tinge of
something older – the dissenting spirit of Defoe and the
humane anger of Swift. Swift he declared to be the writer
he admired with least reserve, and that Swift was Dean of
St Patrick's in Dublin didn't offend his agnosticism.
There's a bad but touching poem Orwell wrote – he sees
himself in an earlier incarnation as a country rector,
meditating in his garden, watching his walnuts grow.

*There was more English than Socialism in his English Social-
ism.*

Very neat, and there's some truth in it. He loved his
country more than his party. He didn't like the tendency
in more orthodox Socialists to inhabit a world of pure doctrine and ignore the realities of an inherited national tradition. Orwell prized his English inheritance – the language,
the wild flowers, church architecture, Cooper's Oxford
marmalade, the innocent obscenity of seaside picture
postcards, Anglican hymns, bitter beer, a good strong cup
of tea. His tastes were bourgeois, and they veered towards
the working class.

*But he couldn't identify himself with the workers. It's horrible
that he should seem to blame the workers for his inability to join
them. I mean, that total condemnation of the proles in Nineteen
Eighty-Four....*

He was sick, remember, and hopeless. He tried to love
the workers but couldn't. After all, he was born on the
fringe of the ruling class, he went to Eton, he spoke with a
patrician accent. When he called on his fellow middle-
class intellectuals to take a step downward and embrace
the culture of miners and factory workers, he said: 'You
have nothing to lose but your aitches.' But those were just
what he could not lose. He had at heart the cause of
working-class justice, but he couldn't really accept the

workers as real people. They were animals – noble and powerful, like Boxer the horse in *Animal Farm*, but essentially of a different substance from himself. He fought against his inability to love them by desperate acts of dispossession – making himself down and out in Paris and London, spending the season in hell which produced the Wigan Pier book. He pitied the workers, or animals. He also feared them. There was a strong element of nostalgia in him – for the working-class life he couldn't have. Nostalgia has come to mean frustrated home-sickness. This got itself mixed up with another nostalgia.

You mean for the past. A vague and irrecoverable English past. Dickensian. That vitiated his Socialism. Socialism ought to reject the past as evil. Its eyes ought to be wholly on the future.

You're right. Orwell imagines a kind of impossibly cosy past – the past as a sort of farmhouse kitchen with hams hanging from the rafters, a smell of old dog. As a Socialist he should have been wary of the past. Once you start to yearn for kindly policemen, clean air, noisy free speech in pubs, families sticking together, roast beef and Yorkshire pudding, the fug of the old music hall you end up by touching your forelock to the squire. You oppose to that past a present full of political dogma, policemen with guns, adulterated beer, fear of being overheard, fish sausages. You remember the hero of *Coming Up for Air*. He bites into one of these horrors and says it's like biting into the modern world. There's a part of Orwell which fears the future. Even when it's Socialist, progressive, just, egalitarian. He wants to oppose the past to it, as though the past were a real world of solid objects.

It's the future that's supposed to be subversive. Yet Winston Smith has his subversiveness all in the past.

Well, the past *is* subversive in the sense that it opposes pragmatic values to doctrinaire ones. The human and not the abstract. Take even the least considerable and most neutral-seeming areas – like, for instance, weights and measures. *Nineteen Eighty-Four* is genuinely prophetic in presenting a Britain that's yielded to the metric system. At the end of the war there hadn't as yet been any official proposal to replace the traditional units with the Cartesian abstractions of France, but everybody felt sure the change was on its way. Inches and feet and yards were too much based on thumbs and limbs to be acceptable in a truly rational world. A prole beer-drinker whom Winston Smith encounters complains of having to drink in litres or half-litres: he wants the traditional pint. But despite the protests of traditionalists, Britain had to be given a decimal coinage. Orwell knew this was going to happen: he puts dollars and cents into Winston's pocket. As the British know, the reality is the heavy dollar still called the pound, with a hundred new pence or *p* in it – shameful liquidation – but the dehumanization remains. Americans have a monetary system that carries an aura of revolutionary necessity, and they'll never understand how the loss of the old shillings and half-crowns and guineas wounded British hearts. For the whole point of the traditional system was that it sprang out of empirical common sense, not abstract rationality. You could divide by any number – 3, 4, 5, 6, 7, 8, 9, 10. If you try to divide by 3 now you get a recurring decimal.

7 and 9?

Yes. You added a shilling to a pound and that gave you a guinea. A seventh of a guinea was three shillings. A ninth of a guinea was two shillings and fourpence, or a Malayan dollar. So long as there were seven days in a week, four weeks in a month, twelve months in a year, and an hour divisible by 3 and its multiples, the old system made sense. But it had to go: it was too reasonable, too human. It also committed the grave error of keeping ancient folk traditions alive. 'Oranges and lemons, say the bells of St Clement's. You owe me five farthings, say the bells of St Martin's.' This old song is a mysterious link between Big Brother's London and the ancient buried one of churches and chimes and liberty of conscience. But in 1984 nobody knows what a farthing is. Everybody began to cease to know in 1960. 'Sing a song of sixpence' – it means nothing. Nor does Falstaff's reckoning at the Boar's Head – a capon, 2s 2d; sauce, 4d; sack, two gallons, 5s 8d; anchovies and sack after supper, 2s 6d; bread ½d.

Why does Orwell make Winston Smith wake up with the name Shakespeare on his lips?

Shakespeare, though still not proscribed by the Party, is subversive. God knows what the Newspeak version of him is like, but the Oldspeak Shakespeare is full of private lives and individual decisions. Shakespeare means the past. But note that Winston Smith evokes the past in a far more dangerous way. He buys, for 2 dollars 50, a beautiful book full of blank paper of a creamy smoothness unknown to his modern world – or, for that matter, to present-day Soviet Russia. He also buys an archaic writing instrument – a pen with a real nib. He is going to keep a diary. He feels able to do this with a modicum of safety because his writing-table is in a small alcove out of range of the tele-screen. He first writes at random, and then lets his thoughts wander. He looks down at the page and finds that he's written over and over again, in total automatism, the words DOWN WITH BIG BROTHER. Mrs Parsons, the woman with the blocked-up drain, knocks on the door but, for all Winston knows, it may already be the Thought Police. Going to the door he sees that he's left the book open. 'It was an inconceivably stupid thing to have done. But, he realized, even in his panic he had not wanted to smudge the creamy paper by shutting the book while the ink was wet.' The subversive act and the materials with which it's been performed – these have become one thing. The past is an enemy of the Party. Hence the past is real. After dealing with Mrs Parsons's problem, he comes back and writes:

> To the future or to the past, to a time when thought is free, when men are different from one another and do not live alone – to a time when truth exists and what is done cannot be undone:
> From the age of uniformity, from the age of solitude, from the age of Big Brother, from the age of doublethink – greetings!

We can talk to the past as we can talk to the future – the time that is dead and the time that has not yet been born. Both acts are absurd, but the absurdity is necessary to freedom.

Conversely, freedom itself is thus proved to be absurd.

Yes yes. Freedom was certainly an archaic absurdity to some of Orwell's contemporaries. Britain and her allies had been fighting fascism, which was dedicated to the liquidation of personal liberty, but one of those allies was herself as repressive of freedom as the enemy. When Soviet Russia became a friend of the democracies –

A brief friend.

Yes. That was when those of tender conscience believed the war had lost its meaning. That was when it was in order for Englishmen to love Stalin and praise the Soviet system. There were certain British intellectuals, especially those associated with the left-wing magazine the *New Statesman*, who even preached totalitarianism on the Stalinist model. Kingsley Martin, its editor, for instance. Orwell summed up Martin's view of the Soviet leader something like this: Stalin has done ghastly things, but on balance they've served the cause of progress, and a few million liquidations must not be allowed to obscure that fact. Means justify the end. That's very much the modern view. It was Orwell's belief that most British intellectuals were given to totalitarianism.

He went too far.

Well, consider – it's in the nature of an intellectual to be progressive, meaning that he'll tend to support a political system that will bring rapid changes about in the commonalty, meaning a disdain for the lumbering old democratic process with its tolerance of opposition. A state machine that can pulp up the past and create a rational future. A very intellectual idea. There had been intellectuals who seemed 'fascist' to Orwell, in love with authoritarianism or at least tolerant of it – writers like Eliot, Yeats, Evelyn Waugh, Roy Campbell, even Shaw and Wells – but the intellectuals who were not fascist were usually communist, which – in terms of state power, repression, the one-party system and so on – amounted to the same thing. Terms like fascism and communism represent no true polarity, despite the war. They could both, thought Orwell, be contained in some such name as Oligarchical Collectivism.

And yet any progressive idea is an intellectual creation. Without intellectuals, with their cries for greater social justice, removal of the profit motive, equal incomes, the death of inherited privilege and so on – would there be any progress at all?

But is their talk of progress truly disinterested? Orwell knew enough, as Arthur Koestler did, of the springs of political authority in Europe. No man, it seemed to them, strove for political leadership solely out of altruism. Koestler had been sent to jail by the system he supported. Orwell fought for freedom in Spain, and he had to run for his life when Russian Communism condemned Catalonian Anarchism. Intellectuals with political ambitions had to be suspect. For, in a free society, intellectuals are among the under-privileged. What they offer – as school-teachers, university lecturers, writers – is not greatly wanted. If they threaten to withdraw their labour, nobody is going to be much disturbed. To refuse to publish a volume of free verse or take a class in structural linguistics – that's not like cutting off the power supplies or stopping the buses. They lack the power of the capitalist boss on the one hand and the power of the syndicalist boss on the other. They get frustrated. They find pure intellectual pleasures inadequate. They become revolutionaries. Revolutions are usually the work of disgruntled intellectuals with the gift of the gab. They go to the barricades in the name of the peasant or the working man. For 'Intellectuals of the world unite' is not a very inspiring slogan.

But why was Orwell frightened of the intellectuals? The intellectuals were not running the Labour Government in the late 1940s.

No. The Labour leaders weren't *New Statesman* fanatics. They'd no desire to turn Britain into a miniature Stalinist Russia. But there was a whisper, perhaps more than a whisper, of the danger that comes from more and more State control, a bigger bureaucracy, the devaluation of individuality that inevitably follows a doctrine of equality. Strictly, a Socialist government can only fulfil its ideal of total public ownership if granted a perpetual mandate. The very notion of Socialism is undemocratic, if by democracy we mean opposed parties, a free vote, periodic general elections. Parliament has increasingly the task of pushing through party legislation and ignoring such issues as the rights of the individual, which Members of Parliament are primarily there to protect. Orwell didn't live to see the compromise which English Socialism now represents – a minimum of public ownership, a social-security apparatus that costs too much, a mass of 'equalizing' laws not easily enforceable, and a necessary thwarting of individual, as opposed to collective, endeavour. But, not even in those first heady days of Socialism, could the concept of Ingsoc have begun to germinate – except in some university lecturer's lodgings.

You think it was purely an onomastic trick?

Yes, the taking over quite cynically of an honourable name and then debasing it. Who, after Hitler, can ever mention National Socialism again without a shudder? The link between the English Socialism of 1948 and that of 1984 is purely nominal. We have to imagine this – that a group of *New Statesman* intellectuals has taken over not just England but the entire English-speaking world. As England, or Airstrip One, cannot be more than a satellite of America, the assumption must be that the *New Statesman* oligarchs have first prevailed in the United States and then, armed with power, come home again. Nothing could be more absurd, and Orwell knows it. There's been a great atomic war, but it has left much of Victorian London still standing – absurd again. There are vague memories of political purges in the fifties, but Winston Smith's own reminiscences – and indeed those of practically everyone else – are of the indistinctness of a fading dream. Absurdity. Amnesia seems to have hit everyone, even when they're not exercising 'memory control'. It finds a sort of counterpart in our acceptance that we don't know, nor do we greatly care, how the revolution happened. It's just a necessary device to get the intellectuals into power. Absurd, comic. I'm back where I started.

So you think there's nothing, as it were, nineteeneightyfourish about Nineteen Eighty-Four? *That it was all there waiting in 1948?*

Yes, in a sense. What was merely in the newspapers or the official records – like torture and concentration camps – had to be imported into Britain. The intellectual totalitarianism had to be fictionally realized. But novels are really made out of day-to-day experience, and Winston Smith's frustrations were ours too – dirty streets, decaying buildings, sickening food in factory canteens, the government slogans on the walls –

Slogans? Like FREEDOM IS SLAVERY *and* IGNORANCE IS STRENGTH?

Not quite like those. Those are pure Nazi Germany. But I remember when I came home from overseas army service that the first peace-time government poster I saw showed a haggard sorrowing woman in black, with the legend KEEP DEATH OFF THE ROADS. Naturally, somebody had crossed that out and substituted SHE VOTED SOCIALIST. We were used to posters put out by the Ministry of Information, mostly ham-handed, not subtly ambiguous like the Ingsoc ones. YOUR FORTITUDE, YOUR PATIENCE, YOUR ENDURANCE WILL BRING US VICTORY. You and us, you see. No wonder we all became bloody purple. BE LIKE DAD,

KEEP MUM. That nearly provoked a riot among wage-earning mothers. Slogans had become part of the British way of life. Orwell gave us nothing new.

Wasn't the warning new?

What warning? He was only telling us what Milton told Cromwell's England – hang on to your liberties. Perhaps not even that. He was playing the intellectual game of constructing a working model of a utopia, or cacotopia. How far, he seems to say, can I push things without seeing the careful structure collapse? He'd already made animals play at the Russian Revolution. Another game. He was being the Swift *de nos jours*. Build your own horrible future, enjoy yourself. The thing works, and Orwell has to be pleased. But the pleasure has nothing to do with politics.

Thank you, Mr er – .

Ingsoc considered

It is, without doubt, an oligarchy of refined intellects that is running Oceania. It cultivates a subtle solipsistic philosophy; it knows how to manipulate language and memory and, through these, the nature of perceived reality; it is totally aware of its reasons for wanting power. It has learned how to subdue personal ambition in the interests of collective rule. There is no Hitlerian or Stalinist cult of personality: Big Brother is an invention, a fictional personage and hence immortal, and those who are contained in him partake of his immortality. The oligarchy has learned how to reconcile opposites, not through dialectic, which is diachronic and admits absence of control over time, but through the synchronic technique of doublethink. Ingsoc is the first professional government, hence the last.

Its doctrines are based on a metaphysic, not a mere ethic. To make a political system emerge logically out of a concept of reality is, of course, as old as Plato. The tricky thing about the Ingsoc view of reality is that it is appropriate to a single mind rather than a collective one. Before the metaphysic can assume validity, a collective must learn the technique of thinking in the manner of a single mind.

Solipsism – which derives from Latin *solus* and *ipse* (lone self, self alone) – is a theory that posits reality as existing only in the self, or, more reasonably, states that only the self can be definitely known and verified. This means that nothing in the external world can be assumed to have independent existence. It goes further than mere idealism, which says that mind is real and matter no more than ideas, but does not necessarily reject the existence of many minds and, ultimately, the unifying mind of God. Solipsism teaches that minds other than that of the *solus ipse* cannot be proved to have existence. It does not, however, go so far as to permit temporal or spatial discontinuity within the individual mind, to deny logic, to admit contradiction or inconsistency. If the single mind is real, its memories cannot be illusions. The past is not malleable: it has true existence in the mind and cannot be altered by the present. Mathematical propositions have unchangeable validity, and 2 and 2 always make 4. The collective solipsism of Ingsoc will have none of this. 2 and 2 may sometimes be 4, but they are just as likely to add up to 3 or 5. This sounds like madness. But the Party teaches that madness is an attribute of the individual mind that will not merge itself into the collective one and accept its view of reality. Winston Smith holds fast to simple arithmetic as truth unassailable even by the Party, but part of his rehabilitation consists in learning how to be convinced – not merely to go through the motions of accepting – that 2 and 2 add up to whatever the Party says. Shakespeare, who foresaw most things, foresaw this:

PETRUCHIO:	I say it is the moon.
KATHERINA:	I know it is the moon.
PETRUCHIO:	Nay then you lie; it is the blessed sun.
KATHERINA:	Then God be blest, it is the blessed sun,
	But sun it is not, when you say it is not;
	And the moon changes even as your mind.
	What you will have it nam'd, even that it is,
	And so it shall be so for Katherine.

The self-willed Winston Smith has to be tamed, and O'Brien is his Petruchio.

The Party's solipsism is far saner – or certainly far more consistent – than anything the term was traditionally held to encompass. The *solus ipse* could be said to enclose space, but time lay outside it and was one of the conditions of its existence. But logically the single mind, if it is the only reality, must contain everything, and that includes time. It also includes logic. The senses are the mere instruments that serve the self, and they are subject to error. That sensory illusions exist none will deny: how can we distinguish between illusion and reality? It is unwise to rely at all on the evidence of the senses. The self only, that non-material verifiable entity, can state what is and is not real. To confer on the self the one attribute it requires to be ultimately real – fixed, unchanging, immortal, like God – it is necessary only to make that self a collective one.

There is something in this notion of an undying, omnipotent, omniscient, all-controlling human entity which lifts the heart rather than depresses it. The history of man is the tale of an arduous struggle to control his environment, and failure always comes from the limitations of the individual, whose brain grows tired, whose body decays. Exalt the collective and diminish the individual, and history will be a procession of human triumphs. Which is precisely what the history of Ingsoc is.

If the collective is to function in the manner of a single mind, all its members or cells must agree as to what they observe or remember. The technique known as doublethink is a device for bringing individual observation and memory into line with whatever the Party decrees, at any given moment, to be the truth. It is the given moment that contains reality. The past does not determine the present; the present modifies the past. This is not so monstrous as it appears. The memory of the collective mind has to be contained in records, and it is in the nature of records to be alterable. Take it further: the past does not exist, and so we are at liberty to create it. When one created past conflicts with another, doublethink has to be brought into operation. It is formally defined in the book attributed to Emmanuel Goldstein, Oceania's necessary and hence unkillable public enemy, and entitled *The Theory and Practice of Oligarchical Collectivism*:

> Doublethink means the power of holding two contradictory beliefs in one's mind simultaneously, and accepting both of them. The Party intellectual knows in which direction his memories must be altered; he therefore knows that he is playing tricks with reality; but by the exercise of doublethink he also satisfies himself that reality is not violated. The process has to be conscious, or it would not be carried out with sufficient precision, but it has also to be unconscious, or it would bring with it a feeling of falsity and hence of guilt. Doublethink lies at the very heart of Ingsoc, since the essential act of the Party is to use conscious deception while retaining the firmness of purpose that goes with complete honesty. To tell deliberate lies while genuinely believing in them, to forget any fact that has become inconvenient, and then, when it becomes necessary again, to draw it back from oblivion for just so long as it is needed, to deny the existence of objective reality and all the while to take account of the reality which one denies – all this is indispensably necessary.

The existence of Goldstein's book – a creation of the Party as much as Goldstein himself – may be taken to be an act of doublethink of a very subtle kind. The Party is literally accusing itself of telling lies through the mouthpiece of an invented enemy. It is disclosing the motive of deception behind the telling of the truth. It is conflating two irreconcilable processes – the conscious and the unconscious. It is the repository of all virtue and yet admits the possibility of guilt. Doublethink is being employed to define doublethink.

Doublethink may not be laughed or shuddered off as a chilling fantasy of the author: Orwell knew he was doing little more than giving a formulation to a thought process that man has always found to be 'indispensably necessary' – and not merely a thought process either: we are more accustomed than we know to reconciling opposites in our emotional, even our sensory, experiences. '*Odi et amo*,' said Catullus: I love and hate the same object and at the same time. Orwell himself once pointed out that meat is both delicious and disgusting. The sexual act is engaged in of the free will; at the same time one is driven to it by a biological urge; it is ecstatic, it is also bestial. Birth is the beginning of death. Man is a double creature, in whom flesh contradicts spirit and instinct opposes aspiration. Orwell recognized his own doubleness very sharply. He was both Eric Blair and George Orwell, a product of the fringe of the ruling class who tried to identify himself with the workers, an intellectual who distrusted intellectuals, a word-user who distrusted words. Doublethink, though rightly presented as an instrument of oppression, seems also a very reasonable technique. Our own attitude to doublethink is inevitably doublethinkful.

Hardly a single human experience is unequivocal. The philosophers of Ingsoc are as good as saying: We recognize that human life is partly a matter of juggling with opposites. We wish that new kind of human entity, the collective, to function as a unity. Unity of thought can only be achieved by forging a deliberate technique for dealing with contradictions. (Note that when you came to that word *forge* you had to perform a very rapid act of doublethink. You were, in a context that suggested cheating, ready to give it the meaning of falsifying a cheque or making counterfeit money. But then you had to give it the primary meaning of making, fashioning, with an aura of blacksmith honesty about it.) Let us control phenomena, not be controlled by them. Let there be total harmony between the past and the present. What is the past, that inert ill-understood mass of vague events, that it should exert an influence on the sunlit reality of now? It is a question of who is to be master.

Doublethink is a serious enough formulation of a mode of mental control, but it is also a grim joke. Orwell, like the rest of us, is sickened by the lies of politicians, but he knows that such lies rarely spring from genuine cynicism or contempt of the mob. A politician is wholly devoted to his party, and he has to find ways of making the worse cause seem the better. He does not want to lie, but he has to. He can evade bare-faced falsehood by gobbledygook or euphemism, by ambiguity or redefinition. There is only one sin, and that is to be caught out. The people complain of high prices and unemployment, and they are told: 'These are the growing pains of a new prosperity.' Sir Harold Wilson, when prime minister of Britain, was asked to give evidence of economic progress under Socialism. He said: 'You cannot quantify an élan.' The Pentagon is given to using expressions like 'anticipatory retaliation', meaning unprovoked assault. The communists use the term democracy to mean the opposite of what democrats mean by it. Orwell ironically deplores a lack of system, of logic and consistency, in political utterances. Compared to the amateurish evasions of most ministers of state, doublethink has a certain nobility.

Ingsoc may be thought of as being too sure of its own strength to have to stoop to dishonesty. It does not like verbal obfuscation: it insists on the utmost clarity of expression, both written and spoken. To this end it has manufactured a special kind of English called Newspeak. This is characterized by grammatical regularity, syntactical simplicity, and a vocabulary shorn of unnecessary synonyms and confusing nuances. Strong verbs have disappeared, so that all preterites and past participles end in –ed, as in *swim, swimmed; fight, fighted; go, goed*. Comparison of adjectives is always on the pattern of *good, gooder, goodest*. Plurals always end in –s – *mans, oxes, childs*. This rationalization was perhaps bound to occur of its own accord sooner or later, without the assistance of the State, but Ingsoc, claiming total control of all human activities, has kindly speeded up the process. The limitation of vocabulary is a godsend or statesend: there are far too many words in the traditional language. *Bad* is unnecessary when we can have *ungood*, and intensifiers can be reduced to *plus* and, for greater emphasis, *doubleplus*. *Doubleplusungood* is a very efficient way of rendering 'terribly or extremely bad', and *plusunlight* expresses what great darkness is really about.

But the chief aim of the Ingsoc philologists is not to prune the language to a becoming spareness so much as to make it capable of expressing State orthodoxy so wholeheartedly that no shadow of the heretical can intrude. *Free* still exists, along with *unfree* and *freeness* and *freewise*, but the notion can now only be a relative one, as in 'free from pain'. *Free* meaning 'politically free' cannot make sense, since the concept no longer exists. A statement about political freedom, like the Declaration of Independence, cannot well be translated into Newspeak:

> We hold these truths to be self-evident, that all men are created equal, that they are endowed by their creator with certain inalienable rights, that among these are life, liberty and the pursuit of happiness. That to secure these rights, Governments are instituted among men, deriving their powers from the consent of the governed. That whenever any form of Government becomes destructive of those ends, it is the right of the People to alter or abolish it, and to institute new Government. . . .

Orwell says that the nearest one can come to a Newspeak translation is to 'swallow the whole passage up in the single work *crimethink*. A full translation could only be an ideological translation, whereby Jefferson's words would be changed into a panegyric on absolute government.' Let us, anyway, try:

> We say that truth writed is truth unwrited, that all mans are the same as each other, that their fathers and mothers maked them so that they are alive, free from all diseases and following not food but the feeling of having eated food. They are maked like this by their parents but Big Brother makes them like this. Big Brother cannot be killed but he is to be killed, and in his place there will be himself. . . .

Nonsense, like saying that the sun will come out at night. Or, for that matter, that Big Brother is doubleplusungood when, by sheer definition, he cannot be.

In 1984 we are only in the initial phase of the control of thought through language. The State's three slogans are WAR IS PEACE; FREEDOM IS SLAVERY; IGNORANCE IS STRENGTH. Orwell has informed us that the term *freedom* can have no absolute, or political, meaning, and yet here it is, with just that meaning, blazoned on the State's coinage. Moreover, the State is using paradox in an untypically witty manner: it is the last kick of wit, we must suppose, before the endless night sets in. We are being told, very pithily, that war is the normal condition of the new age, as peace was of the old, and that it is through fighting the enemy that we best learn to love the tranquillity of our bondage. To be left to choose our own way of life is an intolerable burden; the agony of free choice is the clank of the chains of servitude to one's environment. The more we know the more we are a prey to the contradictions of thought; the less we know the better able are we to act. All this is true, and we bless the State for ridding us of the intolerable tyrannies of democracy. Men and women of the Party are now free to engage in intellectual games.

Winston Smith's work *is* an intellectual game, and a highly stimulating one. It consists in expressing doublethink through Newspeak. He has to correct errors in back numbers of *The Times* – meaning, in uningsoc terms, to perpetrate lies – and to compose his corrections, which often amount to full news items, in a language which, restricting semantic choice, promotes ingenuity. (Incidentally, we may ask why separate copies of *The Times* are allowed to exist, since the collection of them for destruction must be a great nuisance. Why shouldn't it appear as a wall newspaper?) The fascination is that of composing a long telegram. Indeed, Newspeak is recognizably based on press cablese. Orwell must have relished the exchange between Evelyn Waugh and the *Daily Mail*, when that great popular organ sent him to cover the conflict in Abyssinia: WHY UNNEWS – UNNEWS GOODNEWS – UNNEWS UNJOB – UPSTICK JOB ASSWISE. Newspeak is, God help us, fun. Doublethink is, God help us again, absorbing mental acrobatics. There may be dangers in living in 1984, but there is no need for dullness.

Consider the situation for eighty-five per cent of the community – the proles. There is a war going on, but there is no conscription, and the only bombs that fall are dropped by the government, just to remind the population that there *is* a war going on. If consumer goods are short, that is an inevitable condition of war. There are pubs, with beer sold in litre glasses, there are cinemas, a state lottery, popular journalism and even pornography (produced mechanically by a department of the Ministry of Truth called Pornosec). There is no unemployment, there is enough money, there are no oppressive regulations – indeed, there are no laws at all. The entire population, prole and Party alike, is untroubled by crime and violence on the democratic model. One may walk the streets at night quite unmolested – except, presumably, by police cars on the pattern of Los Angeles. There are no worries about inflation. One of the major issues of our time, racial intolerance, is lacking. As Goldstein tells us, 'Jews, Negroes, South Americans of pure Indian blood are to be found in the highest ranks of the Party.' There are no stupid politicians, time-wasting political debates, ridiculous hustings. The government is efficient and stable. There are even measures devised to eliminate from life the old agonies of sex and the oppressions of family loyalty. No wonder the system is universally accepted. Winston Smith, in his ingenuous obsession with the liberty of being able to say that 2 + 2 = 4, and his conviction that the entire army is out of step except himself, is a boil, a pustule, a flaw on the smooth body of the collective. It is a mark of charity on the State's part that he should be cured of his madness, not immediately vaporized as a damned nuisance.

During the Second World War, Orwell bravely wrote that neither Hitler nor his brand of socialism could be written off as sheer evil or morbidity. He saw the attractive elements in the Führer's personality as well as the appeal of a political system that had restored self-respect and national pride to a whole people. Only a man capable of appreciating the virtues of oligarchy could write a book like *Nineteen Eighty-Four*. Indeed, any intellectual disappointed with the wretched outcome of centuries of democracy must have a doublethinkful attitude to Big Brother. Given a chance, confronted by the spectacle of hundreds of millions living, joyfully, resignedly, or without overmuch complaint, in a condition of what the West calls servitude, the intellectual may well jump over the wall and find peace in some variety or other of Ingsoc. And the argument against oligarchical collectivism is perhaps not one based on a vague tradition of 'liberty' but one derived from awareness of contradictions in the system itself.

In the cellars of the Ministry of Love, O'Brien tells Winston of the world the Party is building:

> A world of fear and treachery and torment, a world of trampling and being trampled upon, a world which will grow not less but *more* merciless as it refines itself. Progress in our world will be progress towards more pain. The old civilisations claimed that they were founded on love and justice. Ours is founded upon hatred. In our world there will be no emotions except fear, rage, triumph, and self-abasement.... Children will be taken from their mothers at birth, as one takes eggs from a hen. The sex instinct will be eradicated. Procreation will be an annual formality like the renewal of a ration card. We shall abolish the orgasm. Our neurologists are at work upon it now.... There will be no distinction between beauty and ugliness. There will be no curiosity, no enjoyment of the process of life. All competing pleasures will be destroyed. But always – do not forget this, Winston – always there will be the intoxication of power, constantly increasing and constantly growing subtler. Always, at every moment, there will be the thrill of victory, the sensation of trampling on an enemy who is helpless. If you want a picture of the future, imagine a boot stamping on a human face – for ever....

Winston's heart freezes at the words, his tongue too: he cannot reply. But our reply might be: man is not like this, the simple pleasure of cruelty is not enough for him; the intellectual – for only intellectuals with, behind them, a long deprivation of power, can articulate a concept like that – demands a multiplicity of pleasures; you talk of the intoxication of power growing subtler, but it seems to me you refer to something growing simpler; this brutal simplification surely entails a diminution of the intellectual subtlety that alone can sustain Ingsoc. Pleasures cannot, in the nature of things, remain static; have you not heard of diminishing returns? It is a very static pleasure you are talking about. You speak of the abolition of the orgasm, but you seem to forget that pleasure in cruelty is a sexual pleasure. If you kill the distinction between the beautiful and the ugly, you will have no gauge for assessing the intensity of the pleasure of cruelty. But to all our objections O'Brien would reply: I speak of a new kind of human entity.

Exactly. So he does. It has nothing to do with humanity as we have known it for several millennia. The new human entity is a science fiction concept, a kind of Martian. A remarkable quantum leap is required to get from Ingsoc – which is grounded philosophically on a very old-fashioned view of reality and, politically, on familiar state oppression – to Powerman, or whatever the new concept is to be named. Moreover, this proposed 'world of trampling and being trampled upon' has to be reconciled with the continuing processes of government. The complexities of running a State machine are hardly compatible with the vision – not necessarily a demented vision – of exquisitely indulged cruelty. The pleasure of power has much to do with the pleasure of government, in the variety of modes of imposing an individual or collective will on the governed. 'A boot stamping on a human face – for ever' – that is a metaphor of power, but it is a metaphor inside a metaphor. Winston, hearing the eloquence with which the Ingsoc dream is propounded, thinks he hears the voice of madness – the more terrifying because it encloses his own apparent sanity. But madness never encloses sanity; only poetry, which has the surface appearance of madness, can do that. O'Brien is poeticizing. We, the readers, are chilled and thrilled, but we do not take the poem literally.

We all know that no politician, statesman or dictator seeks power for its own sake. Power is a position, a point, an eminence, a situation of control which, when total, confers pleasures which are the reward of the power – the pleasure of choosing to be feared or loved, to do harm or good, condemn or reprieve, tyrannize or bestow benefits. We recognize power when we see a capacity for choice unqualified by exterior factors. When authority is expressed solely through doing evil, then we doubt the existence of choice and hence the existence of power. The ultimate power, by definition, is God's, and this power would seem non-existent if it were confined to condemning sinners to hell. A Caligula or a Nero is recognized as a temporary aberration, a disease that cannot hold power for long because it can choose nothing but the destructive. The evil dreams of a Marquis de Sade derive from an incapacity to achieve orgasm by any regular means, and we accept that he has no choice but to lay on the whips or the burning omelettes. He makes more sense than

O'Brien's sadism freed from the need for orgasm. O'Brien is talking not of power but of a disease not clearly understood. Disease, of its nature, either kills or is cured. And if this disease is not disease but a new kind of health for a new kind of humanity – well, so be it. But we are the old kind of humanity and not greatly interested. Kill us by all means, but let us not pretend that we are being eliminated by a higher order of reality. We are merely being torn by a tiger or pulverized by a Martian deathray.

Reality is inside the collective skull of the Party: the exterior world can be ignored or shaped according to the Party's will. If the electrical supplies fail that nourish the machines of torture, what then? Is the juice, in some mystical way, still flowing? And what if the oil supplies give out? Can mind affirm that they are still there? There is no science, since the empirical process of thought has been outlawed. Technological skills are all harnessed to the making of armaments or the elimination of personal freedom. Neurologists are abolishing the orgasm, and we must assume that cognate specializations are devising other modes of killing pleasure or enhancing pain. No preventive medicine, no advances in the curing of diseases, no transplantation of organs, no new drugs. Airstrip One would be powerless to stem a strange epidemic. Of course, the decay and death of individual citizens matters little so long as the collective body flourishes. 'The individual is only a cell,' says O'Brien. 'The weariness of the cell is the vigour of the organism. Do you die when you cut your finger-nails?' Still, this vaunted control of the outside world is bound to seem impaired when incurable disease asks the mind to get out, it has outlived its tenancy of the flesh. Of course, logically bodies may disappear altogether, and Big Brother will find himself in the position of the Church Triumphant, souls or Soul static in the empyrean for ever and ever, but with no flesh to thwack or nerves to get screaming.

Nature ignored or ill-treated has a way of expressing her resentment, as the margarine commercials used to remind us. Pollution, says the Party, does not exist. Nature will powerfully disagree. Earthquakes cannot be shrugged off with doublethink. Collective solipsism represents a hubris the gods of the natural order would be quick to punish with failed harvests and endemic syphilis. Orwell was writing at a time when the atom bomb was feared more than the destruction of the environment. Ingsoc, though, has its provenance in an even earlier time, the Wellsian one, when nature was inert and malleable and man could do with her whatever he wished.

Even the processes of linguistic change are an aspect of nature, taking place unconsciously and, it appears, autonomously. There is no guarantee that the State's creation of Newspeak could flourish impervious to gradual semantic distortion, vowel mutation, the influence of the richer Oldspeak of the proles. If *doubleplusungood* or, with a *Macbeth* flavouring, *doubledoubleplusungood*, is applied to an ill-cooked egg, we shall need something stronger to describe a sick headache. *Unbigbrotherwise uningsocful doubledoubledoubleplusungood*, for instance. *Bigbrotherwise*, as an intensifier, can be as neutral as *bloody*. Big Brother, being the only deity, can be invoked when we hit a thumb with a hammer or get caught in the rain. This is bound to diminish him. Pejorative semantic change is a feature of all linguistic history. But – one forgets – one is dealing with a new kind of human being and a new kind of reality. We should not strictly be speculating about something that cannot happen here.

We must take *Nineteen Eighty-Four* not only as a Swiftian toy but as an extended metaphor of apprehension. As a projection of a possible future, Orwell's vision has a purely fragmentary validity. Ingsoc cannot come into being: it is the unrealizable ideal of totalitarianism which mere human systems unhandily imitate. It is the metaphorical power that persists: the book continues to be an apocalyptical codex of our worst fears. But why do we have these fears? We are so damnably pessimistic that we almost want Ingsoc to happen. We are scared of the State – always the State. Why?

Cacotopia

'Wherever you are, you always have to work. There's never any excuse for idleness. Nor are there any taverns, public houses, brothels. There are no opportunities for seduction, no places for secret meetings. Everyone has his eye on you. You not only have to get on with your work, you have to make proper use of your spare time.' That is a rough translation from Sir Thomas More's *Utopia*. It does not sound so bad in the original Latin. In colloquial English it has an Ingsoc flavour. The term utopia, which More invented, has always had a connotation of ease and comfort, Lotus Land, but it merely means any imaginary society, good or bad. The Greek elements which make up the word are *ou*, meaning *no* or *not*, and *topos*, meaning a place. In many minds the *ou* has been confused with *eu* – well, good, pleasant, beneficial. Eupepsia is good digestion, dyspepsia we all know. Dystopia has been opposed to eutopia, but both terms come under the utopian heading. I prefer to call Orwell's imaginary society a cacotopia – on the lines of cacophony or cacodemon. It sounds worse than dystopia. Needless to say, none of these terms are to be found in Newspeak.

Most visions of the future are cacotopian. George Orwell was an aficionado of cacotopian fiction, and we may regard his *Nineteen Eighty-Four* as competing in the Worst of All Imaginary Worlds stakes. It has won by many lengths, with the next worst mare of the night somewhat broken-winded. But without that book Orwell might not have felt inclined to compete.

The book is *We*, by E. I. Zamyatin. Orwell reviewed it in *Tribune* on 4 January, 1946, having at last got his hands on it several years after hearing that it existed. It was always an elusive book, and, if it is easily obtainable now in most languages, that is because Orwell was influenced by it. It is not, apparently, to be found in the original Russian. Zamyatin was a Russian novelist and critic who died in Paris in 1937. Imprisoned by the Czarist government in 1906, he was put into a cell on the same corridor of the same prison by the Bolsheviks in 1922. He disliked most governments and leaned to a kind of primitive anarchism. His title seems to allude to a slogan of Bakunin, the father of anarchism: 'I do not want to be I, I want to be We.' This seems to mean that the antithesis of the powerful centralized State is not the individual but the free anarchic community.

We was written about 1923. It is not about Russia; indeed, it does not portray, even obliquely, any existing political system, but it was refused publication on the grounds that it was ideologically dangerous. One can see why, despite the wildness of the fantasy and the remoteness of the setting. We are in the twenty-sixth century, and the scene is a utopia whose citizens have so thoroughly lost their individuality that they are known only by their numbers. They wear uniforms, and are called not human beings but 'unifs'. As the Orwellian telescreen has not yet been invented, they live in glass houses so that the State police, known as the Guardians, can supervise them more easily. They eat synthetic food and, for recreation, march about to the tune of the State anthem, which blares through loudspeakers. There is no marriage, but sex is allowed at stated intervals. For the 'sex hour' curtains are permitted to be drawn in the glass apartments. There is a sex ration-book of pink tickets: one's partner in the act signs the counterfoil. The Single State, as it is called, is ruled by a personage as remote and vague as Big Brother: he is known as the Benefactor. He is voted to power, but he has no opponents.

The philosophy of the Single State is simple. It is not possible to be both happy and free. Freedom imposes the agony of choice, and God, in his infinite mercy, tried to shut out that agony by shutting Adam and Eve into a glorious garden where they had all they needed. But they ate the forbidden fruit of choice, were driven out of the garden and have had to pay for free will with unhappiness. It is the duty of all good States to bring back Eden and scotch the snake of freedom.

The hero-narrator is D–503, an engineer who tries to be a good citizen but, to his horror, finds atavistic impulses breaking in. He falls in love, which is forbidden. Worse, he falls in love with a woman – I–330 – who leads an underground resistance movement given to such vices as tobacco and alcohol and the use of the imagination. D–503, who is no true revolutionary, is given the opportunity to be rid of imagination, which the State declares to be a disease, by X-ray treatment. Cured, he betrays the conspirators to the police and watches unmoved while I–330 is tortured. All the dissidents are at length executed – by means of the Machine of the Benefactor, which reduces them to a puff of smoke and a pool of water: literal liquidation. Orwell comments:

> The execution is, in fact, a human sacrifice, and the scene describing it is given deliberately the colour of the sinister slave civilisations of the ancient world. It is this intuitive grasp of the irrational side of totalitarianism – human sacrifice, cruelty as an end in itself, the worship of a Leader who is credited with divine attributes – that makes Zamyatin's book superior to Huxley's.

That reference, of course, is to Aldous Huxley's *Brave New World*, which, like *Nineteen Eighty-Four* itself, was written under the influence of *We*. Orwell rejected *Brave New World* as a possible blueprint for even a remote future: he blamed Huxley for a lack of 'political awareness'. Huxley depicts, it will be remembered, a utopia which, like Zamyatin's, has sacrificed freedom for happiness. Perhaps, recalling Dr Johnson's strictures on the loose use of a term which is made to express the joys of heaven as well as a little girl's delight in a new party frock, the term *content* would be better. Pre-natal biological techniques and Pavlovian conditioning are capable of rendering the citizens of the future content with the lots which the State has bestowed upon them. There is no equality. Society is rigidly stratified, from the Alpha-plus intellectual to the Epsilon-minus semi-moron, but immobility is biologically built into the system. The family, which Freud said is responsible more than anything for human discontent, has been abolished; children are produced in test-tubes; all sex is promiscuous and sterile. It is a totally stable society, in which hedonism is the prevailing philosophy. But Orwell considers that such a society would not be dynamic enough to last long. 'There is no power hunger, no sadism, no hardness of any kind. Those at the top have no strong motive for staying at the top, and though everyone is happy in a vacuous way, life has become so pointless that it is difficult to believe that such a society could endure.'

The pursuit of happiness is, then, pointless. Is liberty? Presumably not the struggle for it. Orwell cannot conceive of a society whose rulers are not motivated by the desire to impose their wholly malevolent will on the ruled. This is 'political awareness'. The dynamic of society consists in a resistance on the part of the ruled to the will of the ruler – welcomed by the ruler as an inimical drive that merits suppression, with all its concomitant sadistic pleasures. In stating that this is what society is like, Orwell has history on his side. Why do men seek to rule others? Not for the benefit of those others. To be convinced of this is to be 'politically aware'.

And yet there have been utopians – H. G. Wells, for one – who believed that the just society could be built. The Wellsian future is derided in *Nineteen Eighty-Four* – a clean innocent vision of a world full of Hellenic (or Mussolinian) architecture, rational dress and labour-saving devices, in which reason is in control and such base emotions as a lust for power and the exercise of cruelty are rigidly kept under. Had Orwell really been an Anglican rector, he would have known what term to use for describing it. He would have said that the rational society, with scientific socialism triumphant, was 'Pelagian'.

The terms Pelagian and Augustinian, though theological, are useful for describing the poles of man's belief as to his own nature. The British monk Pelagius, or Morgan (both names mean 'man of the sea'), was responsible for a heresy condemned by the Church in AD 416 which, nevertheless, has never ceased to exercise an influence on Western moral thought. The view of man which it opposes appears, to most people, monstrously implausible, even though it is part of traditional Christian doctrine. This view states that man enters the world in a state of 'original sin' which he is powerless to overcome by his own efforts alone: he needs Christ's redemption and God's grace. Original sin relates a certain human predisposition to evil to the crime of disobedience committed by Adam in the Garden of Eden. As Zamyatin reminds us, Adam did not wish to be happy; he wished to be 'free'. He desired free will, meaning the right to choose between courses of action – in effect, between courses on which a moral judgement could be made. He did not realize that, once free, he was more likely to choose the wrong than the right. He would consult the gratification of his own ego rather than what was pleasing to God. He thus condemned himself to divine punishment, which only God's mercy could rescind.

Pelagius denied this terrible endowment. Man was free to choose salvation as much as damnation: he was not predisposed to evil, there was no original sin. Nor was he necessarily predisposed to good: the fact of total freedom of choice rendered him neutral. But he certainly possessed the capability, with no hindrance from unregenerate forces within, to live the good life and, by his own efforts, to achieve salvation at the end. St Augustine, Bishop of Hippo, reaffirming the orthodox doctrine of original sin and the need to pray for divine grace, loudly condemned Pelagius. But Pelagius has, in more than fifteen hundred years, refused to be silent.

In secularizing these views of man, we tend to forget about sin and concentrate on what is good for society and what is not. The Wellsian brand of Pelagianism blamed criminal impulses on environment. What priests called 'original sin' was a reaction to poverty, slum tenements, enforced ignorance and squalor. A scientific socialism would extirpate what was called crime. Man was not just morally neutral: being a social animal, he wanted to be a 'good', or responsible, member of society; it was his environment that had been getting in the way. But, if there are secular Pelagians (though not so many as before about 1933), there seem to be no secular Augustinians. Those who deny the possibility of moral progress, who insist on the destructive, libidinous urges in man as an unregenerable aspect of his condition, take, of necessity, a traditional theological stance. If anything can be done to improve man, it must come from without – from God, or the Life Force, or a miraculous extraterrestrial virus brought in by a UFO.

The polarity is, however, not all that rigid. We are all both Pelagian and Augustinian, either in cyclical phases, or, through a kind of doublethink, at one and the same time. Orwell was Pelagian in that he was a Socialist, Augustinian in that he created Ingsoc. It sometimes seems that the political life of a free community moves in the following cycle: a Pelagian belief in progress produces a kind of liberal régime that wavers when men are seen not to be perfectible and fail to live up to the liberal image; the régime collapses and is succeeded by an authoritarianism in which men are made to be good; men are seen not to be so bad as the Augustinian philosophy teaches; the way is open for liberalism to return. We tend to Augustinianism when we are disgusted with our own selfishness, to Pelagianism when we seem to have behaved well. Free will is of the essence of Pelagianism; determinism (original sin makes us not altogether responsible for our actions) of Augustinianism. None of us are sure how free we really are.

Invoking two opposed, but interpenetrating, kinds of theology, we find ourselves flirting with terms like *good* and *evil*. These, cut off from their base, tend to become semantically vague though strongly emotive. It is embarrassing to hear a politician use them, less embarrassing – though still disturbing – to hear him juggling with *right* and *wrong*. Strictly, the moral duality which these words represent is within the province of the State, while good and evil relate to theological permanencies. What is right, what is wrong? Whatever the State says. It is right to hate Eastasia and then, in the next breath, wrong. It is right to eat potatoes in a time of glut, wrong to eat them in a time of shortage. The Conservatives are wrong and we, the Socialists, are right – a matter of premises. The laws of the State are always changing and, with them, the values of right and wrong. The need to oppose unchanging values to the State's flighty judgements makes us ready to say that this enactment is good, even though it is wrong, and that one, though right, evil.

It has always been easier to point to examples of evil than of good. An Augustinian might say: inevitably, since evil is in our nature, and good not. *Good*, anyway, is a word with a wide spectrum of meaning: we are liable to confuse ethical good with what, for want of a better term, we must call aesthetic good. One of the great human mysteries is supposed to be provided by the Nazi death camps. A commandant who had supervised the killing of

335

a thousand Jews went home to hear his daughter play a Schubert sonata and cried with holy joy. How was this possible? How could a being so dedicated to evil move without difficulty into a world so divinely good? The answer is that the good of music has nothing to do with ethics. Art does not elevate us into beneficence. It is morally neutral, like the taste of an apple. Instead of recognizing a verbal confusion we ponder an anomaly, or, like George Steiner, assert that a devotion to art renders men less sensitive to moral imperatives. 'Men who wept at Werther or Chopin moved, unrealizing, through literal hell.' There is no real mystery.

When we say, 'God is good,' what do we mean? Presumably that God is beneficent and works directly on his creation to secure its happiness. But it is difficult to imagine and harder to believe. It is far easier to conceive of God's goodness as somehow analogous to the goodness of a grilled steak or of a Mozart symphony – eternally gratifying and of an infinite intensity; self-sufficient, moreover, with the symphony hearing itself and the eaten also the eater. The goodness of art, not of holy men, is the better figure of divine goodness.

The goodness of a piece of music and the goodness of a beneficent action have one thing in common – disinterestedness. The so-called good citizen merely obeys the laws, accepting what the State tells him is right or wrong. Goodness has little to do with citizenship. It is not enacted out of obedience to law, to gain praise or avoid punishment. The good act is the altruistic act. It is not blazoned and it seeks no reward. One can see how it is possible to glimpse a fancied connection between the goodness of Beethoven's Ninth Symphony – composed in deafness, disease, squalor and poverty – and that of the saint who gives his cloak to the naked, embraces the leper, dies to save others. But Beethoven's goodness is outside the field of action, to which the saint is so committed. Art is a vision of heaven gratuitously given. Being quasi-divine, it is beyond human concerns. Unlike the heaven of Christian doctrine, it is as freely available to the morally evil as to the morally good: the equivalent of St Augustine's God's grace, impartially bestowed. This, to the narrower moralist, renders it suspect.

What, then, is the good act? To clothe the naked, tend

the sick, feed the hungry, teach the ignorant. These separate acts add up to a concern with promoting, or restoring, in a living organism its native capacity to act freely within the limits of its natural environment. These acts are always good, but they are not always right. Ignorance is strength, says Ingsoc. The Nazis said: let the Jews shiver, starve and die. The good act admits no differentiation of race or species in its object. It is good to mend the broken wing of a bird or to save the life of a *Gauleiter*. The goodness of the saint is characterized by total disinterestedness; the goodness of lesser beings may have motives mixed, unaware, not clearly understood; but the good act tends to grow wild and be unrelated to expediency, policy or law. The good intention, as we know too well, may have evil consequences. Charles Dickens, involved in a train crash, went around pouring brandy indiscriminately down the throats of the injured, thus killing several. He was not, however, a murderer. But the capacity to perform the truly good act is related to a high degree of intelligence and knowledge. Progress may be regarded as a gradual increase in human capacity to understand motivation and free good intentions from the evil of ignorance.

Evil, in its purest form, shares with good this attribute of disinterestedness. If good is concerned with promoting the ability in a living organism to act freely, evil must be dedicated to taking such freedom away. If we are Pelagians, we accept that man has total liberty of moral choice. To remove that choice is to dehumanize. Evil is at its most spectacular when it enjoys turning a living soul into a manipulable object. To confer death is evil enough, but torture has always been regarded as worse. The State has a considerable interest in dehumanizing. It tends to arrogate to itself all matters of moral choice, and it does not care much to see the individual making up his own mind. It is essential that men in power maintain a distinction between the will of the ruler and the will of the ruled. The will of the ruler must, ideally, be totally free; that of the ruled of a greater or lesser freedom, according to the greater or lesser autocratic nature of the State. The State is the instrument whereby the ruler manifests power over the ruled. In so far as this instrument must meet as little opposition as possible in performing its function, it may be said that evil as manifested in the State can never be wholly disinterested. But Orwell's cacotopia represents the establishment of an authority so sure of itself that it can afford to find its chief delight in committing evil for its own sake – that is to say, slowly, deliberately, systematically reducing men and women to gibbering subhuman creatures screaming under torture. This is the ultimate cacotopia, to which Nazi Germany, Soviet Russia, and a host of little autocracies have tended but which they have never been able to achieve.

It is perhaps typical of Orwell's wholly secular culture that he could see the possibility of evil only in the State. Evil was not for the individual: original sin was a doctrine to be derided. Orwell's Socialism permitted, even insisted, that man should be capable of moral as well as economic improvement. His Augustinian pessimism only applied to that projection of man known as the oligarchical State. The State is the devil, but there is no God. The view that evil is somehow outside the individual still persists in a West that has discarded all but the rags of its traditional beliefs. Evil is accepted, to be seen in the My-Lai massacre, in the Charles Manson slaughters, in the daily rapes and murders that animate the streets of major American cities. But it is comforting to believe that this evil is not built into the human entity, as Augustine taught, but comes from without, like a disease. The devil and his attendant demons own the monopoly of evil, and they are concerned with possessing human souls and lighting them up with all the panoply of evil, from blasphemy to cannibalism. They can, perhaps, be exorcised. But evil does not grow in man himself. The superstitious feel happier about their own backslidings if they can attribute them to the Father of Lies. The Orwellians blame it all on Big Brother.

Orwell seemed to believe that the real world, as opposed to that of his feverish and genuinely diseased imagination, was moving in the direction of bigger and worse cacotopias. States would grow greater and more powerful. Equipped with the most devilish technology of oppression, they would more and more reduce the individual to a gibbering humanoid. The future presented an unequal contest between man and the State, and man's defeat would be humiliating and total. We must now see if his prophecy is coming true.

State and superstate:
a conversation

How does today's world of international politics compare with the one that Orwell envisaged?

Very different. There are superpowers, but they don't find it easy to exercise control over the lesser states. The lesser states have not been absorbed into the big ones. The post-war age has been remarkable for the spirit of devolution, uncountable acts of decolonization, the setting up of a host of independent tyrannies, oligarchies and genuine democracies. True, we talk much of spheres of influence, interlocking systems and so on, but there are no great centralized blocs on the Orwell model, all sharing similar ideologies. And where does the power lie? The literal power that drives machines sleeps in Islamic oil. To Orwell, the Middle East was to be merely part of the trapezial zone of cheap labour for the superstates to quarrel over. Islam is one of the genuine superstates, with a powerful religious ideology whose mailed first punched Christendom in the Dark Ages and may yet reimpose itself on a West drained, thanks to the Second Vatican Council, of solid and belligerent belief.

Dear dear. But you have to admit that the main outlines of Orwell's prophecy have come true. America, Russia and China will do, surely, for the three great nightmare powers, armed to the teeth, ready for explosion.

But not exploding. There've been no dangerous naked encounters. Logomachies, yes, but no nuclear attacks on New York or Moscow or Peking.

No condition of perpetual warfare?

Two minor wars a year on average, true. India fights Pakistan, Israel fights Egypt, Jordan fights Syria. Shooting matches in Palestine, Cyprus, Kenya, Aden, Java, Indo-

China, Algeria, Angola, Mozambique, Goa, Tibet, Nigeria, Greece, Dutch New Guinea, the Congo. But no engagement of the superpowers, except by proxy. Korea and Vietnam. So-called Russian advisers on the Golan Heights in 1967. Both Russians and Chinese training the guerrillas of the People's Liberation Front in South Yemen. But Russian forces have only been directly and openly involved in their own sphere of action – to counter the East German rising of 1953, to put down the Hungarians in 1956, the Czechs in 1968.

But there's the germ of Orwell's Eurasia – sovietized Europe.

How much of Europe? Western Europe became sick of authoritarianism after not only Hitler but years of Prussianism, Hapsburgism. Russia could only build Eurasia by force. And Russia's scared of using too much force. So is America. The great paradox of the period since 1945 has been the intrepidity of the little nations in the waging of little wars and the reluctance of the great powers to face each other directly.

Those looked to me very much like direct encounters, or very nearly so – the Korean armistice in 1953, the missile business in Cuba in 1962.

But the assumption that Orwell made, and he wasn't the only one – big atomic war to be followed by a thug's agreement to keep a limited conventional warfare going – seems to belong to a very remote past. We all feared the Bomb once: it was our daily nightmare. Look at the literature that came out of the late forties and the fifties. Take Aldous Huxley's *Ape and Essence* with its picture of post-Bomb Southern California reverted to savagery, with mutated freaks killed at birth, seasonal sex, the Lord of the Flies, Bomb-bringer, appeased with prayers and sacrifice. Take L. P. Hartley's *Facial Justice*, with a guilt-ridden post-atomic world in which everybody is named after a murderer and all human enterprise is blocked, because all we do is evil. Take *Dr Strangelove*, as late as the early sixties. Take novels like *Fail-Safe*. Orwell failed to see that the terror would come about before a nuclear war could get started. So did everybody else.

He failed to see, also, that mere atomic bombs would be quickly followed by thermonuclear devices of far ghastlier potential. I suppose you could sum up the nuclear age like this – the big powers scared to act except vicariously, or in minor acts of puni-

tion in their own spheres of influence; the little nations warring around the immobile feet of the giants. The giants aware of the ease with which the ultimate blast could be triggered, aware too of the consequences – not millions of dead people but a macroton-nage of ruined electronic equipment on both, or all, sides; the pygmies innocent in their belligerence.

Not innocent so much as shrewdly aware of how far they can go. And how far their economies will permit them to go. It's interesting to note, by the way, that the Orwell war rationale hasn't worked in the nuclear age. I mean the using-up of the products of the industrial machine in wasteful war, in order to keep the standard of living low. That notion came from Nazi Germany – guns not butter. The American economy has been marked by colossal expenditure on armaments accompanied by an ever-growing consumption of pacific commodities. It's as though the intercontinental missile and the colour television set reside in the same area of economic expansion. In the modern age you can't keep the two kinds of ingenuity apart – the lethal and the allegedly life-enhancing. Indeed, it's possible to sum up part of the age in terms of a synthesis of the two – you know what I mean, the cosy television evening with the Vietnam war as part of the chromatic entertainment. The American war adventures have been tied up with teaching the world the merits of consumption. Nothing Orwellian there.

But something Orwellian in American imperialism – the building of a kind of Oceania with the centres of power, as with Ingsoc, curiously hidden, dispersed and anonymous. The CIA a kind of Thought Police. The doublethink of democracy, self-determination, freedom of speech and action reconciled with bullying and brutality. A free Francophone Canada? Unthinkable, shoot the dissidents. Too much American capital invested in Our Lady of the Snows. A communist government in Italy? Not to be thought of. I, a harmless British apolitical writer living in Rome, was well aware that the CIA was tapping my telephone. Doing their job, in the name of global freedom, the travelling men of the Thought Police.

Let's be sensible. There's nothing in the traditions of the United States which predisposes them to authoritarianism on the European model. The hysterical anti-communism of the fifties can be seen as a symptom, though an unpleasant and dangerous one, of an ingrained hatred of centralized authority. You can't deny that America did a great deal to promote democratic self-determination in western Europe. Truman, Acheson, Marshall Aid. There was a kind of arrogant assumption on America's part that she knew best, that God had endowed her with a moral superiority that was the reward of an enlightened democratic tradition, but that's very different from collectivist tyranny.

Well, one thing is true, and this is that authoritarianism is no monopoly of the big powers. Africa is full of nasty little tyrannies. Territories that were supposed to have groaned under the colonial yoke gained liberation only to set up dictatorships. Go to Singapore, where Mr Lee presides over a clean unmalarial heaven of free trade. His political opponents are in jail or abroad on courses of what is called self-education. The police drag longhaired youths to compulsory barber-chairs. The media have that bland, uncontroversial quality you associate with Franco's Spain – society weddings, bonny babies, kittens in ribbons. Cinematic candour is called pornography. I lived in Malta for a few years in an atmosphere of censored books and banned films, lingerie advertisements solemnly snipped out of imported British newspapers so that the youth of Malta might not be inflamed. The Maltese government confiscated my house, still full as it was of possibly incriminating books and papers. There are a host of repressive governments everywhere, their tyranny animated by the hypocrisy of doing what is considered 'best for the people'. O'Brien's candid admission that Ingsoc seeks power for its own sake is, compared with the small tyrannical liars, positively healthy.

Let's think of the bigger, older, genuine democracies for a moment. What we ought to be looking for is signs of inroads on personal freedom. There's no doubt that technologies of oppression exist, of a kind that makes Orwell's snooping Thought Police seem very primitive. Now what worries me is the difficulty of making up my mind about these technologies. I don't want to be led into condemning technology in itself. Take the computer. Norbert Wiener and Warren McCulloch developed it as an aspect of legitimate philosophical investigation into the way the brain works – see how far a machine can simulate a human brain, and then what's left over is the essentially human – but it was inevitable that cybernetics should become a *useful* science, and we all know how usefulness tends to be

342

interpreted – in terms of control over what can be controlled, and that mostly means human beings.

A computer is a neutral thing. Information is a neutral commodity. The more information we have the better. That's the way I look at memory banks and so on.

But once the State gets hold of computers it's led on to the inevitable path of amassing information about its citizens. I don't know whether that's bad in itself, but I'm thinking of what happened in 1971 in safe, free, democratic little England –

You mean the Census?

Look at the things the State wanted to know. Status of head of household, relationship to other members of household, how many cars owned, did the cook have an oven, was the toilet inside the house, country of origin, country of parents' origin, previous addresses, education, marital status, number of children, and so on. Some refused to fill in the form, but the vast majority meekly complied. 800 tons of paper, 105 000 enumerators, £10 000 000 of the taxpayers' money. But only 500 prosecutions. There was a maximum fine of £50 for not answering questions. Alan Sillitoe, the novelist, gave his age as a hundred and one and was fined £25. A man of seventy-three and a woman of sixty-six weren't able to pay the fine attendant on their passion for privacy, so both went to prison. Then it was revealed by the department of the Registrar General that some of this secret information was going to be leaked to commercial organizations. One firm said boastfully that it would have details of 90 per cent of the entire population on its computers by 1980. The police easily get access to this kind of stored information. 152 800 people who'd been patients in psychiatric hospitals have had the most intimate details of their lives computerized. Intelligence levels, whether or not they've ever been in prison, the degree of constraint necessary to get them there, a full diagnosis of the mental ailment, special slots for details of drug addiction, epilepsy, alcoholism –

But is there anything really so sinister about the truth? And, for that matter, about violation of privacy? When young people copulate openly in public places, who are we to ask that our biographies go unpublished?

I don't know, I don't know. But think – the State is only an instrument. Everything depends on who has control of

343

that instrument, which can so easily be transformed into a weapon. It's unwise to assume, even with our heightened wariness of tyranny, a continuation of a tradition of liberalism. A new Hitler could arise in Europe and be overjoyed with the information made available by a civil service thinking in the old terms of restraint and democratic rights. Undoubtedly the computers of the world have Jews neatly listed, as well as dangerous intellectual freethinkers. And even now, suppose a crime has been committed, and a man in middle age is suspected, one suffering from epilepsy with four false incisors –. The nation's blood groups are computerized. The State knows the addresses of all the men with red hair.

You're saying that nobody is fit to be given knowledge. We have to take a chance on this sort of thing. I insist on the neutrality of knowledge. Justice is always as likely to be done as injustice. Besides, I see signs everywhere that the State is losing power rather than gaining it.

In Russia? In China? In the bloody little republics that issue no news?

I mean in those areas where the luxury of freedom has been for a long time taken for granted, as much as clean water and mains electricity. I'm not forgetting, by the way, that the essential thing in life is to live, somehow. That if the only way to get a daily bowl of rice is to be in a stinking jail – well, open up, let me in. That in some parts of the world the antonym to State tyranny is not personal liberty but impersonal chaos. No, I mean the civilized West. America, Britain, western Europe. We've seen no charismatic bull-necked leaders around for a long time. Politicians are generally despised, statesmen derided, a United States president can take a deserved whipping. Orwell believed that the media, especially the new ones like television, would be in the hands of the State, that here was an apt instrument for propaganda, harangues, lordly directives. It hasn't worked out that way at all. Politics can't compete with soap opera or old movies. The posters and slogans we see concern taste-pleasing commodities, not omnipotent Big Brother. We have a bearded Southern colonel who offers us nothing more oppressive than fried chicken, we have handsome open-air smokers of Kool or Kent. The State can't gratify taste or sense or excite sympathetic tears or the rib risible. It knows it can't have our souls. All it can get is our money, and that is, true, a real oppression that didn't seem to interest Orwell (though, I gather, he tried to turn himself into

344

a limited company to protect his royalties from Nineteen Eighty-Four *and* Animal Farm*). The State exerts its power on us chiefly through fiscal tyranny, in the insolence of brutal demands, not graceful requests, in the immorality of taking money for things not necessarily wanted by the payer, and all without contract – give us your cash or you go to jail; as for what we do with it, that's our concern, brother. The State calls up young people to fight wars that nobody wants except the Pentagon and the arms manufacturers. The State shows its ugly face most blatantly in the police, which increasingly uses methods learnt from the totalitarian torturers, but shows itself also more and more not to be an arm of the State so much as a quasi-autonomous force, able to shoot first and ask questions after. But we're not bludgeoned too much into orthodoxy, chiefly because there isn't any orthodoxy.*

What you mean is that there's a lot of power about, but it's not centralized on the Ingsoc pattern. That there are, indeed, forces always ready to diminish State power, though oppressive enough in their own ways. Multinational companies that can make and break governments but don't give a damn about matters of responsibility to thought, art, sentiment, health, morality, tradition. The manipulators, the true investigators into the power of propaganda, meaning doublethink, subliminal suggestion, rendering us unfree in the realm of what we consume. Trade unions. Minority groups of all kinds, from the women's liberationists to the gay sodomites. And where we expect the State, that takes our money, to protect us from the more harmful of the anarchic forces of the community, there we find the State peculiarly powerless.

You mean the gangs that roam mean streets, robbing, raping, putting the boot in. There aren't any of those in Oceania, because the aggressive instincts incident to youth are channelled, as they were in Nazi Germany, into organized robbing, raping, and putting the boot in on the State's behalf. Or perhaps just putting the boot in. What you want is more and more ruthless police, also skilled at putting the boot in. Well, the situation for most of us in the democracies has been neatly contrived by the growth of technology and the advance of violence. What is life? Work followed by television. We dare not go out in the evenings, but why should we, when the whole of life is brought to our hearths?

That's all it is, a coloured TV image – a family hearth.

**When we were permitted coalfires we saw far better pic-
tures in them.**

*Dullness followed by dullness. Real sleep and two kinds of
surrogate sleep. Perhaps we'd be happier loving Big Brother.*

Don't, for God's sake, say that. Don't even think it.
Because it's precisely when we admit to the inadequacy of
our private lives that the State is only too happy to step in
to fill the vacuum you call dullness. A night out with the
boys of Biffsquad Number Seven, dear. Polishing his
boots. It must have been exciting to put on a swastika
armband and go *siegheiling* at a Nazi rally. Life ought to be
adequately fed and fairly dull. That's civilization. And if
we don't really like the dullness, then we'd best do something about expanding our own inner vision. We can go to
a George Orwell class. Armed, of course, against the more
truculent of our fellow-citizens.

*We're not being fair to the State, I suppose. When it doesn't
scare us we sneer at it. Do you believe the State can be, well,
beneficent?*

The Welfare State, which Britain has but America
hasn't, though it fills the postboxes with welfare checks,
all too lootable. It's good to have National Insurance, but
what happens to the exercise of charity? We can't be kind
to the poor when the State kills the very concept of poverty. Industries nationalized, and the workers become civil
servants, unfireable, hence not giving a damn. Without
tooth and claw, no urge to work. All nationalized industries fail. Anyway, how can the State be beneficent when
it's using other people's money? Bureaucracies are self-
perpetuating. Bureaucracies are haughty and inefficient.
What do we need the State for? For the conduct of a foreign policy, which means having an army, and for the
maintenance of civil peace, which means the police.
Always guns and a filing system.

*Let's accept, anyway, that the State in the free West is not
moving in an Orwellian direction. We read what we wish, look at
pornography on the streets, can buy pieces of plastic ordure,
make love without official hindrance. We howl for greater and
greater sectional liberties and usually get them. Yet the State
remains an ogre. Especially to the young.*

Ah, the young.

346

Bakunin's children

It is no new thing to mistrust or fear the State. The nineteenth century went further than our own in wishing to dismantle it as an instrument of oppression. Thinkers like John Stuart Mill saw war as a typical emanation of the State, a terrible evil impossible to individuals or free human communities, and a justification in itself for regarding the State as an unnatural monster. Karl Marx found in it the machinery for capitalist tyranny and believed that it would rust and fall to pieces when the proletariat gained power. Michael Bakunin, Marx's contemporary, dedicated his life to the overthrow of the evil giant, and his spirit is still with us – or rather it has been resurrected, often unknowingly, among the young. Marx regarded him as a fool and a poseur, if not a Czarist secret agent. History, a full century after his death, calls him the father of revolutionary anarchism.

Anarchism has, thanks to him, always carried overtones of violence: you can almost smell cordite in the word. But it resolves coolly and harmlessly enough into its Greek elements – *an*, without; *archos*, a ruler. Bakunin, a Russian aristocrat, large, hairy, emotional, good-hearted, contradictory, clumsy, heroic, has somehow stamped the term with his own personality. He was, unlike Marx, incapable of systematic thought, and this led him to the impulsive doublethinkful, or doublefeelful, adoption of incompatibilities in what he thought of as his philosophy. He loved man, he preached universal brotherhood, and yet he loathed both Jews and Germans. His cult of the hero, beard blowing in the wind on the barricades, had a touch of fascism in it. He rejected authority, and yet for a time could preach revolutionary dictatorship on the Leninist model. He was the rank meat in a more rational anarchical sandwich, tastier than the dry bread of theory that Proudhon offered before him and Kropotkin after. Without him, anarchism would have been merely utopian thinking in books little read: he humanized, or heroicized it. He made the anarchist into a Byron.

Bakunin was born in 1814, before Napoleon met his Waterloo. The despotism that still rode over Europe was matched in Bakunin's mother, whose own reputed tyranny was the cause, or so Bakunin said, of his eventual loathing of all restrictions on liberty. Others, with perhaps more reason, have suggested that his childhood was so idyllic that his subsequent anarchism was an unconscious attempt to get back to the Garden of Eden. He was the eldest son in a family of eleven, idolized by his sisters and brothers alike, but aware of the diversity of tastes and talents possible in a small human community, its capacity for being cohesive despite the contrary tuggings of the temperaments of its members. Why could not the greater human society of the city, the nation, eventually the world, partake of the quality of the family? Bakunin confessed, late in life, to an incestuous passion for his sister Tatyana, a snake in Eden, but normal sexual capacity seems to have been curiously lacking for a man of such hairy volatility. He married, but his wife sought other beds and another father for her children. He perhaps dreamed lust and revolution in the same sector of his brain. His words were always fierier than his acts.

He became a cadet in the Russian army and made, apropos of war, a statement that many of us now would be too hypocritical to accept: namely, that men fight not to win but to revel in the glandular releases of danger: battles are better than the brutal monotony of most people's daily lives. On the other hand, he realized that wars also meant stupid discipline and humiliating regimentation, and it was his revolt against this aspect of army life that primed his revolutionary fervour. He left the army and went to the University of Berlin to study Hegel. The Hegelian definition of the human spirit – 'an I that is a we and a we that is an I' – seems to be reflected in Bakunin's own 'I do not want to be I, I want to be We,' which in turn gives a meaning to Zamyatin's title *We*. Hegel's image of history as a moving towards revelation of the truth, a dialectical process of struggle between ideas, not a mere treadmill of events, fired many of Bakunin's generation both to reject a philosophy that was too much set in the world of spirit and to accept a system that could be applied to the world of brute matter. Socialism needed a metaphysical interpretation of history, and Hegel's dialectic provided the structure for building one. Bakunin made an idiosyncratic dialectic for his own use. History was moving towards the building of a better world, therefore new things were better than old. If you destroyed old things, new things came into being to take their place. Ergo, let us all start to destroy old things. This is what makes the term anarchism carry such terrible, and attractive, overtones.

Bakunin took up revolutionary anarchism as a career. 1848 was the great year of European popular risings (that is to say, risings engineered by intellectuals in the name of the people), and Bakunin followed them around, always just missing their great moments. He was too late to be on the Paris barricades, but he showed such revolutionary fervour in the capital of the new French Republic that he was sent off by its government to start a revolution in Poland. He stopped in Prague on the way and organized bloody battles in the streets – oppressed Slavs versus Hapsburg oppressors, with a foregone conclusion. While in Dresden, still not having managed to reach Warsaw, he was caught up in the Saxon rebellion, captured by the forces of the crown, sentenced to death. Reprieved, he was handed over to the Czarist police, incarcerated horribly in St Petersburg, then sent to Siberia. He got away, tried at last to liberate Poland, failed, led the twenty-four-hour revolutionary commune at Lyons, organized innumerable secret societies, contested the leadership of the First International with Karl Marx, and at length tried to die a hero's death on the barricades of Bologna. The Italian rising collapsed in ignominy, so Bakunin crawled to Switzerland to die in his bed. He died disillusioned. He thought the forces of reaction were too powerful for revolutionary anarchism. But anarchism went marching on.

Limping on, rather, with occasional spastic leaps and gibbers. The immediate followers of Bakunin, obsessed with destroying the old so that the new could automatically replace it, threw bombs, set fire to things, assassinated the functionaries of imperialism, and scared not only the bourgeoisie but the proletariat whose anarchic kingdom was supposed to be coming. Anarchism had a bad press as well as severe thrashings from the forces of reaction. Prince Pierre Kropotkin gave it back something of the philosophical prestige it had lost, emphasizing the intellectual, utopian elements, and at the same time rendering it plausible as a doctrine for the working class. And so a philosophy that perhaps only aristocrats could have contrived slowly made a serious impact, especially in Spain, where it was ingeniously reconciled with trade unionism. Collectivism and cooperativism seemed to be working when the Spanish Civil War broke out. It was with Catalonian neo-Bakuninians that George Orwell fought. There were industrious anarchists in Russia at the time of the Revolution, conveniently forgotten in the official Soviet histories. They worked hard for the Revolution but refused to accept a Bolshevik dictatorship. They were shot in Russia as, to Orwell's unforgettable horror, they were shot in Spain. Anarchism is an unacceptable bedfellow to the Marxists and the capitalists alike. It seems to many still to be too romantic, too much a product of its century, to survive. And yet it produces unexpected saints in unexpected places. Sacco and Vanzetti have certainly been canonized, and not only by fellow-anarchists.

Anarchism has come back to the world, but chiefly with the young. It is characteristic, and probably admirable, in young people to wish to dissociate themselves from both socialism and capitalism, since both have police forces, laws, a concern with materialism, and a respect for property. 'Property,' said the proto-anarchist Proudhon, 'is theft.' Young people tend to idealism, which may be a symptom of the disease called adolescence but also produced the Romantic Revival in literature. They also tend to rebel against their parents, who are dull, worried about money, and have an unhealthy appetite for possessions. Their parents are prepared to send them to fight and die for their country, which means property the young do not own and do not want anyway. The State is, and we yawn saying it, a father-figure. The great divisions in the world are not national or religious or economic; they resolve themselves into one division, which is that of youth and age. The division was mildly dramatized for me in West

350

Berlin a few years ago. Having inspected the whole length of the Wall, I sought a rest and a drink at a table outside a *Bierstube* called *Der Moby Dick*. It was run by the young and patronized by the young. Nobody came to serve me. After half an hour I walked in to the bar and asked why. 'Because,' said a blond young man with a *Herrenvolk* profile, 'you are of the generation that started the war.'

It seemed a fair reason. The fight between youth and age – or, strictly, between puberty and maturity – engenders a dynamic, excites the flow of adrenalin, adds interest to life. It is a more acceptable struggle than the one between classes or nations, and it is romantically bedded in ancient myth. But there is a problem we do not find in the older divisions. When we fight for land or money we are fighting for solid objects in space. The youth–age conflict is a time-war. Youth is time's fool, youth's a stuff will not endure. It becomes maturity or age, its opposite and enemy, and nobody can properly tell at what point the frontier is crossed. Age does not last either, but it ends in death, which is sharp and incontrovertible. Youth is part of a process, but it is important to the young that it be represented as a quasi-permanency, something static, almost spatial. Young people come and go, but youth remains. Any young person needs to achieve definition of his youth through membership of a community of the young. If he is with the young and they accept him, he knows he is young. The old need no communal assurance that they are old, and they expect to die alone.

The youth group is less concerned with doing than with being. It cannot define itself in terms of a continuity of membership, nor is there properly a continuity of culture. The important thing is to sit about and be young together. There are activities on the verge of doing nothing, such as taking mild narcotics or hallucinogens and listening to rock music – both substitutes for art and learning. A bland sense of alienation from the laws and culture of the old can satisfy, with no need of stressing alienation through aggression. Unfortunately, it is the agents of the gerontocracy, or old men's rule, that are aggressive and demand conformity. Youth, content just to be, has to shift from the essential to the existential. The group defines itself in the manner of a mature society – with politics and what is known as a counter-culture. It resembles a commune of the nineteenth century, opposing itself to the established order, though, most unbakuninian, with no hope of overturning it.

That is, of course, an over-simplification. If the youth movements of the sixties can be described in terms of primitive anarchism, this means that anarchism is capable of too many definitions. There have been some young people who have made an intelligent political rationale out of their sense of alienation, such as the 'pragmatic anarchists' of Germany and Scandinavia, mostly young intellectuals. There was an anarchist youth movement in Yunan province in the People's Republic of China, suppressed by the central government in 1968. Bakunin has been specifically evoked by young people in America as well as Europe, carriers of blown-up photographs of the prophet at rallies for the condemnation of everything produced by the old – police forces, television, canned foods, *autoroutes*, war, indiscriminate killing, prisons. Bakunin will serve as the patron saint of any movement that invites voluntary membership and allows equally voluntary withdrawal and is dedicated to harassing the State or else studiously pretending the State does not exist. But the whole purpose of the nineteenth-century anarchic movement was to provide a genuine alternative to the State as an instrument of rule or, mostly, oppression. Youthful communes and even mature *kibbutzim* have, whether they will or not, to acknowledge that the State exists: they themselves exist by the grace and favour of the State. There is nowhere today where the State is not.

In any discussion of the political future of the countries of the Free World, we have to consider seriously the danger that the youth movements represent to the cause of traditional liberty. Such a statement will seem nonsensical to youth itself, which believes it is the sole custodian of freedom in an age when the old seem desirous of limiting it more and more. It is true that age seeks to limit the freedom of youth, but only because this freedom is properly licence. If men are born free, it is only in the Ingsoc sense that animals too are born free: freedom to choose between two courses of action presupposes knowledge of what the choice entails. We gain knowledge through direct experience, like the burnt child fearing the fire, or else through the experience of others, which is contained in books. The voice of the neo-anarchists is that of the film-maker Mr Dennis Hopper: 'There ain't nothing in books, man,' or that of the British pop-singer who said: 'Youth don't need education. Youth susses things out for itself like.' Dr Samuel Johnson, having listened to an exponent of primitivism, said: 'This is sad stuff, sir. This is brutish.' It is cow-like rather than lion-like. It takes a long time to gain, by browsing over a field, the protein available in a quick meal of meat. We old offer the meat of education; the counter-culture goes back to grass.

Education consists in taking swift and economical meals out of the larder called the past. Bakunin, with his eccentric interpretation of Hegel, rejected the past, which was bad by definition, not being new. The young very logically reject the past because it seems of no use to people living in an eternal present. And when the old start to oppress the young, it is of course in the sacred name of the past that the bludgeons are raised. The young do not necessarily reject educational establishments, however, since being taught involves being in communities of their own kind, with teaching as an irrelevance or as a purveying of things to be rejected, such focuses of protest being welcome to the idealism of youth.

It is instructive to note how far youthful anarchism has been able to prevail against central government since the year of the first appearance of *Nineteen Eighty-Four*. No student of 1949 could have dreamt that, twenty years later, university authorities would have been so willing to abdicate traditional discipline. Students have gained remarkable liberties, or licences, by the simple procedure of demanding them. The question of the old was *why*? Of the young it has been *why not*? It is difficult, in an establishment dedicated to reason, to give good reasons why student dormitories should not be mixed, promiscuous copulation should not abound, drugs should not be freely taken. In a society given over to consumption, it becomes, for muddle-headed academics, difficult to separate learning from other saleable commodities. If students wish to study petromusicology (the aesthetics and history of rock music), Basic Swahili, or the poetry of Bob Dylan, they, as the consumers, must have their way. And it is very difficult to make out a cogent case for the study of Latin or medieval economics, or to convince that education is most valuable when we do not too nicely question its content.

Students must naturally delegate the voicing of their desires and abhorrences to elected leaders. Even anarchists require leaders, as Bakunin recognized, thinking of himself. He assumed, like his successors, that new modes of leadership would be untaintable by the vices of the heads of the old tyrannies and oligarchies; a leader of free men and women would be the articulator of their needs, not their oppressor, since the very notion of oppression belonged to a past destroyed. A phenomenon of our age, and a very bizarre one, has been the rise of the student leaders – young people like Daniel Cohn-Bendit, hero of the barricades during the 1968 Paris student revolt, and Jerry Rubin, founder of the Youth International Party. Names not now well remembered used to be briefly in the news when the Dutch Provos or the Spontaneous Maoists of the French high schools extolled the virtues of shoplifting, incest and killing as an *acte gratuit*. We should ask what all this has to do with education. The true leaders of youth should be their pedagogues, qualified to inform them what they have to learn in order to survive as members of a civilized community. The logic of youth's eligibility for choosing its own leaders has, inevitably, been pushed to the near limit with children of twelve finding coeval spokesmen for proclaiming their rights. We have not finished with this extension of rights down the age-scale: it is all a matter of finding leaders.

The student leaders reported in the press are ranting extremists of an eclectic kind, mixing Marx and Bakunin, Zen and the Hobbits in bouts of verbalization with no real programme except more and more licence for the young. The danger is always that they can all too easily be manipulated by maturer, genuinely radical, minds that know what they want. The cause of the students becomes whatever universal cause has lately become urgent. To a great extent, the student rebels of Paris in May 1968 were directed by adult agitators. Youth groups are very useful engines: young people have energy and sincerity and ignorance. They have all the qualities that would make them valuable to the professional agitators who want to bring in Ingsoc. The young could easily be made to love Big Brother as the enemy of the past and the old. He is, after all, careful not to call himself Our Father.

The Orwellian world is one that could have a strong initial appeal to the young. It has a striking anarchic feature – a complete absence of laws. It treats the past as a void to be filled with whatever myths the present cares to contrive. It sets up, as a group to be despised, a vast body outside the pale, devoted to past traditions, reactionary and conservative, essentially *old*. Oldspeak is rejected as having no power to express that eternal present which is youth's province as well as the Party's; Newspeak has the laconic thrust of the tongue of youth. The programme, if not the eventual reality, would find its most energetic supporters initially among the young, all happily ready to destroy the past because it *is* the past, and to accept the Ingsoc revolution as it has already accepted the mixed mythology of Mao, Che Guevara, Castro and Bakunin himself. It is the prospect of revolution that counts, with its connotations of the liquidation of the outdated and the glory of the fresh start. What comes after the revolution is another matter.

If, on the other hand, the new strikes even the innocent and ignorant young as somehow suspect, it can only be scrutinized in the light of standards derived from the past. I mean, of course, those sifted nuggets that add up to what we vaguely call a tradition, meaning a view of humanity that extols values other than those of pure bestial subsistence. The view is, alas, theocentric and rests on an assumption that cannot be proved – namely, that God made man to cherish as the most valuable of his creatures, being the most like himself. It is not the aggregate of humanity that approaches the divine condition but the individual human being. God is one and single and separate, and so is a man or a woman. God is free, and so is man, but man's freedom only begins to operate when he understands the nature of the gift.

Human freedom is the hoariest of all topics for debate: it still animates student gatherings, though it is often discussed without definition, theological knowledge or metaphysical insight. Augustine and Pelagius confront each other on the issue of whether man is or is not free; Calvinists and Catholics shout each other down; even in Milton's hell the diabolic princes debate free will and predestination. The pundits of predestination affirm that, since God is omniscient, he knows everything that a man can ever do, that a man's every future act has already been determined for him, and therefore he cannot be free. The opposition gets over this problem by stating that God validates the gift of free will by deliberately refusing to foresee the future. When a man performs an act that God has refused to foresee, God switches on the memory of his foreknowledge. God, in other words, is omniscient by definition, but he will not take advantage of his omniscience.

The arguments for and against free will can be transposed to the secular plane. So much of man is genetically determined, environment limits him as well as his physical and psychological structure; a seemingly free act may well be the end-product of a process determined by a multitude of unconscious and mechanical factors. Man cannot control his response to a reflex. History is a cyclical movement, and man rides the cycle: he revisits old scenes and repeats old actions. Man is a social creature, and society is a negation of individual freedom. And so on. The view of man as an unfree being is hard to combat, and it is supported by Freud, who found that adult acts were motivated by childhood events cached in the unconscious, and Marx, who saw history as a huge steam engine committed to one track and one destination.

The proponents of human freedom accept a great number of limitations on it, but insist that there are areas where it has to operate, or man ceases to be man. First, man's special nature resides in his capacity to make certain judgements on the basis of certain criteria. He can attach these criteria to experience; he learns the criteria from a combination of experience and insight. He is totally free to apply them. Thus, he can freely choose to declare a thing beautiful or ugly, good or evil, true or false. Writing in his diary, Winston Smith says that freedom consists in being able to say that two and two make four, but this is only one of three available freedoms. It is important to keep the three categories separate from each other, so that a thing is not declared ugly because it is immoral or (*pace* John Keats) true because it is beautiful. There is a whiff of religion in all this: we are reminded that truth, beauty and goodness are attributes of God. But, on a purely empirical approach, nobody would deny that these are valid areas of human judgement.

If man is free to evaluate, he is also free to act on his evaluations. But he cannot evaluate without knowledge, and hence cannot act without it. Education consists in acquiring both the knowledge and the terms of evaluation. Hence we are not free not to acquire an education. It is the first condition of freedom. But education which teaches how to judge and what to judge cannot be regarded as a tyrannical imposition: it is merely tradition, or the past, speaking to the present. If a new political doctrine claims that it is the duty of the rulers to free the ruled from the burden of deciding what is good, true or beautiful, then we know that it has to be rejected, since such decisions can only be made by the individual. When a political party condemns a work of art because it is false (meaning untrue to the party's view of reality) or immoral (meaning untrue to the party's view of behaviour), then we are being given a most spectacular example of trespass on the individual's right to make his own judgements. Such judgements cannot be handed over to a collective: they make sense only in terms of the individual soul.

A human being is free not only to act on his own judgements, but also free not to act on them. Most of all, and this may be the essence of his humanity, he is free to act contrary to his judgements. I am a heavy smoker, but, not finding in myself any of the symptoms of addiction, I consider myself free to smoke or not to smoke. I have been thoroughly schooled in the dangers of smoking and conclude that smoking is bad for me. Nevertheless I defy my own judgement and continue to smoke. The unwillingness to break a 'bad habit' always looks like slavery rather than freedom, but it represents that human doggedness of choice which the Church, if not the State, has always resignedly, even sympathetically, learned to live with. There would be very little literature, whether tragic or comic, without it. The old theocracies of Geneva and Massachusetts offered to free man from his slavery to sin, meaning bad habits, by punishing him. The secular theocracies, or Socialist States, make the same offer, or else substitute 'positive reinforcements' for punishment. They propose taking the health of the citizen, as well as his private morality, into their charge. They cannot properly do this: there are certain judgements which only the individual is qualified to make.

It is out of lack of knowledge of the nature of human freedom, and the conditions which validate its exercise, that many young people are drawn to embrace doctrines of political oppression. If they reject tradition, and the transmission of it through education, they are rejecting their only protection against tyranny. They cannot, in other words, be sure what oppression means. Anarchism, in rejecting the past and assuming that the new is, by a kind of Hegelian necessity, better than the old, opens the way to tyranny. Moreover, the anarchist attributes evil to the State, which is the mere instrument of rule, and fails to acknowledge that the so-called free society must also find a technique for holding itself together. Bakunin saw, more clearly than most of his successors, that danger lay not only in the State but also in any powerful group that knew what it wanted – a fellowship of bankers or scientists, for instance. There is nothing magical about the State, making it uniquely engender a desire to hold on to power. A tyranny can be born out of any social group.

I have seen, in the United States, examples of young people's 'communes' that were dangerous for two reasons. They were based on ignorance of the first principles of agronomy. How to grow grain or look after pigs is something to be learnt out of the past, and the past is rejected. They were ignorant of the nature of the principles which hold a society, however small, together. They assumed the existence of a general will in the group and then found it to be no more than a bag of quarrelling individuals. The strongest of the individuals became a leader and demanded obedience. Often obedience was exacted irrationally and, as it were, mystically. The Charles Manson group was an extreme example of a leader's taking on the properties of a messiah, a kind of bloody Jesus. The acts of violence performed by his followers were fewer in number than those perpetrated by the Nazi State, but one does not measure evil quantitatively. There is no guarantee that the social body that rejects the rule of the State will behave better than those who control the State. Because of the ignorance of tradition on which anarchic bodies are founded, there is every likelihood that it will behave worse.

The anomaly of any commune or *kibbutz* or collective Walden (on the lines of B. F. Skinner's blueprint) is that it both denies and accepts the greater social body: it has torn itself away from the bigger fabric and yet is a pocket of it. Skinner's *Walden Two* grows its own food and generates its own power, but it cannot build either tools or machines. It cannot maintain a symphony orchestra, but it demands the right to hear Beethoven and Wagner on tape or disc. It has a library, but it cannot publish books. The more bizarre youth communes of America have made their dwellings out of Coca–Cola cases and old car bodies – the leavings of the consumer society they detest. Antonioni's film *Zabriskie Point* ended with an apocalyptic vision of the consumer society being blasted, on good Bakunin lines, to smithereens, but the vision was in the mind of a girl with a car and a radio in it. Anarchism is not possible. Bakunin is a dead prophet.

In democratic societies like the United States and Great Britain, whose great crimes in the eyes of the young are consumerism and belligerence, breakaway societies and protest groups often succeed in denting the iron of establishment. In time they modify the laws and even increase bureaucracy. The forces of Women's Liberation and Homosexual Liberation are making it a crime to discriminate in employment rights, which is wholesome and just, but they are prepared also to modify language by fiat, so that if I, a writer, use words that betray even grammatical discrimination, I am in danger of legal punishment. The same is true, of course, of such bodies as Britain's Race Relations Board, which rightly condemns bigotry, discrimination, and 'racist' language but renders the individual not always sure of the limits of his own acts and judgements. The trade unions are a conspicuous example, especially in Europe, of the power that collectives can have within the bigger collective of the nation. Sometimes the power is justly based, sometimes not. A government cannot invoke moral principles when dealing with the perhaps unreasonable demands of a powerful pressure group. And, outside the field of legitimate or tolerated group action, there are the politically motivated kidnappers and skyjackers blackmailing governments in a manner inconceivable on Airstrip One. Soon, we are told, our great cities will be held to ransom. This is the limit of Bakuninism. The cartoon anarchist of the old days, bearded like the saintly founder, carrying like a Christmas pudding a black smoking bomb, has been metamorphosed into a deadly monster. The revolutionaries who want to create Ingsoc differ from traditional anarchists only in lack of innocence and the possession of high intelligence. Ingsoc cannot come about in any of our existing systems of government in the West: it is waiting outside, blessed from heaven by Bakunin.

The individual alone can be a true anarch. Orwell saw this when writing *Nineteen Eighty-Four*, which is an allegory of the eternal conflict between any individual and any collective. Winston Smith, though thirty-eight years old, is very young in his ignorance, though the ignorance is not all his own fault. The only freedom he can think of is the right to say what is true and what is false. As O'Brien rightly says, he has no metaphysics to oppose to the doctrine of the State. Even if he had a coherent system of belief, he could not prevail against the massive engine of the Party. But at least he would have had the stoic satisfaction – like that of the heroes of Seneca – of knowing precisely what he was fighting for in the battle he was bound to lose. The situation is a melodramatic inflation of that which any freedom-loving individual finds himself in today, even in a permissive democracy. The individual, of whom Thoreau is the true patron saint, is always against the State, and his liberties are, inevitably, going to be reduced in proportion as the pressure groups gain more licence. Time that could be given to improving his mind is taken up with form-filling and fighting hopelessly with bureaucrats. His money is taken from him. He cannot travel the world freely, since he is limited as to foreign currency by the exchange control regulations. Comforts like tobacco and alcohol may be taxed out of his reach. But he can still exercise free judgement on epistemological, aesthetic and moral issues and act, or fail to act, on such judgements. He can go to jail because he considers war evil. He can kill, if he thinks, after long consideration, that killing is the only possible response to an attack on his person or loved ones or property. He can steal, commit libel, act or write or draw obscenities. He must, naturally, be ready to suffer for the exercise of free will, even to the lethal limit. 'Take what you want,' says the Spanish *dicho*, 'and pay for it.' The important thing is that he should not act without full knowledge of the meaning of his act. That is the condition of his freedom.

Clockwork oranges

I am aware that there is something intolerably romantic about the above view of human freedom. It posits an inviolable citadel in the human skull, where, however the adversary batters the outer fortifications, the values of individualism subsist. Stone walls do not a prison make. This is very old-fashioned and shows a lack of knowledge of the resources of modern tyranny. The first of the two cinema films made of *Nineteen Eighty-Four* – now, I believe, out of circulation – ended with Winston and Julia shouting 'Down with Big Brother,' while facing the firing squad. This wholly missed the point of the book. The Party is not concerned primarily with liquidating its enemies but with turning them into good citizens. The punishment is not important but the burning-out of heresy is essential. The seventh veil of the recusant mind must be dropped and the final nakedness exposed, ravished, impregnated. And yet, knowing that there is no untouchable citadel, many of us persist in believing, or wanting to believe, that there is a part of every individual soul that eludes the tyrant. Ingsoc knows all about the Christian martyrs, whose bodies were destroyed but voices unstilled. A martyr is, etymologically, a witness. The justice of the new State allows no witnesses.

There are a number of us these days who do not seek deliberately to go to prison but cherish a dream of being sent there to enjoy, paradoxically, true freedom. The stresses of contemporary life grow intolerable, and it is not just the State we blame. There are bills to pay, machines that go wrong and cannot be repaired, roofs that leak, buses that fail to arrive, dull work to be done, an inability to make ends meet, insurance premiums that fall due, sickness, the panorama of the wicked world displayed in the daily press. One longs to be punished, Kafka-style, for a crime that one has not committed but nevertheless is prepared to feel guilty for, and throw over all responsibility. There is a dream of solitary confinement, of writing *Pilgrim's Progress* or *The Ballad of Reading Gaol*. There is even a desire to be bereft of books, paper, pencil, light, and to be forced to sustain sanity by composing in one's head an endless epic poem in heroic couplets. Nor iron bars a cage. What one does in captivity is the true test of how free one is. Ingsoc, however, knows all about the incorrigible wilfulness of the human will and will be cosily with us in the oubliette.

And yet, though Orwell's cacotopia is the epitome of all unfree societies, we hear very little about the scientific takeover of the free mind. What is to happen in 1990 or 2900 or beyond is not yet clear, but in 1984 there are no signs that the brain is to be altered by surgery or psychotechnic conditioning. Admittedly, we have an episode in the cellars of the Ministry of Love where O'Brien shows Winston that it is possible to have the Party's vision of reality blasted into one's brain.

> 'This time it will not hurt,' he said. 'Keep your eyes fixed on mine.'
>
> At this moment there was a devastating explosion, or what seemed like an explosion, though it was not certain whether there was any noise. There was undoubtedly a blinding flash of light. Winston was not hurt, only prostrated.... A terrific, painless blow had flattened him out. Also something had happened inside his head. As his eyes regained their focus he remembered who he was, and where he was, and recognized the face that was gazing into his own; but somewhere or other there was a large patch of emptiness, as though a piece had been taken out of his brain....
>
> O'Brien held up the fingers of his left hand, with the thumb concealed.
>
> 'There are five fingers there. Do you see five fingers?'
>
> 'Yes.'
>
> And he did see them, for a fleeting instant, before the scenery of his mind changed. He saw five fingers, and there was no deformity. Then everything was normal again, and the old fear, the hatred, and the bewilderment came crowding back again....
>
> 'You see now,' said O'Brien, 'that it is any rate possible.'

This is nothing more than a trick, though, a demonstration of what the brain is capable of if it tries. And it becomes clear to us that the unfreedom of Ingsoc depends, in a way not at all paradoxical, on the persistence of traditional mental freedom. For, if O'Brien's statement of the Party's programme is to be believed, the exercise of cruelty depends for its efficacy on being able to work on free minds. There may be satisfaction in being cruel to a dog, but it is a lesser satisfaction than being cruel to a human being, especially when that human being is sharply aware of what is happening and why. Ideally, the torturers of the Party would like to take a Shakespeare, a Goethe, an Einstein – with intellect bright and faculties unimpaired – and reduce him to a shrieking mass of flesh and brain tissue.

Evidently the Party uses techniques learnt from Soviet Russia and Nazi Germany to induce states of hopelessness and emptiness, out of which the voluntary confession of crimes uncommitted and the postures of maudlin repentance will come. And Room 101 represents the crude ultimate in mechanistic terrorization, for 'the worst thing in the world' cannot be withstood, no matter what the inner resources of the sufferer. The technique depends on irrationality, the reflex response to a stimulus which varies from subject to subject – rats for Winston, snakes or black beetles or the noise of fingernails on velvet for another, the materials of terror chosen after loving consideration of idiosyncratic phobias. It is spectacular but implausible.

Implausible in its operation, to judge from Winston's response. The starving rats are about to be unleashed on him: they will jump on his face, tear open his mouth and start to devour his tongue. All that will stop O'Brien's opening their cage is Winston's utterance of the right words. He has not betrayed his mistress; now he must ask that she be eaten by the rats, not he. It is enough. The rats are called off. He has now betrayed everything and everybody. He is cured. And yet we know that enforced betrayal is not betrayal at all, that the conscience will quickly enough exculpate itself, blaming instead the machinery of the nerves that is not in the control of the intellect, and that an even stronger fidelity – reinforced by renewed hatred of the manipulators – will ensue. In fact, Ingsoc's knowledge of the techniques of breaking down individual resistance is crude and elementary. Yet this is in accordance with a philosophy based on doublethink. Big Brother both wants and does not want to be in total control. The victim is not a true victim if he is not allowed a modicum of hope.

The victory of the State over Winston Smith is not achieved through a systematic, or Pavlovian, reduction of his personality to the status of a mere mass of conditioned reflexes. As Orwell makes clear, he has to conquer his resistance to Big Brother through the exercise of his own will, with some help from the Ministry of Love. He has to be shown the inadequacy of his own mental resources, which, in comparison with the rigorous metaphysics of the Party, are nothing – a mere bundle of inchoate vel-leities and catchphrases. He has been shown his essential emptiness, and now he knows that it must be filled with the only thing available to fill it – devotion to the Party and love of Big Brother. Ingsoc depends, then, on a kind of exercise of free will, for acceptance of its authority is nothing unless it is free acceptance.

Winston, during an evening spent at the club, has to listen to an imbecilic lecture on the relationship between Ingsoc and chess. We do not know what the content of the lecture is, but we do know that there is something chess-like about the relationship between the State and its members, as there is something chess-like also in the intellectual techniques which sustain the system. To use doublethink is to play chess – planning a strategy of thought and taking into account its unexpected disruption by an unforeseen move from the Party; to use Newspeak is to play a complex game with a limited number of semantic pieces. The game played by the State against Winston has had prescribed moves if no limitation on length: he has been granted freedom of manoeuvre, but he has had no hope of prevailing against the stronger player. At the end of the story,, Winston sits in the Chestnut Tree Café, pondering a chess problem in *The Times* – white to mate in so many moves:

> Winston looked up at the portrait of Big Brother. White always mates, he thought with a sort of cloudy mysticism. Always, without exception, it is so arranged. In no chess problem since the beginning of the world has black ever won. Did it not symbolize the eternal, unvarying triumph of Good over Evil? .... White always mates.

White always mates because the better player has opted for the white pieces. But black is free to win if he can.

In that its citizens are free to play the game of memory control, of working out the devices of orthodoxy, the Orwellian State bears a direct relation to the one in which English Socialism, not Ingsoc, operates. Human souls have not been modified, prenatally or through infantile conditioning, as they have in the *Brave New World* of Aldous Huxley. Orwell rightly saw that the neo-Pavlovian society, with its members incapable of unhappiness through sexual or social frustration, lacked that dynamic of conflict which animates real totalitarianism – a conflict dependent on the individual's awareness of the impairment of free will at the hands of the tyrant. On the other hand, it did not occur to him that the sustention of power could itself be a product of conditioning, that the Alpha-plus executive of the World State could no more break out of his predestined slot than could the Gamma-minus street-sweeper. Orwell was an inveterate proponent of free will, and even made his nightmare out of it. That Huxley's utopia should be based on happiness rather than fear seemed to him to indicate a lack of élan. You cannot have dictatorship without misery.

The techniques for total manipulation of the human soul were in existence in 1932, when *Brave New World* first appeared. Ivan Petrovich Pavlov had four years more to live, he had done his work, and had been able to see something of the possibilities of its social application. Like his fellow-countryman Bakunin, Pavlov was the product of a great phase of intellectual optimism which could not be held back by Czarist repression – indeed, censorship and obscurantism were a positive stimulus to the revolution of thought. Bakunin believed that men were already good; Pavlov believed that men could be made good. A materialist of the true nineteenth-century brand, he saw the human brain as an organ, in Wundt's words, secreting thought as the liver secretes bile, and no more of a mystery to the scientific investigator than any other organ of the body. The brain, seat of thought and emotion, instigator of action, could be probed, cut about, radically altered, but it must always be altered in the direction of a more efficient mechanism, a machine dedicated to the improvement of its owner's functioning as a human organism. This was the ultimate Pelagianism. The perfectibility of man should be not merely a pious aspiration but a scientific programme. He worked on dogs and discovered that their reflexes could be conditioned: ring a bell when bringing food and the dog will salivate: ring a bell without bringing food and the dog will still salivate. The potentialities of this discovery were enormous, and Huxley saw them clearly. In *Brave New World*, infants of the lowest social group must be made to hate consumer goods they can never afford to buy. Children are encouraged to crawl towards highly coloured toys with gurgles of delight; as they start to touch them, electric bells shrill, sirens hoot, electric shocks are given off by the toys themselves. A few sessions of such conditioning, and the children will hate toys. In the same way, in maturity, they can be made to loathe champagne and caviar-surrogate. This is negative conditioning, conditioning employed in the service of rejection, but positive conditioning is used too. Make sweet scents and lovely music arise out of dustbins and the child is ready to be a life-long refuse operative.

The Soviet State wished to remake man and, if one knows Russians, one can sympathize. Pavlov deplored the wild-eyed, sloppy, romantic, undisciplined, inefficient, anarchic texture of the Russian soul, at the same time admiring the cool reasonableness of Anglo-Saxons. Lenin deplored it too, but it still exists. Faced with the sloth of the waiters in Soviet restaurants (sometimes three hours between taking the order and fulfilling it), the manic depression of Soviet taxi-drivers, the sobs and howls of Soviet drunks, one can sometimes believe that without communism this people could not have survived. But one baulks, with a shudder, at the Leninist proposal to rebuild, with Pavlov's assistance, the entire Russian character, thus making the works of Chekhov and Dostoyevsky unintelligible to readers of the far future.

Lenin gave orders that Pavlov and his family should be lodged in capitalist luxury, fed with special rations, and that every possible technical facility should be granted the master, so that he could devise ways of manufacturing Soviet Man. Pavlov went on working with his dogs ('How like a dog is man,' as Shakespeare, if he had read B. F. Skinner, might have said), looking for the seeds of life in the cerebral cortex, afflicting the creatures with diseases of the nervous system in order that he might, with the utmost tenderness (for nobody loved dogs as Pavlov did) cure them. Meanwhile the Soviet police followed up hints about the induction of neuroses, the driving of the Russian soul to breaking-point. And the ancient point was being made about nothing in itself being good or bad, only the way in which fallible human beings use it. Certainly, humanism was being given the lie: man can be changed; the criminal can be turned into a reasonable citizen; the dissident can become orthodox; the obdurate rebel can be broken. But Soviet Man was not made.

We hear less of Pavlovianism these days than of Skinnerism. B. F. Skinner, a practising behavioural psychologist, teaches, and has written in his book *Beyond Freedom and Dignity*, about the conditions under which human society can alone survive, and these involve changing man through a battery of positive reinforcements. It is never enough to demonstrate to man, on the assumption that he is a rational creature, the rational disadvantages of losing his aggressive tendencies and developing a social conscience. Only by associating a particular mode of behaviour with pleasure can it be made to seem desirable. The other, negative, way, whereby people associate an opposed mode of behaviour with pain, is inhumane. But there is something in all of us that is unconcerned with the manner in which circus animals are trained – whether with sugar lumps or the whip; it is the training itself that disturbs us. We make a distinction between schooling and conditioning. If a child plays truant or shuts his ears or throws ink-pellets at his teacher, this at least is evidence of free will. There is something in all of us that warms to the recalcitrant pupil. But to consider hypnopaedia, or sleep-teaching (which also features in *Brave New World*), cradle conditioning, adolescent reflex bending, and the rest of the behavioural armoury, is to be appalled at the loss, even if rewarded with sugar lumps, of individual liberty. Skinner's title appals in itself. Beyond truth, beyond beauty, beyond goodness, beyond God, beyond life. Big Brother does not go so far.

Arthur Koestler, a man who has endured communist incarceration and torture, and hence is disposed to horror at the very thought of brain manipulation, nevertheless now seems to believe that something will have to be done to change humanity if humanity is to survive. The dropping of the atom bombs on Hiroshima and Nagasaki started a new era – one in which we face the possibility of the death of the race. Because of his strange cerebral make-up, the horror created by man can be the means of destroying man: the supreme product of reason is in the hands of unreason. In his book *Janus* Koestler points to the 'paranoid split between rational thinking and irrational, emotion-based beliefs' and suggests that something went terribly wrong in the biological evolution of *Homo sapiens*. He cites the theory of Dr Paul D. MacLean, of the National Institute for Mental Health in Bethesda, Maryland, to the effect that man was endowed by nature with three brains – a reptilian one, one inherited from the lower mammals, and a third, a late mammalian development, 'which has made man peculiarly man'. These three brains will not gear with each other: the term *schizophysiological* has to be applied to man's central nervous system: man is a diseased creature.

'Man can leave the earth and land on the moon,' says Koestler, 'but cannot cross from East to West Berlin. Prometheus reaches for the stars with an insane grin on his face and a totem-symbol in his hand.' It is not just a matter of inability on the part of the neocortex to control the old animal brain that makes man as he is. It is also the fact that he has a remarkably long period of post-natal helplessness, which makes him disposed to submit to whatever is done to him, and this leads to the blind submissiveness to authority which welcomes dictators and warlords. Man does not go to war to satisfy his individual aggressive urges: he goes out of blind devotion to what is represented to him as a cause. Again, language – that time-spanning creation that may be the highest achievement of the higher cerebral centres – abets the irrational, divisive element which expresses itself through war. Language, out of which high art is made, is also, 'in view of its explosive emotive potentials, a constant threat to survival'.

Koestler rejects the 'reductionist' approach to man, which turns him into the pliable matter of Pavlov or Skinner. But he favours the use of drugs:

> Medicine has found remedies for certain types of schizophrenic and manic-depressive psychoses; it is no longer utopian to believe that it will discover a combination of benevolent enzymes which provide the neocortex with a veto against the follies of the archaic brain,

368

correct evolution's glaring mistake, reconcile emotion with reason,
and catalyse the breakthrough from maniac to man.

Whatever the approach, whatever the therapy, this view
of man as a diseased creature is sincerely held, and the
need for somebody to do something about him is represented, by Skinner and Koestler alike, as extremely
urgent. Man is living on borrowed time; cure, for the night
is coming. Strange that the expert beings who are to
administer the cure are themselves men. Can we really
trust the diagnostics and remedies of these demented creatures? But the assumption is that, though all men are ill,
some are less ill than others. Call, for convenience, the less
ill ones well, and we have two kinds of being – we and
they or, in Prole Oldspeak, us and them. They are ill, we
must cure them.

It was the sense of this division between well us and sick
them that led me to write, in 1960, a short novel called *A
Clockwork Orange.* It is not, in my view, a very good novel –
too didactic, too linguistically exhibitionist – but it sincerely presented my abhorrence of the view that some
people were criminal and others not. A denial of the universal inheritance of original sin is characteristic of Pelagian
societies like that of Britain, and it was in Britain, about
1960, that respectable people began to murmur about the
growth of juvenile delinquency and suggest, having read
certain sensational articles in certain newspapers, that the
young criminals who abounded – or such exuberant
groups as the Mods and Rockers, more playfully aggressive than truly criminal – were a somehow inhuman breed
and required inhuman treatment. Prison was for mature
criminals, and juvenile detention centres did little good.
There were irresponsible people who spoke of aversion
therapy, the burning out of the criminal impulse at source.
If young delinquents could be, with the aid of electric
shocks, drugs, or pure Pavlovian conditioning, rendered
incapable of performing anti-social acts, then our streets
would once more be safe at night. Society, as ever, was
put first. The delinquents were, of course, not quite
human beings: they were minors, and they had no vote;
they were very much them as opposed to us, who represented society.

Sexual aggression had already been drastically burnt out

of certain rapists, who first had to fulfil the condition of free choice, which meant presumably signing a vague paper. Before the days of so-called Gay Liberation, certain homosexuals had voluntarily submitted to a mixture of negative and positive conditioning, so that a cinema screen showed naked boys and girls alternately and at the same time electric shocks were administered or else a soothing sensation of genital massage was contrived, according to the picture shown. I imagined an experimental institution in which a generic delinquent, guilty of every crime of rape to murder, was given aversion therapy and rendered incapable of contemplating, let alone perpetrating, an anti-social act without a sensation of profound nausea.

The book was called *A Clockwork Orange* for various reasons. I had always loved the Cockney phrase 'queer as a clockwork orange', that being the queerest thing imaginable, and I had saved up the expression for years, hoping some day to use it as a title. When I began to write the book, I saw that this title would be appropriate for a story about the application of Pavlovian, or mechanical, laws to an organism which, like a fruit, was capable of colour and sweetness. But I had also served in Malaya, where the word for a human being is *orang*. The name of the anti-hero is Alex, short for Alexander, which means 'defender of men'. *Alex* has other connotations – *a lex*: a law (unto himself); *a lex(is)*: a vocabulary (of his own); *a* (Greek) *lex*: without a law. Novelists tend to give close attention to the names they attach to their characters. *Alex* is a rich and noble name, and I intended its possessor to be sympathetic, pitiable, and insidiously identifiable with us, as opposed to them. But, in a manner, I digress.

Alex is not only deprived of the capacity to choose to commit evil. A lover of music, he has responded to the music, used as a heightener of emotion, which has accompanied the violent films he has been made to see. A chemical substance injected into his blood induces nausea while he is watching the films, but the nausea is also associated with the music. It was not the intention of his State manipulators to induce this bonus or malus: it is purely an accident that, from now on, he will automatically react to Mozart or Beethoven as he will to rape or murder. The

State has succeeded in its primary aim: to deny Alex free moral choice, which, to the State, means choice of evil. But it has added an unforeseen punishment: the gates of heaven are closed to the boy, since music is a figure of celestial bliss. The State has committed a double sin: it has destroyed a human being, since humanity is defined by freedom of moral choice; it has also destroyed an angel.

The novel has not been well understood. Readers, and viewers of the film made from the book, have assumed that I, a most unviolent man, am in love with violence. I am not, but I am committed to freedom of choice, which means that if I cannot choose to do evil nor can I choose to do good. It is better to have our streets infested with murderous young hoodlums than to deny individual freedom of choice. This a hard thing to say, but the saying of it was imposed on me by the moral tradition which, as a member of western civilization, I inherit. Whatever the conditions needful for the sustention of society, the basic human endowment must not be denied. The evil, or merely wrong, products of free will may be punished or held off with deterrents, but the faculty itself may not be removed. The unintended destruction of Alex's capacity for enjoying music symbolizes the State's imperfect understanding (or volitional ignorance) of the whole nature of man, and of the consequences of its own decisions. We may not be able to trust man – meaning ourselves – very far, but we must trust the State far less.

It is disturbing to note that it is in the democracies, founded on the premise of the inviolability of free will, that the principle of the manipulation of the mind may come to be generally accepted. It is consistent with the principles of Ingsoc that the individual mind should be free, meaning free to be tormented. There seem to be no drugs in use on Airstrip One, except temporarily mind-dulling cheap and nasty gin. A strong centralized State, with powerful techniques of terrorization, can keep the streets free from muggers and killers. (Queen Elizabeth I's England hanged rioting apprentices on the site of the riot.) Our own democratic societies are growing weak. There is a great readiness to be affected, in the direction of the loss of authority, by pressure groups of all kinds, including

371

street gangs as much as aggressive students. The lack of a philosophy at the centre (which neither Ingsoc nor Communism lacks) is matched by indecisiveness in dealing with crime. This is human; we leave draconian deterrents and punishments to the totalitarian States. But the eventual democratic response to crime may well be what could be represented as the most human, or humane, or compassionate approach of all: to regard man's mad division, which renders him both gloriously creative and bestially destructive, as a genuine disease, to treat his schizophrenia with drugs or shocks or Skinnerian conditioning. Juvenile delinquents destroy the State's peace; mature delinquents threaten to destroy the human race. The principle is the same for both: burn out the disease.

We must, say both Koestler and Skinner, accept the necessity of change. A new race, *Homo sapientior*, must be created. But, I say again, how far can we trust the therapists, who are as imperfect as ourselves? Whose blueprint of the new man must we follow? We want to be as we are, whatever the consequences. I recognize that the desire to cherish man's unregenerate nature, to deny the possibility of progress and reject the engines of enforced improvement, is very reactionary, but, in the absence of a new philosophy of man, I must cling to whatever I already have. What I have in general is a view of man which I may call Hebreo-Helleno-Christian-humanist. It is the view which the Savage in *Brave New World*, who has been reared in the wilds on a volume of William Shakespeare, brings to the stable utopia of AF 632: 'I don't want comfort. I want God, I want poetry, I want real danger, I want freedom, I want goodness. I want sin.' The World Controller, Mustapha Mond, sums it up for him: 'In fact, you're claiming the right to be unhappy.' Or the right, perhaps, not to find life dull. Perhaps the kind of humanity that can produce *Hamlet, Don Giovanni,* the Choral Symphony, the Theory of Relativity, Gaudí, Schoenberg and Picasso must, as a necessary corollary, also be able to scare hell out of itself with nuclear weapons.

What I have in particular is a kind of residual Christianity that oscillates between Augustine and Pelagius. Whoever or whatever Jesus Christ was, people marvelled at him because he 'taught with authority'. There have been very few authoritative teachers in the world, though there have been plenty of authoritarian demagogues. It is possible, just possible, that by attempting the techniques of self-control that Christ taught something can be done about our schizophrenia – the recognition of which goes back to the Book of Genesis. I believe that the ethics of the Gospels can be given a secular application. I am sure too that this has never seriously been tried.

The basis of the teaching is as realistic as Professor Skinner's, though the terms are rather emotive. Sin is the name given to what the behaviourists would like to cut, burn, or drug out. There is a parallel between the cohesion of the universe and the unity of man. This makes a kind of sense out of the doctrine of the Incarnation. In order that the unity of man may be more than a mere aspiration, love, charity, tolerance have to be deliberately practised. The technique of loving others has to be learned, like any other technique. The practice of love is, we may say, ludic: it has to be approached like a game. It is necessary first to learn to love oneself, which is difficult: love of others will follow more easily then, however. If I learn to love my right hand, as a marvel of texture, structure and psychoneural co-ordination, I have a better chance of loving the right hand of the Gestapo interrogator. It is difficult to love one's enemies, but the difficulty is part of the interest of the game.

The serious practitioners of the game, or *ludus amoris*, will find it useful to form themselves into small groups, or 'churches', and meet at set intervals for mutual encouragement and inspiration. They may find it valuable to invoke the spirit of the founder of the game. Indeed, they may gain strength from conjuring his, in a sense, real presence in the form of a chunk of bread and a bottle of wine. If they believe in the divine provenance of the founder, they will be able to strengthen their sense of the need to promote human love to the end of human unity, since this is a figure of the unity of the divinely created cosmos. Men and women must practise the technique of love in the real world and not seal themselves off into communes or convents. The existence of the State is acknowledged, but it is accepted that it has little to do with the real purpose of living. Caesar has his own affairs, which he considers

373

serious but are really frivolous. The practice of love has nothing to do with politics. Laughter is permitted, indeed encouraged. Man was put together by God, though it took him a long time. What God has joined together, even though it be an unholy trinity of a human brain, let no man put asunder. Pray for Dr Skinner. May Pavlov rest in peace. Amen.

The death of love

When Winston Smith takes part in one of the daily mandatory sessions of Organized Hate, he is aware of how efficiently the emotion of homicidal loathing is aroused in himself by a two-minute montage of noises and images. He is aware too of how the hatred he is made to feel can be used as an indifferent weapon, pointed at anyone or anything. This was perhaps one of the big discoveries of the period in which Orwell planned and wrote *Nineteen Eighty-Four* – that hate could, once aroused, be pointed like a blowgun at any object that the State decreed was hatable. It is, of course, necessary for doublethink that emotions should be automatically transferable from one object to another, without the necessity to take thought and consider why the hatable has now become the lovable, and vice versa. Eastasia changes, in mid-sentence, from friend to enemy, and emotional adjustments have to be immediate. Orwell was doubtless thinking of how the attitude of his own country to Soviet Russia, once as fiendish as Nazi Germany, now a fellow-victim of Nazi aggression, had to change overnight. The great age of hypocrisy had begun.

Evelyn Waugh, in the last third of his *Sword of Honour*, reminds us of how Soviet Russia became not merely an exemplar of democratic freedom but a vessel of holiness. The British State ordered that a jewelled sword be forged in honour of the defenders of Stalingrad, and this Excalibur was solemnly exhibited in Westminster Abbey. The Free World, that had loathed Stalin, now called him Uncle Joe and loved him. When the war was over, of course, hatred was in order again. The free swivelling-around of emotions, as in a gun turret, had become one of the regular techniques of the modern age.

Traditionally, we have always hated a thing because it is intrinsically hatable. Christianity, though it enjoins love of people, commands hatred of certain qualities that may inhere in them – cruelty, intolerance, greed and so on. There was a time when we knew what the hatable qualities were; now we are no longer sure. Traditional vices are presented in the popular press as virtues. A man, film star or tycoon, who has been proud, covetous, lustful, envious and gluttonous and achieved a name in the world through the exercise of such vices, is a hero, not a monster. Tolerance is weakness, cowardice is prudence. The notion of intrinsic loathability no longer exists.

It seems to follow that lovability does not exist either. Love comes into *Nineteen Eighty-Four*, but it is neither the disinterested, generalized love of the Gospels nor the romantic love of nineteenth-century novelists. It is certainly not a love appropriate to marriage vows. Winston receives a note from a girl whose name he does not even know. It says simply, 'I love you.' He at once palpitates with fear and excitement. The love that the girl, whose name turns out to be Julia, claims to feel for him is, we learn, based on a recognition that his political orthodoxy is imperfect, and that his disaffection is ready to be expressed in the only form she knows – a willingness to fornicate. Fornication is forbidden by the State, since it offers a pleasure the State cannot control. To make love physically is an act of rebellion. This imposes on the sexual act a bundle of virtues which it is not, in itself, well able to sustain. But the statement 'I love you' is here as much a mockery of the values traditionally attached to the phrase as is the State's own institution of a Ministry of Love.

The main fictional weakness of *Nineteen Eighty-Four* lies here. There is an insufficiency of conflict between the individual's view of love and the State's. Winston and Julia do not oppose to Big Brother the strength of a true marital union and, by extension, the values of the family. They have fornicated clandestinely and been caught naked in the act. There is a sad moment when Julia, whose sole notion of freedom is the right to be sexually promiscuous, gives Winston a potted history of her love affairs. Winston rejoices in her corruption, and Orwell seems to abet the false antithesis – oppose to the moral evils of the State the moral evils of the individual. And yet, as we know, the

376

history of Orwell's own love life is one of trust and devotion: he was not extrapolating a frustration in his fiction. He was perhaps merely being prophetic. In 1984, whether Big Brother is there or not, the traditional view of love will have disappeared, and through no fault of the repressive State.

One of the achievements of American civilization is the devaluation of the institution of marriage. This has had much to do with the Puritan condemnation of adultery as a deadly sin; the scarlet letter is burnt into the American soul. Divorce is preferable to adultery, divorce sometimes being a euphemism for serial polygamy. But divorce is rarely presented, in American fiction or American life, as the wholly regrettable, unavoidable, last-resort surgical operation of a less permissive tradition. Love is a sort of car that has to be replaced by a newer model. It is an electric light bulb whose hours of illumination are numbered. It is equated, as in the mind of Orwell's Julia, with sexual desire. Sexual desire does not die, but it requires a change of object. Like hatred, it is a gun.

Love, however, could be defined as a discipline. It is big enough to encompass transient phases of indifference, dislike, even hatred. Its best physical expression is sexual, but the expression should not be confounded with the essence, the word confused with the thing. Both Winston and Julia love in the sense that they form a self-contained community whose main activity is the sexual act, the act and its concomitants begetting fondness, companionship, and other benign essences. They know, however, that there is no permanency in the relationship; their only discipline is directed to not being found out. It is a brief phase of superficial tenderness to be ended by punishment. 'We are the dead,' says Winston, and Julia dutifully echoes him. 'You are the dead,' says the voice from the wall. The relationship had death in it from the start. So do many relationships in our permissive age, and the death is not imposed from without; it is self-induced.

Separate the sexual act from love, and the language of love is devalued. An aspect of our freedom is our right to debase the language totally, so that its syntagms become mere noise. Big Brother, though regretting the promiscuity enjoined by our society and abetted by our films and magazines, will be delighted to see the weakening of mari-

377

tal values. Communism has tried to kill the family – with great difficulty in China – since the family is the original of which the State tries to make a grotesque blown-up copy; it is far better for the family to kill itself.

The reduction of love to the sexual act, and then to the promiscuous sequence of sexual acts, has the effect of reducing sexual partners to mere objects. It becomes easy then to regard all human beings, in whatever social connection, as objects, on to whom we can spray whatever emotion is expedient. An object has no individual essence; it is a common noun. Generalization follows – women, not this woman and that; workers, the working class. The shocking demotion of millions of individual souls to a generalized class called the proles is perhaps, after the devaluation of love, the most terrible thing in *Nineteen Eighty-Four*.

If we regard such a bestial corralling as implausible, nevertheless we accept it as the basic condition for the setting up of an oligarchy like that of Ingsoc. If one hundred per cent of the population has to be controlled with Thought Police and telescreens, then the oligarchical State cannot survive: its resources will be insufficient to hold everybody down. It has to assume that the proles are too stupid, cowed, unimaginative ever to represent a danger to stability: if, improbably, a prole demagogue starts preaching revolt, he can easily be picked off. But the whole mystique and technique of Ingsoc accepts without question the inertness of eighty-five per cent of the population. We accept it too; otherwise we would not be frightened of the possibility of the nightmare of Ingsoc's coming true. And by *we* I do not just mean readers of this kind of book; I mean members of the working class who, drinking a pint in a pub after a television adaptation of *Nineteen Eighty-Four*, make jokes about Big Brother watching them. The story is founded on a division that is no mere fictional device, something we are as prepared to accept to get the plot moving as the absence of marine insurance in Shylock's Venice. It was Orwell's revenge on the workers of 1948. They had let him down. More than that, it was an inherited acceptance of an immutable social division that he could no more drop than he could drop his aitches.

The idea of writing *Animal Farm* came to Orwell when he saw a small boy in charge of a Suffolk Punch. What if these great beasts became aware of their power and turned against their puny human masters? The farm animals of the little fable turn against Mr Jones and his family and found the first animal republic. But it was only possible for Orwell to write the book at all by thinking of a revolutionary proletariat as something different from the sort of human being he and his class represented. The common people were different from the middle class, a different sort of animal. They are still a different sort of animal in *Nineteen Eighty-Four*. There is no real human life in them.

Admittedly, Winston Smith cherishes the romantic hope that when change comes it will come from the proles. But it is a vague hope, sentimental and unworthy. If the proles are not to be animals, they are to be a sort of noble savage: they are not permitted to be ordinary human beings, like Winston and his creator. Winston watches a fat prole woman hanging out clothes, singing a popular song turned out by a musicator:

> The birds sang, the proles sang, the Party did not sing. All round the world, in London and New York, in Africa and Brazil, and in the mysterious, forbidden lands beyond the frontiers, in the streets of Paris and Berlin, in the villages of the endless Russian plain, in the bazaars of China and Japan – everywhere stood the same solid unconquerable figure, made monstrous by work and childbearing, toiling from birth to death and still singing. Out of those mighty loins a race of conscious beings might one day come. You were the dead; theirs was the future. But you could share in that future if you kept alive the mind as they kept alive the body, and passed on the secret doctrine that two plus two make four.

'The same solid unconquerable figure ... those mighty loins' – the words are as insulting as the thesis of *Animal Farm*. And the prospect, as O'Brien is to be eloquent in telling him, is absurd.

Either romanticize the worker through deification, which means dehumanization, or despise the worker – they were the only alternatives to an intellectual like Orwell. He had the real Ingsoc stuff in him; he read the *New Statesman* while the workers read *Blighty* and the *Daily Mirror*. The workers did not buy his books. The workers do not buy my books either, but I do not repine. Nor do I make the mistake of supposing that the life of the imagination is somehow superior to the life of the body. The dock-worker and the novelist belong to the same organism, called society, and society, whatever it thinks, cannot get along without either of us.

Orwell was unfortunate in being born on the edge of the ruling class in late Imperial Britain. The gap between himself and the lower orders, who used bad language and smelt horribly, could only be bridged by condescension, by a kind of ritual identification, by the fictional imagination. At the end of his literary career Orwell dropped all pretence of believing in the working class. This, inevitably, meant loss of belief in all men and women, in the possibility of love as a spark capable of leaping over the immensity – five inches or five million miles – between one human identity and another. *Nineteen Eighty-Four* is not a prophecy so much as a testimony of despair. Not despair of the future of humanity; a personal despair of being able to love. If Orwell had loved men and women, O'Brien would not have been able to torture Winston Smith. The great majority of men and women look on like munching cows while Winston screams and the death of freedom is confirmed. This is a monstrous travesty of human probability.

There is no such thing as the proletariat. There are only men and women of varying degrees of social, religious, intellectual consciousness. To view these in Marxist terms is as degrading as to look down on them from a viceregal carriage. We have no duty to cross the gap of blood, education, accent and smell by contracting a penitential marriage outside our milieu, or even by suffering a wet Monday under Wigan Pier. But we have a duty not to turn abstractions like class and race into banners of intolerance, fear and hatred. We have to try to remember that we are all, alas, much the same, i.e. pretty horrible. Orwell has, in *Nineteen Eighty-Four*, opened a gap that cannot exist, and in that gap he has built his improbable tyranny. It rests on air, like a castle in Spain. We are so fascinated by it that we will not use the dissolving power of disbelief and send it silently crashing. 1984 is not going to be like that at all.

Part Two

1985

1 The Yuletide fire

It was the week before Christmas, Monday midday, mild and muggy, and the muezzins of West London were yodelling about there being no God but Allah:

'La ilaha illa'lah. La ilaha illa'lah.'

Bev Jones shoved his way through the multiracial shopping crowd past the screaming Diskbutik, the tinselled supermarket, the former pub that was now a travel agency specializing in trips to Mecca but still known as Al-Bulnbush, turned the corner of Tolpuddle Road on to Martyr Street and arrived at Hogarth Highrise. This was where he lived but, he thought glumly, his heart sinking, you would hardly suppose so, not with that gang of aggressive youths barring the way in. Kumina gangs they were called, these terrors of the streets, *kumi na* being the Swahili prefix that meant teen and, by extension, teenage. Normally they would, at this hour, be terrorizing their school canteens, but there was a teachers' strike on. This was why Bev Jones was not lunching at his own canteen today. His daughter Bessie was home and unattended; his wife Ellen was in hospital. He had to unlock the kitchen and give Bessie a meal. Thirteen years old, physically precocious, she was otherwise young for her age. The National Health doctors blamed it on Yenethlia, a substance prescribed for the easing of childbirth whose side-effects had not been foreseen. 'Nobody's fault,' Dr Zazibu had said. 'Medicine must progress, man.'

Bev grinned ingratiatingly at the seven kumina youths, but his risor muscles responded as though to the massed sucking of lemons. He didn't know any of them; they didn't live here. They were always dangerous, the more dangerous because they were intelligent – more than intelligent, positively learned, some of them. That was the trouble: when the State didn't encourage learning, learning became an anti-social thing. Bev said:

'If you don't mind, gentlemen – I live here.' He was on the second step of the stone stairway; they wouldn't let him get any higher. 'And,' he added, 'I'm in a bit of a hurry.'

'*Festina lente*,' smiled a cocoa-coloured youth in a sweatshirt that showed a huge-fisted flying-cloaked Shakespeare with the legend WILL POWER. Then they had him pinioned. The Latin-speaking youth went through his pockets, singing Latin: '*Gaudeamus igitur, juvenes dum sumus.*' It was a good tenor voice, unforced, resonant. He did not find much in Bev's pockets – an Interbank credit card, a near-empty packet of Hamaki Mild, a disposable lighter, three pound notes, five deckers (or tenpenny pieces). He pocketed all except the lighter. This he flicked and flared at Bev's eyeballs, as if testing his ocular reflexes. Then he yawned, and his belly rumbled. 'All right, tigers,' he said. 'We eat.' Then he set fire to Bev's hair and let his companions beat it out with their fists. Then they all kicked Bev not too hard, gracefully, balletically. It could have been worse. They went off languidly. When Bev got inside the hallway he saw an explanation of the languor. The Irwin boy lay unconcious near the lift door, near-naked, bruised, not too bloody. It had been a multiple pederastic assault, a sevenfold entry. Poor kid. The Irwins lived on the tenth floor and, naturally, the lift was not working. Bev rang the janitor's bell. Mr Withers came out chewing, marmalade on his chin. He chewed still, looking at the bloodied boy.

'You heard nothing?' said Bev. 'Are the Irwins in?'

'No,' said Mr Withers. 'To both.'

'Saw nothing on your screens?'

'The screens is not working. Still waiting for somebody to come round. It's the committee's job to hurry that up. Aren't you on the committee?'

'No longer,' said Bev. 'You'd better call an ambulance.'

'It's a bloody liberty, the whole business.'

Bev climbed to the third floor. It didn't do, these days, to be too compassionate. You could spend all day and night being compassionate to the victims of street, hallway and apartment assault. Compassion began at home. He came to his own apartment, 3B. Home. It was no good ringing, not with little Bessie. Bessie could not manage the complicated multilocks. Bev gave his name to a dim red eye on a wall panel. The device responded to his voice-print and, from a slot, his keybunch came jangling into his hand. It took him forty seconds to open up.

Bessie sat widelegged on the floor in front of the telly. She wore, Bev saw, no garment under her one-piece school frock. He sighed. She'd been masturbating, no doubt, to some beefcake image on the screen. The screen was now flashing, bleating and exploding with a kid's cartoon film – lethal violence but nobody getting really hurt, let alone dying. The six-year old Porson kid on the twelfth floor, having seen Chickweed the Wonder jump from a 120-floor skyscraper roof without damage, had, in smiling confidence, leapt down the stairwell. That had been a year ago; the Porsons had got over it; they had not even got rid of their telly. Bev said carefully:

'Did you telephone the hospital?'

'What?' Her eyes didn't move from the jerking images.

'The hospital. Where your mother is. Did you telephone?'

'Not working.'

'What is not working?' he asked patiently. 'Our telephone? The hospital exchange?'

'Not working,' she said, and her mouth opened in weak silly joy as a mouse in a hat was crushed with a steam hammer and lived to squeak vengeance. 'I'm hungry,' she added.

Bev went to the telephone in the little hallway. He dialled 359 1111 ('I ill': that was how one remembered the hospital number; the prefix was, of course, a different matter).

A tapevox courteously responded. It said: 'This is Hospital Control. At Brentford General salvage and evacuation are still proceeding. No individual enquiries may be dealt with for at least twenty-four hours. This is Hospital C – '

His heart had hardly settled from its triple agitation. The balletic beating, the Irwin boy, the enforced climb. Now it thumped viciously. He dashed to the telly and began to search the channels. Bessie wailed; she beat his ankles with her fists. He got the news. A man with little chin and much hair was saying, against a background of blown-up flames:

' – is taking a serious view of the matter. It is believed that the fire was started by irresponsible elements who have not yet been identified, though Scotland Yard is already at work on the following up of what are described as significant clues. It is felt that deliberate advantage was taken of the firemen's strike, now in its third week, and of the sympathetic strike that broke out yesterday at army barracks in the London area. In the absence of professional anti-pyro services, said Mr Halifax, Minister of Public Safety, citizens must be on the look out for further acts of wanton incendiarism and, at the same time, should acquaint themselves with the fire precaution information made available by their communication services.' Bev, sobbing, '*Oh my God,*' was out of that room and fumbling with the multilocks while the announcer was saying, 'Soccer – tonight's fixtures,' and Bessie, as ever slow on the uptake, was wailing before switching back to her cartoon. An old Popeye was just coming on. She was content. And then she remembered her hunger. But Bev was out of the apartment before her complaints grew loud.

He stumbled sobbing downstairs. The Irwin boy, still unconscious, lay waiting for an ambulance. Mr Withers was probably back at lunch. Bev ran to Chiswick High Street. He saw no taxis. He saw a bus, Brentford-bound, snarled up in the traffic. He boarded it and then remembered he had no money for his fare. To hell; the shock of the sight of the burning sky, his own distress, were not these payment enough? They proved to be as the bus crawled on. The black conductor said: 'You look pretty sick, man. Okay, you pay nother time.'

And then he was there, trying to push through the police, for the police were not at present on strike, and shouting, 'My wife, my wife, it's my wife, blast you.' The sky was puce, damson, gamboge, primrose, daffodil, smoke, flinders of destruction going up like thin black angels, and the heat was a huge shouldering bully. A few windows were square eyes empty of all but flame, sad, at length sadly collapsing. There were a couple of collapsing doctors in singed surgical coats. Beds and stretchers were being loaded on to floats borrowed from the nearby brewery. 'My wife,' cried Bev. 'Mrs Jones, Ellen, Ward 4c.' The doctors shook their heads as if shaking were physically painful. 'You,' cried Bev to an old woman, grey hair burned off, slackly naked under a blanket. 'you know me, you know my wife.'

'Don't let them get away with it,' breathed a known voice.

'Oh, my God, Ellie, Ellie.' Bev knelt to the stretcher that awaited loading. His wife and not his wife. There are parts of the body reluctant to be combusted, but they are mostly bone. He was on his knees beside her and then, desperately sobbing, lying across her, seeking to embrace, picking up a handful of scorched skin and, under it, cooked meat. She could not feel anything now. But that had been her voice. The last thing she said had not been love, I love, look after Bessie, God what a waste, we'll meet. It had been: 'Don't let them – ' 'My dear poor beloved,' he sobbed.

'That one,' said a weary voice high above him. 'for DD. Better out of it. A lot of them would.' Disposal of the dead, evacuation of the living. The brewery floats were chalked DD and EL. Bev was pulled kindly to his feet. 'Can't do anything, mate,' said a kind rough voice. 'It's a crying shame, that's all. It's the world we're living in.'

He went back home. He walked back, seeing in a shop window Bev Jones, his hair singed by a small flame, prophetic, a message, his jaw down, mouth shapeless, eyes fierce. In the hallway of Hogarth Highrise the inert body still lay, awaiting an ambulance that would probably not now come. Bev mounted the stairs.

It was not easy to make it clear to Bessie what precisely had happened, that she was now without a mother, that her mother had been cooked to death by irresponsible elements. That those whose office it was to put out fires had struck some weeks back for more money. That the army had – intimidated or else through genuine ideological conviction of the right to withhold labour – mutinied. But mutiny was an old-fashioned word, its quaint inept syllables (mute, tiny; mew, tinny) to be associated only with old films about the British Navy. It belonged with words like honour and duty. That men and women could withhold their labour on a point of principle was universally accepted as a right, and the right had at last (after certain pointless wrangles about honour and duty) crossed from the shop-floor to the barrack-square. For the moment, he thought, he would say nothing to Bessie. He had quite enough to think about, as well as to suffer, without having to suffer the fatigue of probing for a thinking area in Bessie's brain. Bessie was watching some ancient film about the Americans fighting the Japanese.

She had been eating cereals from a box into which she had poured milk, regardless of leakage, and sprinkled sugar. So much was evident from the floor around her. That was because, in his urgency, he had forgotten to relock the kitchen, in which Bessie could not be trusted. He went quietly to the kitchen now and set about preparing a cooked meal for Bessie. Everybody had a right to a cooked meal at lunch-time. It was long past lunch-time, but the right would stand no nonsense from the feeble arguments of the clock. As for himself, he would not be going back to work today. Tomorrow would be different. Tomorrow would be very different.

He grilled some sausages, reconstituted dried potatoes into a puree, made tea.

'Bessie, dear,' he said, taking her plate in to her. Poor motherless child, watching the Yanks knocking hell out of the Japs. He sat in the worn aubergine-coloured armchair, hands folded, watching her eat. She shovelled it all in near-sightlessly. She belched in finality, scratching her bared pubes. Poor motherless *innocent* child. When THE END came in brassy triumph, he gently switched off the set. She made an animal noise of resentment and put out her hand, but he caught the hand tenderly and said: 'I have to tell you things.'

'But it's Spiro and Spero now.'

'Spiro and Spero, whoever they are, must wait. What I have to tell you is that your mother is dead. She was burnt to death in a fire at the hospital. Do you understand me, Bessie? Your dear mother, my dear wife. We won't see her ever again.' Then he wept, sniffing, *'I'b sorry I cad't help id,'* as he looked for his handkerchief. But the kumina gang had taken that too. His swimming eyes saw Bessie looking at him, mouth open, trying to take it in. She was looking into the future, trying to visualize a life without a mother. She said:

'Who'll cook Christmas dinner for us then?' It was a beginning: she was contemplating a future from which certain familiar amenities had been removed. 'You don't cook as good as mum,' she said. Then she began to snivel. She was taking in more now. 'Poor mum. Poor me.'

'I'll learn, we'll learn together. It's you and me together now, Bess girl.' And he turned eyes of grim pity to her, a child of thirteen who looked twenty and a blowsy twenty at that, over-ripe for the bearing of moronic workers for T U K, or The United Kingdom, or Tucland as Bill, the Symbolic Worker, called it. Bev gauged her capacity to learn anything other than the numbers on the knobs of the television dial, a victim of bad medicine, bad air, bad food, farcical education, a despicable popular culture. A brain that had reached seven and then stood still. Last year there had been compulsory fitting of a ring contraceptive too deep in for her fingers to fiddle with. Well, it was right, he thought, right. *Don't let them get away with it*. If he was going to challenge the system, Bessie was not likely to be much good as a helpmeet.

Having taken in a certain future emptiness, enough to be going on with, Bessie now partially filled it by switching on the tailend of Spiro and Spero. Bev sighed and shook his head. Spiro and Spero were a pair of cartoon dolphins who spoke English on the Chinese model: You Say He Not Come I Know He Come I Know He Come Soon.

He knew that shock was going to strike soon, so he made a cushion. In the kitchen cupboard was a half-bottle of emergency Australian brandy (Beware of Foreign Imitations). He took it down, sat at the kitchen table, and began to sip from it. The tap dripped dully, like life. The calendar facing him showed bronzed naked girls in the snow, their mouths in a rictus of winter joy exhibiting back-fillings. DECEMBER 1984. Ellen had ringed 10 December as the day she was to enter hospital, 20 December as the day she would probably leave it. It had been a matter of Toye's disease, tedious tests anyway to see if Dr Zazibu's diagnosis had been correct, and, if the showings were positive, the excision of the spleen. An altogether safe operation, Mr Manning the surgeon had said, his eyes belying the words. Thank your stars, young man, for the National Health Service. But Bev had looked up Toye's disease in the Public Library. Not at all altogether safe.

He held back his tears and swigged the brandy. A burnt sugar taste was the prefix to the big burning word in the belly, and the word began a vague romantic or sentimental poem of pure feeling: there's a plan, a meaning, an all-provident Providence. He let the tears come and began to enjoy them. Not at all altogether safe. And then he knew that there was going to be no shock. Nothing unforeseen had really happened. Toye's disease. '... Removal of the spleen may effect a temporary remission of symptoms but the prognosis is, in 85 per cent of cases, negative.' He had expected Ellen to die, though not so brutally. As for her last words, as for the thing he had to do – well, a matter of principle had now been given sharp teeth. 'My wife's last words, brothers, don't I have to follow my wife's dying request?' But the principle itself had had sharpish enough teeth five years ago, though soon blunted....

His uncle George and aunt Rosa had emigrated to Australia in the 1960s. They'd been happy enough in Adelaide, that rather strait-laced city, going to church, eating oysters; George efficient at his linotype job. Nearly twenty years of it, dinkum Aussies both, never a tear for the England they'd left behind. And then Rosa had become ill in 1978, the very worst illness, a paralysis that meant her being encased in an iron lung as part of the permanent furniture of the sitting-room of the Gloria Soame (so, as his uncle said in a letter, it was called in Stryne or Australian) on Parkside Avenue.

Then, without warning, the electricity workers struck. *Strike* – the right, terrible word. There was no time to rush her and her iron lung to the hospital with its emergency supply. For want of the animating current she died. Was murdered, George had screamed. And then – Ah, it had been in all the newspapers. He had accused Jack Rees, the strike leader, of murder. The union itself took no blame. The strike had been wildcat, unofficial. Yes, screamed his uncle, but who invented the weapon? My curses on the whole union system, to the deepest hell with syndicalism. And, while I'm about it, let me say that no man has a right to withdraw his labour, not in any circumstances, for only by his willingness to work is a man defined as a man. It was in this evident madness that Uncle George shot dead Alfred Wigg, the General Secretary of the Electrical Workers' Syndicate of the Commonwealth of Australia, while Wigg was getting out of his official car outside his private residence. Jack Rees went free. Uncle George was living out his confused and sometimes violent days in a pleasant green place called the Patrick White Retreat.

And there was another thing – a thing that never got into the British or TUK or Tucland papers, a matter of journalistic discretion of bullying or bribery or the quiet invocation of some regulation about public order. On a January day in Minneapolis, Minnesota, USA (which some said, perhaps jocularly, stood for Unhappy Syndicalized America), with the temperature at 35 degrees Fahrenheit below freezing, the entire city's power supplies were threatened with indefinite intermission unless, by presidential fiat, certain extravagant wage claims were immediately granted the members of the Federal Electrical Workers' Union. Fifteen thousand deaths from hypothermia, very hard to hush up, followed defiance of the threat. And then, as had to happen, the workers got what they wanted. Then other workers tried the same hellish technique in other areas of essential amenity – gas, water, fuel oil, food delivery. The National Guard, which still attached a meaning to the term mutiny, had been called out. Struggles with picket lines, shots fired, finally shame and the restoration of order and decency when Big Jim Sheldon's own son was brutally killed. Bev had known all about it. Bev's cousin Bert had long been settled in Duluth, Minnesota. He had written letters. When letters did not get through it was not because of censorship, only because of postal strikes. There had been no postal strikes at that time; the letters had got, or gotten, through.

And so those dying words – *Don't let them get away with it* –were really the echo of an old song. Bev sighed over the near-empty bottle of Australian brandy as he foresaw himself at last translating a long-rumbling disaffection into action. He did not want to be a martyr for a freedom that, anyway, few believed in any more or even understood. But he felt himself, as it were, buying a ticket for a train whose destination he could not know, the sole passenger. All he knew was that the journey was necessary.

2 Tucland the brave

Devlin peered at the computer print-out. 'Bev?' he said. 'That's really your first name? Not an abbreviation for Beverley or something?'

'It could stand for three things,' said Bev. 'Beveridge, Bevin or Bevan. Those were big names when I was born.

In Socialism, I mean. My father was a great Socialist.'

'Beveridge was a Liberal,' Devlin said. 'But, of course, Social Insurance was essentially a radical idea.'

'A radical idea borrowed from Bismarck's Germany,' said Bev. Devlin frowned at him and said:

'You sound like an educated man.' The term itself sounded old-fashioned, but Devlin was a man in his sixties, and his vocabulary had not always kept pace with the development of WE, or Workers English. 'You don't sound like –' He looked down at the print-out. '– Like a Confectionery Operative. And, ah, yes, of course, it's all here. You actually taught European history. At Jack Smith Comprehensive. It doesn't say here why you gave it up.'

'I gave it up because of the Ministry directive,' Bev said. 'It limited the content of history courses rather drastically. The history of the trade union movement was, I knew, not the whole of history nor even the most important part of it. But I kept my feelings to myself. I didn't make any public protest. I just said I wanted to better myself.'

'Ruining children's stomachs,' grinned Devlin, 'instead of improving their minds. That's what the value judgement boys would say.'

'I *have* bettered myself,' said Bev. 'I'm twenty pounds a week better off. And ought to be thirty pounds a week better off in the new year.'

'Except,' said Devlin, 'that you won't be working at Penn's Chocolate Factory in the new year, will you? Not if you persist with this this this atavism.'

'I have to persist. Wouldn't *you*, knowing the filth of the whole bloody villainy that it's become? What started as self-protection has become an immoral power bloc. We dream through it all, and then we wake. It killed my wife, the blasted filthy immorality of it. Do you expect me to put up any longer with the slimy unquestioning sinfulness of it? I *saw* my wife turned into charred bones and scorched skin. And you ask me to support the filthy bloody fireman's immoral bloody strike?'

'Nobody asks you to do anything,' said Devlin gently. He pushed a packet of cigarettes over. Bev shook his head. 'I must give it up myself,' said Devlin, taking one, lighting one. 'Who the hell can afford it any more?' The picture on the cigarette packet was a vivid, if small, representation of a lung eaten up by cancer. Orders of the Ministry of

Health. Verbal warnings had never done much good. 'The firemen go their own way. The army goes its own way. In principle we approve naturally. We approve of the strike weapon. But try and be reasonable. Don't blame your wife's death on a necessary device of syndicalist principle. Blame it on the wanton swine who burnt the hospital down.'

'Oh, I do that,' said Bev. 'But in doing it I attack the principle of evil. Because whoever did it, they were an evil lot of murdering bastards. If they were caught, they'd be made to suffer – no, not suffer, that's old-fashioned, isn't it? Reformed. But even if I could get them and kill them, and you know how I'd kill them – '

'You'll get over that,' said Devlin, puffing away.

'Even if I could watch them burning, screaming as my wife must have screamed, I'd feel impotent inside, unsatisfied, knowing that evil was responding to evil, that I'd added to the sum of evil, and that evil would still go on – illiquidable, indestructible, primal and final.'

'That's not our province,' said Devlin. 'That's theology, church stuff. You put that very well, very eloquent. Of course, that kind of thing is useful, always will be in a way. Used it myself in my early days, except that I'd say things like, "The evils of capitalism must be liquidated, destroyed," Good metaphorical stuff, theological language. Sorry, I was interrupting.'

'Let me put it this way,' said Bev. 'A man is being abused on a public street – robbed, stripped, beaten, even sexually debauched. People stand round, doing nothing about it. Don't you blame the non-interferers as much as the wrong-doers?'

'Not as much as,' said Devlin. 'They're not doing wrong, they're not doing anything. You blame people for doing things, not not doing them.'

'Wrong,' said Bev. 'You probably blame them more. Because the evil-doers are a permanent part of the human condition, proving that evil exists and can't be legislated or reformed or punished out of existence. But the others have a duty to stop evil being enacted. They're defined as human beings by possession of that duty. If they fail to do that duty, they have to be blamed. Blamed and punished.'

'There's no such thing as duty any more,' said Devlin. 'You know that. There are only rights. Commission for

Human Rights – that makes sense. Commission for Human Duty – bloody nonsense, isn't it? It was always bloody nonsense, and you know it.'

'Duty to family,' said Bev. 'Duty to one's art or craft. Duty to one's country. Bloody nonsense. I see.'

'Duty to see that one's rights are respected.' said Devlin. 'I'll grant that. But if you say, "Right to see that one's rights etcetera," well, it doesn't seem to mean anything different. No, I throw out your duty.'

'So the firemen have the right to stand by,' said Bev very hotly, 'when a hospital's burning down, to stand by and say: "Give us our rights and this won't happen again. Not till the next time, anyway." I say it's a bigger evil than the other evil.'

'Well, now,' said Devlin, stubbing out his fag end, 'you may be interested to know that this fire business at Brentford has already started yielding positive results. The firemen are sitting down today with the Wages Board. Tomorrow the strike may be over. Think about that before you start raging about what you call evil. Nothing that improves the lot of the worker can be evil. Think about that. Write it in the flyleaf of your diary for 1985.'

'Write this in your own diary,' said Bev. 'Write: MEN ARE FREE. You people have forgotten what freedom is.'

'Freedom to starve, freedom to be exploited,' said Devlin with an old, no longer pertinent, bitterness. 'Freedoms I'm very pleased to see belong only to the course in history that you refused to teach. You're a bloody-minded individual, brother,' said Devlin, a growl entering his tone. 'You're a bloody-minded reactionary, comrade. You're demanding freedom and, by the dead or living or non-existent Christ, you're going to get it.' He waved at Bev the official note that Bev's shop steward had forwarded to him. 'The old filthy free days are gone, me boyo,' he said, his Irish coming out, 'except for you and reactionaries like you. You stopped teaching history and you've turned your back on history. Do you not wish to remember that only twenty years ago your union, my union, did not exist? It was struggling to be born, and, by Christ, it got itself born and born in pain but also born in triumph. Men tending the machines that produce chocolate bars and candy crunchies and creamy coconut whatevertheyare were in a worse bargaining position than the miners and railway-workers and foundrymen. Why? Because of reactionaries like you, with your value judgements.'

'This is nonsense and you know it.' said Bev with calm.

'You know bloody well what I mean,' shouted Devlin. 'An archaic and essentially bourgeois ladder of values made it dangerous to let the miners strike too long and freeze the arses of the consumers, but what were called inessentials and marginal goods and luxury products could go to hell and the confectionery workers with them. Well, it's all over now, me boyo. When we go on strike the bakers go on strike with us. No response to a reasonable wage increase demand among the chocolate boys and the populace gets no bread. And there's no stupid reactionary bitch who can say let them eat cake, because if you can't have one you can't have the other. And the time's coming, and it won't be long, it may well be before 1990, when every strike will be a general strike. When a toothbrush maker can withdraw his labour in a just demand for a living wage and do so in the confidence that the lights will go off and people will shiver and the trains won't be running and the schools will close. That's what we're moving to, brother. Holistic syndicalism, as Pettigrew calls it with his love of big words. And you have the effrontery and nerve and stupidity and reactionary evil-mindedness to talk about freedom.' He panted hard and fiercely lighted himself another cigarette. Bev spoke mildly. He said:

'I ask only for the rescission of the closed shop. I demand, as a free human being, the right to work without being forced into membership of a union. Isn't that reasonable? People like me, who oppose the closed shop on moral principle – '

'It's not moral principle, and you damned well know it. It's not thought or conviction, it's rage, and I'm not blaming you for the rage, I wouldn't blame any man, but I *am* blaming you for converting the rage into what you think is a belief. What I say is: give it till after Christmas. Get drunk, stuff yourself with turkey, nurse your hangover, then go back to dropping little bits of hazelnut on to your chocolate creams or whatever they are – '

'My rage,' said Bev, 'as you rightly term it, is the mere emotional culmination of a long-growing belief that the closed shop is evil, that it's unjust to force men into being mere cells in a gross fat body that combines the torpid and the predatory, that a man has a right to work if he wants to work without having to jump at the shop steward's whistle, and that, given certain circumstances, a man has a *duty* to work. A duty to put out a fire, if that's his trade. A duty to – ' He was going to say: drop nuts on chocolate creams, but he saw the absurdity of it. And then he did not see the absurdity of it. A child dying and wanting only one thing: a box of Penn's Assorted. And everybody on strike and not a box left in the world, and the defiant worker, braving the threats and the blows, going to his machine – No, it wouldn't work. Principle, principle was the thing.

Devlin got up and walked over to his watercooler. His office was very rational, with flimsy basic furniture in primary colours, and it was very dry and warm. On the wall was a framed poster – the original Bill the Symbolic Worker, not just the first pull but the coloured drawing itself, done by a man called Tilson. Bill was a handsome, tough, intelligent-looking, sharp-eyed generic operative in a cloth cap with curly hair escaping from it, blue-overalled, an indeterminate tool like a wrench in hand. Bev saw, as Devlin stood in the light of the window, drinking water from a paper cup, that Bill might well have been modelled on Devlin when he was, say, thirty years younger. He said: 'Is that you?' Devlin looked sharply and, it seemed, balefully at Bev. He said:

'That? This? Bill? Not quite me. My son.' There was something in his tone that made Bev able to say:

'Dead?'

'Dead to me. With his bloody ballet-dancing and his pansified pretty ways.'

'Homosexual?'

'He might well be for all I know. The bastards he got in with are brown-hatters, bugger them.' Devlin saw he had gone beyond his immediate terms of communication with this bloody-minded one here, who was now grinning rather nastily and saying:

'That must make for a terrible conflict inside you, Brother Devlin – knowing that the prettily pansified are as tightly corseted in their unions as the boilermen and the truckdrivers. Male models, I mean, and dancers, and even the Gaypros.'

'The gay what?'

'The homosexual prostitutes. Minimum rates and so on. I'm old-fashioned enough to get a certain ironic pleasure out of knowing that Bill the Worker there is probably handling a spanner or whatever it is for the first time in his life. What a world you've made.'

'I think this has gone on long enough,' Devlin said. He went back to his desk and picked up the report delivered by Bev's shop steward. 'You tore up your union card in full view of your brothers. You loudly proclaimed your disaffection with the system. Your brothers were tolerant, knowing that you were not your normal self. I don't think, in the circumstances, disciplinary action is called for –'

'What kind of disciplinary action?'

'Read the regulations. Clause 15 section d subsection 12. A fine not less than double and not more than five times your annual subscription. We let that pass. The tearing of the card is nothing. It's like in the old Christian days when people got baptized. Tear up your baptizmal certificate and it doesn't make you unbaptized. You're a union member, and that's it.'

'Until I start to go my own way and not hop to the whistle.'

'You're a union member and you can't unmake it. The records say so and the records are like the tablets of the Mosaic law. But – ' And he looked at Bev sternly, a bald man with a tired and fleshy grey face, droll eyes despite the sternness, a mobile mouth that briefly chewed air or some tiny residue of breakfast cached by a hollow tooth and now released by it. Bill the Symbolic Worker smiled down at Bev with gentle encouragement.

'But,' Bev completed what in effect was meaningful enough. 'when I next neglect to participate in industrial action – '

'There's a strike of the millers on Christmas Eve,' said Devlin. 'I hope you'll have got over this nonsense by then. If not, you can call that the shooting of your bolt.'

'You'll see,' said Bev, getting up.

'It's you that's bloody well going to see, brother,' Devlin said.

Bev left the office of the general secretary of his union, or former union, and took the lift from the twenty-third floor to the foyer, which still had the look of the old Hilton hotel that this building, New Transport House, had formerly been. There was not a single union in the syndicalist network of the whole country that was not represented here, from chimney-sweeps to composers of electronic music for films. A great plaque above the reception desk said THE TRADES UNION CONGRESS OF THE UNITED KINGDOM. Beneath it was a logogram – a simplified map of the country with the simple inscription TUK = TUC. This was why Great Britain had been christened, by a jocular columnist in *The Times*, Tucland. It was a nomenclature seriously and gratefully seized by the great union chiefs, or their copywriters, and it featured in the Anthem of the Workers:

> Muscles as tough as leather,
> Hearts proofed against the weather,
> Marching in friendly tether,
> Cradle to·grave,
> Scorn we a heaven hereafter –
> Build it with love and laughter
> Here, firm from floor to rafter –
> Tucland the brave.

Needless to say, few of the workers knew the words. Outside, a warm drizzle just beginning, Bev looked up at the towering stained stucco to the flag flapping at the top – a silver cogwheel on a blood-red background, a hammer and sickle no longer implying a world union of workers but standing for the Advanced Socialists who, in the sacred name of labour, sought to build, or had already in Europe long built, repressive state systems which denied syndicalism. Aneurin Bevan, probably the primary namesake of Bev, since Bev was a son of Wales, as Bevan had been, had once said, though never in public, wise words: 'Syndicalism is not Socialism.' Meaning that when the workers were their own employers there was no one to fight against. In Tucland the ancient division of capital and labour continued to subsist, and would probably do so for ever, whether the capitalist was the private boss (a fast-disappearing figure) or the State.

Bev couldn't help smiling as he strained his neck, still looking upward at the flying wheel, remembering that ownership was incompatible with the philosophy of labour, and that the TUC rented this building from the Arabs. Where would Tucland be without the Arabs? The oil, at a price ever more exorbitant, flowed in from Islam and kept Tucland's industries going. And Islam was not

only the hot desert but also the cold ocean, for North Sea
oil had been mortgaged to the Arabs for a government
loan when the International Monetary Fund had closed its
cashboxes to Britain for the last time, and the loan had
been called in and the mortgage foreclosed, and the crescent moon banners waved from the chilly derricks. The
Arabs were in Britain to stay. They owned Al-Dorchester,
Al-Klaridges, Al-Browns, various Al-Hiltons and Al-
Idayinns, with soft drinks in the bars and no bacon for
breakfast. They owned things that people did not even
know they owned, including distilleries and breweries.
And, in Great Smith Street, soon would stand the symbol
of their strength – the Masjid-ul-Haram or Great Mosque
of London. To remind Britain that Islam was not just a
faith for the rich, plenty of hard-working Pakistanis and
East African Muslims flowed in without hindrance, for the
adjustment of the immigration laws (which had had too-
stringent quota clauses) in favour of the Islamic peoples
was a necessary political consequence of Arab financial
patronage. Yet the workers who had forgotten their Christianity were supposed to sing, 'Scorn we a heaven hereafter'. They ought, thought Bev in a flash of insight, to be
more fearful than they were of a people that believed in a
heaven hereafter.

3 You was on the telly

Like good Muslims, the British millers who produced
what Britain called flour – a fine white dust with car-
cinogens but little nutritive content – struck at sunset, not
at dawn. At dawn on Christmas Eve there was no bread,
for the bakers locked the doors on their flour-stocks and
also went on strike. The confectionery workers went on
strike too. Housewives, who were not yet unionized, grew
angry when they found no loaves or cakes around and
rioted in the High Streets. The Wages Board responded at
three in the afternoon by promising favourable consideration of the millers' demands for triple-time pay for night-
work, and the strikes were ended half an hour before the
Christmas holidays were due to start for regular day

workers, so that all could toast the festive season in the boss's time. There was still no bread for Christmas.

Bev, shoulders straight, chest out, legs like water, reported for duty as usual at eight in the morning at Penn's Chocolate Works. There was a picket waiting for him. There were policemen, chewing their straps. The police, though reluctantly, grabbed a man who threw a small stone at Bev, even though he missed.

'Whose side are you bloody rozzers on?' went the shout.

'You know the law as well as what I do,' said the sergeant unhappily. A van from Thames Television drew up. Bev waited. His act would have no validity unless available for the world to witness. This was the new way. It's Really Real when it's Seen on the Screen. Jeff Fairclough got out, hands deep in smart burberry, red hair waving in the breeze. A man with a hand-held camera and a recordist with a Stellavox followed. Fairclough and Bev nodded to each other. He had telephoned Fairclough the previous evening. Fairclough had once been a colleague, a teacher of English until the advent of the new WE syllabus. ('Usage is the only law. *You was* is the form used by eighty-five per cent of the British population. *You was* is therefore correct. The pedantic may reflect that this was the regular form used by pedants like Jonathan Swift in the eighteenth century.') Bev and the team marched through the open gateway. The strikers put on a great act of snarling and cursing for the camera. The sound recordist didn't record. They could get the bloodying and buggering from stock. Bev led the way to the executive wing. Young Mr Penn, very nervous, came forth to meet them. The Stellavox man put his headphones on, switched on, gave a thumbs up to Fairclough, who said: 'Action.'

'Good morning, Mr Penn. I'm reporting for work as usual.'

'You can't, you know it, we're closed. There's a strike on.'

'*I'm* not striking, Mr Penn. I claim my rights as a free man. I'm here to work.'

'You can't. You damn well know you can't. Be reasonable.'

'Are you denying me my basic right as a worker?'

'Don't be so bloody stupid. You know bloody well what the position is.'

400

'Are you a Quaker, Mr Penn – a member of the Society of Friends?'

'I don't see what the hell that's got to do with anything. Now bugger off.'

'You're dismissing me, Mr Penn? On what grounds? Redundancy? Inefficiency? Insubordination?'

'I'm not dismissing you. I'm giving you the day off.'

'You deny one of the basic tenets of the Quaker chocolate manufacturers – an employee's right to work, his total immunity from any exterior coercion that persuades him not to?'

'You know the position as well as I do. You're in a closed shop. You can do nothing about it and neither can I. Can't you at least go through the motions, man?'

'I'll go through the motions with pleasure. Open up and let me get to my machine.'

'But the power's off. Oh, go away.' Mr Penn was in deep distress.

'You think this is just?' said Bev. 'You think you're being just in the way your ancestral co-religionists were just?'

'It's not the point, I tell you. This is the modern age.'

'You and I, Mr Penn, have entered into contractual relations. As employer and employee. Do you propose breaking that contract?'

'Right,' said Mr Penn grimly. 'Come with me.' And he led the way (the cameraman ahead, walking backwards) to the works. Soon Bev stood by his cold machine among other cold machines, being interviewed by Jeff Fairclough.

'So this, Mr Jones, is your way of denouncing the principle of strike action. Don't you consider you're being rather old fashioned?'

'Is justice old fashioned? Is compassion? Is duty? If the modern way approves the burning to death of innocent people with firemen standing by and claiming their workers' rights, then I'm glad to be old fashioned.'

'You realize, Mr Jones, that you're inviting your dismissal from your job? That, moreover, no other job can possibly be available to you? That the closed shop is a fact of life and applies to every single gainful activity?'

'The individual worker has the right to decide whether or not to withhold his labour. My curse on syndicalism.'

'You've just condemned yourself to permanent unemployment.'

'So be it.'

The camera stopped whirring. The recordist switched off and packed up. 'Was I all right?' asked Bev.

'You was fine,' grinned Fairclough. 'But God help you.'

They left. The picket, held back by unhappy police, jeered and threatened. Bev was given a lift by Thames Television to his bank, where he drew out £150, noting that he now had a credit balance of £11.50. He went to do the Christmas shopping. Poor motherless Bessie must not be deprived of her right to seasonal stuffing. She knew what Christmas was about. Her class teacher, Mrs Abdulbakar, had told them the whole story. Nabi Isa, last of the great prophets before Mohammed (may his name be blessed), whom it was in order for the Peoples of the Scripture to call Jesus, had been born to tell the world of the goodness and justice of Allah Most High. Therefore you had to stuff and make yourself sick.

Bev was in the kitchen drinking Christmas Eve whisky when he heard Bessie call: 'Dad, dad, there's this man that looks like you.' He went in and saw himself on the news, but he did not hear himself. The appropriate teleworkers' union would have been at work there, threatening strike action if heresy were allowed to be spoken to the world. He saw himself with Mr Penn and at his cold machine for about ten seconds as a brief pendant to the regional news, and he heard the flippant newsreader say something about here's one man that we can wish a merry Christmas to but not a happy New Year, and then, to the tune of Chopin's Funeral March on wa-wa trumpets, they cut to a chalk-scrawled hanged man on a wall. And that's the end of the local news. Bessie said: 'He's like you, dad.' Bev said:

'He has to be, girl. He *is* me.' Bessie looked at her father with an awe she had never before shown: my dad on the telly.

'Why was you on the telly then?'

Bev sighed and wondered whether to tell her all. No, let it wait. Let her have her Christmas stuffing, poor kid. So they sat together that evening chewing dates and cracking walnuts, her eyes glued to the screen, his restless, sometimes closing unhappily, and they saw *White Christmas* with Saint Bing and Rosemary Clooney, and when *Arab Hour* came on they switched over to a new musical version of Charles Dickens's *A Christmas Carol*, in which Ebenezer Scrooge was not reformed into a model paternalistic employer but, scared by his ghostly visitants, saw what the bloody power of the workers was going to be bloody well like, mate, and celebrated Boxing Day by being cowed by the new Clerical Workers' Union under its leader, Bob Cratchit. Then Bev served them both, on the floor in front of the telly, with the electric fire glowing away, a nice big cold Christmas Eve meal of ham and mixed pickles followed by sherry trifle he'd made with old dry sponge cakes and eggless custard, and they drank Australian sherry (Beware of Foreign Imitations) and big mugs of sweet tea. There was a late late movie called *The Bells of St Mary's*, with Saint Bing again as a straw-hatted RC priest and Ingrid Bergman as a nun, but it was so cut about as not to make much sense, and then Bessie went to her squalid bed (Bev had neglected the laundry) and woke her father up at four in the morning screaming about a man with claws and three heads. She had wetted the bed in her fright, and Bev in some unease let her come into his, his and poor dead Ellen's. The poor girl was naked, having soaked her already soiled nightdress, and this made Bev very uneasy. When she had got the nightmare out of her head (there were other details than the three-headed man, such as horrid white snakes and hands clutching out of dirty pools of water) she grew calm and said:

'You was on the telly, dad.'

Then she approached him in a frank amorousness that he had to fight off. Poor kid, she was going to be a hell of a problem. He decided to cool her down by telling her what the situation was. It wouldn't spoil her Christmas: she'd have forgotten it all by tomorrow morning. He said:

'Listen carefully, Bessie my love.'

'Yes darling, I'm listening. Put your hand there.'

'No, I will not. Listen, bad times are coming. I'm going to be out of a job. There's going to be no money coming in at all, not even from the National Insurance. They'll probably throw us out of this flat because I won't be able to pay the rent. The bad times are coming because it's my stupidity that's making me jobless – that's what they'll tell you – '

'Who'll tell me? Put your hand there.'

'Your teachers and the other kids whose parents will have told them all about it. But you have to understand why I'm doing it, Bessie. No man has to be crucified. Jesus didn't have to be. But there are some things that a man can't submit to, and I can't submit to what the unions mean. Do you understand?'

'What's croosy whatever it was? Why won't you put your hand there?'

'Because you're my daughter, and there are certain things not permitted between father and daughter. I want you to understand what I'm telling you, Bessie. Your poor dying mother said: *Don't let them get away with it*. And, although it must seem mad to you, that's why I'm setting myself up against the whole power of the unions. I can't beat them, but I can at least be a martyr to the cause of freedom, and some day, perhaps not till I'm long dead, people will remember my name and perhaps make a kind of banner out of it and fight the injustice that the unions stand for. Do you understand me, Bessie?'

'No. And I think you're mean. Why won't you put your _ '

'Well, perhaps you'll understand this, Bessie. You'll have to go into what they call a Girl's Home.'

'A what?'

'A place where the State will look after you, all girls together, until you're old enough to get a job.'

She thought about that for at least a minute, then she said: 'Will there be the telly?'

'Of course there will. No home complete without one, not even a State Girl's Home. You'll get your telly all right.'

'Perhaps they'll have one of these new wide ones.'

'I shouldn't be surprised.'

'They can show the big wide pictures on them, like that one we saw that time with the monsters.'

'You mean *Sky Rape*?'

'Was that what it was called? You and me and mum saw it.' A tone that might have been called victorious came into her voice. 'And now it's me that's here and not mum. Put your hand there. You've *got* to.' Bev turned over wretchedly and pretended to go to sleep. Bessie beat at his back with her fists for a time and then seemed to settle to masturbation. The sooner she got in that Girls' Home the better. The sooner – The first *waktu* of the day started from the Chiswick mosque. No God but Allah.

Next day Bev cooked the stuffed turkey and the cauliflower (it had cost £3.10) and the potatoes and heated up the canned Christmas pudding, while Bessie divided her attention between the telly and her presents – a transistor doll with long provocative legs and an insolent leer, an earplug stereo radio twin set, the Telennial for 1985. After dinner, which Bessie conceded was as good as what mum could do, they listened to the King's Speech on the telly. King Charles III, a rather podgy bat-eared man in his late thirties, a near-contemporary of Bev's, spoke of this happy and sacred time and God bless you all and, at the end, he grinningly wiggled a finger offscreen and Her Majesty the Queen (not to be confused with Elizabeth II, the retired Queen, now Queen Mum) came on, a pretty dark woman with many pearls, also grinning. The King put an arm round the Queen and both waved at the viewers as though they, the viewers, were going off in a train. Then there was *God Save the King*.

In the evening, while they were eating their cold turkey and ham and fried-up spuds and cauli, accompanied by champagne cider, and watching *Holiday Inn*, once more with Saint Bing (whom Bessie took to be a kind of obligatory Christmas presence), the electricity went off. The film rushed at the speed of light to an horizon where it became a pinpoint and then vanished, the electric fire glowed duller and duller and then became irritable noises of contraction. They had no candles, they were really in the dark. Bessie howled and wailed in real anguish.

'*Now* do you understand?' growled her father. '*Now* do you see what I'm fighting against?' She howled that she thought she saw, but the poor motherless child was incapable of generalization. Medicine must progress, man.

4 Out

On 27 December Bev went back to work and at once the all-out whistle blew. Obedient to the contract with the union, the management formally dismissed Bev. Bev went to the Labour Exchange, where he insisted on seeing the Director, not the mere chewing girl underlings with dark after-Christmas rings under their eyes. He informed the Director of his position, and the Director brusquely told him that he could not be registered at the Exchange since he was unwilling to abide by the fundamental condition of employment in any of the scheduled trades, which meant all imaginable trades except that of poet. Formally unemployed and unemployable, Bev went to see about the drawing of unemployment benefit under the provisions of the National Insurance Act. He was told that he was not entitled to anything since he had wantonly rejected employment inasmuch as he refused to accept the conditions of employment as laid down in the Trade Union Enactment (Compulsory Membership) Act of 1979. Bev said:

'I have paid money into the fund. Every week since I began work at the age of twenty – '

'Why did you start so late?' asked the shrewish fat blue-rinsed woman behind the bars, irritably tapping her pencil on the little counter.

'I went to university. I took a degree.'

'Compulsory payment into the National Insurance fund does not automatically entitle you to receive benefits. Certain conditions have to be fulfilled, and you are unwilling to fulfil them.'

'Then what do I do? Do I starve?'

'You fulfil the conditions.'

Bev went to a pub for a half-pint of bitter and a cold sausage with free mustard. He telephoned his Member of Parliament, or rather his secretary, and arranged for an appointment in the late afternoon. Parliament was not sitting: the Christmas recess was on. Mr Prothero would see Mr Jones at his five o'clock 'surgery'.

J. R. Prothero MP was a smart sleek man in early middle age, dressed in tweeds as for a country week-end, smelling of an aftershave lotion that was aggressively urban. He smoked a pipe which he had difficulty in keeping alight; the ashtray before him was a communal grave of dead matches. He listened to Bev's story and said:

'What do you expect me to do about it? Change the law?'

'Laws *are* changed. It's a slow job, I know. The House of Commons, I was taught, is where unjust laws are opposed and just laws propounded.'

'You must have been taught that a very long time ago.'

He had his pipe alight now and sucked two or three times. Then it went out. 'Damn and blast.'

'Why don't you give it up?' said Bev.

'Give what up?' said Mr Prothero with sudden sharp and defensive suspicion.

'Smoking. It's not worth it, with tobacco at £3.50 an ounce, and you obviously don't enjoy it.'

Mr Prothero relaxed. 'I thought you meant – you know.'

'Well,' said Bev, 'You must have asked yourself often enough what use Parliament is. I'll confess I've come to you with no hope. Like a fool, I suppose, living in the past when Members looked after their constituencies. But I have to suck a bitter pleasure out of the hopelessness of it all. I have to go through the motions of believing that democratic freedom still exists. It's like trying to believe in one's wife's fidelity when you see her lying on the hearthrug with the milkman. Till death us do part. Government for the people. Silly, isn't it? Nostalgia.'

Bev saw that Mr Prothero's inefficiency with pipe-lighting was, in a way, volitional. He kept striking, and, unlike so many of his constituents, he struck to no avail. But the fruitless process gave him an opportunity to put off answering awkward questions or, as now, being even minimally helpful. Still, he said at last, putting down a still cold pipe: 'You can't fight history.'

'Ah, interesting. And who makes history?'

'Movements. Trends. Elans. Processes. Not who, what. What's happened in Britain has not happened through bloody and wasteful revolution. We've gone our democratic way and not, in the process of changing, seen any violent signs of change. And then one morning we wake up and say: The Rule of the Proletariat is Here. What has still not happened in countries where nasty revolutions took place has happened here without trouble. I don't know what Karl Marx would say if he came back, but – '

'Marx would say that the desired thing hasn't happened, that the means of production are not in the hands of the workers, that capitalism has not been destroyed.'

'It's being destroyed,' said Mr Prothero. 'Fast. There's hardly a firm in the country that hasn't passed into the hands of the State. The State's the great employer.'

'Exactly. And against the employer is set the employee. The State's the dirty horrible boss and the unions fight it as though it wore a top hat. And they always win, that's the trouble. The government's a mere machine for printing paper money. Look at the state of inflation. And is one single voice in parliament raised against the imminent ruin of the country? It's time some of you risked your jobs and spoke out for liberty and decency and, yes, plain old-fashioned common sense.'

Mr Prothero picked up his old enemy and tried once more to set fire to it. The graveyard of dead matches was rising into a tumulus. He gave up bitterly and said: 'There's the Whips. We just vote in the bills or abstain from voting. Our constituencies aren't regional any more, whatever they're called. Our constituents are a cross-section of the whole syndicalist system. It's no good anyone complaining. That's the historical process nobody can oppose. It's not like in the days of Fox and Burke and Wilkes. There's just two collectives.'

'It might as well be one. The notion of opposition is a farce. Socialists and Conservatives – nothing but names with a nostalgic historical meaning. What difference is there now between your ideologies? Whoever's running the government, the workers can reduce it to impotence. Do what we say or we strike. And,' his voice grew deep and harsh, 'there's a day or two of token resistance in the name of holding back inflation or keeping our exports competitive. Then more money printed with nothing to back it. Token resistance to show the government's really governing. Except that it's not token resistance to those who die of hypothermia or, Jesus Christ help us, hyperthermia.'

'I'm sorry about what happened,' said Mr Prothero pitilessly. 'You must be feeling very bitter. The firemen go back to work tomorrow, if that's any consolation.'

'Unfortunately, I don't have another wife for them not to burn to death. All right, forget it, I have to forget it. I come to you now to ask – to demand, I suppose – that you do something about me. A man jobless and likely to be for ever, unentitled to State benefit, because he's followed the dictates of his individual conscience and refused to yield to the collective will.'

'You know damned well I can't do anything,' said Mr Prothero, clutching his pipe peevishly. 'You're fighting history. I've got more sense than to try to fight it. Strictly speaking I'm forbidden even to open my mouth in a *token* way on your behalf. Because you're outside the law. Union membership is a basic condition of franchise. You're not represented any more.'

'I join the little old ladies and the lunatics and the criminals?'

'There's a Senior Citizens' Union, as you damned well know. Lunatic – criminal – yes, I suppose those terms apply. You're on your own, brother.' It was not clear whether *brother* was used out of Socialist force of habit, or with the contemptuous irony it sometimes carried in old American movies. It certainly conveyed clearly to Bev his condition of brotherlessness. Bev said:

'I expected all this, of course. In a way I'm courting my own ruin. Call me a witness, which, in Greek, is *martyr*. But I had to go through the motions – pretend that an engine is still working when it's only a disregarded item in a museum. I hope my situation gives you bad dreams, Mr Prothero. Screw you. And get rid of that bloody stupid pipe.' Then he went out.

He went back to his flat where Bessie, still on holiday, was eating the remains of the cold turkey with her fingers and gawping at Red, Rod and Rid on the television. He sat down wearily and wondered whether there was anything he could sell to put off the coming day of eviction. There was nothing except Ellen's clothes and a couple of old suitcases. The furniture belonged to the landlord, a faceless collective with computers that would brook no appeal to such human weaknesses as compassion. The eviction notice would come in a week or so, and then the RPs or Rent Police or bullyboys would arrive to enforce the eviction. He did not even own the television set: it was rented from Visionem Ltd. The end of the month, which was also the end of the year, was coming up. Repossession Day. He said:

'Bessie, I think the time has come. Get your things together.'

'What for? It's Dish and Dash in a minute.'

'Very well. After Dish and Dash, whatever they are. You and I must go you know where.'

'Where?' Her eyes had not left the screen.

Bev went to the kitchen and drank the last of the Christmas whisky. Anything to sell here? He opened a drawer: all landlord's cutlery. Wait, what was this? It was a flick-knife, rather a good one, sharp and solid, the blade quick to respond to the flickswitch. It had been put there to keep it away from Bessie. Where had he obtained it? Ah, yes – the two six-year-old boys once on this very street, threatening a five-year-old girl. Why? For no purpose except sheer disinterested terrorization. He had hit the boys and grabbed the knife. If his MP had, more or less officially, assigned him to the criminal classes, he might as well be criminally armed. He put the knife in his trouser-pocket. Then he went to drag Bessie away from whatever it was that followed Dish and Dash. She did not wail. it was only the news. 'Let's be quick,' she said. 'There's *Sex Boy* on soon.' Home was anywhere, so long as there was a telly.

5 Culture and anarchy

The new year came in with bitter weather. Bessie was snug in a Girl's Home in Islington, whence she travelled daily to school in what her father, having already seen some of her co-inmates, ironically called a virginibus. Then she travelled back to tea and the telly. Bev himself slept where he could – in Salvation Army hostels, in railway termini and, on one occasion, in Westminster Abbey. His bit of money soon ran out – £7.50 in notes and deckers. The decker was the old florin that the Victorians had introduced with a view, later wisely abandoned, to decimalizing the coinage – ten of them to a sovereign. The decimalization of the 1960s, to force Britain into line with the rest of the European Community, had brought one hundred new pence (called, with proper contempt, *p*), but these, with the advance of inflation, had soon lost their meaning. Ten deckers to a pound, and no finer division. Soon, Bev foresaw, the Tucland quid would be like the Italian lira, only theoretically fissile. For a decker he could buy a small box of matches, if he wished to, though he did not see the use. Tobacco, the lonely and idle man's comfort, was beyond him. A bun or sandwich was at least £1.00. The Salvation Army gave him, on condition that he first prayed over it, a bowl of skilly. He grew pretty wretched, dirty and bearded. He had expected to be able to spend much of the day in the reading-rooms of public libraries, but there were not many public libraries around these days, and such as existed still were full of old snoring men.

'The workers don't need libraries,' said a kumina boy. 'They need clubs.'

'I'd club the bastards,' growled another. A small gang of them had stopped Bev with an evident view to bashing and robbing. Bev felt no fear and the boys must have sensed it. He leaned against a torn wall-poster of Bill the Symbolic Worker (some graffitist had added the inevitable cross-bar to the T in TUCLAND), right hand in pocket clutching flick-knife. He smiled and said:

"*Sunt lachrimae rerum, et mentem mortalia tangunt.*'

They'd surrounded him on that, examining, sniffing, breathing on him.

'You know Greek too, man?'

'*Me phunai ton hapanta nika logon.* Sophocles,' said Bev. 'From the *Oedipus Colonus.*'

'Meaning?'

'It is best not to be born.'

From some of the boys came a deep exhalation, as from some satisfying inhalation. The kumina leader, black with an Aryan profile, pulled out a pack of Savuke Finns and said: 'You want a cank?'

'Thanks, but I had to give it up.'

'You out of a job? Union mashaki? You antistate?'

'Yes yes yes.'

There were seven of these kumina boys, not all of them black. The leader said: 'Ah.' For across the street, Great Smith Street in Westminster, where the foundations of the new Mosque lay white in frost, an unwise man was walking alone purposively, a man with a place to go to. 'Ali and Tod,' said the leader. The two named walked over and tripped the man expertly, booted him in the left side, then frisked him as he lay. They came back with thirty-five pound notes. 'Right,' said the leader. 'You come, Tod. The rest at Soapy's around eleven, okay?'

'Okay.'

'Okay, Tuss.'

So Tuss and Tod, a yellowish frail-looking boy who

danced up and down with cold, took Bev to the Unemployed Canteen off Westminster Bridge. Here they fed him with ham sandwiches, sausage rolls, macaroons and tomato soup in a cup. The woman behind the counter said they had to show their certificates of unemployment before they could be permitted to take advantage of the low, subsidized, prices, but the boys merely snarled. Tuss said to Bev, while he wolfed:

'You ever heard of Mizusako?'

'Japanese? Inventor of a violin method?'

'That's very good. But you're a couple letters way off. Violence is more like it. Method, yes, a method.'

Tod said earnestly: 'The trouble he said is separating culture from morality. Because culture's developed by societies and that makes it preach social values. I mean, he means, books don't preach villainy. They preach being good.'

'Books shouldn't strictly preach anything,' said munching Bev. 'Knowledge and beauty – they're outside ethics. Who is this Mizusako?'

'He's in jail somewhere in the States,' said Tusa, smoking very aromatically. 'He went the rounds of the campuses preaching disin disint shit disinterest shit shit shit – '

'Disinterestedness?'

'Hell of a mouthful. But yes, that's it. Free learning, free action. He talked of a UU.'

'You You?'

'An underground university. Paid for by robbery, which has to mean violence. Teaching useless things. Latin, Greek, history. We got lousy education, right?'

'Right.'

'Lousy because it's Labour. Lousy because it levels. No clever boys wanted. There's certain things it won't allow, because it says they're no good to the workers. Now it follows that the things they won't allow must be the only things worth knowing. You get that?'

'There's a sort of logic in it.'

'We go to school, we lot, till we're sixteen. That's the law. Okay, we go and we don't listen to the crap they call sociology and Worker's English. We sit at the back and read Latin.'

'Who teaches you Latin?'

412

'There are these antistate teachers about. You a teacher?'
'History. Very useless.'

'Okay, there are these thrown out of schools for not wanting to teach the crap they're supposed to, right? They wander, like you're wandering. We give then the odd wad like we're doing to you. Then they give us a bit of education in return. Real education, not State school crap.'

'You want something now?'

'One thing,' said Tod. 'How did we get into this mess?'

Bev took a deep breath and then coughed on macaroon crumbs. 'The workers say it isn't a mess. Do your parents say it's a mess?'

'They say nothing,' said Tuss. 'They consume. But it's got to be a mess, because it's so fucking *dull*.'

'I accept that.' Bev couldn't help grinning at the downrightness of Tuss's statement. 'Let me try to explain the mess very quickly and simply. Since the beginning of history there've been the haves and have nots. In politics two main parties developed – one for ensuring that the haves continued to have and, indeed, to have more; the other for turning the have nots into haves. No rich, no poor, just enough for everybody. Levelling, egalitarianism, the just society. Socialism. We have a Socialist State now. We've had one pretty continuously since 1945. Who were the have nots? The workers, the proletariat. They were ground down by the haves, or capitalists. The workers organized themselves into bodies too big for the capitalists to exploit. Unions. Right, the capitalists tried to use non-union labour. The time came when this put them outside the law. The unions had and have the upper hand. The formerly exploited are doing fine. What's wrong with that?'

'There's got to be something wrong,' said Tuss, 'if life is so fucking *dull*.'

'Here's where things went wrong,' said Bev. 'There used to be an Independent Labour Party in England, the old I L P. Then there came a new Labour Party, which destroyed the old. The new Labour Party started off as the political executive of the Trades Union Congress. Part of the union subscription went to the support of the party – very reasonable. Now the aim of Socialism is to socialize. To abolish, as far as possible, private ownership. Instead of railways and mines and steel making huge profits that all go into the pockets of wealthy shareholders, the profits go to the State, which can thus give more money to the workers and put some by for development and improvement. The only trouble is that nationalized industries never make money. Why not? Because there's no urge to make profits.'

'We know all about that,' said Tuss somewhat irritably. 'Bureaucrats and nobody getting fired and sitting pretty.'

'Now I come to the Great Contradiction,' said Bev. 'With a Socialist State you don't strictly need unions any more. Why not? Because the workers are officially in power, and who do they have to defend themselves against? East European Socialism has no unions, and that's logical. But British syndicalism, once started, has to go on existing. It needs its opposite still. Of course, there are still a few private bosses around, but the State is the main employer. You still have the old dichotomy of employer and employee. The workers have to regard their own political executive not as an aspect of themselves but as an entity they have to oppose. They oppose, and the opposition has to give in, because it's not a true opposition. Hence all wage demands are met and inflation flourishes.'

Both boys looked gloomily dissatisfied. 'That explains nothing,' said Tod. 'It doesn't explain the crap we get at school. It doesn't explain us and you sitting here.'

'All right,' said Bev. 'The worker's struggle in the nineteenth century was not solely economic – it was cultural too. Why should the bourgeoisie have the monopoly of taste and beauty? People like Ruskin and William Morris wanted the workers to be *enlightened*. With the Marxist stress on the basic reality of culture and of history too being economic, well – well, pretty wallpaper and free reading-rooms didn't seem so important. Discriminate consumption disappeared as a doctrine. The thing to do was to consume – but what? Whatever gave or gives the easiest gratification. Diluted taste. The manufacturers are always ready with some watered-down parody of a genuine individual creation. To buy should be to gratify. You buy a book you can't understand, and you get angry. You *ought* to understand it, you've paid for it, haven't you? Things have to be made simple, easy sources of gratification, and that means levelling-down. Every worker with money is entitled to the best that money can buy, so the best has to be redefined as what gives gratification with the least effort. Everybody has the same cultural and educational entitlement, so levelling begins. Why should somebody be cleverer than somebody else? That's inequality. There are no nineteenth-century progressives around, telling the workers about the beauties of Homer's verse. As you know, some of the old workers actually learned Greek. And Hebrew. It was called self-improvement. But that means some selves improve and others don't. Monstrous inequality. Hence your lousy school curriculum. Hence the dullness. Napoleon may have been a monster, but at least he wasn't dull. What can great men like Julius Caesar and Jesus Christ do for the worker?'

'We're not in jobs,' said Tuss bitterly, 'and we never will be. We're not sheep, we don't follow the ram's bell. We face a life of crime and violence. Culture and anarchy. I wish to Christ I could get them to fit. Read Virgil and then rip some guy up. I don't like – what's the word?'

'Inconsistency,' said Tod.

'You can't avoid it,' said Bev, though uneasily, 'if you're human. You're committed to crime if you're against the Workers' State. My MP told me that.'

'Crime of two kinds,' worried Tuss. 'Robbing Robin Hood style, like you saw tonight. The *acte gratuit*.'

'Who told you about the *acte gratuit*?'

'A guy called Hartwell.' said Tuss. 'He talked to us some place, I forget where. A great man for the gin. He told us about Camus – a French Algerian guy, a footballer, you may have heard of him. This guy kills a guy and then he knows he's a human being. He's done a thing there's no reason for doing and he sees that that's what makes him free. Only human beings can do the *acte gratuit*. Everything else, and that means the great fucking big universe and all the stars, it all has to follow like laws. But men have to show they're free by doing things like killing and chopping.'

'What we do isn't *gratuit*,' Tod said. 'It can't be. If we're antistate we have to be properly antistate. That means kicking against the law because it's a State thing. Like Latin and Greek are antistate things. So violence and Shakespeare and Plato go together. They *have* to. And literature teaches revenge. When I read *Don Quixote* I went round slashing every guy that wasn't thin and tall and a bit dreamy. I left the little fat ones alone too.'

'What's that big Greek word you said yesterday?' said Tuss to Tod.

'Symbiosis?'

'That's it. Without us how would the Christniques get on?'

Bev's head reeled. All these things happening. 'Explain,' he said.

'These kids,' said Tuss, 'that started the UC or Underground Christ. In that bit of the District Line that's been closed up. They have what they call a love supper, with real shagging, boy and girl, boy and boy, but the feast bit is only mkate and the odd drop of vino. Sometimes we nick it for them. They say the bread and wine is really Jesus. Then they go out looking for trouble.'

'Christian violence?' said Bev, now ready to believe anything.

'No no. They go out wanting to be cracked. Then they practise the Christnique of loving your enemies. That's where we come in. We get sort of friendly, that's the trouble, don't slash hard enough. Let them get their own vino,' he said with sudden viciousness.

'The only things of importance,' Bev said, still with uneasiness, 'are subversive. Art is subversive. Philosophy too. The State killed Socrates.'

'Yeah, I know,' frowned Tuss. ' "Crito, we owe a cock to Aesculapius.' "

'*O Kriton,*' translated Bev back, '*to Asklipio opheilmen alektruona.*'

'Again, again,' urged Tuss, grabbing Bev's worn greatcoat lapel. 'Christ, those are the real words, that's really the poor guy talking.' Bev, who still owned a stylo, wrote it down in Roman transliteration on Tuss's cigarette pack. Tuss devoured the words, then he said: 'I get a shiver when I read the words in English. Right down the backbone. Now it'll be a shiver all over. I had to bash up those Greeks that ran the stinking restaurant in Camberwell. Because of that. Then I found the guy that ran it was called Socrates. Mockery, I said, and I put the boot in proper.'

Bev shivered inwardly when the image of the ravished and torn Irwin boy came back to him. He'd suffered and died because he wasn't a character in literature? Or perhaps he wanted it, an extreme Christinique? Who knew anything of the dark heart of man? 'Aren't you afraid of getting caught?' he asked. 'Of being put away?'

'No.' Tuss shook his head many times slowly. 'Not scared. It's the final test, to see if you can live like alone inside your skull. That's one reason for stocking it up, to see if it can feed off itself. That's real freedom, being alone in a cell and there's all your brain to travel in, like a country. But nobody gets caught. The nguruwes keep out of our way.'

'I don't know the word. Police?'

'Pig in Swahili. The chanzirim – that's Arabic, that's worse – they don't want blood on their uniforms. *O Kriton,*' he began to read, '*to Ask –* '

' "Pay the debt, therefore. Do not neglect it," ' said Bev. 'That's how it goes on.'

'Give it me in Greek. Give it me real. I want the past in front of me like it was all really there.'

'I can't remember the rest,' said Bev, 'sorry. You're right about the past. We owe no debt to the present or the future. Keep the past alive, pay the debt. Somebody has to do it.'

6 Free Britons

It was the following night that Bev, frozen, came to a disused factory off Hammersmith Broadway. In the factory yard, railed and gated off from the street, ragged men sat round a fire. A reek of charred meat flooded Bev's mouth with saliva. The gate was open.

'No room, no room' said a scholarly-looking man in a stained and ancient British warm, tartan trews and muddy Wellingtons. But his eye was kindly. Bev, without invitation, sat on an old oil drum.

'Antistate?' he said. 'All?'

They looked at him warily. 'Your vocation?' said the scholarly-looking man. Bev told him. The man nodded. 'My name is Reynolds,' he said. 'I am fifty-nine. Had I been willing to keep my mouth shut for a month or so longer I would have retired in the normal way and received my State pension. Comprehensive School, Willingden. Senior teacher of literature, sir.'

'Look, prof, we've heard all this,' whined a bulge-eyed man with a perfectly round head shorn and shaven, as if against ringworm.

'You cannot hear it too often, Wilfred. Besides, I'm addressing Mr Jones here. The set books laid down for the advanced level of the State Leaving Certificate examination were as follows. Poetry: the lyrics of a boy called Jed Foote, member of a singing group called The Come Quicks that sang them; a volume of songs by somebody, American I think, called Rod something. Drama: a play called *The Mousetrap* by the late Dame Agatha Christie – still apparently running in the West End forty years after its premiere. Fiction: a novel called *The Carpetbaggers* – or to be exact *A Shorter The Carpetbaggers* by Harold Robbins, and some nonsense about the errors of social climbing by Sir John Braine. I ask you. Literature. I resigned.' He looked round the circle as for applause.

'Most courageous,' said Bev. 'Might I have a little of that meat there? I'm starving.'

'Let him nick his own,' snarled a black man.

'Charity, charity,' said Reynolds. 'He will do his share of nicking tomorrow, if he joins our band. Here, sir, this is chuck steak and hard to masticate but nourishing. I think a roasted onion rests somewhere among the bluebleak embers.' He picked for it with an iron rod and rolled it out towards Bev. It was oozing juice through its black overcoat. Bev ate gratefully. Wilfred grudgingly, at Reynolds's ocular urging, lent Bev a bottle of rotgut, a coughing fit in every globule. They talked and ate. A thin man with a cap named Timmy read, to general groans, from a worn pocket copy of the New Testament.

'Every bleeding night we have this,' said Wilfred.

'It's to drill it into you,' said Timmy. 'The bargaining principle is forbidden the workers by the Lord hisself. "Didst thou not agree for a penny?" That's clear enough and it's the word of God, so stick it up your jaxy and keep it there.'

'If there's to be reading aloud,' said Reynolds 'hear the word of Alexander Pope.'

'We don't want no RC stuff,' whined Wilfred.

'You see?' said Reynolds. 'You join the ignorant. Banned in the Ealing Public Library because the Library Committee chairman said some nonsense about the Secular State and if you want Popes go to Rome. But you will listen, my friend.' He read out with evident pleasure:

'Lo! thy dread Empire, CHAOS, is restor'd;
Light dies before thy uncreating word;
Thy hand, great Anarch! lets the curtain fall
And universal Darkness buries All.'

'CHAOS,' said Bev. 'Consortium for the Hastening of the Annihilation of Organized Society. Pope didn't have to fight society. He gloried in exalting it. The elitist society, of course. Meanwhile the loaf-stealers hanged and the beggars scratched their sores.'

'Do you mind?' said the religious man. 'I'm eating.'

Reynolds said: 'And yet what springs out of universal justice? The universal darkness Pope never knew. Pope knew what the great enemy of life was and is.'

'Dullness,' said Bev.

'Ah,' said Reynolds with pleasure. 'No dullness now. Welcome, Szigeti, welcome, Tertis.' Two men with fiddle cases joined the group. One of them produced a kilo of pork sausages from his overcoat pocket. 'Prick them first,' said Reynolds. 'I can't abide burst bangers.'

The newcomers ate and then opened their cases. A violin and a viola. They played a charming duo by Mozart and then a Bach two-part invention. Their standards were high; they were very mature men; they were professionals without union cards. Tertis said;

'You could see how it was going to go back in 1977. Covent Garden, I was first viola. They stopped the damned opera after the second act. Said it was going on too long. They wouldn't accept overtime, all goes in tax anyway they said. I protested.'

'That was nothing,' said the violinist. 'They blew the whistle three bars after the start of the last movement of the Ninth. The singers needn't have come. And the whistle wasn't pitched in the right key, either. Royal Festival Hall, September '79. Jesus help us.'

Don't let them get away with it. Bev's wife's voice crackled out of the fire. 'What do we do?' Bev asked.

'We wait,' said Reynolds. 'We wait for one of history's

419

little surprises. I propose turning in, gentlemen.' To Bev he said: 'This factory closed down when it couldn't meet the '79 wage demands. The government didn't find it worth while to take it over. It was a mattress factory. We found plenty of mouldering mattresses in the warehouse. If you sleep here, you will feel very much like the filling of a sandwich. Trevor,' he said sharply to the black, 'you said something about knocking off some blankets.'

'Not easy, man.'

'You must really take our situation more seriously, Trevor.' To Bev: 'Have you any particular speciality, sir?'

'In thieving?'

'We don't like that word. We prefer euphemisms like nicking, knocking off, finding, scrounging. Were you ever in the army?'

'I was born,' said Bev, 'at the beginning of the Long Peace.'

'I see. The army gave me, brief as my service was, a wholesome attitude to property. Well, we'll see. Come, let me find you a place to sleep.' He produced a candle-end and lighted it at the fire.

The empty hull of the factory was cavernous and rusty. It rang hollow and forlorn. Reynolds lighted a smoking oil lamp with his end of candle. He showed Bev how to sleep – on a mattress with two other mattresses laid over him laterally. Bev felt warm but dirty. 'Does one wash?' he asked. 'Surely, successful nicking depends on a decent appearance?'

'For retail winning, yes. For wholesale, filth does no harm. When a meat truck is unloading, you present a dirty shoulder and receive a side of beef, then you take it into the store or shop in question and leave the back way. Sometimes there are problems. We can give it to you the easy way tomorrow, if you wish. A beard does no harm. A cat lick in cold water. But decent dress is essential for the knocking off of supermarket goods. We have what we call the C and A. Wilfred's little pleasantry – the Coat and At. Kept clean and ready in plastic. No shortage of plastic, plastic everywhere, free and indestructible, like God. Ah, on cue, as they say. Father Parsons, Dr Jones.'

'Mister, mister,' protested both at the same time. Parsons, who had just walked in, evidently drunk, inclined courteously, a skeletal man well muffled, nearly seven feet high. 'A very nearly altogether satisfactory evening,' he said. 'Some of the violent youth of Camden Town stood me whisky in exchange for a swathe of church history. They were sincerely interested. Very pro-Latin. Very much against the Lord's Supper as mere commemoration. Then the landlord of the pub said no religion in here and no politics neither. One of the youths said what else is there worth discussing, up your pipe mate or some such locution. Trouble, fighting, a timid brace of policemen. It spoilt the evening rather.' He yawned with loud relish: 'Yarawwwgh.' He fell on his mattress fully clothed and slept. One by one, two by two, the cheerless cavern filled with sleepers. Snores, chokes, groans, odd muttered or screamed words. No life, thought Bev before he too dropped off, no life for anyone.

In the morning black Trevor stole milk and yoghurt from a dairy float for breakfast. Bev washed in an oil drum half-full of rain water, wiped himself on what Reynolds called The Towel. Then he was dressed in the Coat and At – a decent nicked burberry and a pert trilby – and was ready for knocking off a few supplies from a supermarket. 'Observe the poacher's pockets,' said Reynolds. 'Win, for the most part, flat things. Here is one pound.' He tendered a note cheery with the boyish smile of King Charles III, merry monarch. 'You obviously have to buy *something*.'

So Bev, heart beating hard, his first crime ever, entered the nearest Foodmart and stowed dehydrated soups and vegetables, sliced bacon, pressed meats, cheese. The place was full of shopping women. One, in metal curlers and head scarf, was saying to another: 'There's nothing in the papers anyway, except that I like the cartoons, but it's Coronation Flats on the telly tonight, and I think they ought to have more consideration, the rotten lot.' It appeared that all the communication media had struck. Why? Bev bought a kilo wrapped loaf for £1.00. None remarked on his bulges. He went out elated.

The fire in the factory yard was going nicely. Reynolds knew all about the strike. 'Tea bags?' he said to Bev. 'Good, we'll brew up in that filthy kettle. I like the tang of rust. Yes, well, this was warned of. As you know, only card-carrying members of the National Union of Journalists are permitted to write for the newspapers and periodicals. In *The Times* last week there was a review of some work – American, inevitably – on Egyptology. The review was inept, ignorant, illiterate, but its author was an NUJ man. *The Times* had the effrontery to publish a very long letter – fifteen hundred words or thereabouts – by some wanderer like ourselves, pointing out the ineptness, ignorance and illiteracy. Frankly, I don't see how it got past the printers. Hence the strike. Hence the shutting down of radio and television services. There has to be an abject apology. Oh, and also some kind of gratuity to NUJ funds to sweeten the sour insult.'

Derek, a fair youth in decent clothes, came to the fire smiling. 'I've got a job,' he said. 'Start tonight.'

'That's not bleeding possible,' said Wilfred.

'All too bleeding possible,' said Derek. 'A private press, flat bed, very hush hush. Tosh, you know Tosh, met him just off the Broadway. Gave it me out of the corner of his mouth. A bloke, well-dressed said Tosh, slash speaker, gave him a quid and asked if he knew about printers. Hush hush, like I say. Private residence. On Hooper Avenue. I get met at the corner of the street. Nine tonight.' His hands were already going through the motions of loading a stick with type.

'How much?' asked Reynolds.

'Five quid above union.'

The long day proved not to be as dull as Bev had expected. There were intellectual discussions with Reynolds, Father Parsons, and a new man, an Assyriologist useless to the State, named Thimblerigg. Wilfred nicked or won a small sack of potatoes for roasting in the fire. A clarinettist warmed his instrument by that fire and then played the first movement of the Brahms sonata. Father Parsons, clerical collar on, got altar wine from a religious supplies store on forged credit. Trevor came back from foraging with two plastic-wrapped blankets from a street market. 'More tomorrow, Trevor,' said Reynolds, fingering the synthetic wool.

The following morning the streets were full of copies of a new newspaper, distributed free. Father Parsons brought it in with the milk. It was called *Free Briton*, and there was a copy for each of the company that sat sipping tea from old cans and toasting bacon and bread on the fire. There were only four pages; the type was of an almost forgotten elegance that went piquantly with the inflammatory contents. It was a newspaper without news, except of the proposed formation of the Army of Free Workers. Reynolds read part of the editorial aloud for Trevor's benefit, Trevor being but a slow reader:

' "This once great country has suffered enough from the indolence, insouciance and downright obstructiveness of the workers' unions. . . ." '

'What them big words mean, man?'

'Never mind, Trevor. Let me summarize. There is a gentleman here who calls himself Colonel Lawrence.' Reynolds mused a moment. 'Pseudonym? It could be his real name, of course. Still, it suggests – never mind. This gentleman, Trevor, is forming a private army. As His Majesty's Forces are no longer trustworthy, being unionized and ready to go on strike at the first strangulated note of an ill-blown bugle, there is need, says the good colonel, for a trustworthy paramilitary organization that stands outside the law – law, however, which Colonel L. proposes be changed by a great outcry of the people, backed and encouraged by the Free British Army, as it is to be called. This army is already partly officered, but it awaits recruitment to the ranks. The ranks are as follows: private freeman, free two-striper, leader of thirty, company democrat, battalion democrat-major. The commissioned ranks seem orthodox enough – junior captain, senior captain, major and so on. The promotion rate is rapid and depends on ability rather than mere time-serving. The pay rates seem to me unbelievable.'

'How much, man?'

'Private freeman gets £150 a week, but pay is geared to inflation levels.' Reynolds was thoughtful again, frowning. 'The aim of the Free British Army is to maintain essential services when strikes hit this dear dear land, as the colonel calls it. Free soldiers take a solemn oath – to obey their superiors in everything. They vow to serve their country unquestioningly. There is even an army song – *I vow to thee, my country, all earthly things above*. Familiar, that. A very fine tune, I seem to remember, by some Swede or other.'

'Gustav Holst,' said the violist Tertis. 'Pure English, despite his name. The tune comes from *The Planets*. The Jupiter movement. E flat, three-four, maestoso.'

'And where do you sign on, man?'

'Trevor,' said Reynolds earnestly, 'I hope you are not thinking of joining a fascist organization. Freedom, Free Briton, private freeman – eyewash. This Lawrence man wants a kind of Hitlerian takeover. I beseech you in the bowels of Christ, keep away from it.'

'I could use that kind of money, man.'

'Where is the money coming from?' asked Bev.

'Obvious, I should have thought,' Reynolds said. 'Look on Page 4 – at the bottom.' Bev looked and read:

> Let us be ever mindful of a truth that the Syndicalist State counsels, nay forces us to neglect. Above our duty to country stands our duty to God, and the higher duty contains, in a mystical sense, the lower. God made us to fulfil on earth in human action the divine attributes of which our natures partake – to put beauty, truth and goodness above getting and spending. I do not mean the cricket-playing gentlemanly God that the Anglicans have created. I mean the God of the prophets, from Abraham to Mohamed. . . .

'Now,' said Reynolds, 'do you see where the money's coming from?'

7 Nicked

Bev was too ambitious. Young in nicking or knocking off, he was over-encouraged by his little successes in supermarkets. He should not have attempted to win that £15 bottle of Burnett's Silver Satin from the drinkshelf. The telescreen caught him tucking it away. When he joined the pay-line with a 50p half-kilo brown loaf he was himself joined by a hard-faced handsome girl with attractive streak-blonde hair, not unlike poor Bessie's. She said:

'That bulge in your pocket. May I see it, please?'

'What bulge? Where? Private property, mine. I regard this as an intolerable infraction of.'

'You were observed taking a bottle of gin from that shelf. Do you propose paying for it?'

'I propose putting it back.' Bev took out the bottle and tried to make his way to where he'd nicked it from. There were a lot of people looking at him. One old woman tuttuttutted. 'Having counted my money I discover that I haven't enough after all. It's terribly expensive.' The girl barred the way. The supermarket manager appeared, grim as a surgeon in a white coat. 'Putting it back,' Bev said, 'if you'll kindly allow me.' But they wouldn't allow him. The manager said:

'All right. Caught red-handed. Get the police, Miss Porlock.'

'Yes, Mr Allsop.' She went, a pretty-legged girl.

'Look,' said Bev, 'you're making a fool of yourself. I've stolen nothing. It would be theft if I got it past the paydesk, right? But I haven't. You'll have a hell of a job proving anything.' And he tried again to put the bottle back where he'd scrounged it from. The manager pushed him. The manager called:

'Alwyn. Geoffrey.' Two other men in white coats came from their work of shelf-packing. It was as though Bev were going to be forced into submission to a dangerous surgical operation. He panicked and tried to leave, gin bottle in hand. Then he turned back on a reflex of honesty and tried to give it to Alwyn, who looked sympathetic, a sly nicker himself probably. Alwyn, as if to disclaim complicity, thrust it by. 'Grab him, Geoffrey,' said Mr Allsop. Alwyn, who was now shown to be really Geoffrey, laid hands on Bev. Bev was not going to have that. He fought off the hands with the bottle's firm base. Miss Porlock arrived with two policemen, young men with gangster moustaches. They came for Bev and breathed hot sweet tea on him. They grabbed. Bev was not going to have that. He raised his bottle once more. The bottle was seized by one of the constables and given to Miss Porlock. Bev fought. The customers watched. This was as good as the stricken telly, almost. Bev tried to shove through the customers in line at the paydesk, some of whom shoved him back. The police got to him again. Bev scratched. His nails had not been trimmed since Christmas. He achieved a bloody hairline on a left cheek. 'Ah no,' said the constable, 'not that, chum.' They got him with a knee in the groin. They frogmarched him off.

The sergeant at the station two streets away supped tea and nibbled a cream horn while he wrote down Bev's various misdemeanours in a large slow hand: attempted robbery, resisting arrest, assaulting a policeman, being in possession of a weapon (they had found the flick-knife), having no fixed abode. 'Gertie,' said the sergeant to a policewoman, 'get this geezer's testiculars from CR.' CR was Central Registry, where Bev's entire curriculum vitae lay waiting in a computer for instantaneous disgorgement. 'Jones, B.'

'Number?' said the policewoman.

'What's your number, cock?'

'Union number? Birth registration number?'

'All your numbers, chummy.'

'To hell with numbers,' said Bev. 'I'm a human being, not a bloody number.'

'Be reasonable,' said the sergeant, 'the whole place is swarming with Joneses. Very difficult to find, even with a B. Come on, lad, co-operate.'

'Why should I help a bloody machine?' said Bev. One of the two constables thumped him.

'Right,' said the sergeant, writing. 'Uncooperative. Let's have your fingerprints.' They forced him to press inky whorls on a card, and the card was taken off to be photo-telexed to CR. 'You forgot anything?' said the sergeant to one of the constables. 'Sure you got the story right? You forgot to say he pulled the shiv on you.'

'It's a lie,' said Bev.

'You have to co-operate,' said the sergeant kindly. 'Co-operation is what life is all about, my son. Take him away in the usual manner, lads.'

Bev was, in what he took to be the usual manner, thumped towards the cells. He thumped back. The sergeant, sighing as though at the irredeemable folly of man as represented by Bev, made a new entry. The charge sheet had grown to quite a sizeable document. 'Right,' said the constable whom Bev had scratched in the super-market, 'you wait here, cocker, till court in the morning.' He shoved Bev in a small heaven of warmth and cleanli-ness, with two made-up bunks and a chamber pot. There was even a basin of water and a rough towel and a hunk of green soap. As for the iron bars, it was the rest of the crazy and evil world that was shut in, not he. He stripped off and washed all over. He was given a plate of blind hash and a mug of sweet tea by a surly man in an apron. He lay on the upper bunk and meditated. The early winter dark came and dim fluorescent lighting simpered from the ceil-ing. He slept.

He woke to hearty noise. Two different constables and a new sergeant were thrusting into the cell with some difficulty a soiled and drunken man. They apparently knew him well. 'Come on, Harry,' said the sergeant, 'be a good lad. Your bunk's nice and ready. Get your bloody head down.' The man's head was not in fact bloody, but it was bald and scarred and contained areas of crinkly skin as though it had at some time been burned. The man sang:

> 'They shoved him down and they shoved it up
>   Till his cup was well-nigh overflowing,
> And this went on till the crack of dawn
>   And all the time their cocks were crowing.'

He interspersed his blurred and tuneless lines with, 'Fuck you, matey,' and, 'If it isn't old Bert, Bert's my pal Bert is,' and, 'Just one more and make it a boilermaker,' and, 'I've supped some stuff tonight, I have that.' He was thrown on to the bottom bunk. Bev sighed, foreseeing a sleepless night. The sergeant, a thin man with the look of a Methodist minister, said:

'We know all about you, you non-union bastard. I've read your little dossier and filthy reading it is. You've got old Ashthorn on in the morning and I hope to Christ he pulverizes you.' He then locked the cell-door, saying to the drunk: 'That's right, Harry, keep that swede well and truly crashed.' Harry snored. Bev tried to go back to sleep. The snores turned into the pleasant sound of a sawmill in a country place: the sun was hot, even for August, and he and Ellen sat on the bank of the stream, their feet laved by the kindcold flinty element. Little Bessie, four years old, chased a red admiral. How beautiful Ellen was: clear skin, wide green eyes and snub nose, laughing wide mouth; her body spare but shapely in its pippin-russet brief summer dress. A covey of partridges drummed. The sawmill had stopped. Bev was shaken very roughly awake. Harry was on his feet, shaking.

'You got a drop for an old pal?' he said. 'I've a thirst that rasps. I can bloody hear it rasping like a real rasp.'

'There's water over there,' said Bev, trying to turn over.

'Water? Water for me? Handled thousands of millions of gallons of the bloody stuff in my time, but never not one drop down the gorge except by accident. All right, if you won't help, you won't, so bugger you, matey.'

427

Bev, wide awake now, said: 'What's that about water?'

'Never touch it, me, except by way of the job.'

'And what would the job be?' asked Bev, getting down from his bunk. 'Would it be by chance the job of a fire-man?'

'Hit it first time, matey. Station B15. Here, I'm fucking parched.' He went to the cell-door and yelled through the bars: 'I'm dying of bloody thirst. Beer'll do. I know you've got a dozen Charringtons there, I saw them, you bas-tards.' There was no response. All was dark. Bev, now standing, his arms loose, said:

'Murderer. You murdered my wife, you bloody mur-derer.'

'Eh?' Harry turned in tottering surprise. 'Don't know your wife, matey. Never murdered a woman in my life. Killed one or two with kindness, but that's different. What you on about, then? Christ, I suppose I shall have to.' And he went to the water jug, raised it, glugged it down. 'Terr-ible stuff,' he panted.

'You struck,' said Bev. 'You let the Brentford Hospital burn down. My wife was a patient there. I saw her. I saw her just before she died.' He came for Harry with thumbs ready to gouge. Harry was drunk, also pot-bellied, but he had no difficulty in knocking Bev's hands off.

'You're barmy,' he said. 'We don't start fires, we put 'em out. You get that, you see it?'

'You didn't put this one out. You murdering bastard.' He struck out but missed Harry's face. It was the sort of face that might look better upside down. 'You went on strike and let people die in agony.'

'Look,' said Harry, 'blame the bastards that set fire to it, right? It was the murdering Micks, the IRA. One of my mates heard them on about it in a boozer in Shepherd's Bush. He lunged and got done for his pains. We don't like fires, matey. The fewer fires there are, better we're pleased. So don't start on about that business, get it?'

'You went on strike,' said Bev, 'that's all I know. She was just burnt bone and scorched skin. My wife. That's what you did with your bloody strike.'

'Listen,' said Harry, now rather sober, 'you got to jump when they say, right? You hear the bells going down and you shin down the pole and don't ask questions. Same when they blow the whistle. You're going on strike, they say. Right, so that's what you do. If you don't, you're out of it, right? I've got five kids. I've got a missis that'll play screaming buggery when I get home tomorrow morning. I've got a job, and it's the thing I can do. I got to do it. I need the money, and what with prices shooting I need more all the time. So you put the fear of Jesus into everybody by going on strike, and then you get what you want. What's wrong with that? Besides, it's not me and my mates that says right we'll strike. It's what they tell us to do and we have to do it.'

'You bloody murderer,' said Bev, feebly, doubtfully.

'I know how you feel. The fire should have been put out, right. We thought the army was doing it. Christ, that's what an army's for. Then those bastards strike, what we didn't expect. We don't want their bleeding sympathy. Scared shitless of the job is what I'd say, so they get out of it by talking of the cause of our civilian brothers. In the army you're supposed to jump to it and get fucking shot if you don't. My dad always said that, he was in the Desert Rats as they were called, and by Christ he was right. Look, I've slept it off, I want out.' He began to rattle the bars loudly, yelling: 'Bert, Phil, Sergeant MacAllister.' Bev sat on the one rickety Windsor chair and sobbed without tears.

8 Sentence of the court

Old Ashthorn presided, as foretold, in Number 3 Court. He was a fierce wattled martinet in his seventies, bald but with clumps of hair like wool-balls above his ears. Next to him sat an assistant magistrate, a plain flat-chested woman with a drab hat on. The clerk of the court was loud and insolent. Bev was addressed as plain Jones. The constable with the bloody hairline on his cheek, which, Bev could have sworn, had been cunningly emphasized with lipstick, read out the charges in the gorblimied form that the desk sergeant had dressed them up in. They sounded pretty bad. Miss Porlock from the supermarket confirmed everything except what was supposed to have happened at the station. The clerk of the court handed up the flick-knife to old Ashthorn who, with frightening expertise, kept shooting in and out the blade, on which dried blood stains had been imposed, presumably by the police. He dared Bev to say something in answer to the charges.

'I admit the attempted theft,' said Bev.. 'But I have no job. The Workers' State denies me unemployment benefit. I have to live. I have to steal.'

'You have to steal *gin*,' said old Ashthorn, flashing the bottle (Exhibit A) in the artificial light. 'Not bread, but gin. And a very good gin, too.' He made a cage of his long skeletal fingers and beetled very sternly. His colleague read everything on the label of the bottle. She nodded, as in awe, at the long claim to excellence. 'You tried to evade lawful arrest,' said old Ashthorn. 'You carried a bloody weapon.'

'*Not* bloody. That knife has never been used.'

'Speak when you are spoken to, Jones,' cried the clerk of the court.

'That's precisely what I did,' said Bev. 'He spoke a lie, and I corrected it. Is there something wrong with that?' The assistant magistrate whispered something at great length to old Ashthorn, who kept nodding and nodding.

'You have broken the law,' said old Ashthorn. 'Society must be protected from people of your type.' Bev came as rapidly to the boil as a pan full of alcohol. He said:

'My type? What do you mean, *my type*? I'm a scholar forbidden to transmit my scholarship. I'm a widower whose wife was burnt to death while the firemen of London sat on their arses and picked their teeth.'

'You will apologize to Mrs Featherstone for using that word,' bellowed the clerk of the court.

'I apologize, Mrs Featherstone,' said Bev to the assistant magistrate, 'for using that word. Words are terrible things, aren't they? Far more deadly than fires allowed to burn on while firemen sit on their fundaments. I am not a *type*, your worship or honour or whatever you like to be called. I'm a human being deprived of work because I stand by a principle. I object to being a unionized sheep.'

'You understand what you are saying?' said old Ashthorn.

'Perfectly well. Justice has been corrupted by syndicalism. Not only justice in the wider sense but justice as meted and administered in the courts. Send a union man to jail and you have a strike on your hands.'

'This is insolence,' said the clerk of the court loudly and insolently.

'Shall we say,' said old Ashthorn, 'that it is merely untrue? Shall we also,' he said to Bev directly, 'be reasonable? The law is founded on reason. It would be unreasonable to fine you, since you have no means of paying a fine. This is your first offence – ' He checked with Bev's cybernetic *curriculum vitae.* 'It seems to me evident enough from your behaviour that you have not previously been in a court of law. I am not empowered to send you to prison. Even if I were empowered, a spell of imprisonment would in no wise alter your situation. You are, you say, forced to steal. Justice *in the wider sense* demands that your circumstances of life be so modified that the urge to commit crime is quelled and eliminated. You are to be placed on probation. Mr Hawkes,' said old Ashthorn, 'would you be good enough to explain the probationary process to the er er to the.'

A brightly polished man stood up. Bev had thought him merely to be an idle frequenter of court-rooms; now he was revealed as a court officer of some sort. He was chubby, beautifully dressed, self-satisfied in the manner of a Welsh tenor singing *Comfort ye my people.* His accent was Welsh. He said: 'Yes, your honour.' He smiled at Bev. He said: 'Let us substitute for the term probation the more meaningful word rehabilitation. Have you heard of Crawford Manor?'

'No,' said Bev, 'I have not.'

'*Sir*,' said Mr Hawkes, completing Bev's statement for him but with a kind of apologetic good humour. 'Crawford Manor is a rehabilitation centre set up by the TUC and part-financed by the Treasury. You will be given an opportunity to reconsider your position. You will in no manner be coerced into a resumption of your former union status. Your course of rehabilitation will, it is trusted and, indeed, foreknown, present the nature of *rights* which you seem to regard as tyrannous impositions so cogently that you will, I have no possible doubt, be only too eager to be welcomed back into the comity of the nation's workers. Have you anything to say?'

'I won't go,' said Bev,

The magistrate said: 'I'm afraid you have no alternative.'

'Your friend here,' said Bev, 'said there would be no coercion.'

'No coercion in the rehabilitation process,' smiled Mr Hawkes. 'But I fear that enrolment is compulsory. After all, can you deny that you have broken the law?'

Bev considered that. He saw that there had to be dragging of some kind – a fine from his pocket, his body to a jail. You committed a crime, you accepted the dragging consequences if caught.

'All right,' said old Ashthorn, 'next case.'

The constables looked murderously at Bev as he left the box. Mr Hawkes smiled.

'I go now?' said Bev sullenly.

'You go in three hours time. You take the 13.20 from Charing Cross. Crawford Manor is just outside the village of Burwash, in East Sussex. There will be transport for you and the rest of the party from Etchingham station. Mr B – '

'What a mess,' Bev interrupted. 'there was a time when the powers were separated. Now you bastards control the judicature as well as the – '

'Mr Boosey, as I was trying to say, awaits you outside this court-room. He is your conducting officer.' Mr Hawkes suddenly changed his tone and his manner. He said in a low sibilant voice: 'See sense, *wus*. You can't win, boy. Got you we have then and don't bloody forget it.'

'Fuck you, shitbag,' said Bev.

'Better that is, boy *bach*. Talking like a worker you are now. Go on, *bachgen*, take your non-unionized pong away.'

9 A show of metal

There were twenty-one of them on the train, including Mr Boosey, a man like a failed private detective who sat nursing a big mottled fist like a weapon he was dying to use. But, yawning and stretching on Charing Cross station, he had revealed, perhaps intentionally, a leather holster under his jacket. Most of the party doubted that there was a gun in it. This was England, where only criminals went armed.

Most of the twenty were men of education, few of them very young, some mild and hopeless, hanging on to principle like an expired credit card. But there were some religious fanatics, including a Scot with jutting brows who set himself to provoke Mr Boosey from Tonbridge on:

'Sae, ye dullyeart horse-punckin, ye'd hae it that the Laird's worrrd is kilted in a tippit?' He waved his Bible at the Lord's creation beyond the window, mostly concealed as it was by broken factories and dirty smoke, 'Eh, rawny banes?'

'I dinna ken what you're jabbering aboot, Joke,' said Mr Boosey. 'If it's a pee you want you'll have to wait till we get there.'

'Ach,' the Scot sneered, 'he's nocht but a quean's bycomes an' a drutlin' druntin' para-muddle.' He then turned to high-pitched Kelvinside English and said: 'What I wish to convey, brother, is that you and your lot have decided that the Word of the Lord God is all washed up and if the Lord Jesus was alive today he'd be leading the carpenters out on strike.'

'If you want to shout the odds about what's in the Bible, wait till you get where we're going. I'm just taking you there, right?'

A young half-starved-looking Midlander with great pale eyes began to sing *Onward Christian Soldiers.* Nobody joined in. He said, in a Black Country whine: 'Throwing us to the lions. The twentieth-century martyrs.' Nobody said anything. Mr Boosey took out some throat tablets but did not offer them around. He began to suck. The Scot said:

'Ach, yon thieveless sook-the-blood. Ye scaut-heid reid-een'd knedneuch mawkin'-flee.'

'You watch your tongue, Jock,' sucked Mr Boosey.

The train stopped at Tunbridge Wells. A tall member of the party in a black raincoat stood up and said: 'We change here, surely.'

'Sit down,' said Mr Boosey. 'I checked. We don't change.'

'Are you ordering me to sit down?'

'I'm telling you.'

'I think,' said the tall man, looking very coolly at Mr Boosey, 'I'll get out just the same.'

'Try it,' said Mr Boosey. 'Go on, just try.' And then it was confirmed that the leather holster beneath his jacket was not just for show. Mr Boosey pointed at the tall man a black oiled Sougou .45. The man sat. All marvelled. Mr Boosey said:

'You lot have got to remember that you're criminals.'

Bev said, marvelling: 'I never thought it possible. Gun law. Tell me, Boosey, what kind of a hermaphrodite are you?'

'Watch it,' said Mr Boosey. 'I've got a handle to my name.'

'Aye, that's guid. A scrat.'

'I mean no sexual insult by the term,' said Bev. 'Kipling used it of the Royal Marines, His Majesty's jollies, soldier and sailor too. You're an officer of the law and an officer of the TUC. A confirmation of achieved tyranny in a train going to Etchingham.'

'Batemans,' said a man in dark glasses, 'has been taken over. You'll see when we get to Burwash. The poet of empire's home is now a regional computer centre. May Puck of Pook's Hill split it with an electronic murrain.'

'Look, you lot,' said Mr Boosey, with quiet ferocity. 'I'm doing a job, get it?' He looked across the aisle to take in the rest of his party, even those who sat reading the *Free Briton*, good as gold. 'A job, that's what I'm doing. A job.' He seemed to have nothing further to convey. A uniformed guard came down the aisle calling:

'Everybody out. Train proceeds no further. We're on strike.'

The probationer criminals were interested in Mr Boosey's response to this. He should by rights have said, 'Good, brother.' Apparently, the day of holistic syndicalism not having yet arrived, he was not expected himself to go out on strike with the rest of the Conducting Officers' Union or Guild or whatever it was. But he was surely not expected to frown in irritation.

'Lead us,' said the tall man in the black raincoat, rising again. 'Lead us, brother, whither thou wishest to take us.'

'Look,' said Mr Boosey to the guard, 'will the telephones be working?'

'Working just now when the news came through from the Transport Union, but if you want to phone you'd better put some jildy in it.'

'Kipling,' said the dark man in glasses, 'is not dead.'

'But if it's a bus or something you're after,' said the guard, 'you know the position as well as what I do.'

'Jesus Christ,' said Mr Boosey.

'That is not the tone of a believer,' said the boy from the Midlands.

'You're right there, lad,' said the guard. 'Come on, let's have you all out.'

Mr Boosey looked dangerous as he got his charges out on to the down-line platform of Tunbridge Wells Central. It began to rain. There was distant thunder. A swarthy squat man who had not previously spoken said:

'Tonnerretruenotuonotrovaotunetdonnerdonder – '

'Shut it, you,' snarled Mr Boosey, 'do you hear?' The guard hovered, interested.

'Foreigner, is he?' he said. And then: 'You going up to the Manor, as they call it? Because if you are it looks as if you'll have to walk there. March them along the line, no law against it. Quickest distance between two points.'

A ruddy man with a very dirty raincoat and a copy of the *Free Briton* sticking out of its pocket said jocularly:

'Get fell in, you horrible lot.'

Before Mr Boosey could take charge, the squad had gleefully gotten down on to the rails and started to march south. 'Here, here, bugger you,' called Mr Boosey. The guard was amused.

They moved in double file. Bev's partner was the tall man in the black raincoat, a former county librarian, his name Mr Mifflin. It rained drearily. Mr Boosey cursed. At Stonegate the ruddy man said: 'Five minutes break every hour. Army regulations.'

'Keep going. You're not in the frigging army now.'

Near Etchingham Mr Mifflin said: 'Shall we make a run for it?'

'He has a gun.'

'True. Let's see if it's loaded. *Now.*'

The gun was loaded. Bev felt something whistle past his ear. He and Mr Mifflin came back sheepishly from the green embankment they had attempted to mount. 'Now you know,' sweated Mr Boosey. 'Now you know that the time for your bleeding childish nonsense is over and done with. Now you know who's bloody well in charge.'

10 Two worlds

Mr Pettigrew stood near the blocked-up fireplace of what had once been called the Joshua Reynolds salon and surveyed his audience of 150. They all knew who he was: they could not, in spite of themselves, but feel flattered. The great TUC theorist, the permanent chairman of the TUC Presidium, lean, tow-haired with an equine forelock, younger-looking than his forty years, beamed at them and eyed them dimly while he polished his glasses on his tie (blood-red with gold flywheels). He put his glasses on and the eyes, clicking into focus, were seen to be sharp and of a terribly clear grey. Formidable eyes, thought Bev. Mr Pettigrew said, in a reedy donnish voice:

'Brothers.' Then he smiled and shrugged with great grace. 'I find it hard to use the term with the requisite sincerity. Sisters. No, it won't do, will it?' The seventy-odd women in the audience seemed to agree. Giggles, little chortles. 'To call a female fellow-worker *sister* seems to announce the preclusion of what our American friends call a meaningful relationship. There is room for many things in what is rather absurdly nicknamed Tucland, but I don't think incest is one of them.' Laughter. Careful, careful, said Bev to himself; don't laugh, don't be seduced by the charm, he's the enemy. 'So I say: ladies and gentlemen. There are no officious shop stewards standing by the walls to rebuke me.

'Ladies and gentlemen, you have been summoned here because you are exceptional people. You would call yourselves, perhaps, individualists who put the single human soul before that strange abstract group entity called the Workers' Collective. You have known struggle, you have known pain. The principle of the unique importance of the individual soul, the untrammelled free individual will, has led most of you to a state of desperate loneliness – the loneliness of the outcast, the criminal, the vagrant, the sane soul shrieking through the prison bars reared by the insane. I know, none better. You have faced every day and, more terribly, every night in the distortions of bad dreams, the intolerable human dilemma. I have faced it also, perhaps with less courage than you.

'What is the nature of the dilemma? It is this. That humanity craves two values that are impossible of reconciliation. Man – or, to use the term recommended by the Women's Liberation Movement, Wo Man – desires to live on his, sorry, zer own terms and at the same time on the terms imposed by society. There is an inner world and there is an outer world. The inner world feeds itself with dreams and visions, and one of these visions is called God, the enshriner of values, the goal of the striving single soul's endeavours. It is good, nay it is human, to cherish this inner, private, world: without it we are creatures of straw, unhappy, unfulfilled. *But*, and I must emphasize this *but*, the inner world must never be allowed to encroach on the outer world. History is full of the wretchedness, the tyranny, oppression, the pain occasioned by the imposition of an inner vision on the generality. It began, perhaps, with Moses, who had a vision of God in a burning bush, and, through it, initiated the long trial of the Israelites. St Paul sought to impose his idiosyncratic vision of the resurrected Christ on an entire world. So with Calvin, Luther, Savonarola – need I go on? And in the secular field, we have seen, or read of, the agony caused by the enforcing of some mystical conception of the State on millions in Europe, on untold millions in Asia.

'Do I make myself at least a little clear? I have nothing against the inner vision so long as it is controlled by mer who holds it, kept sealed from the outer world, cherished behind locked doors. The outer world cannot accept the inner vision without pain, for the values of the outer world are of a substance so different from the inner one that they cannot meet – as phosphorus and water cannot meet – without dangerous conflagration. Now, you will ask, what are the values of the outer world? They are simple, and their simplicity is the inevitable attribute of a generality. They consist in what all Wo Men possess in common – the need to live, which means the need to work and to be paid for that work. When we speak of a Workers' State, a Workers' Collective, we would, if we could, expunge from the term the cynical political connotations which have been added to it by the Marxist oligarchs. By a Workers' State we mean no more than a system in which the basic human right is permitted to prevail – the right to work and to be adequately paid for that work. The very concept implies, perhaps, a contradiction. For if the State is the possession of the workers, then the worker's long struggle for justice has been won, since the means of effecting justice is in zer hands. But every day sees signs of the continuation of the struggle, and the struggle will go on for ever. The opposition between Employer and Employed is a basic tenet of our system. The State becomes increasingly the Employer, hence, by simple logic, what is theoretically for the worker is in practice against mer. I repeat, this dichotomy is essential. Essential, because a dynamic is essential to sustain the progressive amelioration of the worker's lot, and only out of opposition can a dynamic be generated.

'It should be clear to you now, I think, that this simple philosophy of the worker's rights does not have to be identified with the philosophy of Socialism. It is true to state that Socialism favours the workers more than the happily defunct metaphysic of grab and capitalist privilege; indeed, the Socialist movement, as I need not remind you, is the movement of Labour, is based upon justice for the worker. But a movement is different from an enthroned system. A Socialist government, especially one that rules virtually, like our own, without opposition, has ceased to struggle. And yet, to sustain its dynamic, it is obliged to struggle. Thus, it struggles to increase the Gross National Product, to stem inflation, which means, in effect, to discipline the worker. Dedicated to Work, it has no especial trust in the Worker. On the other hand, a basic philosophy held in common by the Workers' Collective and the Socialist Executive ensures that the principle of simplification, of the consultation of the need to satisfy, through the machinery of government, certain fundamental requirements of the Worker, is more or less adequately fulfilled. I mean, of course, the provision of a national health service, an educational system that meets the general need but eschews the special ones of the inner world of individualists like, ladies and gentlemen, your good selves. And, of course, a social security network from which you, ladies and gentlemen, have – through your failure to set up a strongly policed frontier between the inner and outer worlds – wantonly cut yourselves off.'

He smiled, as though ironically citing an official view with which he did not necessarily agree. He continued to smile, somewhat dreamily now, as he said:

'Soon, I have no doubt, gently, imperceptibly, with none of the smoke and noise of revolution (for revolutions are always bred in the inner world), we shall see a withering away of the unwritten political constitution which was always held to be one of Britain's instinctual masterpieces. A parliament has become a time-wasting formality, as you know. We need only an executive and a civil service. A political college is already in process of formation, wherein the executives of the future will be trained. This executive will require, for the mystical purposes of continuity, a permanent head. If you're thinking it will be Bill the Symbolic Worker, you are, of course, mistaken. A monarchy suffices, an entity outside politics. The devotion of the British Worker to the British Royal Family is of long standing, and it expresses an instinctual sense of value of a nominal executive that is outside the sweaty world of the political professionals. Our fellow workers in America are already turning against the republican principle, seeing in the presidency a mere monstrous absolutism that is the ultimate fulfilment of the dirty struggle for political power. Who knows? – soon the Declaration of Independence may be repealed, and the English-speaking peoples of the world – or should I say the speakers of Workers' English? – reunited through a common purpose under a common head.

'But this is for the future, and I apologize, ladies and gentlemen, for a digression that is not to our immediate purpose. What is our immediate purpose? What aim do we seek to encompass during your stay – alas, enforced; would that it could have been voluntary – at Crawford Manor? Primarily, we wish you to feel in your hearts what you are perhaps ready enough to accept with your reason. We wish you to feel equality in your pores. The equality of the outer world, in which there is no privilege and where the very notion of the exceptional man or woman – the Hitler, the Bonaparte, the Genghiz Khan – is an abomination. What of the exceptional artist, you may say, of the scientist or genius, the thinker whose new vision threatens to burn up the old? Such will not be strangled at birth, I assure you, as the principle of egalitarianism gains

439

the strength which it still struggles to achieve. Art, thought, research belong to the inner world, the private sector of life. The exceptional genius thrusting into the outer world – heesh is not wanted, but that does not mean that heesh is not valued. But the value does not belong to the world of the workers, and the value must seek its own encouragement in that inner world which you, ladies and gentlemen, sought to confuse with the greater one which you thought to reject but which, you find, rejected you.'

He became suddenly stern and loud, and Bev knew that he was probably mad. Mr Pettigrew cried:

'You have sinned. Sinned, yes. Sinned against equality, sinned against fraternity – '

'But not against liberty.' Bev looked round, embarrassed, to see who had so rudely interrupted. He was astonished to find that it was himself. There was a murmur in the audience, and the murmur grew. It was hard to know who the murmur was against. But Mr Pettigrew at once seized the word and drew all eyes and ears to his now large-eyed and gesticulating person.

'Liberty,' shouted Mr Pettigrew. 'You do not even know the meaning of the term. You have swallowed whole the triple shibboleth of a misguided foreign revolution. You have failed to see that two of its terms belong to the outer world, but that the other has no meaning except in the inner. Liberty – who denies you liberty? Liberty is a property of the private universe which you explore or not as you please, the universe where even natural laws are suspended if you wish it so. What has it to do with the world of working and earning one's bread? You chose an impossible liberty, seeking it in the outer world, and you found nothing but a prison.' There was a chill silence, in which eyes were averted from Bev, as though even a look might bring dangerous contagion. Mr Pettigrew, with frightening speed, relaxed, grinned boyishly, took off his glasses and wiped them again on his tie. 'Liberty,' he said, vague-eyed. 'It's use in Workers' English is the right one, the only one. I have taken a bloody liberty in talking so long this evening.' There was a slight gasp, chiefly from the ladies, at the shocking intrusion of a colloquialism that Mr Pettigrew's oratorical style had not seemed capable of encompassing. 'I have played the dreary demagogue. It is not, I assure you, my true forte. I hope we shall have opportunities to meet while you are here and share for a space our blessed inner worlds. Good night.' He said this glassed again, sharp-eyed.

And oft he went, to applause. Bev did not applaud.

11 Spurt of dissidence

There were a few rooms in Crawford Manor where inner worlds could be visited. Some of these rooms had a bed in them and could be locked from within. There did not seem to be any bugging devices, visual or auditory. You were welcome to take bloody liberties there during your leisure periods. Bev had learnt, during a session on Workers' English with the very humorous and erudite Mr Quirk, that the terms *leisure* and *pleasure*, though not etymologically cognate, could be used interchangeably in WE, though in practice the second word had swallowed the first. In AWE, or American Workers' English, such assimilation had not taken place, since the words had never rhymed in America. Workers in Britain, anyway, talked of being at pleasure during their pleasure hour, and that, since it was current usage, must be regarded as correct. Bev was pleasuring and being pleasured by a pleasant girl in her thirties named Mavis Cotton. He had met her before in the old days when she and he had been on a History Teaching Course at Ambleside, and both had agreed that it was a load of rubbish.

They lay back naked, sighing with satisfaction, on the bed. Bev had to admit to himself that, in his five or six bouts in this room with Mavis, he had known more sexual satisfaction than in all his years of marriage to Ellen. They had had a pleasant enough year together, though never ecstatic, the whole world burning up, before Bessie was born. After that birth, which had been a difficult one, she had shied from his embraces. He had remained loyal but frustrated. After all, he'd told himself, sex wasn't everything. Now, he saw, sex was a great deal. It was ironical that he should have to make this discovery in a place dedicated to that Outer World of abstractions which denied ecstasy. But, of course, no, not ironic: this paradise of the

441

nerves was free to all, nothing elitist about it. And yet –
wasn't there really perhaps a kind of Workers' Sex that
owed nothing to erotic education, self-betterment, sex
horny-handed, thrusting, bestial? Perhaps there would be
a lecture on that before the course ended. Mavis said:

'You was good. You did that proper.'

He looked at her, smiling and frowning. 'I never know
whether you're being facetious or not. With your WE, I
mean.'

'Oh, yes and no. Or, I suppose, neither do I. My father
spoke like that. A terrible man for aitchlessness. Who was
it said how easy it would be for the middle class to become
proletarianized? You have nothing to lose but your
aitches, he said.'

'George Orwell,' Bev said. 'My uncle fought with him in
Spain. God, fifty years back. Orwell died very unpleasantly at Pamplona or somewhere. Planning, so my uncle
said, a book about homage to Catalonia till the very day he
was shot. He spoke rather refined, my uncle said.'

'What are you going to do?' asked Mavis.

'What are *you* going to do? Have they convinced you
yet?'

Mavis said nothing. She twined a long hank of her black
silk hair in her shapely, rather rosy, fingers. Then, 'Yes
and no,' she said. 'I can see myself standing up there
lecturing on the Tolpuddle Martyrs and forgetting about
imperial expansion and Brunel and the 1851 Exhibition. I
can even hear myself doing it in WE. 'They was fighting
like for their rights, wasn't they, and they was not allowed
them rights.' Because I can go home then and play my
Bartók records and read Proust. The Inner World.'

'And when your Bartók records are worn out, who will
press new ones? Who'll play Bartók? The Inner needs the
Outer. Books have to be printed. I bet you had a long
search in the second-hand barrows looking for Proust. The
whole business is based on false premises. There's only
one world. If you can't fire some kid in one of your classes
with an enthusiasm for Gibbon, who's going to read him?'

'I can always bring in some aside about the fall of the
Roman Empire and read a paragraph of Gibbon and – '

'If you can find Gibbon around. And then you'll be had
up for bourgeois irrelevancies and watch it sister this is
your second like warning. Don't you see how it's going to

442

be, has to be? The universities are going to lose their sub-
sidies if they don't turn themselves into cats – '

'Into – ? Oh, CATs.'

'And a Centre of Advanced Technology isn't going to be
allowed to regard literature as a technology, even though
it is. Look at the authors already out of print and likely to
remain so. The levelling's going to reach the limit. Not
even technical brilliance in the performing arts is going to
be allowed. Them kids what sings and plays the guitar
does all right, don't they, earning millions though they
loses it all in tax, and they never had a bleeding lesson in
their bleeding puffs.'

'You do that very well. WE, I mean,' She rolled over
and lay half on top of him, her sweet warm breath and her
searching tongue-tip in his ear. 'And,' she said, 'the other
thing.' She looked at her wrist-watch, the only clothing
she had on. 'Oh, my God. It's 15.55. Seminars.' She leapt
off the bed and grabbed her one-piece garment – the siren
suit or uniform overall they had jocularly been issued with
on arrival, the quartermaster saying: 'Some of you poor
buggers looks a bit the worse for wear, here, a nice bit of
denim with the complimongs of the ouse.' Bev said:

'And if one doesn't go to one's seminar?'

'If yer don't go, ducks, yer gets beat up proper in a cellar
wiv very strong lights burning away on yer bleeding
body.' She hadn't quite got it yet: a whiff of refined vowel
spoiled her demotic, but she'd learn. Bev looked somewhat grimly at her, arms behind his head. She'd learn,
and she wasn't the only one. Some had learnt already.
That religious Scot, for instance, had been ably argued at
by a genuine theologian who'd persuaded him that the
twelve apostles were the first trade union, that Christ had
been martyrized for the principle of free organization, that
the Kingdom of Heaven meant a proletarian democracy.
There was one old man who had taught everybody something – a reformed dissident now on the staff of this centre
of rehabilitation. He had given a very moving talk in WE
on his sufferings, saying:

'I held out, brothers and sisters, to the bloody limit. And
I saw after six months of begging and tramping the roads
and sleeping beneath hedges and in the nick and out of it
that I was a bloody fool and a flaming idiot. I had a trade
and a good one – hydraulic-press checker – and here I was

443

not doing what I could earn good money for, and the money was getting better all the time, I could see that from odd bits of dirty newspaper I picked up here and there. I was wasting my life and, what was a bleeding sight worse, I was depriving others of what I could do, I was in a manner of speaking wasting the resources of the community. Forgive them long words, but they're the right words, brothers and sisters, and if you can think of better ones just let me know. I didn't believe in jumping to the whistle, but then I saw the light. I even heard like a voice out of the sky. 'It's your hand holding the whistle,' it seemed to say, 'It's your breath blowing it. There's no such thing as a solitary worker, you're all one big body. Horrible to think of an organ of the human body sort of deciding to go its own bleeding way. You want to raise a nice hot cupper to your lips and you're dying for it, being parched, and then your thumb goes into rebellion and says it won't help to lift it. Horrible, horrible.' Them was the words, or something as near like as make no bleeding difference. I saw it was not somebody else making me jump, it was me telling myself through the mouth of somebody I'd set up to do it for me. I had visions of workers marching together. I saw the power flaming from them like a flame like of fire. There'd been a time when the government had said: 'Haw haw, crush him, he's only a bloody workman, we've got the bastard in our power,' but now I saw it was all different. I saw that I had the power, and my mates with me, and I've never looked back since.'

Very moving, almost as moving as the films they'd been shown, very well made creatures of TUCFILM at Twickenham, historical films of the Struggle that made you want to cry out with rage. But nothing, neither film nor lecture nor group discussion, had yet dared to make the point that denied all history, centuries of religious and humanistic teachings alike: the right of man to loneliness, eccentricity, rebellion, genius; the superiority of man over men.

'Okay, love, I'll jump,' said Bev, and he donned his uniform with its TUC badge of a silver flywheel on a ground of shed workers' blood. He put on his issue slippers. The 16.00 hour bell shrilled. They kissed, they parted, she to her seminar, he to his.

'I know what is still in the minds of most of you,' said Mr Fowler to his group of twelve. They sat informally in what, in the days of its aristocratic ownership, had been the Blue Room. It was now distempered in buff and very plain, and even the old baroque cornices had been chipped off. 'You're seduced still by the traditional notion that to give one's total allegiance to a collective is to deny one's rights as a human being. You're holding out, a lot of you, against what you regard as the philosophy of the anthill.' Mr Fowler beamed, a beaming sort of man in these sessions though, strolling on the paths outside, he frowned much and muttered to himself, and concentrated the beam on Bev. 'You anti-anters have to provide an argument powerful enough to shake us collectivists, but none of you has yet done so. Am I not right, me old Bev?'

Bev shuddered at the facetious colloquialism, then growled briefly, then said: 'I want to approach this business from a perhaps illegitimate angle – '

'Bastardize all you will, Bev boy.'

'You, I mean you, Fowler. You're not a worker. I'd say you were a product of a middle-class home, father a clergyman perhaps, with a middle-class education – '

'My father,' said Mr Fowler, 'was an agnostic. A bank inspector, if you must know. As for my education – '

'Middle class,' said Bev. 'You've never practised a trade, am I right?'

'Teaching is a trade, as you know. Books are the tools of it. As for class, your term is outmoded. There are only employers and employees.'

'What I mean is – why,' asked Bev, 'do you put the generality in front of the individual? Why do you so passionately blazon this belief in the Syndicalist Society?'

'I've explained all that. Because it is the will of the majority and the aspirations of the majority that must count in the modern age, that the cult of minority power, interests, culture – '

'Of course I bloody well know all that,' cried Bev. 'What I want to know is this – what's in it for you?'

'There is nothing in it for me except the happiness of seeing fulfilled – '

'Come off it, Fowler. You don't like the majority. You don't like beer, football pools, darts. A spell on a factory floor would give you neurasthenia. You don't give a monkey's for the worker's cause. What are you getting out of all this? For that matter, what is the great bloody Mr

445

Pettigrew getting out of it?'

'What am I getting out of it, Mr Jones?' It was Pettigrew's own voice. All turned. Pettigrew was sitting on a plain wooden chair by the door. He had made a sneaking entrance at some point in the session unacknowledged by Mr Fowler in smile, nod or bow. Bev, abashed, turned and stoutly said:

'Power.'

Mifflin the librarian and that other travelling companion of a fortnight back, the Midland youth who had whined about Christian martyrdom, both seemed to make 'That's torn it' gestures with their mouths. The rest of the group looked among themselves with smiling eyes of anticipation: this bugger's up for the chop, he is that. Pettigrew rose and came forward, nodding pleasantly at Fowler. He took one of the standard-pattern easy chairs and said:

'Of course. Power. So obvious one doesn't even bother to think about it. Why do people become shop stewards, union leaders, group chairmen? Because they want power. A more interesting question is: why do they want power? Can you answer that, Mr Jones?'

'Because,' said Bev, 'the exercise of power is the most intoxicating of narcotics. Sexual power, the power of wealth, the power which can grind to a stop the wheels of industry at a mere lifting of a finger, that can hold a whole nation dithering in fear, the power of the blackmailer – what does it matter what kind of power it is? It's always the same potent drug, desirable for its own sake. And it's usually a substitute for a more wholesome kind of fulfilment. A compensation for the failure of the creative urge, or for sexual debility, or because one's mother doesn't love one enough.'

'Because your mother doesn't love you enough,' said Pettigrew. 'Do get rid of that impersonal pronoun. It's the most tiresome vestige of Bourgeois English. Yes,' he then said, 'one kind of power instead of another. You've told us nothing new, Mr Jones. There has to be a dynamic. But the power invested in the leaders of the new community is, you must admit, not dedicated to human destruction. It's not Nazi or communist power. We have no concentration camps or extermination chambers. The power of the leaders of our collective is the power of the collective itself. It has never yet done anything that has not benefited that collective. The strike weapon, the most evident instrument of power, has, without exception at least in the last forty years, always succeeded in bettering the worker's lot. Can you deny that?'

'Yes,' said Bev, 'I can. The bettering has all too often been purely nominal. Wages shoot up and prices follow. The vicious spiral, as it used to be called. Small firms can't meet new wage demands or go smash because they're strike-bound and can't fulfil their orders. Okay, they're nationalized, there's a blood transfusion of public money. But where does that money really come from? From increased taxes the workers immediately strike against. It's not true capital, it's only paper money.'

'How old fashioned you are, me old Bev,' beamed Mr Fowler. 'Capital isn't money. Capital is resources, energy, the will to create. Money is nothing.'

'Interesting,' Bev beamed back. 'Money is nothing, and yet it's the only thing that the workers care about.'

'Substitute the word *consumption*,' said Pettigrew, 'and you've said all that has to be said about the Outer Life. Yes, the workers want to consume, they have a right to consume, and the Syndicalist State uses power to fulfil that right. They had little enough chance to consume during those glorious historical epochs you were prevented from stuffing the heads of the kids with, and sulked because you were stopped.'

'Consumption,' said Bev bitterly. 'And what consumption. Colour television and food without taste or nutriment, workers' rags that call themselves newspapers and substitute nudes for news, low comedians in working men's clubs, gimcrack furniture and refrigerators that break down because nobody cares about doing a decent job of work any more. Consumption, consumption and no pride in work, no creative ecstasy, no desire to make, build, improve. No art, no thought, no faith, no patriotism –'

'Me old Bev,' said Mr Fowler, 'you forget a very simple truth. That the techniques of modern manufacture do not allow for pleasure or pride in work. The working day is a purgatory you must be paid well for submitting to, paid well in money and amenity. The true day begins when the working day is over. Work is an evil necessity.'

'It was not that to me,' said Bev. 'I enjoyed my work. My

447

work as a teacher, I mean. My work as a rather better paid dropper of nuts on chocolate creams was a mere nothing, a sequence of simple bodily movements above which my mind soared in speculation, meditation, dream. But to educate young minds, to feed them – '

'To feed them rubbish,' said Pettigrew. 'Force-feed them with innutritious fibre or downright poison. Your chocolate creams were a more honest fodder, Mr Jones. Listen to me, sir.' That *sir* was like a promise of steel whips. 'You were wrong to enjoy your work. Even the Bible says that work is hell: "In the sweat of thy brow shalt thou earn bread." You are at your old business of confusing two worlds.'

'There's only one world,' cried Bev.

'One world is coming,' nodded Pettigrew, 'but not the one world you mean. Holistic syndicalism, the fulfilment of the ancient battle cry about workers of the world uniting. You mentioned patriotism, which means what it always meant – defending the property of a sector of the international bourgeoisie against an imagined enemy, for the only enemy of the worker was the ruling class that sent him off to fight against other workers. This is old stuff, Mr Jones. The age of war is over, along with the age of the blown-up national leaders. The age of the imposed mystical vision, the madness, the cynicism. Done, finished.'

'And now we have the age of dullness,' said Bev. 'I wonder how long it can last? Because it can't last for ever. There's something in man that craves the great vision, change, uncertainty, pain, excitement, colour. It's in Dante, isn't it? "Consider your origins. You were not made to live like beasts, but to follow virtue and knowledge." You've read Dante, I don't doubt. Read him and rejected him because he's nothing to say to the workers. *Homo laborans* replaces *Homo sapiens*. Caliban casts out Ariel.'

'Gentlemen,' said Pettigrew to the group, for there were no ladies in it, 'I'm glad you've had this chance to listen to the arguments of one kind of dissident. Conceivably, some of these arguments were once your own. We're coming to the end of this rehabilitation course. Next week, after a four-day break for the staff, the next one starts. During these last few days, I have the task of visiting your discussion groups or syndicates and putting straight questions: how are things with you now? Simple things are required of you before you effect your re-entry into the world of work. First, a choice of job. Our Employment Officer, Miss Lorenz, is at your disposal with a list of vacancies. Second, the issue of a new union card, meaning a reinstatement, a resumed citizenship of Tucland. Third and last, a formal recantation of heresy – chiefly, I may say, for our own propaganda purposes. A whole-hearted acceptance of the closed shop principle and a rejection of the delusion of right to unilateral action.'

'So,' said Bev, 'in effect you ask us to set up a new morality in our hearts. A hospital burns down and the firemen stand by waiting for their £20 rise. We hear the dying screams and we say: This is right, this is in order, first things first.'

'No,' cried Pettigrew with such force that the word struck the opposed wall and came bouncing back. 'No and again no,' more softly. 'You see the breakdown of a public service and you regret that this should be so. You regret the stupidity of the public employer that has allowed things to get so far, that has refused to listen to the just demands of the workers and has now forced them to use the ultimate terrible weapon. You look beyond your immediate vision to the reality.'

'To a man whose wife has perished in a burning building,' said Bev bitterly, 'such a mystical vision is hard to attain.'

'And yet,' said Pettigrew, 'there have been moments, and very recent moments too, when you have said to yourself: I cannot altogether regret what happened.'

'What do you mean?' Bev felt his heart tumbling into his belly and blood pumping up to his throat.

'You know what I mean.' Pettigrew looked at him steelily. 'We here are entitled to know what inner worlds you enter. After all, you are in our charge.' He turned to the rest of the group. He said: 'Do any of you still have misgivings? If so, speak honestly.' Nobody answered because they were preoccupied with the shock of seeing Bev leap on to the great Mr Pettigrew and belabour him with his fists. Pettigrew's glasses flew off and were heard to tinkle tinily on the floor. He tried to get up from the chair where Bev had him pinned, blinking and gasping. Fowler, not now beaming, was on to Bev's back, disclosing a strength

none of the normally beamed at would have suspected.
Nobody came to assist Bev. Two men, metalworkers, once
very bloody-minded, came to assist Fowler.

'You damned traitors,' breathed Bev, while Pettigrew
looked with woe at his broken glasses and Fowler panted,
straightening his tie. A metalworker said:

'You're mad, mate. Fucking nutcake case, do you know
that?' Pettigrew said:

'Perhaps, Fowler, you'd get me one of my spare pairs.
In the left-hand drawer of the desk in the office.' Fowler
went. Pettigrew tried blearily to focus on Bev. 'Strangely
or not,' he said, 'this will not be held much against you.
It's a last spurt of dissidence. I think you're going to find
yourself cured. Group, dismiss. I'll see you all sometime
tomorrow.'

---

12   Clenched fist of the worker

Supper that evening was a solid worker's meal of cod
deep-fried in batter with chipped potatoes and a choice of
bottled sauces, spotted dick and custard to follow. Tea was
served, as usual, in half-kilo mugs. Everybody looked
strangely at Bev, not knowing whether to approve his belligerence or not, since none really liked Pettigrew though
they feared him; some seemed to be fearing the worst for
Bev, sucking their teeth thoughtfully at him as they
lighted up their penultimate issue fag of the day. Pettigrew was not present at what he facetiously called High
Table. Mavis said to Bev, as they entered the cinema
together after supper:

'How could he know?' Bev whistled a few bars of *I have
heard the mavis singing*. Mavis was quick. 'Don't be a
bloody idiot. I'm not a nark. Do you honestly think I go
round telling the staff who I sleep with.'

'How many do you sleep with?'

'That's none of your flaming business, Jones.'

'Sure you're not the Official Whore of Rehabilitation?'

She cracked him a damned flat-handed slap for that and
bounced off to sit with some of the girls. Bev, his cheek

tingling, sat alone but not neglected. There were many sad or wondering eyes on him before the lights dimmed. The curtains opened to show a wide bloody screen and a turning silver flywheel, with the first two measures of *Tucland the Brave* stereoing out in hunting-horn harmonies. TUC-FILM presented *The Fury of the Living*. The story was conventional but it was given painful force through the technique developed by Paramount's experimental workshop in the seventies, whereby the minute blackness between frames, normally filled in by continuity of vision, had been eliminated, and the images on the screen struck like raw actuality. The subject might have been chosen specially for Bev, since it was about a factory fire service going on strike in order to secure better equipment and working conditions, and the rest of the employees going out in sympathy. The dirty employers, who had planned its demolition anyway in a programme of improvement and expansion, set on fire their own warehouse, making sure first that the pretty young wife of Jack Latham, one of the strikers, was imprisoned in a washroom there. None believed this when told: a filthy employer's trick, no more. The strikers watched the warehouse burn, and then Jack Latham heard his wife screaming: 'Jack, Jack, save me, Jack,' and after that actually saw her arms and hair waving from the flames, but his mates held him back: a filthy trick, don't look, don't listen. So the warehouse burnt out, and the strike remained unbroken, and the workers had won. But in the charred ruins Jack found his wife's asbestos identity-disc and went wild with grief and attacked his own mates. And his mates admitted: yes, they had known. But a calmly wise elder, a veteran of the cause, put him right: the cause needs martyrs, the cause is sanctified by their blood or their black heavenward-soaring flinders. But why the innocent? Why should the innocent. . . .? Jack screeched from the four walls and the ceiling of the cinema. Bev went out.

Bev went out, a thing not previously known, and encountered two bruisers in official overalls. One of them said:

'Well, mate. Not satisfied with the entertainment provided?'

'I've seen it all before,' said Bev. 'Indeed, I've lived through it.' And he made off towards the dormitory,

'Indeed indeed,' said the other, a man with unusually close-set eyes and no lips, 'indeed.'

'Well, it adds to it,' the first said, barring Bev's way. 'We don't like what you did to Mr Pettigrew earlier on. None of us here does.'

'Who,' asked Bev, 'is *us*?'

'Mr Pettigrew,' said the second, 'is the boss.'

'There are no bosses any more,' said Bev. 'There are representatives, delegates, secretaries, chairmen. But no bosses.'

'For your type,' said the first, 'there has to be bosses. Boss language is all your type understands. This way.'

Bev was gloomily pleased that the organization was at last showing, as he had always suspected it would, the quiet face of violence. He was elbowed to a lift he had not previously seen used. It went down, as was to be expected. It stopped, and opened directly into a cellar that still held wine bins, though all now empty. There were a plain deal table and three chairs. There was strip-lighting, already on. Another man, not tough looking, was standing thoughtfully under the light, cleaning his nails with a match. 'Ah,' he said, looking up, without enthusiasm. 'This him?'

'Him, Charlie. What they call an educated taff. He's going to do something nice for Mr Pettigrew. It will bring tears of joy to Mr Pettigrew's eyes, it will that.'

'Ah, that,' said Charlie. He tucked his match away in the top pocket of his overalls and, from the broad and deep thigh pocket, brought out a folded piece of foolscap. 'It's here to be read. Then signed. But read first. Sit down, Taffy boy. Read it careful.'

Bev sat and read:

I hereby acknowledge that, after a most useful course of rehabilitation at the Trades Union Congress Education Centre, Crawford Manor, East Sussex, I have been brought to a very clear understanding of the errors I formerly cherished concerning the aims and organization of British Syndicalism. I have no hesitation in recanting those errors herewith and wish it to be known, publicly if need be, that henceforth I will be a co-operative member of my union and an ardent supporter of the principles for which it, with its brother unions, stands.

Date: *Signed:*

Bev said: 'I'm not too happy about that verb at the end.

Mr Pettigrew's work?'

'It's nice and flowery,' said Charlie. 'It's a good piece of writing. Here's a pen here.' He held out a ballpoint. 'All you have to do is shove your moniker down. I'll put the date in.'

'Does this happen to everybody?' asked Bev. 'Does everybody have to come down here to sign? Or am I specially favoured?'

'Some comes here,' said Charlie, 'but not many. It looks like you're the only one on Course 23. It's good reports on the rest, but you seem to be a right bastard.'

'Did Mavis tell you that?' asked Bev.

'No names has to be mentioned. And if you're thinking this is Mr Pettigrew's idea, then you've got another think coming. Mr Pettigrew is above this cellar business. He grieves if anybody leaves here still a bloody-minded bastard, though them wouldn't be his words. He's innocent, Mr Pettigrew is, and has to be protected like from the rough side of life. So now you know what's to be done, Taff, and, if not, what has to happen, so let's get it over, shall we?'

They all nodded sadly as Bev tore up the document. The lipless man said: 'Charlie here has got plenty more of those.'

'Not all that number,' said Charlie. 'You'd better start, lads.'

They started. They were good at their work, which left no marks. Bev lay panting on the floor, trying to draw air in, and the air just wasn't available.

'Come on, lad,' said Charlie. 'All you have to do is sign. You can do what you like when you leave here, but for God's sake, lad, don't be more of a swine to Mr Pettigrew than you've been already.'

Bev found enough breath to say, *'Fuckyou.'*

'Dear dear dear,' said Charlie. 'Naughty words. Try again.'

'Did you bring the pliers, Bert?' asked the first tough. 'The dentist's ones? This geezer's got a fair number of pegs in his cakehole.'

'Left them upstairs,' said the one with no lips. 'Shall I get them?' To Bev he said: 'Always used those when I was in the police. Hurts more than just knocking them out and it shows less.'

'Later perhaps,' said the other. 'We'll see how we get on now.'

'Perhaps he'll sign,' said Charlie. 'Come on, Taff, be reasonable.

'*Bastardsfuckyou.*'

'Oh, all right then, ungrateful little swine.'

I can always recant the recantation, said Bev's brain clearly as he was kicked and thumped. I'll sign, but not just yet. I'll wait till they start the tooth-pulling. I can stand this, I can stand any amount of – The brain itself was astonished as its lights began to go out, having just time to say: 'No need to sign after all.' Then there was nothing.

13   A flaw in the system

Bev had been the only patient in the little sickbay; he had, indeed, been very nearly the only inmate of Crawford Manor. His course had ended, the reformed had gone off to the world of resumed work and consumption and syndicalist loyalty, the staff had taken their four-day break. But Bev had had a male nurse with a doctor's telephone number, and the male nurse had dished him up coarse meals made mostly of corned beef and onions, no invalid diet. But Bev was no longer really an invalid. Tomorrow, when the new course started, he would be free to go. But Mr Pettigrew did not wish him to go, not just yet. Mr Pettigrew did not take breaks. He worked all the time. He and Bev, Bev in an issue dressing-gown, had been together nearly all day for three days, either in the ward or the up-patients' tiny sitting-room. Bev wanted to know about the medical report, Mr Pettigrew wanted Bev to sign the document of recantation.

'I say again, Bev, that you were found in the grounds at night in a condition of syncope. The medical officer diagnosed slight anaemia. Our psychiatric consultant considers that the loss of consciousness might well have been caused by profound psychic tension, a struggle between selves, as it were. I incline to the latter view.'

'I was beaten up. I want that to go on the record.'

'You may have been. I can well understand that some of your er fellow-students might have wished to use violence against you. But to allege that violence might have been administered here, officially, is wholly monstrous. Violence is not a proletarian weapon. It is the monopoly of capitalism and totalitarianism. Besides, there were no marks on your body – except such marks as were obviously occasioned by your falling heavily on to a gravel path.'

'The lack of marks,' said Bev wearily, for the tenth time, 'is a sure sign of professional violence. But how can one man's truth prevail?'

'That is very nearly a sound aphorism,' said Mr Pettigrew. 'How can one man prevail in anything? Truth and virtue and the other values can only rest in the collective. Which brings me again to our unfinished business. I wish you to be manumitted, clean and reformed. Comprehensive School B15, Isle of Dogs, is only too anxious to have you. Your union card is ready. Sign, please please sign.'

'No,' said Bev.

'You know the consequences. The consequences have been presented to you very candidly.'

'I know,' very wearily. 'I'm an unreformed criminal. I can only survive by living the life of a criminal. And if I'm caught next time, there'll be no course of rehabilitation.'

'Next time,' said Mr Pettigrew gravely, 'it could be a matter of indefinite confinement. I'm not saying *will be*, but I *am* saying *c* – '

'I beg your pardon?' Bev interrupted him in large-eyed incredulity. 'You mean if I steal another bottle of gin – or try to; Christ, that's all I did last time: tried to – you mean I get a life sentence? I don't believe it. God, man, that's going back to the eighteenth century.'

'In the eighteenth century you could have been hanged for stealing a loaf, let alone a bottle of – '

'Gin was cheap then,' said Bev in the schoolmaster's way that not even impending death can kill. ' "Drunk for a penny, dead drunk for twopence, clean straw for nothing." '

'Hanging then was done without regret. We're not in the so-called Age of Enlightenment now.'

'We're certainly not. Universal darkness buries all.'

'You ought to know that the concept of penal servitude

455

has drastically changed in the last ten years. Prison with hard labour is not permitted by the TUC. Labour of any kind entails union representation. We cannot allow prisons to be sweatshops. Very well, there is only one kind of confinement available now.'

'You mean solitary? Solitary for life?'

'Oh no. The TUC would not permit any such fiendish punishment. May I put it this way – that the distinction between the place of penal detention and the mental home must, of necessity, progressively narrow. Which represents, in terms of the amenities of enforced confinement, an improvement. Mental homes don't become like prisons, I mean – it's the other way round. You can see that this had to happen.'

Bev looked at him with wide eyes of horror for at least five seconds. 'The bin? The asylum? Impossible, you have to establish insanity.'

'Would insanity, in your case, be so difficult to establish? You're recidivist, atavistic, a confirmed criminal, a danger to the community. You reject the sanity of work.'

'I reject,' said Bev in a small voice, 'the insanity that goes along with work in your syndicalist state. I'm entitled to my eccentric philosophy.'

'You admit the eccentricity? Yes, of course, you have to. The gap between eccentricity and insanity is easily bridged. Put away – think of it – with paranoids and schizophrenes and cases of general paralysis of the insane – that's how you'll be, Bev. Not indefinitely for punitive reasons, but because it's impossible to quantify the time in terms of a judicial sentence. *Indefinitely* meaning until somebody thinks it worth while to initiate the long bureaucratic process of approving your discharge on the grounds that adequate familial custody and care will be available. *Indefinitely* not in the sense of permanently but because there's no rational period of confinement shorter than an indefinite one. All a question of somebody caring. The State won't care. The TUC won't care. Why should it care about one who's thrust himself deliberately away from the protection of its maternal bosom? As for family – you have no family, Bev.'

'I have a daughter.'

'You have a daughter – Elizabeth or Bess or Bessie. She presents another problem. The State Institutions for Children in Need of Care and Protection are, unfortunately, overcrowded and, being desparate as to vacancies, they must consult a strict table of priorities. There seems to have been a mistake made in the documentation that accompanied the admission of your daughter to SICINC G7 in Islington. You said, apparently, something about being distraught over the death of your wife and unable to look after your daughter. It was naturally understood that the arrangement would be temporary. It was not appreciated that you had decided to deunionize yourself and join the beggars and vagrants and criminals. You are not one of the legitimately unemployed. You have no claim on the beneficent offices of the SICINC system. Your daughter must leave. She can, of course, accompany you in your derelict hopelessness, but to subject a child to that situation is a crime in itself. Sign, Bev. Join the comity of workers. Teach what you have to teach, draw your pay. Organize voluntary evening classes in the history of the Renaissance and the Reformation. Show sense. *Sign.*'

He had the document and the pen ready. The pen was an attractive one, a stout ink-barrel of old-fashioned vulcanite, the nib sturdy and gold and blackly moist.

'No,' said Bev.

Pettigrew kept his temper. 'Very well,' he said. ' "Between the stirrup and the ground – " You still have till tomorrow. One more thing. The MO says you must watch your heart. He wasn't too happy with what he heard. You're not fit to cope with the stresses of the life of the outcast. Tomorrow morning you may dress in whatever clothes you possess and report to me in my office at nine. I would pray, if prayer was in order, for some angel of good sense to descend on you in the night.' He got up, smart in his tweeds (for this was, after all, the country), and settled his glasses and pushed back his tow lock before giving a valedictory sad shake of the head. Bev said:

'As, in one capacity or the other, I'm to re-enter the outside world, would it be possible for me to have news of it? We've been sealed off for the last – '

'The strike of the communication media continues, and rightly. You need no outside news. You have enough to do this evening without reading rags or gawping at the box. Think, man, think, think.' And he left.

Bev did not think. He merely mused on various possible

futures. He was quite certain that he would never give in. If the worst came to the worst, London afforded many spectacular opportunities for martyr's suicide. But how about poor Bessie?

He tossed much of the night but had one period of still sleep in which he dreamt, irrelevantly to his troubles, of angelic trumpets blowing over the city (of course, Pettigrew had put angels into his head) and then a voice crying: 'The kingdom is fulfilled.' Workmen in strange robes were hacking at barrels, and golden liquids gushed out to flow bubbling along the gutters. Banners with unreadable inscriptions flew from high buildings. There was a distant thunder of horsemen, and the thudding hooves came nearer though the riders remained invisible. 'They're coming,' cried Ellen, restored and whole, 'but for the sake of the All High don't let them get away with it.' Then the hooves were deafening. The sky, blood-red, turned primrose. Bev awoke sweating.

It seemed, from the light, to be about seven in the morning. He rose, bathed and shaved with the issue razor, then put on his old clothes and shoes. Carrying his ragged overcoat across his arm, he left the sickbay and walked the corridors and descended the stairs that led towards the eating-hall. He grieved distractedly at the low estate to which this eighteenth-century manor had fallen. What beauty of line and texture had been left in wall, pillar, curve of staircase had been wantonly rubbed out with buff distemper, posters, cheap syntex carpeting, a three-metre cut-out representation of Bill the Symbolic Worker. All that beauty, all those exquisite possessions of the tax-ruined Crawford family – gone, sold to Americans or Arabs. No room for beauty, for beauty was always for minorities. Pettigrew and his like were at least consistent: no vestige of the privileged past to be left, even though this could not but be a self-inflicted wound on those who, knowing what privilege meant, must also know that the spiritual and imaginative transports they had started to liquidate (all that nonsense about the Inner World!) were what human life was about. Perversion, masochism, martyrdom. Taste and intelligence vociferously denied by those who, possessing them, knew they were the ultimate value. Such men were fanatical. Such men were dangerous. Approaching the eating-hall, Bev knew in his tripes that he would be pursued to the limit. *Pursued by his own kind.*

Two tables were already full with early arrivals for the new rehabilitation course. As Bev filled his tray at the counter – tea, yoghurt, buttersub, toast white as leprosy – he saw Mr Boosey the conducting officer slurping his tea while waiting for three eggs to be freshly fried. Mr Boosey recognized him and grinned unpleasantly.

'Put you right, have they? A good boy now?'

'Sod off,' said Bev. 'Shove your gun in your fetid left armpit and squeeze the trigger, bastard.' Mr Boosey growled. Bev looked for a place and saw Mr Reynolds smiling up at him. Bev sat. Reynolds said:

'Yes, I thought this was what must have happened to you. It happens to everybody, I'm told, sooner or later. Are you converted?'

'No. What were you caught doing?'

'I stole a whole ham. I ate much of it too, with some of our old friends of the community. Then they came from the grocery store with the police and said: That is the man. *Ecce homo.* Will I find it amusing here?'

'A lot are converted,' Bev said. 'Be on your guard.'

'Drugs in the tea? Positive reinforcements? Torture?'

'*I* was tortured,' said Bev. Reynolds went pale as the yolk of his fried egg. 'But I leave here as I came.' Reynolds nodded and nodded. He said:

'You remember my little black friend, Trevor? Illiterate, or near, but very stubborn about human rights. Well, he joined this free army or whatever it's called. Came round flashing a bottle of *bought* gin and his first month's pay. A generous boy, happy as a king. Not a real army, man, he said. We ain't got no guns. A clever organization, I'd say. Not easily bannable. You can't even call what they wear a true uniform. Rather a smart suit really – green, belted, with a yellow enamel badge of rank on the lapel. Green for England, I suppose – '

'Yellow for Islam,' Bev said. 'You seem interested. Did you think of joining?'

'My dear boy, at my age? With my arthritis? How old are you, by the way?'

'Thirty-eight in February.'

'Consider it. They need instructors, they say, but in what God knows. Trades, I gather. Black Trevor used to be a builder's labourer. I'm in the Engineers, man, he says, proudly of course. It sounds better than being a class three hod-carrier or whatever he was. Perhaps they need history courses too. It was history you taught, wasn't it? Wait – ' He pulled from inside his ruined brown-bread-coloured suit a crumpled copy of the *Free Briton*. 'Everybody reads it,' he said. 'There's nothing else to read. I gather they put out radio and television programmes also. Formidable people. You'll find addresses and phone numbers in there somewhere. Not that the telephones are working at the moment, of course. The trains started just in time for our trip here. What a filthy mess it all is.'

'Have you,' asked Bev, 'any money?'

Reynolds looked at him sternly. 'Not here,' he said. 'Is it forbidden to go unescorted to the toilets?'

In the toilets Reynolds handed Bev three ten-pound notes. 'This is one little crime that went undiscovered. Not even the frisking police found this lot. They rarely look inside one's socks. As for a surgical stocking – I regret the crime in some ways. An old lady coming from the bank. Still, they've driven us to it, the swine. I'm sorry it's not more. It won't take you very far.'

It was with perky confidence that, jump on nine, Bev went to Mr Pettigrew's office. He wouldn't starve for a day or so. He would consider joining the Free Britons. He said, before Pettigrew uttered a word:

'No. I'm not signing.'

Pettigrew's little office was something like a presbyterial interview-room, though there was no crucifix on the wall and no musty smell of unwashed soutanes. Pettigrew said:

'A special dispensation is sometimes granted. You are more than welcome to take the course again. Miss Cotton would help you. She seems genuinely fond – '

'No,' said Bev.

'Well,' said Pettigrew, and he rose from his chair for the commination. 'I must deliver the secular equivalent of a curse. Everything possible has been done for you. On the bathroom scales this morning I noticed that I had lost several hectograms. My appetite is failing. I have never met such painful obduracy.'

'Am I entitled to a travel warrant?'

'Go and see Miss Lorenz, it's nothing to do with me.

Get your travel warrant and go. Never let me see your face again. You're a flaw in the system, a blight. Death will come for you soon, make no mistake about it. You've cut yourself from the blood supply of the commonalty and must fall off, a piece of stinking gangrenous flesh. I can smell your putridity from here. Get out, you piece of death.'

'You're mad, Pettigrew,' Bev said. 'You prophesy my end, so let me prophesy yours and the end of the system you and your kind have brought into being – '

'Get out. Now. At once. Or I'll have you thrown out – '

'You'll come up against reality, Pettigrew. The reality of no more goods to consume, no more fuel to burn, no more money to inflate. The reality of the recovered sanity of the workers themselves, who know in their hearts that this cannot go on. The reality of the invader whose insanity will flood a sphere more fanatical than yours. If I'm to die, I say: so be it. But you believe that death is really life – '

'Charlie,' called Pettigrew loudly. 'Phil, Arnold.' His cry was a supererogatory act, for he had his finger pressed on a button on his empty desk.

'Ah,' smiled Bev. 'The thugs are coming. I've finished, Pettigrew. I'm off.'

'Finished, yes, yes, finished, finished, that's what you are, finished and ended and done for.'

Bev left just as the thugs started coming in. Charlie nodded at him without rancour. 'Still not signed?' he said.

'Not yet,' Bev said. 'Mr Pettigrew seems to need you. A small fit of hysteria.' And he dashed off to get his travel warrant.

He breathed deeply of the free January air as he left Crawford Manor. He walked briskly and came to Batemans, Kipling's old house, now a cybernetic centre. Somebody there had remembered the poet, for there was a kind of wayside pulpit near the entrance to the grounds, the text as follows:

OH IT'S TOMMY THIS, AN' TOMMY THAT, AN' TOMMY GO AWAY,
BUT IT'S THANK YOU, MR ATKINS, WHEN THE BAND BEGINS TO
PLAY.

Bev walked into Burwash village, needing a bus to get to the station at Etchingham. There was no bus for another three hours. He thumbed at passing cars, of which, the price of gasoline being what it was, there were not many.

461

Eventually a green Spivak stopped. A gaunt man leaned out to say:

'Where?'

'Well, London.'

'Where in London?'

'Anywhere.' Bev realized that he didn't honestly know where. Islington would come into it, but not just yet.

'Hop in.'

'Thanks.'

The gaunt man drove with skill. His ethnic group was hard to place: Armenian? Greek? Some obscure people of northern India? But it was he who asked the questions.

'One of the dissidents they treat at the Manor?'

'Right. Still a dissident.'

'Trade? Profession?'

'Confectionery operative. Before that, schoolmaster.'

The man digested this. 'And you don't like things as they are,' he at last said. 'Well, you're not the only one. It's all got to change.' His accent also was hard to place. Sharp and patrician, but with a round foreign *o* that could come from anywhere. 'You'll see it soon, I think. Terrible change, terrible.'

'What's *your* trade?' asked Bev, 'or, of course, profession?'

'I'm with Bevis the Builders,' said the man. 'We specialize in the erection of mosques. I've built mosques all over the world. I built that one off the Via della Conciliazione in Rome. You know Rome?'

'Unfortunately, I've never been able to afford to travel.'

'Rome is not worth knowing. Not now. There you see what bankruptcy is really like. At present I'm engaged on the Great Smith Street contract.'

'Ah,' said Bev. 'The Masjid-ul-Haram.'

'You speak Arabic?'

'*La. Ma hiya jinsiyatuk?*'

The man chuckled. 'First you say no, then you ask me where I'm from. Call me Islamic, no more. Islam is a country, just as your Tucland is a country. Ideas and beliefs make countries. The big difference between Islam and the materialistic syndicalist states is the difference between God and a bottle of beer. Does that shock you?'

'Not at all.' Bev's dream was regurgitated in small gobbets.

462

'You shivered. Are you cold? Shall I turn up the heating?'

'No, no, thank you. You talked about terrible change. I was reacting belatedly.'

'I shudder too when I think of it,' said the man. 'But I do not shudder for myself. No no no, not for myself.' A light snow began to fall.

14   All earthly things above

The address was Number 41, Glebe Street, in Bev's own, or erstwhile, Chiswick. He checked it again with the last page of the *Free Briton* before ringing the bell. It was a very shabby terraced house with a neglected front garden and overflowing dustbin. A girl chewing something, frizzy auburn in a green suit with a yellow badge, opened for him. 'You'll have to wait in there,' she said, head-jerking towards a door to her right. But, clattering down the carpetless stairs, came a moustached man with papers in his hands, green trousers, white shirt. He looked foxily at Bev while he handed the papers to the girl, saying:

'Five of each there, Beryl. Good God, don't I know you?'

That was to Bev. Bev said: 'Wait. You did that last inspection. HMI. Your name's Forster.'

'Faulkner. Yes, indeed, I was one of His Majesty's Inspectorate. Welsh, aren't you, some Welsh name? You come for a job?'

'I came to see about the possibility of a commission of some kind. Jones is the name. Master of Arts, University of – '

'I'll get my jacket,' said Faulkner. 'Very fuggy in there. I'm due for a break. I've got a thirst I wouldn't sell for – Beryl, tell the Democrat-Major to carry on for a bit, will you? This gentleman and I will be at the Feathers.'

In the lounge-bar of the Feathers, Faulkner, whose yellow lapel badge was embossed with the black square of a major, drank off his gin and tonic thirstily and called for more. Bev ravaged a plate of cheese and chutney sandwiches and sipped at a double scotch. 'The price of it,' said Faulkner. 'Still, it won't be for much longer.'

'You mean the price is going to go down?'

'I mean that there just won't be any,' said Faulkner. 'There'll be a hell of a row, but it has to happen. Never mind, never mind, first things first.' He surveyed shabby though clean-shaven Bev. He was natty, pretty, vulpine, his polished black hair short and parted as with a ruler. 'You one of the naughty boys, then? All right, don't tell me. I was had up for my hundred-page report on the state of secondary level science teaching. If you don't like it, I said – you know the rest. What sort of job are you after?'

'What sort of jobs are going?'

'Entries to commissioned rank are dealt with at the top. That's the way his lordship wants it. I can't ring Al-Dorchester, but he's certain to be there tomorrow. You can go along with a note.'

'His lordship?'

'Oh, we call him that. The boss. Colonel-in-chief. Law-rence isn't his real name. He's not even Anglo-Irish, or whatever T.E. was. The money's good. The money is very very good.'

'Accommodation?'

'You married?'

'My wife was burned to death just before Christmas. When the firemen were on strike. I have a daughter. Thirteen. Mentally retarded. A victim of one of the easy-birth drugs. Look, could I have another one of these?' His whisky glass shook in his hand.

'You certainly could.' He waved at the barman. 'A pretty girl, is she?'

'In a blowsy way – oh God, I shouldn't say that about my own daughter. Sexually precocious, of course. A telly-addict.'

'She sounds like any other girl of thirteen,' Faulkner said. Then: 'When you go to Al-Dorchester, take her along.'

'Why? Thanks.' He took his new double and squirted soda in.

'They'll want to know everything there,' he said vaguely. 'I'll write you the note now.' He scribbled something on a message pad, tore, folded, gave. Then he said: 'How religious are you?'

'*Religious?* Does that matter?' Faulkner waited. 'Well, I was brought up Primitive Methodist. Dropped it, of course. I'm nothing now. God's abandoned the world.'

'Ah,' said Faulkner. 'Not everybody would say that. I'm Unitarian. It helps. His lordship will want to know. He'll inveigh against a society gone mad with materialism. He believes the only answer is a return to God. He'll want to know how you feel about that."

'Accommodation?' asked Bev again.

'The usual. No married patches, I'm afraid. But take that daughter of yours to Al-Dorchester. Ask for the Abu Bakar Suite. Where are you staying?'

'I've only just been let out of Crawford Manor. My rehabilitation course didn't work. But I've thirty pounds.'

'That won't take you far. We have a sort of miniature transit depot by Turnham Green station. Officers only. I can fix you up for the night if you like.'

'You're kind.'

'No, just doing my job. We need good officers. Plenty of recruits for the lower levels. *Leading* an army is always the problem.'

'How much of an army is it? Thanks.' He had been given a third double scotch. Faulkner surveyed him coolly before answering. Then he said:

'Like the Salvation Army in a way. But we're not for derelicts. We're for energy and patriotism, skill and God. We're the alternative State. We have no arms. We've no desire to function outside the law. Not, that is, until the law puts itself beyond reason.'

'It's done that already,' Bev said with gloom.

'No. Use your imagination. Or just wait. I don't think you'll have to wait long. Events have a peculiar genius of their own. Whatever the mind imagines, the mind itself is primarily a boggling machine. Wait. One for the road?'

The transit depot had formerly been a small biscuit factory. Bev found several six-bed chambers, with very clean lavatories and a kitchen that provided bread and cheese and very strong tea. There was no officers' bar. Talking to Lieutenants Brown and Derrida, Captain Chakravorty and Acting Major Latimer, Bev discovered that they were waiting for postings to provincial barracks – Darlington, Bury St Edmunds, Durham and Preston. Chakravorty estimated that the strength of the Free Britons was now above 50 000 and growing, but it was, he said, sadly under-officered. The problem of placing arms caches worried Latimer. He was convinced that it would soon be necessary to be armed. He was recommending crash instruction in the use of automatic weapons, with dummy guns if need be. But they needed an arsenal network and they needed to be able to ensure the free passage of arms. 'We'll have to wait till G Day,' he said, 'but that's cutting it very fine.'

'G Day?' puzzled Bev. They looked at him as at one who was unforgivably ignorant, but then Derrida said:

'Of course, you're new, you can't know. General Strike Day. Ours as well as theirs. There's going to be terrible opposition.'

'And where will the arms come from?' asked Bev. They held back their laughs, but Chakravorty said:

'That's something you ought to know. There's no excuse for that kind of ignorance.' He said no more. He yawned genteelly and said it was time to turn in. He had to take a train at 05.15, picking up a Drains and Sewage detachment half an hour before.

Bev was up early enough. He had to get Bessie before the 08.15 virginibus took her to school. He rode the underground railway – a diminished service but not now on strike – from Turnham Green to the Bank, and then changed lines for Highbury and Islington. The Girls' Home was off Essex Road. He had bought a newspaper at Turnham Green, the media strike over, and found it full of blanks where the printers had not allowed certain items to be published. The front page news concerned the beginning of a construction workers' strike that day. There was a pugnacious photograph of Jack Burlap, the union leader, saying that sweet reason had failed and the twenty-hour week and the £20 rise reasonably requested had been brutally thrown out at a joint meeting of the National Productivity and National Wages Boards. They knew what was coming, brothers, and now here it is.

Bessie, waiting with her friends for the virginibus, chewing roundly on something, listening to raucous rock on a gipsy-looking girl's transistor radio, did not at first recognize her father. Then she said, 'Dad,' and embraced him lusciously. She was clean in a short blue skirt and a provocative red sweater, was much fined down in body except for her breasts. 'He was on the telly, my dad was,' she told her friends, 'The strike's over,' she told her father. 'It was terrible, wasn't it, Linda, having no telly. But tonight it's *Road Floozy*.' The gipsy girl was turning the selector. Talk came through an instant and another instant and another as she sought noise:

'Sheikh Abdulrahman said he was ... under no circumstances would the strike be permitted to ... Great Smith Street was scheduled for....' And then music, loud, crude, brash. Bev said:

'Put the news back on. It sounded important.'

'Up your fucking arse,' said the gipsy. 'Bus is coming, Bess.'

'You, Bess, are coming with me,' said Bev. 'Get packed.' Bessie howled. Her friends climbed aboard, miming sexual assault on the driver, who wearily said, 'Stop that lot now.' Bessie sought to follow them. Bessie's friends got off to rend Bev with their nails. Bev said:

'A day out. Lunch. Cinema.'

'It's *Road Floozy* tonight.'

'I'm talking about *today*.'

'So I don't have to pack, do I?'

'I suppose not.' Bev and the driver exchanged a nod of large frustration. 'We'll get you things, whatever one means by things.'

'Lipstick? Manegloss?'

'Come on,' said Bev. He still had, after his tube-fare, twenty-five pounds in his pocket. He took her to a Crumpsall's Yumbox and watched her eat sausages with her fingers. She told him about her life at the Girls' Home, which meant mostly what television programmes she had seen. The strike had been terrible, strikes shouldn't be Allowed by Law, but Miss Bottrell had put on film shows. And they didn't have a wide-screen telly there, anyway, which was a fucking cheat, and there was only one set, and there had been scratching and hair-tugging and gouging about what they should all look at. But it would be all right tonight, they all wanted to see *Road Floozy*. She did not seem to remember her mother; she was vague about her old address; her father she remembered because he had been on the telly. She spoke of Red Azel and Dirty Nell and Black Liz and the night they had got a boy into Dorm B and thrown his clothes out of the window and made him do things to them, but he couldn't do much and it wasn't as good as the telly. Bev sighed.

He gave her lunch at the Pig-in-a-Blanket on Tottenham Court Road and watched her eat sausages with her fingers. She ate two helpings of Cream Corn Heaven with Old Piggy's Chocsauce. Bev had enough cash left to take her to the one o'clock showing of *Sex Planet* at the Dominion, and she wanted to see it round again, but he said:

'No. We're having tea now,' knowing that they weren't unless it was going to be stood them, 'at one of the finest hotels in the world. And don't ask if they have telly there, because they do.' He counted up his deckers. They could afford to ride to Green Park. From there they must walk. By the tube station the *Evening Standard* was being sold. A headline said: MOSQUE SCABS THREAT. Bev couldn't afford a copy.

High above Al-Dorchester on Park Lane a yellow flag flew, with the name of the establishment in beautiful Arabic script, and floodlights flooded it with light. Bev and Bessie went through the swing-doors. The vestibule was full of Arabs, some in robes, others in badly cut Western suitings. In the long lounge tea was being taken. Bessie said:

'Look at them lovely fancies.' Weary British waiters pincered cream horns and éclairs on to the plates of disdainful male Arabs. Bev said:

'Sit down there.' And he shoved her into a canary-coloured armchair while he went to the desk to ask about Colonel Lawrence. Colonel Lawrence was expected at any moment, he was told. He went back to Bessie. Bessie complained:

'You said we was going to have tea. I want some of them cakes.'

'Be quiet child. I haven't enough money.'

'You promised.' She beat on his chest with a sturdy fist. Some tea-taking Arabs looked amused. One man, in snowy robes and corded headpiece, gazed through dark glasses long and with no discernible expression. He said something to a big-eared young man in an atrocious brown suit. The young man nodded and came over to Bev. He said:

'His Highness says you join him for tea.'

'Well – ' Bev was doubtful. Bessie said:

'His Highness?'

468

'He says you join him for tea.'

'Then tell his Highness ta,' said Bessie, and she pulled Bev vigorously up from his chair. They went over. Bev inclined to His Highness.

'Sit,' said His Highness. 'Sit.' There was a clapping of hands. Two waiters appeared with silver teapots and fancy cakes. Bessie couldn't wait for the pastry-tongs. She grabbed. His Highness smiled with reluctant indulgence. He spoke long Arabic with many throat-clearings and glottal checks to a fat man in a navy blue double breasted of which the bosom sagged sadly. The fat man said, nodding:

'Gamil, gamil. Harusun?'

'What precisely is – ?' Bev began, and then he was aware of a stirring in the lobby. Somebody important had arrived.

'Al Orens,' said His Highness. Bev said, rising:

'Excuse me. An appointment. I – '

'You leave her,' said the fat man. 'She eat. She be safe.' As an earnest of this he clapped his hands for waiters. Bev now saw Colonel Lawrence for the first time. He was immensely tall, had a Mediterranean nose and a northern pallor, was dressed in a green suit with discreet yellow piping on the lapels, wore a black cloak. He had an entourage of five or six, white, brown, black. To an aide of an aubergine colour he spoke rapid Arabic. He bowed to the Arab tea-takers with deferential grimness, making for the lifts. He carried a riding-crop. Bev went, pulled out his note of introduction, addressed the aide:

'Sent by Major Faulkner – '

'Okay, you come up. Long wait maybe, maybe not. Many things going on now. You take next elevator.' Too tall for the ascending box, Colonel Lawrence seemed to bow towards Bev. The door closed. Bessie was on her, surely, seventh éclair. His Highness encouraged her gently to eat. Bev took the next lift.

The room where he was made to wait was a sumptuous lounge half-transformed into an office. Office? More like a map-room, war-room, operations-room. Two girls in green, one of whom greeted Bev with, 'Hi,' were dealing with, respectively, a telex machine and a typewriter whose carriage moved the wrong way (of course: Arabic). A map of the United Kingdom was on one wall, on another a map of Greater London. There were flags stuck on these maps. In the Westminster area was a black lozenge with the moon of Islam in the middle. Of course, the new mosque. The typing girl, very English rose and yet a great clatterer of Arabic script, got up and took a Coca Cola from a drinks-fridge. She offered one silently to Bev. Bev was thirsty.

He was standing with a black bottle stupidly in his hand when Colonel Lawrence came in. The eyes that looked down on him were speckled and flashed irregularly and disconcertingly. 'There is little time,' the voice was a reedy tenor, the accent vaguely Scottish, 'for formalities. Things are beginning. I have a strong recommendation from Major Major – '

'Falk er ner,' said the aubergine aide.

'You are, I gather, highly literate. Have you had journalistic experience?'

'I edited the university magazine for a year. But listen, sir, I would like – '

'You would like to know terms of engagement etcetera etcetera. There is no time, I say. This is the evening of the double strike. We need full eye-witness information ready for press by at latest 22.00. We wish you to go to Great Smith Street.'

'I fear, I'm afraid – '

'Afraid? Ah, I see. Give him money, Redzwan. Give him, ah, one of our anonymous raincoats. Take a taxi. Take a notebook and a pencil. You seem, if I may say so, to have nothing. Soon, I promise you, if you are obedient and faithful, you shall have everything.' Colonel Lawrence, aide following, strode back to the neighbouring room. Bev frowned and swigged his coke. The typing girl, without looking up, said:

'He's like that.'

Bessie was still stuffing, but more slowly. 'Oad Oozie,' she said. The entire Arab company watched benevolently. 'Telly,' she said. Bev said:

'I have to go. Work. For Colonel Lawr – '

'She be safe.'

Bessie, drugged with goo, looked up at her father and did not seem to recognize him. The white raincoat perhaps. The oversize bowler hat that was really a lightweight steel helmet. Bev went to the door and the Cock-

470

ney doorman whistled him a taxi. Bev gave him a five-pound note. Sophisticated by Islamic prodigality, the doorman scowled. Bev rode off through the winter evening. There was not much traffic. The price of petrol, the cost of cars. Hyde Park Corner. Grosvenor Place. Victoria Street. The taxi-driver sang some bitter recitative to himself. The corner of Great Smith Street, Westminster Abbey just ahead. Of course, the great mosque must challenge the ancient temple of the people of the scriptures, British branch. Bev heard the noise of crowds. He gave the driver a ten-pound note and told him to keep the change. 'Ain't no bleedin' change.' Bev gave him a twicer. 'Ta, mate.' And there it was facing him: the start of the great confrontation.

The crowd was angry and was hardly to be held back by an unhappy police cordon. Mounted constables clacked up and down. There was much light. Huge generating trucks fed huge brutes of floodlamps. By the light of these men worked. How many? A hundred? More? Two sky-high cranes were gravely busy, their gantries gyrating, their cabled grabs placing great blocks of masonry with delicate care. A brace of concrete-mixers ground and growled. Workmen in aluminium bonnets climbed ladders and descended them. An electric hoist took up a whole brickie gang to a boardwalk. The crowd of strikers yelled filth at the scabs. A loudspeaker truck rolled into Great Smith Street and a voice hurled and echoed:

'The building of the mosque must proceed. It is not a supermarket or a high-rise apartment block. It is a temple dedicated to God. To God, the God of the Jews and Christians and Muslims alike, the one true God of whom Abraham and Jesus and Mohammed were the prophets. I say again, the work must proceed. The wage offered is twenty pounds above the new rate sought by the Builders' Union. Be free, be free Britons, do the work you can do. We need your skill, your energy, your devotion.' A television team drank in the strikers' response: fists of anger, stroked bristled chins of indecision. The voice of Jack Burlap countered. Jack Burlap himself was there, on top of a truck, a loud-hailer to his face like an oxygen mask.

'Don't listen to the swine, brothers. It's the old capitalist trick. No guarantee, no contract, no security, no right to withdraw labour. You blackleg bastards up there, listen to the voice of reason. Get off that filthy job, you're playing into the bastards' hands. You're done for, you've given up your freedom, they can kick you off the job when they want to. It's wog money, it's dirty Arab oil. You're finished, brothers, you stupid swine, you've given up your buggering birthright.'

'You hear the voice of reason?' cried the loudspeaker van. 'The voice of intolerance, rather, of racism and chauvinism. You Muslims, you hear yourselves called dirty wogs. You Jews and Christians, will you allow your brothers in God to be reviled and spat upon? Be free, throw off your chains, honest godly work awaits you.'

A huddle of strikers tried to overturn the loudspeaker van. The police held them off. Jack Burlap addressed them:

'Now then, you police, do your duty. Don't turn against your comrades. You know the law, and I don't mean the law of the courts and the statutes. I mean the law of labour. You're workers too. Join your brothers. What's happening here is fragrant infringement. Don't let it happen – '

He was drowned by an unearthly blast of music. Eyes and open mouths sought its source. Loudspeakers, but where? A thousand mixed voices, a Berliozian orchestra, brass bands added:

> I vow to thee, my country,
> All earthly things above –
> Entire and whole and perfect,
> The service of my love....

A police sergeant on a prancing mare reined in the better to hear what was coming through on his walkie-talkie. He put down the instrument and nodded at a waiting constable. The constable blew a whistle thrice shrilly. Everybody out. The police were on strike. Jack Burlap seemed to halleluiah against the music, as though at a personal triumph. Perhaps union leaders were now interchangeable, inevitable result of holistic syndicalism. The cordons broke. Odd policemen removed helmets to wipe brows. The mounted cantered off.

> The love that asks no questions,
> The love that stands the test,
> That lays on the altar
> The dearest and the best....

The strikers howled or deeply moaned. They moved in on the holy building site. The music stopped in mid-minim. And then –

A platoon of men in green suits, lieutenant and leader of thirty ahead, marched down Great Smith Street at a light infantry pace. A brace of outriding motor-cycles grunted and spluttered. Another platoon followed. The police, shambling off, did not interfere. The green men carried no arms. In files they fought their way through to the making of new cordons. They were, Bev now noticed, all green-gauntleted. The right hand that had to strike out at occasional strikers seemed unusually heavy. It cracked dully on jaws. One hit a skull whose owner dithered and went clumsily down to be trampled on. Knuckledusters, of course. Bev felt sick. Another green platoon came from round the corner, this time doubling. The two cranes kept gravely to their lifting, one, setting down the other. Concrete heaved like simmering porridge. The builders went on building.

15   An admirer of Englishwomen

'NOT armed,' said Colonel Lawrence. 'That is important.'

'I say armed,' said Bev. 'Arms aren't necessarily guns. Your troops used violence.'

'A hard word,' said Colonel Lawrence. 'Try and see this thing in proportion. Ah.' His telephone rang.

'Impossible,' Bev said. The colonel widened his nostrils in a sort of triumph. He picked up the receiver. He listened. He smiled. He said:

'Your shorthand man? Good. Mr Jones will dictate.' To Bev he said: 'We've certain lines open. They will stay open. Our newspaper is to have eight pages tomorrow. Come, to work.' Bev improvised fluently from his notes. He had never expected to be a pressman. It was easy, money for jam.

'That,' said Colonel Lawrence, 'is contrary to my instructions. He had listened keenly to Bev's dictation. '*Not* armed. Never mind. Major Campion will know what to do.' He said thanks into the handset and then replaced it.

'Censorship, eh?' Bev said. 'The not so *Free Briton*.'

'Mr Jones,' said Colonel Lawrence, 'we will discuss later the true nature of freedom. And, in respect of yourself, the freely assumed constraints of army discipline. The *Mr*, by the way, means acting full lieutenant. For the moment, can you be trusted to write the editorial? Phone it through, Major Campion will make such adjustments as are needed. He knows my style. I must go out now.' He shook his aide Redzwan, dozing in a chair. Redzwan came up fighting. 'I must inspect the stricken city.' He went over to the window and looked out on a black London. There was light here in Al-Dorchester, though. It was dim and fluctuating, but it would get better: they were at work in the cellar adjusting the generators. 'The situation you know – before dawn the strike will be general. The first British General Strike since 1926. Point out the great difference between then and now. Now there are no communications, no law and order. In 1926 there was at least an army that kept its oath of loyalty and a non-syndicalized police force. Ours is now the only organization capable of maintaining minimal services. Say that when the TUC leaders see sense they will be more than welcome to the hospitality of these columns – '

'You mean that, Colonel? Your organization thrives on a TUC that doesn't see sense. You want this strike to end? Remember, you or your Islamic màsters started it.'

'*Your* organization, *your* masters. Tomorrow we must see about your formally taking the oath of obedience.' The telephone rang. Redzwan picked up the receiver. His jaw dropped. He handed it to Colonel Lawrence with great staring eyes on him. Colonel Lawrence said: 'Yes?' His face too lengthened. '*Allah ta'ala*,' he prayed. 'Yes. Yes. I agree.' He hung up and looked tragically at Bev. 'Tungku Nik Hassan has been assassinated,' he announced.

'Tungku – ?'

'Malay. From Brunei. Head of the Pan-Islamic Commission in the Haymarket. There are mobs of striking workers with nothing to do but attack various buildings flying the flag of the star and the crescent. This was inevitable, I suppose. I just did not think it would start so soon. Say something in the editorial about the deplorable racism and bigotry and, indeed, atheism that have become associated with – '

'Wait,' Bev said. 'How was he killed?'

'He was struck on the head with a length of lead piping. The Tungku courageously ventured into the mob, trying to make them see reason. He was an eloquent man, his English always of the most persuasive. Put it in about his virtues – ' The Colonel's nostrils were wide.

'You smell a special danger, don't you?' Bev said. 'Britain is now wide open to the punitive invader. The services are on strike. NATO will dither, the constituent countries worrying about their oil supplies. Are the Arabs coming?'

'The Arabs are here, Mr Jones.' Colonel Lawrence made his eyes project something fearsome on to the map of Greater London on the wall. 'Retaliation, Mr Jones. Do you think the Holy War ended in the Middle Ages?'

'Look, Colonel sir. What exactly are you after? A free Britain or an Islamic Britain? I have to know. You've appointed me as your provisional mouthpiece.'

'The only way out of Britain's troubles, Mr Jones, is a return to responsibility, loyalty, religion. A return to Gqd. And who will show us God now? The Christians? Christianity was abolished by the Second Vatican Council. The Jews? They worship a bloody tribal deity. I was slow in coming to Islam, Mr Jones. Twenty years as one of His Majesty of Saudi Arabia's military advisers, and all the time I kept, as was my right, to my father's Presbyterianism. Then I saw how Islam contained everything and yet was as simple and sharp and bright as a sword. I had dreamt of no Islamic revolution in Britain but rather of a slow conversion, helped by an Islamic infiltration expressed in terms of Islamic wealth and moral influence. Slow, slow. The working man's beer grows weaker, since so many of the breweries are in pseudonymous Arab hands. One cannot impose prohibition with a sudden stupid Volstead Act. Pork is swiftly pricing itself out of the market. But sometimes the North African blood that is my dear dead mother's cries out for fast action, while the Scottish side of me counsels care, *festina lente*. We will talk more of these matters tomorrow. But for now I fear the swooping of the sword.' He turned his eyes, alive with rivet-sparks, away from Bev and on to Redzwan. 'The striken city,' he said. 'Come.'

Alone, for the two girls were snatching sleep on camp

beds somewhere, Bev leaned back in his chair and yawned, arms behind his head, trying to think out the opening of his editorial. There was a knock and the door opened. A slim Arab entered, a Savile Row suit of quiet grey on, gold wristwatch, cufflinks, Gucci loafers. 'Mr Jones?' he said, in a very fair British upper-class accent.

'I don't think I've had the pleasure – '

The Arab sat down gracefully on a hard chair. 'My name is Abdul Khadir,' he said. 'His Highness's personal secretary. Which Highness, you will want to know. The answer is: His Highness Sheikh Jamaluddin Shafar ibn Al-Marhum Al-Hadji Yusuf Ali Saifuddin. You had the honour earlier of taking tea with him, so he tells me. The question I ask now is: does she possess a passport?'

Bev stared. 'Who? Why? What are you talking about? Oh my God. I'd forgotten clean about her. Where is she now?'

'Sleeping. Happily, I think. Alone, I must add. She watched the television programmes. The strike did not begin until well after the termination of a particular programme she had expressed much desire to view. She viewed it. She ate much. I think I can say she sleeps happily. His Highness leaves tomorrow – ah, I see it is already tomorrow. As she will be a member of His Highness's entourage, perhaps there will be no need of a passport. Still, His Highness has this democratic concern with the obeying of regulations.'

'You mean,' Bev said. 'I just don't,' he said. 'I don't think I. She has no passport, no. She's never had a passport. Please,' he said, 'explain.'

'I must first explain about His Highness. He is at present Chairman of IOU. It is a rotating chair, as you will know.'

Bev's brain swam. 'IOU?'

'The Islamic Oil Union. In Arabic, of course, the initials are different. His Highness's territories, as you will know, comprise – '

'Spare me. A hot territory, with oil and Allah. Muezzins and yashmaks. No need to tell me precisely where he sits on his revolving chair and watches the mineral fatness gush. Somewhere in Islam let us say.'

'Somewhere in Islam will do very well. Of course, the chair does not literally rotate.'

'And what does His Highness require of my daughter?

God knows, she has little enough to give.'

'Concubinage for a probationary period. And then marriage. His Highness already possesses four wives, which number represents the statutory allowance. Probationary concubinage until the marital vacancy is arranged. Do you object to the term?'

'What does Bessie say about it?'

'Besi has no objection. She does not know the word. Besi has, anyway, no option but to obey her father. I may say she thinks already very highly of His, ah, Highness. She has never before, she gives us to understand, seen such a capacity for bestowal. She is yet to encounter his library of videotapes in Ghadan. Western television programmes are very popular in His Highness's gynaeceum. His Highness travels widely throughout Islam. Also throughout the infidel world. His tastes are enlightened. But he is mostly in Islam. He pays frequent visits to London.'

'You seem to regard London as part of Islam.'

'It is the commercial capital of Islam, Mr Jones. I have a document in preparation for you to sign. It is being engrossed at the moment, in English and in Arabic. We could meet perhaps for breakfast here tomorrow. Here, of course, there is no strike. This is regarded as Islamic territory.'

'Is there anything for me in all this?' Bev asked coarsely.

'Satisfaction,' said Abdul Khadir, 'that your daughter is well provided for. I do not think your England is a good place to bring up a daughter. Unless, that is, the father has much wealth. Money? You require payment? You consider your daughter an object for sale? May I remind you that you have not been asked to provide a dowry.'

'You said something about concubinage. Aren't concubines bought and sold?'

'*Probationary* concubinage. It is not uncommon in Britain, and here there is no talk at all of money. But you may take it as certain that there will be marriage. His Highness has a great regard for Englishwomen.'

'She's only a child.'

'She is thirteen years old, Mr Jones.'

Bev sighed and then felt a qualified elation cautiously approaching. He was free, by God or Allah. He had now for shouldering only the burden of himself. He said:

'If the bar were still open we could drink on it.'

'The American Bar here has been long abolished, Mr Jones. Alcohol, in our faith, is *haram*. On the other hand, I have an adequately stocked drinks cabinet in my suite downstairs. If you would care to – '

'Thank you,' said Bev. 'On second thoughts, no. I have work to do. In the name of Allah and a Free Britain.'

'We will meet at breakfast, then. Your delightful daughter is looking forward to breakfast, she tells us. She has a great fondness for the *naknik* – no, that is the Hebrew name. *Sougou* is the right word.'

'*Sou* – ?'

'Sausage. It is common among Western children. She will not be allowed to have pork ones, of course, but she will hardly notice the difference. She did not notice it tonight.'

16   Strike diary

G1

Near the Cherry Blossom Boot Polish Factory, Chiswick, I got the first physical impact of strikers' enmity towards Islam. Three Bentleys going to Heathrow, flying Muslim flag. Sheikh in middle one, me and Bessie in third, father and daughter saying farewell. We stopped to let two loudspeaker vans go down Devonshire Road. Ten or so strikers threw stones at us, shouting wog bastards, up Allah's arse and so on. Our offside rear window starred and, from the noise, bodywork dented. Bessie open-mouthed with joy as though seized by scruff and thrust bodily into TV scene of violence. I expected we'd shrug it off, go on to Heathrow, but HH did not shrug it off. He was out of the car, giving Arabic orders. Two chauffeurs, Pakistanis probably victims of East End paki-bashers, dragged two Nimr automatic repeaters from trunk of Car 2. Clicked their weapons to ready and waited for signal to fire. I tumbled out of car yelling No no no no for God's sake, got into fireline. Stonethrowers ran like bloody hell, one Paki ran a few yards and spluttered shot at them, got one in leg, other in chest. One dead certainly. HH shrugged, dark glasses on, cigarette in Dunhill holder. Guns stowed, continued to Heathrow, leaving 1 dead 1 wounded. Bessie said it was like Grimm's Law or some such bloody TV nonsense, then wondered if she'd be in time to see Pornman that night, very vague indeed as to where she was going.

Heathrow Terminal 3, Islamic corner where nobody on strike. We whizzed straight on to tarmac. Sheikh's Nisr jet waiting, fuel nozzle to breast. Giant jets everywhere becalmed, no control tower staff, no customs, passport formalities. Whole airborne army could land here without opposition. Felt tremor of fear. Two Arab Wizzahs were there, mechanics peering into their innards, wooden crates being unloaded. Major Latimer, man met at Turnham Green, posting to Preston cancelled, was there with swagger stick and two trucks. Weapons he said – Okottas, Ghadibs, Vihainens, also British Mark IV Angries. Real army now, he said. If bastards want trouble bastards can have bloody trouble. Wind whipped up Bessie's skirt to arse level. Latimer went click click in soldier's vulgarity. My daughter, I said. Sorry old boy, nice piece of goods, daughter or not. I said ila allaqaa to HH, my prospective son-in-law, kissed poor or lucky Bessie. She said: I'm hungry, dad. They'll serve elevenses when you're aboard, Bessie. But I'm hungry NOOOOOOW! Last words Bessie spoke to me. Went back townwards in Bentley No. 3, starred and dented.

Strike absolutely and totally bloody general. Went round getting news. Rain, mud, piled refuse, squalor of streets growing. Women crowding and scratching to get into supermarket, Free Britons trying to control. Strangely, some of the strikers help. Hope there. Bloody ideological nonsense from top of unions must fail sometime, workers basically decent, must see sense. Later saw windows smashed of liquor store not by strikers but by Free Britons, coming out loaded with booze. Free Briton NCOs tried to make them see sense, barked orders, got the usual Up yours Jack and so on, then put on knuckledusters, waded in. Very nasty, very necessary. At Great Smith Street work on mosque goes on, but workers on mosque obviously unhappy at being marched to and from shifts by platoons protecting them from angry mobs. How long can this go on? File news, write editorial, cautious, no word about being armed or the necessity of violence. I have wads of cash in pocket worth little at moment. Loaf of bread £5. Bit of chuck steak £9.50. A Free British bakery is being set up in, appropriately, Bread Street. Have own bedroom Al-Dorchester.

G2

Ill-printed bulletin going the rounds with facsimile signatures of appropriate ministers of the crown, saying that builders' demands have been met – 20 hour week, £20 rise. That is to get that particular bit of unrest out of the way. Great Mr Pettigrew himself turns up at Gt S. Street to harangue from loudspeaker van mosque workers. Join your brothers, leave this illegal workforce, back into union, your action paralysing whole country. Some of mosque workers scratch heads, doubtful, unhappy, but NCO foremen shout and prod them back to labour. Which is worse – obeying NCOs, WOs, officers or jumping at shop-steward's whistle? Pay better in Free Britons? Yes, notice posted on worksite of £25 rise in soldier's pay. Half-hearted cheers.

Food supplies remain a problem, though not in well-stocked Al-Dorchester, in front of which now barbed wire and sentries armed with Chanzir 45s. Col. Lawrence says all ammunition blank, but I do not believe. He wants me to take oath of obedience, come properly under military discipline, but I say no time, too much to do. A certain Syed Omar, mufti for Central London, comes into office to deliver statement to be published in *Free Briton*. Col. L translates for me. Gist: must be clearly understood that mosque erection is holy work not subject to secular laws or covenants, that the site may be British soil in geo or topographical sense but in deeper or spiritual sense this is Islam, holy ground, promise made to the whole Islamic world that Great Mosque of London, chief Muslim temple of all of West, would be opened with great ceremony on first day of Shawwal. Promise must be kept, strikes and industrial disputes generally most frivolous, let British people and their governors clearly understand that Islamic leaders will stand no bloody nonsense or holy words to that effect.

Car of Syed Omar pelted with stones and rubbish on his way home from Al-Dorchester. Small irregular patrols going the rounds of the town, armed with pistols, staves, coshes, anything, all Muslims, Pakistanis, even Northern Chinese, Anglo-Saxon converts to faith, women too, no Arabs, nothing to do with Free Britons, protecting Muslim shops, residences, mosques of course. An infantry detachment from Lockheed Barracks, against instructions of army shop-stewards, marched round East End, with auto weapons taken from armoury broken into, tried goodheartedly to organize distribution of flour supplies for communal street baking. Candles, when obtainable, cost £10 each. Much breaking-up of property – furniture, shop fronts etc – to light street fires. Frozen mud everywhere today, people slipping and cursing. Free British sentry slipped outside Al-Dorchester on to arse, gun went off accidentally, mortally wounded woman who turned out to be Lady Belcher, wife of TUC peer. Hell of a row. Tanks reported rumbling through streets of Birmingham. More arms certainly coming in at Heathrow and other airports. Cannot get much news from provinces except of riot, killing, gaspipe leaks, explosions, water supplies frozen. Hot argument with Col. L about his lying about sentry blank ammo. He says: I hate violence but you can see situation. You can see also no compromise possible re mosque. I say end of strike in your hands and those of your bosses, whoever or wherever they are. Call off blackleg Free Briton labour, let unionized labour take over. He says: So this your view, eh? You've changed, by Allah. Not really, I say, have always believed in a minimum of protective unionization, am, after all, a historian, but object to rigidity. He says: once for all, no possibility of compromise, Islamic leaders will not accept unionized labour, the British union leaders must be made to see reason. See reason in nozzle of gun, I say. Don't like this situation one bit, I say.

Curious event in Piccadilly. Devlin's son, model for Bill the Symbolic Worker, turned up by Eros statue dressed as in poster and recognized as such, very very drunk, stripped off naked despite cold and indulged in homosexual cavortings, saying Bugger the Workers, Workers, come and be buggered. Posters of Bill the Symbolic Worker all over town being defaced, great pricks and dirty words spraygunned on. Woman I met in street sobbed at me and said you must help, I have to get to Darlington, have no money, terrible things happening in Darlington they tell me, married daughter there, very worried. I gave her my travel warrant issued at Crawford Manor, blank but signed, and she nearly grovelled in gratitude. How ridiculous really. No northbound trains running beyond Leamington, manned by Free British engineers. Warrant probably useless anyway. But anything with royal coat of arms on, as warrant has, being issued by State Rail Authority, is a talisman of sanity and stability. Some day she may be able to use it, poor woman.

Remembered Kumina boys – so long ago it seems – telling me of UU or Underground University. Saw one in action today in broken and totally looted supermarket, Latin literature being taught to gang of attentive toughs. Striking sec. school teachers come along to protest at blackleg education, scholastic scabs etc, and UU students show how violence, not gratuit though, necessary to protect human right to be taught Virgil and Horace. Gesta sanguinaria (?).

G3

It is quite certain that feeble government no longer in existence. Mr Sheen, Prime Minister, was heard yesterday on Free Brit radio asking both sides to see sense, Islamic authorities to temper fanaticism, TUC for that matter to temp. fan. Today story came through very rapidly that he had resigned and that King had done nothing about asking anybody else to form new government. Makes no difference. Proves conclusively that we have never had a govt in Tucland except for going through motions of delaying enactments demanded by TUC. Constitutional situation interesting, though. Has monarch right to leave country govtless? Traditionally he must ask some member of majority party, usually recommended by retiring PM, to take over Cabinet, reshuffle, form new Cab. Will next stage be deposition of King and promotion of Mr Pettigrew as (Temporary?) Head of State? End of Constitution?

Increasing demand in streets, esp outside Gt Smith St mosque site and United Arab Embassy, for Arabs to leave Britain. Get rid of bloody wogs etc. Race riots on small scale, perhaps to grow greater. Free Britons openly using arms. Story of tanks in Birmingham proved false. They were small World War II Bren carriers. Food growing short at Al-Dorchester.

Persistent rumours from East Coast of Arab planes, or at least planes with star and sickle moon glinting in winter sunlight, trying to land but NATO forces buzzing them off. Too fantastic to be true. Bombers? Troop carriers? I will believe nothing of this nonsense.

G4

Hunger, chaos, thawed mud everywhere, uncollected debris, water pipes bursting, unofficial warnings of tainted water supplies, gas explosions. Unrest among Free Britons. Today being pay day, pay parades lined up punctually at FB centres at 09.00 hours. Moratorium on pay declared. No cash available. Violence. Arab leader spoke Oxford English at conference in Al-Dorchester ballroom (Sheikh Isa Ta'ala? Name seemed to be in doubt) about awareness of unpopularity of Arabs and Muslims generally in angry strikebound Britain, but Islam had known hostility throughout its long existence and there was no intention of withdrawal of Arab presence. Much Arab money tied up in British property. The Sheikh, statutory dark glasses on, cigarette in Dunhill holder lighted by brown-suited aide, seemed uneasy. I gained impression from Free Briton higher-ups, other Arabs, anonymous men who might have been from TUC or MPs or higher civil servants, that there had been serious discussion of kind of Pan-Islamic take-over under Sultan or Kalif or President, in accordance with instructions of The Prophet to plant the flag of the faithful in the land of the infidel. Feared opposition from USA cartels with substantial, if dwindling, financial interests in Britain. Much talk of CIE, which I did not understand. Found out later that the letters stand for Channel Islands Experiment. Cannot believe. Cannot at all believe what I was told.

Apparently a French-speaking Algerian force collected in Avignon and Orange, backed by money from Saudi Arabia, took over the islands of Alderney and Sark some months back. Muzzled press and radio, no news leaking to either French or British mainland. Enforcement of Islamic law, closing of bars, splitting of beer and liquor casks in streets, golden fluids singing down the gutter, banning of pork and other pig products, conversion of main churches into mosques, conversion of Jesus Christ into Nabi Isa, penultimate great prophet but no more. Much hostility on part of Channel Island citizens, blood chasing golden liquor down gutters. So – my dream! General conclusion that experiment was a failure, that enforced conversion impracticable. French government persuaded seignories of Sark and Alderney to hush up incident, embarrassing to French. How little we know, God help us, how little we are told. It seems unlikely, anyway, that there is going to be an imposition of Islam here. Festina lente.

G5

A very nasty incident today and a very unpleasant row with Col. L. Five or six mosque workers wanted to pack the job in. They hated being marched to and from barracks and being yelled at, cursed, and threatened with violence. They wanted to re-enter the ranks of the unionized construction workers and quit the Free Britons. They were marched off under heavy guard and not seen again. I wanted to know what had happened to them. Col. L knew but would not tell me. Disciplinary action necessary against the defaulters of any army, he said. What kind of disciplinary action has been taken? I wanted to know and still do. Not important, he said. They have been punished. Mutiny totally impermissible. Shot, have they been shot? No, of course not, we do not shoot our own people. But these, I said, are not your own people, these are just people in it for the pay. Tell me, I want to know. You have no right to know. It's time you took that oath of allegiance. Tell me, I said, and to hell with your bloody oath. Do not swear at me, Lieutenant Jones, and so on.

I decided I would quietly walk out.

I can join the looters. I can join the dead. I can teach history in one of the UUs. There is great confusion now, a blurring of the conflict, an indistinctness of frontier. Free Britons mingle with the strikers (having first discarded their uniforms and put on looted mufti) to restore a bit of human decency. Many of the strikers want to go back to work. There is a strong collective desire for a nice piece of meat, a quiet bottle of beer, an evening with the TV. Union speakers on top of trucks (fewer now, there being no petrol around) are howled down. But, of course, they are also cheered. The mosque workers work surlily. They are supervised by NCOs who carry pistols but use coshes. The illness has to be resolved. How?

17 His Majesty

The thirteenth night of the General Strike was the night of the big fires. Those who believed that these had been started by the Sons of the Prophet were disabused by the spectacle of the bright destruction of the tall thin building in the Strand (a building so slim and sharp-apexed that the Arabs themselves called it the Mibrad Azafir or 'nail file') devoted to Islamic popular culture. Many, indeed, could see clearly now why the Free Britons were backed by Arab money: it was primarily so that, in desperate times like these, Arab property could be protected or salvaged by a body that resided outside the syndicalist covenant. The fire services did not, of course, break the strike but they rendered their equipment available to such as wished to fight fires, though they grumbled about this being a bloody liberty. The Free Britons were driven to fire-fighting almost literally at bayonet point. But, in the middle of the night when the fires were at their brightest, cash suddenly reappeared from sources unknown and pay parades were held in the streets. Some of this money unfortunately went up in flames, but for all that the fire fighters fought fires from now on more willingly, though not with a more notable expertise.

It was the Irish Republican Army at work, of course. But was it that same band of eternally and illogically disaffected who sent over the bombing planes? The fires of the night of G13 had evidently been laid by hand, but, at 02.35 the night following, the fires that ravaged the dock area and even set blazing some of the idle freighters on the Thames had an aerial provenance. There had been in history, so said the experts, only one Irish airman (the one celebrated by W. B. Yeats in a famous poem); the IRA was essentially a land force; where would they find the money to buy or borrow bombing planes?

Puzzled and perturbed, Londoners followed an invisible and inaudible bell-wether to Trafalgar Square on the morning of G15. This was the traditional forum where grief and worry could find expression, resentments could be aired, words of reassurance spoken by one leader or another. Four docile couchant lions brooded and, high in air, the one-eyed, one-armed (and, as the vulgar had it, one-arsed) hero of a great sea battle seemed to drink of air that today was like chilled Pouilly Fumé. Bev stood on the periphery of the vast muttering ragged bruised, convalescent – could one, he wondered, say convalescent – crowd. Jam-packed and grumblingly patient. Hopeful, though, of something. On the plinth of the pillar there was as yet nobody. But, of course, nobody officially knew anything. There had been strong rumours of a meeting here, but rumours are only noise. The loudspeakers trumpeted dumbly to the corners of the square. What a target, thought Bev, for a phalanx of day bombers. But the sky was clear and empty. Bev saw Mr Pettigrew in the crowd, along with burly union leaders. What stopped them from getting up there and starting a fluent harangue about something? But everybody waited. The air was full of pigeons, comically bombing with putty-coloured faeces or vainly seeking low-level landings. There were ironical cheers when someone got one with an airgun, deadly accurate. There were also growls about leaving the poor bloody birds alone. Then there was a rustle, a growing hum of expectancy, incredulity. Vehicles were coming along the Mall. The more agile of the waiting Londoners leapt on to the plinth to get a look. 'It's the King!' somebody yelled. Everybody laughed, nobody believed it. And then some believed, and soon everybody, and cheers began. Some rude children near Bev began to sing:

> 'God save our gracious cat
> Rub his belly in bacon fat
> God save our'

The royal Rolls-Royce, with the Royal Standard flying, gently nosed into the square, with behind it a plain van. The plain van opened up first, and overalled technicians with the monogram CIIIR jumped out. Why weren't the buggers on strike like every other bugger? Royal servants, not allowed. Up for the chop if they did. Leads and cables snaked. The royal car opened and His Majesty King Charles III got out. Lean moustached men in good subfusc suits escorted him to the plinth. A microphone was placed in his woolly gloved hand. He wore a tight blue Melton overcoat of vaguely naval cut. There were cheers and countercheers. The King grinned. His ears were pink with cold. He said, and all listened:

'What I'm doing right now is against the law, I suppose, but it strikes me that we've all been a bit against the law lately. What I mean is I've no constitutional right to stand here and speak. I mean, the monarch's only supposed to be a kind of figurehead and only say what his government tells him to say. The trouble is, we don't seem to have a government at the moment. Any of you seen a government about lately? I looked under the bed this morning, but whatever it was I found there, it wasn't a government.'

He shouldn't do that, thought Bev, he shouldn't play for laughs. But he's getting the laughs. When will we bloody British learn to take things seriously?

'As there's no government,' said the King, 'and as I'm constitutionally a sort of head of the State, I thought I'd better come along and say a few words. I mean, nobody's working at the moment, you can all spare the time to listen. Not that I'm going to say much. One thing I have to say, though, is that Sir Malcolm McTaggart, the royal physician, is a bloody blackleg. He broke the strike this morning against the orders of the shop stewards of the British Medical Association. I asked him to. Had to. You see, my wife, the Queen that is, is just starting to give. I mean, any minute now we're going to have an addition to the family. I think we might call him Bill.'

There was an affectionate uproar. A little chinny man with glasses on, just in front of Bev, yelled:

'Another bloody mouth to feed.'

'What I want to say is this,' said the King, 'and thanks very much for that er loyal expression of er you know what I mean, is this. That this bloody nonsense pardon my French has gone on long enough. I think it's time we all went back to work.' Cheers and jeers. 'And I'm not just politely asking the Navy and Army and Air Force to go back, I'm *telling* them. If they don't want the King to be their commander-in-chief, then they'd better stop calling themselves the Royal this and that and the other. Right, let's see them jump to it. Because if they don't jump to it it's going to be a bit late to do the job they're paid to do, which is defending the country. I mean, look at what happened last night and the night before. The whole damned country's wide open for anybody who wants to walk in. We're not mugs at Buck House, you know, not all of us. Some of us know what's going on. For instance, there's this business of a number of big battle wagons prowling the oceans round our shores, and they don't belong to the Sons of the Prophet, oh dear me no. There's an aircraft carrier been spotted just off Cromarty, and the Arabs don't go in for that sort of hardware. You all know who these things belong to. No, not the IRA, not them. And don't think our pals the Americans are going to flush them out in accordance with their North Atlantic Treaty Organization commitments. There are a lot of big American business concerns in that particular country, and that means a lot of hard Yank cash. It's a country they don't want to start a shooting match with. Too useful. It's one of the few countries in the world where the workers don't go on strike.'

Boos, cheers, laughter. The King said:

'Anyway, I want to see the boys in blue and khaki jumping to it and shouting *Sah* and getting on with the job. We all know there's a little army been flitting about, and with our own army we don't have any need for private armies, thank you very much. So this organization is disbanded as from this moment on, and anybody who belongs to it and has weapons and ammunition had better start handing it all in to the nearest police station. Which means we want to see our brave bobbies back on the beat as from the moment I step down from this pedestal here. As for the work that's been going on in Great Smith Street, seat of the old Colonial Office and now site of the new mosque, that's strictly a union job as from now on. I had dinner last night with one or two of our Arab pals. It was a whole sheep and they gave me the eye, which they consider a great delicacy. Delicious, well, no, not really. I put it in my pocket when they weren't looking, still got it here somewhere – never mind. The point is that a mosque may be a sacred place and all that, but when it's just bricks and mortar it's no different from a supermarket or a public urinal – bigger, of course. When it's finished it can be as holy as they like. As for now – sorry, chaps, I said, but you see what happens when we start making exceptions to the rule. They saw the point all right, decent chaps really, and they're going to let us carry on doing things our own way. I know there've been some hard words said lately and a few blows, but apologies have been offered and accepted on both sides. If you don't believe me about us having our own way, just take a shufti at Great Smith Street and you'll find things nice and normal, with nobody doing a stroke.

'We've got to stop all this nastiness between the different races, you know. I shouldn't really have to tell you that. I mean, the future peace of the world depends on everybody respecting everybody else's colour and creed and what have you. I mean, race means very little really. When I think of the racial mix of my own family my head starts to spin. Scottish and German and Greek and God knows what else. There'll be Israeli and Arab before it's finished – if, that is, it's allowed to carry on and produce constitutional heads of State and so on. But that's up to you. Everything's up to you. That's what they mean by that big word democracy.

'So I think everything ought to be okay now. Tonight, so they tell me, the telly will be starting again. Of course, not according to what's printed in the *TV Guide* or whatever it is – I never buy it, I just switch on and take what's going – I go to sleep, anyway – anyway BBC1 is doing *Gone With The Wind*, uncut, and that sounds like a nice way of filling in an evening. Of course, we need a bit of electricity, but I don't doubt we'll have that by lunch-time. That's about all, I think. I suppose I'm going to be for the chop now, though God knows who from, since we haven't got a government yet. Ah well, never mind – '

One of the moustached thin men passed up a message. The King's face became suffused with boyish joy as he listened. Then he told his subjects:

'It's happened. I'm a father. A fine lad. Mother and infant both doing well. God bless you all.' He waved his woolly gloved hand and got down from the plinth. His chauffeur held the car door open ready for him. The car pushed gently through the crowd. The crowd sang fervently as the National Anthem began to pulse from the loudspeakers:

'Send him victorious
Appy an glorious
Long to rine orious
Gawd sive ve – '

They sang with perfect WRP (TV) – Workers' Received Pronunciation (Thamesside Variety). Then they all got down to thinking of the possibility of going back to work.

18   His Majesty's pleasure

'Jones,' said old Ashthorn, presiding, as previously, in Number 3 Court, 'you've been up before me already at least once – '

'At most once,' corrected Bev.

The clerk of the court, loud and insolent, bawled:

'Watch your tongue, Jones.'

The assistant magistrate, a plain flat-chested woman with a drab hat on, though not the same woman as on the previous occasion, whispered something to old Ashthorn, who sourly nodded. He said: 'You still do not seem to have pondered sufficiently the errors of ah ah your ways. I have before me a record of recalcitrance and ah recidivism and ah what's this word?'

'Atavism probably,' Bev said. 'I recognize the hand of the great Mr Pettigrew.'

Old Ashthorn humphed and puffed and then said: 'You have been given every opportunity, every. You remain what it says ah here. What have you to say for yourself this time?'

The clerk of the court bawled:

'Come on, Jones, we've a lot of work to get through.'

'Yes, of course, that strike of court officers has left you with a nasty backlog. Felicitations, by the way, on your latest salary award. Sorry. Well, then, I'd like to express satisfaction that this time I'm up for achieved theft instead of, as before, merely theft attempted but unaccomplished. Boodle's Gin, your honour, is a fine cordial and I enjoyed it. I wish also to say that I do not accept the jurisdiction of this court. The British judicature in all its branches has become the mere legal instrument of State Syndicalism. Let me add – '

'All that is down here too,' said old Ashthorn. 'And it is all ah ah irrelevant, not to say impertinent.'

'Very well, then, I protest against the sentence you are now compelled to impose – '

'You know nothing, sir, of the sentence till the sentence has been delivered. You have said enough, I think.' The assistant magistrate whispered to him. 'Yes, I quite agree,' said old Ashthorn. 'More than enough. The sentence of this court is that you be detained in a state institution for as long as His Majesty's pleasure shall determine.'

'I knew the sentence,' said Bev, 'before you uttered it. I protest.'

'Take him down,' bawled the clerk of the court to Bev's police attendant.

He had not done too badly really, thought Bev as he travelled north in a closed van, a white-coated orderly beside him, a conducting officer in grey next to the driver. It was spring now, very nearly Shakespeare's birthday, and he had lived free, though dirty, for nearly the whole of a hardish winter. He had not given in to the swine. As for now, was he really beaten? Hardly, since he remained unsyndicalized despite all their entreaties and bludgeonings. He could live freely in the large periphery of his brain. He knew precisely what was going to happen to him.

'Here it is,' said the orderly. 'SI-5, Purfleet Castle as was. Hear them birds sing, see that lovely green and them daffodils,' for the van door was now open. 'Consider yourself bleeding lucky to be here and not in the bleeding jug.'

'Anybody's free to enter,' said Bev, 'so long as they see sense.'

'Shut your fag-hole,' said the conducting officer. 'Get out there and get in.'

Bev was handed over by the white-coated orderly to a couple of men in cleaner white coats. They had clipboards and the frowns of the overworked. Bev was sent in for a physical check-up.

'Go on, bend down proper. We've got to see right up. That's more like it.'

Undernourished, underweight, physical tone poor, right lung somewhat spotted, heart to be watched, teeth dreadful, in dire need of a bath.

A clean Bev in an institutional dressing-gown had his mind gone over by a Dr Schimmel and a Dr Kilburn, the latter a woman, washed-out blonde, thin and sharp. He tried to get the matrix tests wrong, but his wrongness was so consistent as to be adjudged right. Dr Schimmel said:

'What's the matter with you, man? You could live a sane healthy productive life if you wanted to.'

'I know. But that would mean approving of an insane morbid slothful State philosophy.'

'That's undemocratic. Insanity is defined as a rejection of the majority ethos. You proclaim insanity in words and actions.' Both doctors frowned over the thick dossier that had accompanied Bev on his journey.

'What are you going to do to me?' asked Bev. They did not answer. Bev said: 'Look, I can't see where I've gone wrong. I was brought up under a system of government that was regarded as the triumph of centuries of instinctual sanity. I see the world changed. Am I obliged to change with it?' Both looked at him in quiet satisfaction, as though the asking of that question was a kind of capsule confirmation of his insanity. Dr Kilburn said:

'You're part of it. Your error is in supposing that the human observer can be separated from the things observed. Your aberration, to use a charitable term, is that you resist change.'

'I won't resist the change that brings the world back to sanity. To an acceptance of justice and the wholesomeness of spiritual and aesthetic ideals.'

'Yes?' said Dr Schimmel encouragingly.

'Consider,' said Bev, 'the British Constitution. I believe that the people should be represented, as they have been for centuries. All we have now is an upper house legislature crammed with TUC life peers. The House of Commons is withering away. The monarch, as head of the executive, presides over a cabinet made up of alumni of the TUC Political College. The elective principle has disappeared.'

'The people,' said Dr Schimmel, 'elect their union representatives. Isn't that fair enough?'

'No,' said Bev, 'for life is more than what nowadays

passes for work. More than a fair wage and a dwindling selection of ill-made useless consumer goods to spend it on. Life is beauty, truth, spiritual endeavour, ideals, eccentricity – '

'Ah,' said both doctors.

Bev felt very tired. 'It won't do, it won't, it won't, it won't.' And then: 'Forget it. It's like addressing a couple of brick walls. Do what has to be done. I'm in your hands.'

Don't let them get away with it. The man who slept in the next bed, formerly a professional signwriter, made a beautiful job of inscribing those words in Gothic letters (upper and lower case) on a panel cut from a shirt-box lid (institutional shirts, grey, medium, 10). This had, with permission from the wardmaster, been affixed with tacks to the wall above Bev's bedside locker. Nobody enquired as to what the words signified: they were taken as an emblem of Bev's derangement.

The food was plain and adequate. There were football or cricket matches in the ample grounds. There was even a library made up of books that had escaped liquidation in the State taking over of ancient aristocratic country seats. Volumes of seventeenth-century sermons, Thomson's *The Seasons*, Pope, Cowper, *The Rights of Man*, John Milton, nothing later than about 1789.

Don't let them get away with it. Don't let who get away with what?

They rarely bothered with news of the outside world. Mr Thresher, who had been a television news reader given, in his later (literally) days, to ribald asides on the items he retailed, kept his hand pathetically in by announcing in the day-room public occurrences that might or might not be fictitious:

'British inflation is running at the rate of fifty-five per cent per annum. This was stated unofficially by Dr Erlanger, World Bank economic adviser, at a conference in Chicago of United States economists. The figure was neither denied nor confirmed by the Tucland authorities.' Or:

'The National Union of Comprehensive School Students has reached an amicable settlement with the National Union of Teachers as regards the relegation of school-teachers to an advisory capacity in the conduct of State education. The help of the teachers in devising school syllabuses of a more realistic content than has hitherto prevailed will be gladly accepted, said Ted Soames, National Secretary of NUCST, at a press conference, but students will consider themselves under no obligation to implement the advice given – '

'Ah, shut it,' Mr Cauldwell, a boilermaker, would shout, looking up from his game of checkers with Mr Toomey, a ruined cobbler.

' – Among projected school courses at the secondary level may be mentioned sex drill, porn hard and soft, strip-cartoon teaching of trade union history – '

'Shut it, or I'll bleeding bash you.'

But Mr Cauldwell was frightened of Mr Ricordi, a thin frail man who had run a bookshop and was believed to have the Evil Eye. Mr Ricordi would turn it on him, and Mr Cauldwell would gulp and go back to his slow game. Or:

'The Islamicization of the Isle of Man, or Gazira-ul-Ragul, has, thanks to the fervour of Nabi Mohamed Saleh bin Abdullah, formerly Joseph Briggs, been effected with comparative smoothness. Protests at the imposition on the community of total abstinence from alcoholic liquors were to be expected, but scientific demonstrations of the absence of alcohol in Manx beer, the stimulant-depressant LMP having been long substituted for it, convinced the community that no real hardship was being imposed.'

'Shut it shut it, or you'll get my fucking fist in your fucking face,' Mr Ricordi having gone out for a moment.

Don't let them get away with it.

They wouldn't get away with it, not indefinitely. They couldn't. You can't take without at the same time giving. Bev was prepared to get out there and fight again, preach, get his own army together. Was this a sign of dementia? The only way he could get out was to have his family claim him. That meant Bessie. He got a letter to Bessie, sending it through the London agents of the Arab ruler who was his son-in-law, potential or actual, or else merely the man who had debauched, and was perhaps intermittently still debauching, his daughter. Six months later he got a postcard, its glossy picture showing camels and street beggars: 'der dad i am alrit ere tely very gud i am ok luv besi.' The next letter he wrote received the following reply:

Dear Sir,

I am directed to inform you that no one of the name of Elizabeth (Bessie) Jones is resident in any of His Highness's establishments. Conceivably you are mistaken as to either the name or the address, perhaps both.

Yours very truly....

From the Astana, Ghadan, the 12th day of the month Shaaban, in the year of the Hijrah, 1364.

Mr Coombes, a Jehovah's Witness, tried to escape. He was powerfully reminded that he was undergoing an indefinite period of penal servitude. The perimeter wires were electrified. The institution had its own generators; there was no hope of their being rendered harmless through a strike. Mr Coombes, a tough man in his late fifties, was badly burnt. One of the medical officers told him he was lucky he had a strong heart. There were also big dogs which Bev could hear howling sometimes in the night. Presumably the supervision of the inmates could be left to these animals if the human staff were to go on strike. Dogs had, as yet, no union. Anyway, the human staff had it cushy and showed no desire to withdraw what was euphemistically termed their labour.

The long days that grew into months and years were enlivened by the deaths of the older inmates and, very occasionally, the entrusting of some of them to the care of their families: farewell tea parties, with an extra cake each. New inmates brought news of the outside world; the news did not greatly interest such veterans as Bev. One day none other than Colonel Lawrence appeared. He had been convicted of manslaughter. Discharged from his army, he had found work as a State interpreter, under his real name of Charles Ross. Frustrated for one reason or another, he had broken a habit of abstinence that had lasted a quarter of a century, and, drunk in a pub, had quarrelled with a Persian. He had not intended to kill the Persian, he said; the skull of his victim had, at the autopsy, been shown to be preternaturally fragile. Anyway, here he was.

The Persians, he said, were going to go to war with the Arabs. The Islamic union had been broken. The Iranians were Aryan and the Arabs Semitic, and blood was thicker than a Koranic *surah*. The Shah, whom the Americans had long considered to be the only reliable magnate of the

Middle East, was well armed with what the Pentagon called a nuclear capability. The Arabs, who had never been favoured customers of the American armourers, would be at the mercy of Iran. Iran would take over all the oilfields of the Middle East. The Arabs, aware of American partiality to Iran, were withdrawing their megadollars from the American banks. There was bank panic in the United States, with little depositors lining up for cash and finding their local banks declaring a moratorium. The Federal Reserve was printing too much money, desirous of quelling the panic by increasing – in fact, doubling – the cash flow. Too much cash in the United States. Twice the amount of cash chasing the same quantity of consumer goods. Stores closing down, their shelves emptied, an awareness among the economically literate that inflation was spreading like a southern Californian fire. Other currencies responding to dollar inflation. The sterling situation unbelievable. Bankruptcy on its way. The end of syndicalism? At least three and a half million unemployed in Tucland. Nothing much heard of Mr Pettigrew these days. Deposed? Assassinated? A burly man called Big Tim Holloway heard much in the land, ranting about workers' unity and the wicked capitalists.

Bev had taken to teaching history to a small interested group, giving a lesson on Elizabethan England every afternoon in one of the day-rooms. Later he gave a course on England in the seventeenth century. It seemed reasonable to push on to the end, all from a memory that grew ever more defective. He seemed, even to himself, to be dealing with the history of another planet. But he and his students escaped daily to this unreal past, as to a fuggy room from a biting wind. The First World War, recovery, Wall Street crash, rearmament, the rise of totalitarianism. The Second World War and after. History dangerously began to approach the present. The present could not be summarized, explained, even well understood. A great river seemed inexplicably to be dissipating itself into a vast number of muddy little streams and creeks. One afternoon he sat hopelessly in front of his class – Mr Tyburn, Mr Gresham, Mr Hooker, Mr Merlin, Mr Lyly, others. He said:

'Shall we start again? Shall we go back to the rise of capitalism and try once more to trace the cracks in the structure, to discover where everything began to go wrong?' Mr Hooker said:

'I think we've had enough.'

Bev nodded and nodded. After supper that night he went out into the grounds. That heart was weak, watch that heart. He stumbled through the unknown pasque-grass to that part of the electrified perimeter that was framed by two knotty apple trees. Those trees had given sour crabs for a long time. They would survive a while, and that was a small comfort. The moon, defiled by politics, its poetry long drowned in the Sea of Storms, had but recently risen. Bev addressed to it certain meaningless words.

But, of course, they all got away with it; they always would. History was a record of the long slow trek from Eden towards the land of Nod, with nothing but the deserts of injustice on the way. Nod. Nod off. Sleep. He nodded a farewell to the moon. Then he bared his flesh-less breast to the terrible pain of the electrified fence, puzzling an instant about why you had to resign from the union of the living in order to join the strike of the dead. He then felt his heart jump out of his mouth and tumble among the windfalls.

A note on Worker's English

Worker's English represents the rationalization of a general pattern of proletarian language, formulated by Dr R. Stafford and Dr A.S. McNab, of the Ministry of Education, during the 1970s, and made compulsory as a subject and as a medium of instruction in State schools, under the provisions of the Democratization of Language Act, 1981. The basis of the language is the urban workers' speech of the Home Counties, with a few additions from the industrial Midlands and North-West, but with very few elements of rural dialect. The primary aim of Drs Stafford and McNab was less the imposition, under political or syndicalist pressure, of the language of the dominant social class on the rest of the community than the adaptation of an existing form of English to the fulfilment of a traditional language planner's aspiration – namely, the development of a rational kind of language, in which grammar should be simplified to the maximum and vocabulary should achieve the limitations appropriate to a non-humanistic highly industrialised society. What appeared, in fact, to be the implementation of part of a political programme was actually a social achievement with no political bias, with the two philologists concerned activated by a scientific desire for the reduction of entities and only secondary ambitions in the fields of class domination and pedagogic economy.

The simplification of such elements of inflection as parts of verbs, declension of pronouns, irregularities of pluralization in nouns could, it was admitted, be pushed a great deal further than the forms actually formulated in *A Grammar of Workers' English* (His Majesty's Stationery Office, 1980), but it was recognized that certain traditional

499

irregularities had been long condoned by considerations of prosody, apart from the fact that the British working class, itself a development out of the Anglo-Saxon serf class, accepts the patterns of vowel-gradation, characteristically Teutonic, at a deep level, whose genetic, as opposed to cultural, provenance has still to be sufficiently examined. Thus, there seemed no necessity to rationalize *man/men*, *woman/women*, *mouse/mice* etc., into pluralizing patterns on the *cat/cats*, *dog/dogs*, *box/boxes* formula, though, in later developments, there may be some attempt to make such rationalization an optional, and even creditable, feature of Workers' English.

That a considerable economy has been effected in verb conjugation may be seen chiefly in the invariable negative form *ain't*, which serves to negate the present tense of both *to be* and *to have:*

He ain't there = He isn't there
He ain't been there =He hasn't been there

The preterite of *to be* takes the invariable form *was* (*I was* etc, but also *we was* etc), though the present tense remains, at present, identical with that of the verb in Bourgeois English (BE). In strong verbs, preterite and past participle are usually the same in form – as in *I done it; I ain't done it* – though the choice of form from the two available in BE follows a seemingly arbitrary procedure:

I seen it; I've seen it	(BE past part.)
I done it; I've done it	(BE past part.)
I ate it; I've ate it	(BE pret.)
I swum; I've swum	(BE past part.)
I forgot; he's forgot	(BE pret.)
I wrote; he's wrote	(BE pret.)
I fell; it's fell	(BE pret.)
I drunk it; I've drunk it	(BE past part.)

Considerations of syllabic economy seem to determine the preference for the shorter of the two forms available (*wrote*, not *written*; *forgot*, not *forgotten*), but there is no ready explanation of *seen* for *saw* and *done* for *did* in the demotic tradition embodied in WE. It should be noted also that there has never been, in that tradition, any impulse to level strong verbs under weak forms (*I eat; I eated* etc); the ablaut transformation – as also in certain nouns – is rooted deeply in the language of the workers, and the rational

dard to which other varieties (rural, industrial and colonial) aspired. The following sentences are considered orthographically correct:

Enry Erbert Iggins, being ot and in a hurry, ad to ang is at up in the all.
E's a orrible unk of atefulness.

On the other hand, the aspirate is to be retained as an emphasizer, only initially however, in such statements as, 'I said, eat up my dinner, not heat it up' (the meaning here being diametrically opposed to the meaning conveyed by a speaker of BE when uttering this sentence). This means that the presence of an emphatic aspirate has absolutely no etymological or lexical significance, being a purely prosodic device:

The law is a hass.
You're a hugly great hidiot.

Coincidentally, of course, emphatic aspiration may match phonemic usage in BE, but the statement, 'You're horrible,' in WE represents no return to BE pseudo-gentility of utterance. The phoneme *ng* in verbal-noun terminations having been traditionally replaced in demotic, as well as rural genteel, usage by *n*, this usage is now formulated as regular. The fricatives found initially in *thin* and *then* are to be regarded, considering their absence in the phonemic inventories of most metropolitan speakers, as optional in speech, being replaced by *f* and *v* respectively, though the digraph is retained in writing and printing.

We come now to the question of vocabulary and that principle of economy of lexis which, instinctually consulted in traditional demotic, is to be more deliberately and rationally applied to the development of WE as a living and progressive language. Generally speaking, the speaker or writer of WE is expected to possess a trade vocabulary, wherein amplitude and exactness may constitute factors of efficiency and safety (thus, the generic *thing* or *wotsit* or *oojah* or *gadget* will not serve in the designation of parts of a machine which have opposed functions), and a social vocabulary whose elements are of mainly Teutonic origin and serve to denote physical and emotional states and processes. WE is not concerned with the abstractions of philosophy or even science, though, for rhetorical purposes, an arbitrary sub-lexis of polysyllables of Latin or

weakening of strong verbs, desirable to the regularizing philologist, would find no acceptance among WE speakers, who would consider such formations as 'childish'.

The verb *get* – not always considered elegant in bourgeois education, so that *rise* has been preferred to *get up* and *enter* to *get in* – is regarded as a useful form in WE and its increased use in verbal phrases may, it is hoped, enable a vast number of verbs to be eliminated from the language. Indeed, it is believed that, with the exception of such verbs as *to be* and *to have*, practically all existing verbs can be replaced by a *get*-phrase. Thus:

drink = get some drink down
eat = get grub in your guts
live = get some living done
eliminate = get rid (shot) of
fuck off = get the fuck out of here
sleep = get your head (swede, loaf) down
read = get some reading done; get your head into a book; get a bit of bookwork into your fat lazy swede, etc.

Admittedly, it may be necessary to employ a verbal noun or gerund in a *get* phrase, but the indicative mood of the great majority of verbs can, in time, be rendered supererogatory.

Pronouns in the demotic English of industrial regions have rarely shown a willingness to imitate the invariables of rural dialects, (*give un to I; he do hate she*, etc.), and only the levelling of the demonstrative adjective *those* under the form of the demonstrative pronoun *them* and the occasional use of *us* for *me* – as in *give us one of them bottles there* – may be adduced as indicative of a need for rationalization in this area. An attempt, in early pedagogic experiments with WE, to replace *she* and *her* with the invariable Lancashire *oo* (from Anglo-Saxon *heo*) was greeted, even in Lancashire industrial towns, with strong resistance.

Before considering the semantics of WE, a word may be said about its phonetics. It is felt that no legislation from the State's philologists is required as regards pronunciation, whose regional variants are accepted as unlikely to impair the unity of WE. Only one traditional BE phoneme has been omitted from the consonantal inventory, this being the aspirate, and the typographical signal of its absence – the apostrophe – is regarded as a regrettable relic of an age when Bourgeois English posed as a stan-

even Greek origin is available, whose lexicographical definition is regarded as otiose. Examples of such terms are *verification, obstropulosity, fornicator, supercodology*:

> I ask you in all bleeding verification whether or not you think it's bloody fair.

> I've had enough of his bloody obstropulosity and I'm bleeding well going to do the bastard.

> That fucking fornicator got his hands in my coat pocket when I'd got my eyes on the dartboard.

> Don't get working on any of that supercodology when I'm around, mate, or you'll get a bunch of fives in the fag-hole.

(Here in deference to the BE reader's habits, traditional orthography is used.)

Generally speaking, statements in WE are expected to be of a tautologous nature, thus fulfilling the essential phatic nature of speech; as modern linguistics teaches us, non-tautologous statements are either lies or meaningless:

> I like a nice pint when I've done my work, because a nice pint's bloody nice, mate.

> The working class is all right, because they're a very nice class of people.

> I love that girl, I can't hardly keep my hands off of her.

> They want to get rid of that new left-half, because he's no bleeding good.

(It will be noticed that qualifiers of emphasis formerly regarded as obscene have full lexical status in WE.)

As an example of the expressive capacities of WE, a rendering of the opening of a well-known speech in Shakespeare's *Hamlet* may here be appended:

> To get on with bloody life or not to, that's what it's all about really. Is it more good to get pains in your fuckin loaf worryin about it or to get stuck into what's getting you worried and get it out of the way and seen off? To snuff it is only like getting your head down, and then you get rid of the lot, anyway that's how we'd like to have it. . . .

The passage from the Declaration of Independence which Orwell regarded as untranslatable into Newspeak yields easily enough to WE, though its meaning is somewhat modified:

> This is true, and there's no arguing the toss over it, that everybody's got the same rights to belong to a union, to live for ever, to do what the hell he wants to do, and watch TV, get drunk, sleep with a woman, and smoke. It's the job of governments to let the unions give union members what they want, and if the governments do not do what the unions want, then they have to get kicked out.

Epilogue: an interview

Do you really think this is going to happen?

A question to be answered by waiting a few years. It's always foolish to write a fictional prophecy that your readers are very soon going to be able to check. Take it that I merely melodramatize certain tendencies. In Britain, the unions are certainly growing stronger and more intolerant. But by the unions I probably merely mean the more belligerent union leaders. I leave out of account too, as Orwell did more spectacularly, the good sense and humanity of the average worker.

I'm an American, and it seems to me absurd that the USA could ever become Unhappy Syndicalized America. American society will never be tyrannized by the unions.

Probably not. I was extrapolating certain experiences of my own in the field of American show business. The tyranny of the musicians' union, for instance, on Broadway. It's hard to prophesy the future of the United States. That cacotopia of Sinclair Lewis's, *It Can't Happen Here*, still seems to me to be the most plausible projection, though it was written in the thirties. At least it shows how a tyranny can come about through the American democratic process, with a president American as apple pie, as they say – a kind of cracker-barrel Will Rogers type appealing to the philistine anti-intellectual core of the American electorate. Core? More than the core, the whole fruit except for the thin skin of liberalism. My old pappy used to say: Son, there ain't no good books except the Good Book. Time these long-haired interlettles got their come-uppance, and so on. And so book-burning, shooting of radical schoolmasters, censorship of progressive newspapers. Every repressive act justified out of the Old Testament and excused jokingly in good spittoon style.

I think we're past the naïveté of letting mere novelists do the prophesying. They're fantasists, they don't really examine trends. The futures they present couldn't possibly have their beginnings in the present we know.

True. Novelists have given up writing future fiction. They leave that to the think-tank people. What fantasy-writers like to do nowadays is to imagine a past when history took a turning different from the one it did take, and then create an alternative present based on that past. Keith Robert's *Pavane*, for example, and Kingsley Amis's *The Alteration* both posit that the Christian Reformation never got to the Anglo-Saxons, with the result in both of the killing of the empirical spirit, which means the death of science. And so a modern world without electricity and a powerful theocracy ruling it from Rome. Amusing, stimulating, but a time-game. Prophecy is no longer the province of the fictional imagination, as I say, as you say. The question is: are the futurologists of MIT and elsewhere doing the prophetic job any better?

It's not a question of prophecy. Professor Toffler tells us that the future's already here, in the sense that a technology and a way of life are being imposed on us that belong neither to the past nor the present. A lot of people, he says, are in a state of shock at what they regard as things alien to the present. When your thinking and feeling and, above all, your nervous system reject certain innovations, then the future's arrived and what you have to do is to catch up with it. The symptoms of rejection are hysteria or apathy or both. People drug themselves out of the present which is really the future, or else exile themselves into pre-industrial cultures. Violence, madness, neuroses of all kinds abound. We don't define the future in temporal terms, but in terms of the new stimulus that overstimulates to dementia. The future's a solid body we've never seen before — something dumped on the shore for the wary natives to sniff at and run away from. Then they come back, see what it is, accept. The future has become the present. Then we await the next new solid bodies, with the inevitable syndrome of temporary rejection.

But what we fear from the future is not new solid bodies but war and tyranny.

Which function by means of solid bodies. Is there going to be a tyranny in the United States — not a tyranny of the syndicates,

like the British one, but a good old-fashioned Orwellian Big
Brother?

If it happens, it will happen through war.

*Is there going to be a war – not the little contained wars of
which we have, on average, two a year, but a really big
Second-World-War-type war?*

Your compatriots Doctors Kahn and Wiener, of that
Hudson Institute which was looking after the year 2000 for
us, give us a table which shows how limited and total wars
tend to form into a time pattern. An alternation of eras
devoted to the two kinds of war, like this:

1000–1550 limited war – feudal, dynastic
1550–1648 total war – religious
1648–1789 limited war – colonial, dynastic
1789–1815 total war – revolutionary nationalist
1815–1914 limited war – colonial, commercial
1914–1945 total war – nationalist, ideological

And since 1945 we've had thirty-odd years of limited wars
conducted for various, often spurious, reasons – territorial, anticolonial, ideological, what you will. If history really
follows a pattern of alternation, we can't have an indefinite period of limited wars. We have to break out on a
world scale once more sometime. Consider that thirty
years is the longest period the modern world has had
without a global war. Perhaps our economic troubles, the
inexplicable yoking of recession and inflation for instance,
stem from the fact that we don't know how to run a peace
economy. War economy is different—we have precedents.
I've dreamed of a Malthusian world war conducted with
conventional weapons—one that can only break out when
the world's planners realize that the global food supply is
not going to feed the global population. Instead of famine
and riot we have a pretence of nationalist war whose true
aim is to kill off millions, or billions, of the world's population. I even wrote a book in which Enspun fights Chinspun –

What are those, for God's sake?

The English Speaking Union and the Chinese Speaking
Union. The third great power is Ruspun, and you know
what that is. Actually, the war is made up of local extermination sessions called battles, in which men fight women.

A real sex war. And then the cadavers are carted off to be processed into canned food. The recent bout of enforced cannibalism in the Andes proves that human flesh is both edible and nourishing, despite the new dietetic taboos which condemn it as so much poison. The processed human flesh is sold in supermarkets and called Munch or Mensch or something. People will eat anything these days.

Seriously, though.

In a way I was, am, being serious. That kind of war would be a just war and a useful one. But the world will have to wait till the year 3000 to see it. As for the new world war that's waiting in the womb of time, a healthily developed foetus, who can say what will spark it, how destructive it will be? We've already played at this war in film and fiction, indicating that there's a part of us that desperately wants it. What nonsense writers and film-makers talk when they say that their terrible visions are meant as a warning. Warning nothing. It's sheer wish fulfilment. War, somebody said, is a culture pattern. It's a legitimate mode of cultural transmission, though the culture transmitted is usually not the one we expect –

How?

To take a trivial example, popular Latin American song and dance flooded North America and Europe in the forties and after because of the need of the United States to make Latin America a 'good neighbour' – we know how much sympathy for the Nazis there was in the Argentine, for instance. This meant that we all had to see *The Three Caballeros* and Carmen Miranda, dance congas and sambas, sing *Brazil* and *Boa Noite*. To be less trivial, Americanization of both Japan and Germany could best come about by defeating them and confining their post-war industrial production to pacific commodities. Soviet Russia transmitted her brand of Marxist control to Eastern Europe. War is the speediest way of transmitting a culture, just as meat-eating is the speediest way of ingesting protein. It used to be possible to see war as an economic mode of exogamy on a large scale – transmit your seed and produce lively new mixes, avoid the weary incest of perpetual endogamy which is the dull fruit of peace. The greatest war picture of all depicts the Rape of the Sabines. War uses international politics as a mere pretext for fulfilling a deep need in man, which he's scared of admitting because he doesn't like to relate the enhancement of life to the meting out of death.

The Third World War?

It could start anywhere. It will pose as an ideological war. It will use conventional weapons. It will end in a truce with a million men and women dead but the great cities untouched. Flesh is cheap and is growing cheaper all the time. Great cities contain valuable artefacts, which cost dear and had better not be bombed. Computers for example. We've read so many scenarios about the next war; you don't want another. What interests me is how a species of totalitarianism could come about in the United States through uneasiness about the enemy at the gates. A communist revolution in Mexico, helped by the Chinese, might set America dithering, looking for spies, deploying her immense cybernetic and electronic resources to keep citizens under surveillance. The enhanced power of the presidency, the temporary dissolution of Congress. Censorship. Dissident voices silenced. And all in the name of security. No war is necessary, only the threat of war and, in good Orwellian style, the notion of an enemy, actual or potential, can be the device for justifying tyranny. Orwell was right there. War is the necessary background to State repression. War as a landscape or weather or wallpaper. The causes don't matter, the enemy can be anybody. When we think of a future world war, we get quickly bored with working out the causative details, since these could literally be anything. India drops a bomb on Pakistan. An East German coup breaks down the Berlin Wall. Canada resents American capital and American military installations and tells the US to get the hell out. You remember how H. G. Wells made the Second World War start? He wrote a book in the middle thirties called *The Shape of Things to Come*, a history of the future and mostly, as it had to be, absurd. But he had the war start in 1940 on the Polish Corridor, which was astonishingly accurate. A Polish Jew is eating a hazelnut, and a bit lodges in a back hollow tooth. He tries to get the fragment out with his finger, and a young Nazi interprets the grimace as a jeer at his uniform. He fires a shot. The Jew dies. The war starts. That the causes of war are so vague, that the priming incident is so trivial—don't we have here a proof that we want war for the sake of war?

I was born in 1951, but I had a vivid dream the other night about the First World War. Not about battles. I was in a London restaurant and there was a calendar on the wall showing the month to be February and the year 1918. The place was crowded, and I was sitting drinking tea, very weak tea, at a table where two ladies were talking. They were dressed in the style of the time as I've seen it in films and photographs—the décor of the dream was amazingly accurate. One of the ladies said something like, 'Oh, when will this terrible war be over?' Of course I knew exactly when. I very nearly said: '11 November this year,' but held myself back just in time. That isn't the point of the dream, though. The point is that I felt the period. I could smell the under-arm odour of the ladies, the dust on the floor. The light bulb seemed to belong to that period and no other. When I consider the future, I don't care much about the generalities – the type of government and so on. I want something more existential, the quality of quotidian living – Do you understand me?

I understand you very well. If dreams can't do it for you, novelists and poets ought at least to attempt it. Here we are in this room in this flat in London. The year is 1978. I've worked in this room since 1960, and it hasn't changed much. The desk and chair are the same, also the carpet, which was tattered enough, God knows, when I first laid it down. It should be possible to hang on to this furniture, if not this typewriter, until the year 2000. Unless there's a wholly destructive fire, or unless the town planners pull down this block of flats, there's a sort of guarantee that things in this room will remain as they are. I, of course, may be dead, but these dead things will outlive me. So, you see, we're already in the future. We leave this room and go into other rooms. How much else will be the same? The television set, I'm pretty sure, will have been replaced many times over by 2000.

I saw a photograph of President Carter and his First Lady watching television. They were looking at three programmes at the same time. It struck me that that would be the pattern of future viewing. In the United States, certainly with so many channels, it seems a pity to confine yourself to one. We'll learn the gift of multiple viewing. And listening. This will be a definitive change in our modality of response to a stimulus –

But there'll be no change in our assumption that the domestic TV screen will be the chief source of entertainment and information. The death of big-screen cinema, and the substitution of big-screen television. More and more newspapers closing down. Stereoscopic vision? Expensive, for a long time. That's going to be the trouble with a great number of innovations – price. I don't see money going very far. I don't see a real grip on inflation, even by the end of the century. Unless a new Maynard Keynes comes along. I think that governments are going to make the price of drink and tobacco prohibitive, to save us from ourselves, but that they're going to permit the free sale of harmless stimulants and depressants. Something like Aldous Huxley's soma –

What do you see on your wide screen?

Old movies. Two or three at a time, as you suggest – why not? *Casablanca* and *Emile Zola* and something silent, like Fritz Lang's *Metropolis*. New movies lacking in overt violence, but candid as to the sexual act, which will be presented to the limit. Arguments in the press, and on talk shows, about the difference between the erotic and the pornographic. Also news. Industrial unrest, inflation, pump-priming (that means our total war may be coming). Kidnapping and skyjacking by dissident groups. Micro-bombs of immense destructiveness placed in public buildings. More thorough frisking at airports and at cinema entrances and on railroad stations – indeed, everywhere: restrictions on human dignity in the name of human safety. New oil strikes, but the bulk of the oil in the hands of the Arabs. More and more Islamic propaganda. Islamic religion taught in schools as a condition for getting oil. The work of finding a fuel substitute goes on. Gasoline very expensive. Jet travel on super Concordes, swift but damnably expensive. Life mostly work and television.

And outside the house where you sit watching it?

Old buildings coming down, more and more high-rises. All cities looking the same, though lacking the raffish glamour of old Manhattan. Not many people in the streets at night, what with uncontrollable violence from the young. Women in trousers and men in kilts – not all, of course. Yves St Laurent makes kilts cheap and popular, arguing that men are not anatomically fitted for pants, though women are.

And what will 2000 smell and taste like?

The air *has* to be cleaner. It's a sign of grace on the part of America that America is aware of pollution, whereas so much of Europe, Italy for instance, pollutes without knowing or caring. England got a terrible shock in 1951, when smog killed off not only human bronchitics but prize exhibits at the Smithfield Cattle Show – cows and bulls worth far more than mere human beings. This mustn't happen again, so London was made into a smokeless zone. London air is breathable now, which it wasn't in the time of Dickens, and fish are returning to the Thames. When we're shocked sufficiently, then we're prepared to act. The air of the future will smell of nothing. Alas, food will increasingly taste of nothing, except additives. The steady decline of the taste of food, which I've marked since boyhood (I *remember* what the food of the twenties tasted like), goes on. The human body will become a better-cared-for instrument, but it will be less dedicated to pleasure than the syphilitic body of the Renaissance. Even the pleasure of sex has diminished, since there's so much of it available. Sex to me, as a young man, was unattainable caviar. Now it's hamburger steak and children of ten are allowed to eat it. The permissive age will last through 2000, and films and magazines will work hard at devising new variations on the basic copulatory theme. There's a limit, I should think. There's a law of diminishing returns. Abortion will be cheap and easy. A gloriously apt correlation between the disposability of the foetus and the availability of sex, since both proclaim the cheapness of human flesh.

Religion?

The Christian ecumenical movement will have reached its limit, meaning that Catholicism will have turned into Protestantism and Protestantism into agnosticism. The young will still be after the bizarre and mystical, with new cults and impossible Moon-type leaders. But Islam will not have lost any of its rigour. G. K. Chesterton published a novel called *The Flying Inn* at the beginning of this century, in which he fantastically depicted an England flying the star and crescent, with drink forbidden and two men and a dog rolling a barrel of rum round the roads, in constant danger from the Muslim police, trying to keep the memory of liquor alive. I see a distinct possibility of the fulfilment of the vision, say about 2100. Supernature abhors a super-vacuum. With the death of institutional Christianity will come the spread of Islam.

I'd say that universal communism is a greater likelihood.

Isn't the term communism a vague verbal counter, all overtones and no fundamental note, in the minds of most Americans? History may, not much later than 2000, prove that the Marxist sequence was wrong. He thought revolution would come in the highly industrialized countries, with the workers turning against the capitalist oppressor. The answer to capitalist oppression has been syndicalism, not revolution. Revolution comes about in the underdeveloped countries, and it may be that the historical sequence is poverty, communism, capitalism. Take your choice of tyrannies – you're free to. I prefer the mild tyranny of the consumer philosophy. The underdeveloped nations have no choice. Communism is what happens to Lower Slobovia, not the United States.

Orwell says that Newspeak is fundamental to Ingsoc, that Newspeak in a sense is Ingsoc. Isn't it possible that the way language is developing, or deteriorating, we're preparing our minds for an incapacity to make rational choices, leaving them empty to be filled by some dictatorial philosophy?

There's a huge fissure in language. On the one hand, you have the rigidities of science and technology, where terms or words or symbols mean precisely what they say, on the other you have increasing vagueness, an oscillation between total inarticulacy and polysyllabic high-sounding gibberish. In American English you have a distressingly schizoid yoking of slang and jargon, like, 'Right, now let's zero in on the nitty-gritty of the implied parameters of the ontological, shit what's the word, right, yah, constatation.' I notice a tendency to pure verbalization, especially in public utterances, which we always expect to be lying or evasive. I mean, a statement can *sound* as if it had a meaning, so long as there's a coherent syntactical structure. The words have just got to be organized into a pattern of some kind, but it doesn't matter what the words mean.

Example?

Well, a newsman asks a president or a cabinet minister if there's going to be a war, and the reply is something like, 'There are various parameters of feasibility, all of which merit serious examination in the context of the implications of your question, Joe. The overall pattern of strike capability on both sides of the hypothetical global dichotomy is in process of detailed scrutiny, and the tem-

513

poral element involved cannot, of course, be yet quantified with any certainty. Does that answer your questiôn, Joe?' And Joe has to say, 'Thank you, sir.' Apart from what we can call the Language of Professional Evasion, there's an increasing tendency in ordinary communication to use technical language which has not been clearly understood. Things like 'a meaningful relationship,' which ought to mean a love affair, and 'you're overreacting,' which probably means: you're being damnably and unneccessary rude. Then there are all the acronyms, which a lot of people use without being able to reconstitute into the component antilogarithms – God, now I'm doing it. I mean, SALT and MASH and CHAOS.

What's CHAOS?

Council of the Hagiarchy of Anathematists of Onanistic Sex.

What will the English language be like in, say, the year 3000?

As sound? As semantemes and morphemes? Let's consider sound first. Remember there are many forms of English, all with equally respectable ancestries, but it seems that, on both sides of the Atlantic, we're accepting a kind of educated norm – newsreader's English, call it. It's not all that different in London from what it is in New York. New York English is conservative as to its sounds; it's closer to Pilgrim Father English, or Shakespearean English. London English has moved on a bit, bringing in the long *a* of *baaaath*, for example, and making *home* sound like *heume*. Now, I always say that if Chaucer knew about the inherent instability of long vowels, he'd be able, in 1400, to predict what speech would be like in 2000. He'd know, for instance, that *mouse*, which he pronounced like the French *mousse*, would end up like the German *Maus*. What I mean is, it's possible to make rough prophecies about phonological change in English. You can't, by the way, necessarily hold change back by fixing language through film and tape and cassette. Spoken language tends to go its own way. I'll make one prediction about vowel sounds in the year 3000 – they'll all tend to move towards the middle of the mouth, approaching the sound we make at the end of *lava* or the beginning of *apart*. Consonants haven't changed much since the year 1000, and I don't think there'll be much change a thousand years ahead, but vowels will sound more and more like each other. *Light* and *loud* will be differentiated mainly by the final consonants. All this must sound frivolous, but you want to get the *feel* of the future –

How about language as meaning?

Have you noticed one curious, and rather endearing, thing about *Nineteen Eighty-Four* – the penchant for rural metaphors or similes that Orwell passes on to his characters? O'Brien talks of taking the child from the mother as we take an egg from the hen. The three superstates are spoken of as leaning on each other to keep each other upright, like three stooks in a hayfield. Winston and Julia have no doubt that the bird they heard singing was a thrush. There's too much country knowledge in this story of the ultimate urban culture. What's happening with our language already, and is going to happen far more, is the steady elimination of rural particularities, so that *elm* and *oak* and *sycamore* will have no very clear meaning, and all trees will be summed up as *tree*. Birds will be *bird*. Flowers will be *flower*. Language will become more and more abstract in its vocabulary, and its speakers will occasionally erupt against this in more and more ingenious obscenities, but obscenities too will be very generic. There'll be a large everyday technical vocabulary to replace the old natural one – words for the parts of a refrigerator, a tape deck and so on. But language will be cut off from its roots in basic physical experience. Language of the brain rather than of the body.

How about words like love, honour, duty, God, fidelity, treason, hate, infamy?

It is going to be extremely difficult, in the absence of a traditional system of moral values, to give words like that any precise meaning. There's a vague emotional connotation attached to each, but little more. It's here that the danger lies. Any dictatorial regime can take hold of these words, exploit the emotional response they excite, but provide its own definitions. 'God is the supreme being. I am the supreme being. Therefore I am God.' Yeah, man, but you ain't, you know, like spiritual. 'What do you mean by spiritual?' You tell me, man. 'With pleasure.'

Koestler says that we can only get rid of national enmities based on international misunderstanding by having a world language. Is that possible?

We already have a world auxiliary – English. It's the

515

language of commerce and air traffic, for instance. Ogden and Richards made, in the thirties, a reduced form of English, limited to about 850 words, called Basic. The British Government bought the rights to it, and it was in that that Orwell saw the possibility of language clear and simple and orthodox imposed on the people by the State. There can be an agreed imposition of a kind of Basic in all the countries of the world – a second language taught compulsorily in schools. But that can never be allowed to *replace* the first language.

Can governments tell us what words to use and what not to use – as with Newspeak?

They're certainly telling us what words we may *not* use. And it's not the governments so much as the pressure groups working on the governments. I don't doubt that, in Britain, there'll be a Restriction of Language Act. Certain racist terms, like *kike* and *sheeny* and *wog* and *wop* and, most terrible of all, *nigger*, are already taboo, as the four-letter obscenities used to be, and the next step is to make them illegal. The Gay Liberation movement – which ought to be prevented, by law if need be, from limiting a fine old word to a coy, giggly, totally inaccurate and quite arbitrary signification – will demand that terms like *poofter*, *fag*, *pansy* and so on be made illegal. Even your bowl of pansies on the dining-room table may be against the law, unless you call them geraniums. And then there are the forces of Women's Liberation, which demand a reorientation of generic pronouns, so that *he* and *his* cannot be used for either sex, and for that matter the generic term *man* – which in German corresponds to the pronoun *one* – must be replaced by some fabricated monstrosity like *manwoman* or, better, *womanman*. The Rights of Womanman. Already *chairman* has become *chairperson*, and there has been a response from accoucheurs, who want *midwife* turned to *midperson*. Now the Women's Lib philologists are probably working on *tallboy*, *carboy*, *chessman* and, conceivably, *talisman*. We're moving in the direction of increasing restrictions on speech as well as action, but few of these spring from a Big Brother kind of lust for centralized control. They derive from what, I suppose, must be termed a democratic situation.

We have an anomaly before us, then – pressurizable governments aware of their weakness, and yet increasing loss of liberty?

The governments of the West – and this may apply soon to the governments of the Soviet bloc – are less concerned about political orthodoxy than with people paying their taxes. Fiscal tyranny is not the worst tyranny you can get, but it's nasty enough, and it's going to get worse.

It only applies to people with money, and the great majority of the world's inhabitants earn too little to be taxed. Hadn't we better cease thinking narrowly about the future of the West – whether or not there's going to be more freedom or less – and concentrate on the future of the planet?

It's too much. As Voltaire said, we must cultivate our own Hesperides.

Hesperides?

Gardens of the West. Progress won't come through dilution, everybody being poor together.

Are you pessimistic about man, or manwoman?

Man has survived the first thirty-three years of the Era of the Bomb. He'll survive whatever new horrors are in store for him. He's remarkably ingenious.

And if he doesn't survive?

There remains Life. You remember the words of Lilith at the end of Shaw's *Back to Methuselah*? I do:

'Of Life only is there no end; and though of its million starry mansions many are empty and many still unbuilt, and though its vast domain is as yet unbearably desert, my seed shall one day fill it and master its matter to its uttermost confines. And for what may be beyond, the eyesight of Lilith is too short. It is enough that there *is* a beyond.'

That's what I believe in – mind, free mind, trying to understand itself as well as the world without, and to hell with the little men who try to stop free enquiry and the State is all that matters and no one has a right to hear Beethoven while the Third World starves.

You're under arrest.

I beg your pardon?

You're under arrest.

You're joking. Yes, joking. I knew somehow you were joking.

But for a moment you thought I was serious.

Yes, I did. God help me, I did. You think even the right to free speech may be a lulling device of Big Brother? You think he's really watching us? That he'll emerge as the persona of some great industrial combine, an international octopus, just when we least expect him?

We have to be on our guard.

I'll accept that.

Monaco 1978